to an American Doctor of Linguistics and, along with their five-year-old daughter, he is her test-subject. He has lived abroad for ten years, working and studying in the USA, New Zealand and Russia, and has been a pretty bad stand-up comedian, produced mime shows for Japanese TV and written theatre for the Shakespeare festival, produced in London and Verona.

His first novel *The Last Winter of Dani Lancing* is now in development with Warner TV, working with the creator of *Dirty Pretty Liars* and the head writer of *Dexter*.

To find out more visit: www.pdviner.com

Praise for The Last Winter of Dani Lancing:

'Genuinely intriguing' *Guardian*

'An entertaining thriller, but also a moving examination of loss, memory and morality' *Sunday Mirror*

'Brilliant! P. D. Viner's writing is audacious, clever and bold. I think he'll go far' Sophie Hannah

'An exciting thriller that is also deeply moving. A hugely impressive debut' Mark Billingham

Also by P. D. Viner

The Last Winter of Dani Lancing
The Ugly Man (digital short)
The Sad Man (digital short)

summer
of ghosts

P.D. VINER

EBURY
PRESS

3 5 7 9 10 8 6 4 2

Ebury Press, an imprint of Ebury Publishing
20 Vauxhall Bridge Road,
London SW1V 2SA

Penguin
Random House
UK

Ebury Press is part of the Penguin Random House
group of companies whose addresses can be found at
global.penguinrandomhouse.com

First published in 2014 by Ebury Press
This edition published in 2015

www.eburypublishing.co.uk

A CIP catalogue record for this book is
available from the British Library

ISBN 9780091953331

Printed and bound by CPI Group (UK) Ltd,
Croydon, CR0 4YY

Penguin Random House is committed to a sustainable
future for our business, our readers and our planet.
This book is made from Forest Stewardship
Council® certified paper.

To my parents.
It's all your fault.
Thank you.

ZERO

'Guv! The body is through here,' Detective Inspector Jane Thorsen calls before she turns away and is swept up in the maelstrom of white-clad figures who busily sweep the room for every last trace of the life that has been extinguished there.

Detective Superintendent Tom Bevans remains on the threshold, but he doesn't, or can't, move to join her. He watches as the rest of the SOCO team pass him to enter the building. They carry test kits, evidence markers, cameras, tapes, tarpaulins and a body bag. The double doors are held open by two large fire extinguishers wedged against them, so the cold of the night can seep into the building like a virus to the lungs. Tom hugs his arms around his chest and, suspended in the wool of his coat, there is the tang of smoke. He loves Bonfire Night; the 5th of November – fireworks, greasy burgers and a burning man. He's had such a great evening. He recalls how close he stood to the giant bonfire as it was lit. The wood caught with an earthy sweetness and within seconds flames darted high, crawling up to kiss the body at the summit.

Remember, remember. Fireworks exploded high in the sky above him and orange flames danced in his eyes as—

'Guv,' DI Thorsen calls from the doors, breaking the spell. 'SOCO have taken samples and photographs; the area's secured, we can examine the victim.'

'Okay,' he calls to her. She nods and turns back. For a moment, involuntary sadness jags across his face and then is gone. *No more hiding in the past*, he tells himself. Slowly he walks into the school, to see a dead girl. As he passes under the oak-lined entranceway, above his head the school motto is carved into marble. *Rather death than false of faith*. Really?

The SOCO team have created a pathway that spirals to the body, avoiding the direct route and any contamination of evidence; zig-zagging around the blood spatter, but there is so much blood to avoid. Jackson Pollock turned killer. Thorsen reaches the body in moments and then turns to watch Tom as he signs the logbook and checks the date and time. It is 2.35 a.m. 6th November 2006. With his arrival, he is the senior investigating officer on site. She feels her hackles rise a little at the slowness of his approach. Most SIOs are pretty confident, arrogant even. She expects the officer-in-charge to storm in, barking orders and demanding an update; then to rush to the body. But Bevans enters the crime scene like a reluctant guest at a wedding, unsure if he is on the bride or groom's side, moving slowly, as if he does not want to disturb the air as he passes through it. He takes a few steps and pauses; she can see him soaking in the atmosphere, reading the room. It makes her feel a little self-conscious as she had just barged in and made a bee-line for the body. DI Thorsen needs instant gratification.

Tom scans the room as he traverses it, very impressive for a city centre school – even an independent one. The main hall is about half the size of a football pitch, with dark wood-panelled walls that hold large crests of the four houses that make up the school. The floor is an intricate herringbone of interlocking wood, with about ten per cent of the whole room being taken up by a raised stage. On it sits a piano, covered with a green cloth. To the right are stacks of plastic chairs, maybe four hundred in all. It's been a while since he was in a school hall. When he first joined the police one of his jobs was to visit classrooms and talk about being aware and safe on the streets. The kids called him *Officer Tom* and he had a badger glove puppet that knew all about road safety. Later, when he was a family liaison officer, the badger knew all about bullying and peer pressure, self-harming, anorexia and incest. The glove puppet committed suicide eventually. Very sad.

Tom reaches the middle of the room and stops. He can see Thorsen standing by the body; she looks impatient. He'll get there. He looks up, and through a large skylight, can see the moon hanging in the sky and, to the side of it, the wishing star. He closes his eyes for a second and wishes he were a real boy. He looks over at the long fluorescent strip lights that hang from the ceiling and illuminate the room with a dodgy puke-yellow hue. They buzz like a swarm of bees. 'Were the overhead lights on when the body was found?' he calls out to the assorted officers scattered around the room.

'Don't think so, guv,' Fat Eddie calls back louder than anyone else. Jane Thorsen confirms it with a shake of the head. Tom files it away for later and speeds up his movement to the body; as the SOCO floodlights finally burst into life – banishing all shadows from the room. Tom joins the spiral pathway that leads to her.

'Oh.' The breath is pushed from his lungs as he reaches the dead girl. She is naked, more than naked if that is possible. She has blonde hair, though it is mostly red with blood now. Her arms are stretched out from her body and the legs are splayed. He wants to close them, to cover her with a thick blanket and warm her up. This death is so undignified; there is so little respect.

Poor little dead girl. He catches himself creating stories for her, imagining a life full of ... Stop it Tom, that's how you make yourself crazy. He will do better by her if he forgets she is someone's daughter/sister/friend and regards her merely as an intellectual challenge, a series of problems to solve; *not as the poor little dead girl.* He cannot consider the family and their tears, the corrosion of loss and—

Concentrate on what you see, he tells himself. *Focus.* He can see that loops of plastic have been used around the wrists and ankles. *Good, what else?* There are no signs of a struggle, her wrists are not bruised or cut, he would guess that she was tied while unconscious – drugged, and never regained consciousness. That, at least, is something. Later, when he talks to the parents, he will be able to tell them that she did not suffer, and he will probably be telling the truth. That will help. It will help both them and him to get through this.

You and your bleeding heart. A memory cuts him for a moment; it had been an accusation Dani had made, such a long, long time ago. *Concentrate.* He drags his attention back to the body: her pale skin is scratched in places and there appear to be bite marks around her breasts. Love bites? The phrase makes him want to laugh. There is not one drop of love here. He cranes forward and looks at her head, above her right eye, where the claw hammer entered. He can see its trajectory, swung with real force sweeping up into her skull, dragging bone and blood and brain-matter out and up, making a spire, a crenelated tower of red and pink, like a Disney Princess castle. A part of him wants to lie down next to her and hold her. But it is too late. There was no one to hold her hand or sing a lullaby to her while she died. She was alone, except for the monster who did this. He hopes she wasn't scared.

In his peripheral vision he sees DI Thorsen has just finished talking with the SOCO team commander; she shakes his hand and then walks up alongside Tom. Together they stand sentinel over the fallen girl.

'What do we know about her?' Tom finally asks his DI.

'No name yet. We found some clothes,' Thorsen takes a deep breath, 'School uniform.' Tom flinches. 'We think they're hers. There's a prefect's badge, so if they are, then she's in the sixth form. The headmistress is on her way and I've got Jenkins looking through the school office for photos. Either way we should have a name soon.'

He nods. 'When she gets here hold her at the gate. Once the body is ready to move, the headmistress can view the body away from the crime scene, if she is up to it, but I don't want her to see the wounds – just the face.' *Just the sweet face.*

'Guv.' Jane nods. Then the two of them stand silently over the body, each wrapped in their own thoughts. For Tom, he feels the buzz of anger in his chest. *She was a schoolgirl.* It makes his heart burn. Such a waste of life, such a vile, vicious act. Jane Thorsen can only stand there for another minute. She is armoured against the grief but needs to be moving, doing something. It isn't good to wallow – it isn't healthy to get attached to the dead. She wishes Tom Bevans knew that. She watches how he reaches out to them and makes it personal. He makes them promises and sometimes … Oh what does she know; his success rate is phenomenal isn't it. He turns rocks over and finds them, the men who harm, scuttling in the shadows like beasts. Tom

Bevans has saved countless young women. He is an inspiration to all these young officers. So why does she want to put her arms around him, and tell him it will be all right? With a heavy sigh she goes to look at more blood spatter.

Tom stands still, the anger washing through him like fire in his veins. He stares into her dead face for five minutes. From the outside he must look like he is studying everything about the victim, but in reality he is just trying not to cry. If he lets one tear break through the levee they will not stop. So often he feels like this, in the presence of the dead. He sees them all stretched out before him. Dozens of them, all the way back to the first dead girl. To Dani, who he loved. Who, pathetically, he still loves. *Pull yourself together*, he hisses to himself, just as another officer walks over to him and hovers by his side.

'DI Jenkins.' Tom greets him without a smile.

'I don't know if you've been apprised of the course of events this evening?' Jenkins asks with a nasally twang.

'I think I have the gist; the victim's details were entered into the HOLMES computer and a flag was triggered. The locals called us in.'

'Pretty much. A local response team found the body at just after 11 p.m. They called an ambulance, even though they were pretty sure the girl was dead.'

Tom can't help but sweep his eyes across the floor – blood and brain-matter everywhere. Of course she was bloody dead.

'Then they called in the local CID and suggested a SOCO unit was dispatched straight away. The area gold commander okayed the request about ten minutes later. After that they secured the building and searched the ground floor.'

'When did the local CID arrive?'

'They didn't. Before they got here the case details were inputted and the case was kicked over to us. The local CID team stood down. They never even entered the building.'

Tom sighs wearily. He should be pleased that the protocol worked so well; the fact that no other team has been in to mess with the crime scene is excellent. However, it means that there is another killer out there targeting young women. It means there are at least two dead women. 'What was the trigger?' he asks Jenkins, even though he is afraid of the answer.

'One previous victim: Spall, Heather Spall. Sixteen years old.'

'When?'

'Five weeks ago, in Leeds.'

He nods, it could have been worse – could have been years. 'What are the similarities?'

'We've only got the bullet points so far – but the positioning of the body—'

'Including the use of the plastic ties to splay the legs and arms?'

Jenkins consults his notes. 'Yes, the initial reports seem to tally.'

'What else?' Tom asks, feeling his chest flutter a little.

'The murder weapon in the Leeds case was also a claw hammer. Cause of death: blow to the back of the head, hammer exit above the right eye.' He pauses. 'The Leeds case also states bites to the breasts.'

'Sounds pretty strong.' Tom starts to move away from his DI, thoughts already racing, then he swings back to ask: 'Do we have an ID on the victim yet?'

'DS Matthews thinks he has a match from the school office files. But—'

Tom nods. Sometimes it is just impossible to match a dead face to a photograph. So much of who we are is our vitality, the twinkle in the eye and the smile on the lips. Drain the life away and she could be any one of a hundred blonde teenagers.

'Okay. Do we have any arrival time on the headmistress?'

'A local squad car is bringing her in; she couldn't drive herself. Shock.'

'Let me know when she arrives.'

'Yes, sir,' Jenkins turns to leave, but Tom stops him for a second.

'Is Dr Keyson here yet?' Tom asks, hoping his chief pathologist might get to see the body in situ, not just in the sterile environment of the morgue.

'No, but he's been called.'

'Okay, well don't wait for him to get the body removed if SOCO are ready. But I do want him to get up to Leeds and examine the body there as quickly as possible.'

'Assuming there is one, guv.'

'Yes, well if there isn't a body, then he can get all photos, police reports, pathologist and coroner's reports. Then he can start comparing our girl with the Spall girl. I want to know for certain that these cases are linked.'

'Okay.' Tom turns to walk away but – *what is nagging at him?* 'Wait!' He calls out, Jenkins stops. *Something isn't right.* Slowly the cogs turn in Tom's head. 'You said a response team found her?'

'There was a 999 call.'

'Who called it in?'

'We believe it was the victim. When the response team got here the place was dark. They had to force entry, they almost left without finding—', he tilts his head towards the dead young woman.

'What exactly did the caller say?'

Jenkins opens his notepad and flicks back through it. 'Here's the transcript: The call operator picked up at 10.54 p.m. and before they could ask what service was required there was a girl who, according to the operator, was hysterical. She said: "Help, we are at St. Mary Magdalene School. Help. He's coming." Then the phone was dropped but not turned off.'

Tom is quiet for a second. 'Has the phone been found?'

'No, guv.'

'Has the building been combed?'

'Every room. It is a big building though, there are lots of hi—'

'She said "we are".'

Jenkins suddenly realises what he's getting at. 'There's another victim?'

'Or a witness.' Tom feels cold creep into his chest. 'Christ.' In a whirl, Tom jumps up onto the stage and claps loudly. 'Listen up. Everyone quiet. QUIET!' The noise in the room drops. 'There may be a second victim somewhere in the building, hurt or in hiding. They could be in a cupboard, under tables, unconscious or—' He suddenly has flashes of a film he saw about Columbine, how the students and teachers hid in any rabbit hole they could find, any place they could crawl into. 'I want every inch of this building searched – look for overturned desks, any kind of barrier that could have been built to keep someone safe and look for blood, on the floor, on door handles – anywhere and everywhere. Make noise, friendly noise. Call out your names, first names, tell the world and their wives that you're police and that the area is safe – there is no need to hide. Anyone wearing protective suits take them off so you don't scare any potential witness. Forget evidence gathering, this is the highest priority. GO.'

Tom catches DI Thorsen's eye across the room; she flashes a quick smile to him and runs off to round up the rest of the core Operation Ares team. Tom jumps down from the stage and for a second he halts by the unknown girl. 'Who is out there,' he asks the lifeless girl, 'a friend? Will there be another body tonight?' The thought makes him sick. He turns slowly and walks to the double doors at the other end of the hall, pushes through and into a dark corridor. He slips a torch from out of his pocket and heads up the stairs.

'There's no need to hide. The police are here. My name is Tom.' *They call me the Sad Man, because later tonight I might have to tell your parents you are dead.* He tries not to think such ugly thoughts but he cannot keep them away, 'Detective Superintendent Tom Bevans. I am here to help you.' *I am here to save you.*

My hero. A memory of Dani slices through his mind – her mocking him when she first saw him in his uniform; she had hated him joining the police.

'Tom. Tom Bevans.' He keeps calling out his name as he moves from room to room. He even starts to sing, thinking it might convince her he can be trusted. Killers don't sing, do they? After ten minutes he can hear DI Thorsen calling from another corridor. Then DI Clarke and DI Jenkins join in – lastly DS Eddie Matthews starts to shout out. They are the main Ares team. The fantastic five or the five stooges?

They finish searching the first floor and then head up to the second, which seems to be all art rooms. Everything is dark. They fan out at the top of the stairs, switching on their torches and picking a classroom.

'Don't be scared. My name's Jane,' he hears Thorsen call out in a sing-song voice.

'I've got some chocolate,' Fat Eddie shouts, sounding more like the child catcher than a sympathetic police officer.

Tom walks to the end of the corridor and enters the furthest of the art rooms. He slides his hand across the wall inside, trying to find the light switch, but there is nothing. All these rooms are probably operated by a master switch. *Damn.* It is almost pitch black; very little light creeps in from the moon hanging in the sky outside. Tom plays his torch through the room. Squares of smears and squiggles are hung on strings that span the walls like spider webs. One half of the room seems different; the art is no longer in two dimensions but three. Malformed children appear to perch on the windowsills like gargoyles. On a table, hands and arms stretch up into the air like zombies rising from the gr— *Change the record, Tom.* He's scaring himself. Sculptures. Clay and nothing more.

'My name is Tom.' He calls into the air. 'I am a policeman, there are a few of us here in the building – we heard your phone call and came to help.' He listens. There is nothing. 'We found your friend.' Still nothing. He turns to try the next room and as he does so something glows for a second and is gone. He steps slowly back, a single ray of moonlight hits the floor at just the correct angle and – it could be art. It looks moist and red. He squats down to it. There is a footprint on the floor. It is a bare foot. He kneels down and touches a finger to it. He brings it up to his nose and inhales; sweet, not paint, it's blood. He plays the torch beam across the floor, looking for more signs to show where somebody may have gone. There is nothing.

'Hello sweetheart. It's the police, is somebody hurt in here? We're here to help.' Nothing. Maybe they would trust a woman more. He runs back to the door and shouts out, down into the long black corridor. 'Thorsen, I'm in Art block B. Room 4. I think—' There is a sound, the faintest of buzzes – like a mosquito settling on your neck, about to strike. He thinks it is a mobile on silent. 'Jane, get down here now,' he shouts to her, then turns back to room 4. Tom looks across its length and shines the torch ahead of him. On the floor, pushed behind a cabinet, he sees some fabric has been thrown back there. He slides his hand as far as he can, under a desk and pulls out a school shirt. It is smeared with red, still tacky. He is pretty sure it is blood. He holds his breath and strains into the darkness. There is nothing. He stretches his hand out to the cabinet and grips the door, shifting his weight to his back foot in case anything wants to jump out at him. Then he slowly twists the handle, and yanks it open. Empty. There is nowhere else in the room that could be a hiding place – unless. In a corner stands a kiln. A fat, squat bell-jar. It stands about 4 feet high, an oven for baking and glazing, but there will be shelves, compartments, nobody could hide in it, could they? Tom walks over to the kiln. The door is slightly ajar. He raises the torch and examines the handle. It could be glaze. It could be paint. It could be blood.

'Where are you, guv?' Jane calls out.

'Here. Ceramics and pottery. There's a kiln.' As he says it, he feels something inside shift, like a kick to the metal sleeve. 'Fuck.' He whispers to himself, gripping the door handles and leaning back, it starts to shift. Using his whole bodyweight the doors begin to swing open. It is deep, in five sections, the middle one being the biggest but still only twelve or fourteen inches high. At that second Jane reaches him and together they peer into the black of the kiln. It is like a concrete bunker, with its walls jagged and sharp, pitted from hundreds of firings as glass has melted, bubbled and erupted – covering the sides with miniature blades.

Tom bends down to look deeper into the abyss. There is something there, a shape, he cannot tell. He slowly lifts the torch and its light touches the kiln wall.

'Jesus Christ,' Jane breathes. They can see blood and flesh on the walls, ripped and gouged from a human body. He lifts the torch higher to see all the way to ... *Oh Christ* there is a body, wedged inside. Naked, a girl, dead. He reaches in to touch and—

'Fuck!'

Her eyes spring open – deep blue in contrast to the blood red of her face. Her mouth opens and—

'Aaaaaaaaaaaaaaaaaaaaaaaaaaaaaaaaaaa!' she screams. High, shrill, total panic.

'It's okay, love, it's okay. I am a policeman. There is no need to be afraid.' But she continues to scream; he tries to get his hands in to her but she beats at them. She is sobbing and wailing. Her arms hitting the walls and shredding more, blood spills and starts to trickle out of the kiln. Tom jumps back – he is making it worse. She is terrified of him.

'Jane, you try.'

Thorsen slowly raises her hands, palms out to the girl. 'Shhhhhh ...' she coos, as if to a baby. 'Come on, my love. Safe now, you are safe now.' She reaches inside, slowly, always with open hands. She reaches close enough to touch the girl and stops. She waits for the girl to reach out to her. 'It's okay, Jane is here. You're safe. It's all over, all over.'

Tom steps back, away into the shadows so as not to frighten the girl. Fat Eddie pokes his head around the door but Tom shoos him away. He watches DI Thorsen stand there, strong and calm, waiting for this poor injured child to reach out to her. Finally she does take hold of her hand. Her screams begin to melt into sobs, uncontrollable sobs as the girl allows Jane to pull her out. It is difficult, like a cork in a bottle. She takes more skin and flesh off as she moves. Tom can see her pain – it is heart-breaking.

'Come on, darling, almost out,' Jane continues to coo and cajole. Always keeping the pressure on her to move forward, even though she can see the pain in the girl's eyes. She keeps moving, and blood trickles before her – it is like she is being born again. From the tiny confines of the kiln she emerges, a bloody mess. Tom pulls off his coat and has it ready to wrap her in.

'Christ, Tom, something softer,' Thorsen hisses. Tom looks at his coat, wool and scratchy and smelling of smoke. He drops it and runs to the supplies cupboard, his torch beam dancing ahead. He pulls open the doors; inside is a basket with a sign that reads *fabrics*. He tips the basket over and watches the smaller pieces flutter, but there is one large piece – it is white cotton, like gauze – for a bloody bride. He takes it and dashes back, just as the head emerges, then the shoulders. 'Christ,' he whispers.

'Come on darling, almost there.' Thorsen coos softly. One last push and she is out into the world. She looks as if she has been flayed alive.

'Good girl, good, good girl,' Jane keeps soothing her. Tom throws the fabric over her shoulders and between the two of them they swaddle her. Her legs are unsteady and Jane slowly drops her to the floor. She is shivering. Tom cannot take his eyes off her as blood begins to soak through her makeshift shroud. This is not Turin, he can't see the face of Christ in the blood – he sees a monster. Tom pulls his *airwave* radio from a belt loop, and speaks softly into it as Jane hugs and cradles the girl.

'We need urgent medical attention – witness found, alive but hurt and in extreme distress. She has major lacerations to the skin. We need a sterile body suit, bandages, and sedatives. A&E need to prep for skin salve, could be derma level trauma, skin grafts – like a burn, friction burn. Please be quick,' he releases the transmit button. He puts the airwave down, *alive*. She is a miracle, but she is also a witness. He kneels down close to her, close enough to smell her blood.

'Can you tell us your name?' he asks her. She shakes. All she knows is pain and shock.

'Later, guv,' Thorsen says insistently.

'Was it you who called the police?'

He thinks she nods – it is hard to tell, she is shaking so much.

'W, w, w,' she tries, but that is all she can say.

'Guv—'

'I know.' His eyes flare at Jane, he is pushing too hard but he has to. Christ, can she not see that he has to do this? 'Did you see his face?' he asks the girl.

She shakes, he cannot see her eyes – there is only blood. Her hair is soaked with it – he can't even tell if she is blonde – possibly redhead, possibly. In the street outside he hears the siren, they are almost here. Great for her, they can take her pain away – but downstairs there is a dead girl who needs to be avenged. In Leeds there is another girl and a family who have been in pain for a month already, that pain needs to be salved. He has to push, to be the bad guy. She opens her mouth to say something and—

Boom! The overhead lights flare into life. The girl squeals and hides her face. Tom's eyes sting after so long straining in the dark – shitty timing.

'No, please, please, it's only the lights.' Tom leans forwards, his shadow stretching over her. 'I know you are hurting.' He leans in, so close his mouth almost touches her ear, and whispers to her. 'I am so sorry but I need to ask if—' he hears their boots on the stairs '—you can identify him. If you can describe him.'

'Paramedics coming through,' a voice calls out from beyond the room. The sands have almost run out.

'Please help me,' Tom whispers to the girl as the double doors at the far end of the room burst open, and two medics enter with a stretcher. 'The man who did this, was he known to you, a teacher or someone's dad?' Tom asks, his voice urgent and insistent.

'Step back from her,' the lead medic calls, not liking the way a Detective Superintendent is leaning over an injured and traumatised girl. Tom looks up at him, his eyes pleading for another minute.

'Let me just ask—'

'Please step away.' The paramedic's face is stone. He stretches down a hand to help Tom up, but he pushes it away and turns back to the girl once more.

'We only have a second.'

'NOW.' The medic grabs Tom by the shoulders.

'Back off!' Tom yells at the medic firmly. 'I know what you need to do but I must have a few seconds here.' Tom turns to her and as lightly as he can he places his hands on her shoulders.

'Your friend is dead,' he tells the girl.

'GUV!' Thorsen and the medic grab him and lift him back from the girl. *Did he go too far?*

'I need your help to save others,' he tells her.

Jane gets between Tom and the girl. He can see she is upset with him, but the living have a lot of people looking out for them, while the dead have so few. The medic grips him hard and Tom holds up his hands to get him to back off. He does – Tom's palms are blood red. Tom sinks to his knees for one final try.

'Please, please,' he speaks softly to the girl, but her eyes are closed and she seems to have slipped out of consciousness.

'Step away,' the medic asks and pulls at his shoulder simultaneously. Tom nods slowly and lets himself be moved back, away from the only witness. The medics immediately move in to tend to her. Tom looks across at Jane, she pulls her eyes away from his. A gurney is slid alongside the girl. With an incredible tenderness she is lifted onto it and a mask is placed over her face. In seconds she will be anaesthetised and the pain will be gone. Tom steps forward and with his softest voice tells her: 'Don't worry – we can talk tomorrow, after you've been cleaned up and had a great night's sleep.' Her eyes snap open – they are the deepest blue but full of fear – she whimpers and shakes her head. She tries to free her swaddled arm, reaches out to grab Tom. He holds out his hand and she grips it; her fingers hold him strongly. Her mouth opens, behind the plastic of the mask. He can see she has braces on her teeth, she looks so young, he couldn't tell from the bloody mess. She is desperately trying to get something out before the drugs take hold. 'B … b … b … b-b-b-beautiful,' she says slowly through the obvious pain.

'Beautiful?' Tom repeats. He can see her eyelids flutter as the drugs slide her under. 'I need to get her back.' He yells at the medic and grabs the mask away from her face; the medic grabs his wrist in a vice-like grip.

'That is enough,' the medic says to Tom, flexing a fist at the same time.

The second medic slides in and replaces the mask. 'Don't worry love, you'll be asleep in a second.' His voice like honey. 'Just count to five.'

One. Tom counts in his head, *two* …

She struggles as blackness slimes into her mind. 'He said—' *Three*, her eyelids flutter. *Four*. '—skin, beautiful skin,' *Five*. She is unconscious.

'Beautiful skin,' Tom repeats. *Remember, remember.* A voice-in-his-head whispers.

'I won't forget,' Tom answers back. 'I promise.'

But he does forget, he forgets for a long time, more than four years. And then—

Four-and-a-half years later

Friday 17th June 2011.

Remember.

Tom's eyes flick open, panic sweeps through him as the final beats of the dream die from his chest. He is breathing heavily, bathed in sweat – his heart pounds. He was in the kiln, glass tearing at his skin as he pushed himself out – birthed in blood, surrounded by their ghosts who were calling to him, asking why he had forgotten them; why they were yet to be avenged. *Why is it taking so long?* More than four years in the wilderness. 'Christ,' he mutters, his throat dry and cracked. He looks to the clock by his bedside, it is early; too early – almost the night before. Today is important, he needs to be sharp and calm; not strung out from lack of sleep. Today he has to get his life back on track and—

Remember.

Tom can't tell if the voice is just in his head or in the air around him. 'I do remember, I remember everything,' he tells them, but he knows the ghosts won't let him sleep now. He sits up and swings his legs off of the bed. Maybe he'll polish his shoes and iron his clothes ready for his appointment.

'Detective Superintendent Bevans?' the man asks with a syrupy-sweet voice, standing as he does so. Tom Bevans does not reply immediately. Instead his eyes flit across the unbearably beige office – taking in the diplomas and qualifications that cover almost every available inch of wall space. *Over-compensation*, Tom thinks, as he scans the room and his eyes alight on the bookshelves; they seem to contain at least a dozen copies of one book: *Opening the Criminal Mind* by Dr A. V. Harrison.

'Dr Harrison.' Tom extends his hand over the large oak desk and the psychiatrist takes it with a grip like a damp dishcloth. He gestures to a soft armchair, and Tom sits, thankful there is no couch to lie on.

'Please tell me why you believe you are here today,' Harrison asks and then sits back in his ergonomically designed steel and leather chair and looks out of the window at the blue, cloudless sky.

To convince you I'm not a lunatic, Tom thinks, but keeps his mouth closed; this is important, not something to play games with. Instead he is quiet for a few seconds while he sizes up the man who must judge him. A podgy face, mostly covered by a thick, reddish beard and owl-like glasses, with a mouth that seems to want to look sincere but finds it hard not to look superior and judgemental. Tom's assessment of the man is that he is not to be trusted with Tom's secrets, or anyone's quest for sanity.

'Did you not understand the question, Detective Superintendent?' Dr Harrison asks as he makes notes on a large yellow pad, which is turned away from Tom. His tone reveals what little he thinks about the IQ of senior police officers.

Tom pauses, unsure what to say, what to reveal to this man. 'Dr Harrison, I understand that what I tell you, what we say here is private.'

'Detective Superintendent, that is true, but only up to a point. Whilst I may keep private from your superiors anything you confess to me, from an indiscretion or lapse of judgement to a predilection for dressing like a nineteenth-century whore in the comfort of your own home.' He laughs at the image he has created. Tom assumes it is meant to put him at his ease – it doesn't. 'I am still here, primarily, to assess whether you can return to your duties without proving a threat to yourself, your team or the general public. That is what I have been tasked with here, consequently I will use all you tell me in making that assessment.' He pauses. 'So Superintendent Bevans, you have been off active duty, ever since—'

'30th December 2010. Almost six months ago.' Tom finishes his sentence.

Harrison takes a deep theatrical breath. 'Six months. What have you been doing all that time, Detective Superintendent?'

'I have spent some time volunteering in a hospital, a specialist head trauma unit. I help the staff. I feed the patients and I read to them. I have been there three or four days a week for the last few months.' Tom sees Harrison's eyes narrow and the man makes a note on his pad. It is the truth, of course, about Tom volunteering in the hospital, but not the whole truth. Outside a cloud limps across the sky and smothers the sun; the room they are in gets quite gloomy.

'Sad Man.' Dr Harrison says the name with some relish and watches Tom's face spasm, for a second, in response. 'That is what your colleagues call you, isn't it. Sad Man?'

Tom feels his jaw clench involuntarily; he hates his nickname. It is all because of the tears. Other officers freak out when they see him cry, but he has no control, the tears just bleed from his eyes at the slightest provocation. He was worse when he was a family liaison officer – he cried all the time then, but nowadays it is better. A bit better, maybe. He has seen two therapists – in secret of course – hoping they can help him. One of them prescribed drugs that made him thirsty and unhappy. The other said: *empathy is a gift*. He finished with both quickly. He has learned to live with the tears and the weird looks he gets from colleagues, and the whispers of *there goes the Sad Man*. It is no big deal.

'Some perhaps have called me Sad Man, in the past. Fewer now and never to my face,' Tom tells the psychiatrist.

Harrison smiles; he can see why Detective Superintendent Tom Bevans has that nickname – he looks as if he is filled to the brim with life's pain, like the figure in Edvard Munch's painting *The Scream*. His hair is white, his skin looks like shattered porcelain that has been painstakingly glued back together, but it is his eyes that make the biggest impression, they appear to burn in some unfathomable way; mineshafts to some inner hell that has corroded him, etched pain into his physical being. Harrison can see how the lost and vulnerable would trust him; he reminds them of themselves.

'Why do your colleagues use it?'

Tom does not want to respond to that intrusive question. He would like to sit in silence, let the time run away, like sand through his fingers, but if he wants to return to duty he has to play the game; show a little of the wizard behind the curtain, but not too much. Just a tease, all a tease. As Freud might say: 'It's all tits and ass.' Tom takes a deep breath.

'Soon after I joined the force the woman I loved was abducted and murdered.' Tom thinks to himself, *while I was weeping for her, the wind changed and I was stuck like this*. But he cannot say that to this man, so instead he tells him: 'I was deeply affected by her death, emotionally and physically.'

Harrison nods and makes more notes. 'This girl—'

'Her name was Dani, Dani Lancing.'

'Dani. My understanding is that you founded your sexual crimes unit as some form of monument to her?'

'No. My experience with loss and grief led me into a role as a family liaison officer dealing with the bereaved. My founding of the unit came from that work – not some desire to build a shrine to any one person.'

Harrison nods and makes a note. 'I have read your service notes. Frankly, I was amazed.' He looks up and holds the other man's gaze. 'I believe you have investigated scores of murders and, in each case, you personally have broken the news to the parents that their daughters—'

'Sons too, sometimes.'

'You have broken the news yourself, that their children will not be returning home,' he pauses, and Tom thinks he sees a glint of excitement in the psychiatrist's eye, 'surely at your elevated position of authority you have other officers who are better placed to inform and counsel the parents?'

Tom makes no attempt to reply.

'Do you enjoy heart-break, Detective Superintendent?'

'Do you, Dr Harrison?'

A shaft of sunlight across the desk brightens between them.

'Operation Ares.' Harrison chews on the name. 'You named your unit after the Greek god of war. Are you a man of war, Detective Superintendent Bevans?'

'The unit is not named after Ares. The unit *is* Ares – we go after the men of war: those who hurt and kill and take what they want from those they perceive as weaker than themselves. We try to protect women who would otherwise be victims, and if we cannot protect them, we avenge them.'

'Vengeance? Quite an emotional response to your work, Detective Superintendent.'

'Yes. Yes it is.'

Harrison nods to himself and makes another series of notes. Tom wonders if they are not merely items for a shopping list.

'Why did you suddenly take a six-month leave of absence last December – no notice given?' Harrison drops the hand grenade of a question and waits for the fall-out. Tom smiles what he hopes is a realistic and sane smile. He understands he cannot tell him the truth of that night, six months ago, when in the snow of a terrible winter, alongside her parents, he had finally discovered the truth about the death of Dani Lancing. Her mother, Patty, had kept at the case like a dog with a bone. For more than twenty years she gnawed and gnawed at it, desperate to find Dani's killer, until it finally shattered and the marrow of truth spilled out; but there was a cost. The cost was two people dead and another man with his skull bashed in, a man who had once been Tom's best friend – Marcus Keyson; a man who is now little more than a vegetable, slowly withering away to nothing in a hospital bed. Tom cannot tell Harrison any of this, cannot describe the guilt that haunts him.

He had not delivered the blow that felled Keyson; it had been some crazy accident, but that night and its tragedies had made him realise that his career, the career that he thought was so damned pure, was actually based on lies and pain. And for Tom, there had been an even more terrible realisation that night – that Dani had never really loved him. For twenty years he had thought himself her protector, but now he had to come to the realisation that he had done great harm in her name, all for a love that was a sham. He had maimed an artist, Bix, who had date raped her – Tom had sliced his face in two. A journalist, Ben Bradman, who had written appalling slurs about her, found himself in prison for selling contaminated drugs – framed, of course. For Dani. All for Dani. *The things we do for love.*

For ten years after Dani's death, Tom mourned her loss and tried to make amends by saving other girls. When he finally founded Operation Ares, that first morning before any other member of the staff arrived, he wrote her name in giant letters with a spray can on the main wall of the office. Then he screwed four large notice boards over the top so only he knew her name was there. She was his ghost in the machine, the reason he worked so tirelessly – for the dead girls.

His unit operated with the highest of standards and values; they were a phenomenal success. Their detection rate was far higher than any comparable serious crimes unit anywhere in the country – over time Tom had actually forgotten about the lies and the pain he caused trying to save Dani. He had forgotten that everything he had built was set on a foundation of pain. Then six months ago it all came home to roost, the truth of Dani's death and the crippling shame of his own guilt. It broke him. For weeks he stayed in the same clothes, not washing, not eating and barely sleeping. One night he beat his forehead on the wall until he lost consciousness. He lived rough in the park for a week and howled in the middle of the night; the sound was inhuman. He recalls, as a child, watching something on TV, something on *John Craven's Newsround*, a report from the zoo where an elephant had given birth, but after a day, the baby died.

The mother howled for twenty-four hours – they called it a death song. The mourning of the animal was heart-breaking, and as a child it had made him cry. Now he realises it was that same song that he had howled into the night. The song of loss and grief. For Dani, Patty, Jim, Marcus and himself. But none of that can be told to Dr Harrison. Stories like that will get him put in the nut-house, not back on active duty. There can be no sharing the harrowing tales – this is the 'lite' version of his last six months – because he must get back to work, he really must.

'Burn-out. I needed to recharge. It just hit me all of a sudden, like monumental flu,' he tells Harrison, and it isn't a lie, not really. He had burned, deep inside he had roasted. 'I couldn't drag myself out of bed, I could barely move, all I wanted to do was sleep.'

Harrison nods slowly, classic reaction to trauma. He has seen it often in rookie police officers but rare in someone so senior. 'So you just took yourself off for a – what, little holiday?'

Tom holds his face impassively. 'It was hardly a holiday, I believe I suffered a grief overload.' It is a plausible story, Tom thinks. He's been reading about trauma in the military for the last week, to prepare himself for today's show.

'And so you rested, meditated yourself through it?'

'Nothing spiritual. I just think I needed some time for reflection and rest,' he smiles at Harrison, 'I feel more balanced now, grounded. I'm ready to go back to work.'

'Are you sure? Back to that same cycle of desolation, grief and loss? Back to the stresses of leading a murder investigation, to seeing young women who have been violated and killed?'

Tom frowns, unsure if Harrison asks this with a psychiatrist's eye, or more that of a father who could not bear to view the body of his own child laid on a slab. Tom hears the emotion creep into the man's voice; so few people can imagine spending a lifetime with the dead, and those who loved them.

'Back to helping people, Dr Harrison. Helping people in pain.'

Harrison narrows his eyes. He is confused about this man with the cracked face, this sad man. He can see in his file that he is an exemplary officer; he has more citations for bravery than he has seen in any other senior officer he has worked with. He has also reported five colleagues to the Directorate of Professional Standards and had three colleagues fired from the force. The man seems whiter than white, too white – too inflexible? Harrison cannot help but let a smile crawl across his face – it is an interesting question. But he stops himself sliding down that fanciful path, for he is a scientist not a storyteller. He must judge this man's capacity to work with an open and clear mind.

'You feel you are well enough to lead a team of—'

'Forty-seven men and women.' Tom completes his question. 'Yes, yes I am.'

'Why?' It is a simple enough question, Harrison thinks. Why would a man who has seen more than twenty years of pain and grief – seen the very worst of humanity – want to get back in?

'Do you believe in ghosts, Dr Harrison?'

There is the stab of a smile, slightly supercilious, from the mental health professional. 'Do you mean an oogy-woogy dead man in a sheet, maybe holding their head under their arm?'

Tom Bevans scowls his reply.

'I am sorry, Detective Superintendent Bevans, I should not mock the belief of others, even spiritualism.' He drops his pad onto his desk with a bang that shoots up a dust cloud to glitter in the sunlight that cuts his desk in two. 'I believe in guilt. I believe in regret, shame, lust, anger. A whole plethora of emotional wounds we may build pathologies from, become *infected* by, if you like.' He pauses, removing his glasses to clean them. 'Ghosts. An interesting word.' He retrieves the pad from the desk and makes a note. 'But in answer to your question, I suppose in some form, I do believe in ghosts. At least I appreciate that human beings can feel haunted by their actions, or their inactions. Why, do you see dead people?'

'Of course not. I mean that the dead, those who are murdered – ejected from the world before their time – need someone to help them, champion them.'

'And that person is you?'

'And my team. We work with the living but we answer to the dead.'

'You really believe that?'

'Yes.' Tom pauses, drawing his thoughts together. 'Dr Harrison. You seek to help people, those who have lost their way, those who are troubled and in pain – you release them from their anxieties.'

'I hardly think—'

'You must get a buzz from it, feel like you are valued – that this is how you better society, how you grease the wheels of life and living.'

Harrison nods. He does understand, sort of.

'This is me, what I do, how I make the world a better place. I have a job to do and I am ready to go back to it.' Tom knows that he will not be at peace until he confronts what he did to the men he hurt and, more importantly, remember and avenge the dead women he promised to help.

Harrison puts his pen down; maybe he has underestimated the intelligence of this man whose eyes burn with what looks like an almost religious zealotry.

'So, Dr Harrison. Can I return to active duty?'

ONE

Tuesday 21st June 2011. The first day of summer.

The young woman fractures as he twists, her body cut in two and smeared to nothing. Then, as if by magic, a half-turn and – hey presto; she slides back into focus in the centre of the tele-photo lens: Pia.

The blond man in the leather coat, who has been paid a lot of money to follow her, walks at a safe distance, always holding her centre frame as she ambles in a crowd of other chattering students. Finally they stop and settle in the long grass. Some of them pull apart loaves of bread, while others peel slices of ham or orange triangles of cheese from plastic pouches. There is a crack, like a gunshot, and champagne oozes over someone's hand.

The blond man is ready, finger poised on the fire button. But now all he can see of the girl is the top of her head, angled towards him as she talks to someone lying down; the curls of her chocolaty hair hiding her face.

'Just look up, sweetheart,' he pulls on the cigarette, drawing smoke deep down into his lungs. 'Just—' he holds the smoke, trapped, as slowly she raises her chin. 'Beautiful …' her face is perfectly held in the viewfinder, her complexion a flawless cinnamon, '… skin.' He smiles as his finger tightens on the shutter and fires, fixing her for eternity. 'Perfect,' he trills to himself and the smoke curls up over his cheeks, through his hair and into the sky. He relaxes and drops the camera, tilting the screen to look at the image. He toggles in close, checking the focus: needle-sharp. He has her at last.

He takes one final look at the group as they talk and drink, all so young and happy. *Fucking students*. He turns and walks back down Arthur's Seat, the hill winding down to the city and his car. He can't wait to leave Edinburgh, he never feels comfortable outside London. There's no place like home.

When he reaches his car he sits in the back and opens a silver case, sliding his laptop out and onto the seat beside him. From the camera, he removes the CF card and slots it into the computer. He types *Pia* as a tag for the photo, and renames the file: Pia Light. Then he emails it. He throws the butt into the gutter and locks the laptop back in its case. Now he waits, there should be a message soon; it will either be *keep close to her*, or *kill her*. Either way is fine with him, as long as he gets a crack at her father too. He locks the car and with a swish of his leather coat walks off in search of some food that's not deep fried.

TWO

Above the secretary's desk there is a calendar, a George Clooney calendar. Twelve whole months of being watched over by the handsome brown-eyed man. Tom smiles; we all have our fantasies. Today's date is circled, in small print it reads Tuesday, 21st June 2011; British summertime begins. Then in thick marker the secretary has written, *chiropodist appointment*. Tom hopes the appointment is for Deputy Commissioner Raymond Grayson. Tom likes the idea of his boss having a nasty corn dug out with a scalpel.

'—ur turn,' he half hears the secretary speak to him.

'Sorry.' Tom snaps out of his daydream. 'I didn't hear you.'

'He will see you now.' The secretary points to the door and Tom walks inside.

'First day back and – what the fuck is this Tom, beautiful skin?' Grayson asks with obvious distaste as he leans back in the expensive, posture-enhancing leather chair, behind the massive steel desk, in the largest office at New Scotland Yard.

'That was how we talked about them, inside the unit, it was our codename for the three dead girls.' Tom pauses, feeling heaviness settle in his chest. 'They were reported to be the words the killer said to the second victim.'

'There was a witness?'

'There was.' Tom sees Grayson's face crease, hard to tell if it is just plain disappointment or outright contempt. Tom can see that he wants to ask – *if there was a witness, then why didn't you catch the bastard?* If only it had been that simple.

'A young woman was in the school with the second victim. She didn't speak except to say—'

'Oh let me fucking guess, beautiful skin.'

Tom tries to let the sarcasm go. 'He may have planned to kill her too, we don't know. She alerted the police and then hid.' The image of the blood- and flesh-streaked kiln is burned into his memory. It makes bile etch at his throat, even after several years. 'The girl was deeply traumatised by the—'

'Yeah, yeah, I get it, tragedy, tragedy, tragedy.' Grayson rolls his eyes dramatically.

'We kept the name from leaking to the press, it would have been too sensational, too hurtful for the families, *the beautiful skin murders*.'

On the desk lies a green folder. With a pen the commissioner pokes at it, as if the insides are toxic. Maybe they are, Tom thinks.

'More than four years, these killings are over four years old?' Grayson asks.

'Three killings that stretch from October 2006 to February 2007.'

'And there's been nothing with a similar M.O. since?'

'No.' Tom thinks he can see where this is going.

'Do you have any intelligence to suggest there will be a further victim?'

'I have no—'

'Or any new evidence that has come to light from another investigation?'

'Sir, I—'

'Christ, Tom.' He slams the pen down on his desk. 'I have put my arse on the line here. Out of the fucking blue, you disappear – in the middle of five investigations – and are off work for months, bloody months, then you ask to come back. So we go by the book and you see the shrink. His report is inconclusive, he said you were,' Grayson opens a folder and thumbs through a report on his desk, 'yes, here we are: "evasive and argumentative". Tom, if I read that report on almost anyone else, they would not get to waltz back into running a serious crime team.'

'I agreed to the follow-up sessions; I'm seeing him every week.'

'And in the meantime you are back on active duty and are you grateful? Do you thank me by bringing flowers and chocolates, or even coming back and catching me a killer? No, you walk back in and apply for a cold case to be reopened – doubling the workload for your team with something you failed to solve four years ago.'

'That isn't fair—'

'Your job is to solve ongoing crimes, not dig back into ancient history. I hear there were some unsolved murders in Whitechapel a while back – do you want to have a crack at those too?'

'Sir, I realise this is outside the remit of my unit but the investigation of these three murders was hampered—'

'Yes, I remember, Tom.' He says Tom's name like you might to shame a naughty child. 'I'm not losing my marbles yet. I remember when the shit hit the fan back then, when one of your men was arrested for serious breaches of conduct and charges of conspiracy to pervert the course of justice. Your whole unit was suspended if I remember correctly.'

'You have most excellent recall sir.' The sarcasm is lost on Grayson, who just nods. 'But I am sure you will remember that only one person was found to have acted inappropriately and he was dismissed. No other member of my—'

'Tom, give it a rest,' Grayson cuts him dead. With an exasperated sigh he hauls himself out of his chair and walks to the window, his left leg dragging behind him. Grayson's story has always been nerve damage from an IRA bomb. Tom is sure it's just gout. The deputy commissioner stares out over the city and watches the worker ants toiling down below. He no longer sees people and lives, but crime statistics and potential offenders. *Christ,* he thinks, *I could really do with a smoke.* He turns back to face Tom squarely. 'How many murders are your team currently investigating?'

'Three, sir.'

'Does that mean you are so underworked that you can open cold cases?'

'Sir—'

'Because if it does, Detective Superintendent, then I will relieve you of a couple of your thumb-twiddling officers and put them to work solving some of the other thirty murders the Met are dealing with at the moment.'

'Sir, with all due respect—'

'Bevans, with fuck-all respect, NO!' The older man curls his lips, almost in a snarl. His eyes flash angrily and he takes a half step forward. Tom is worried for a second that he'll beat his fists on his chest like a wild gorilla warning another male off his territory. He finds it all a bit demeaning – he won't do alpha male battles.

'Yes, sir.' He backs down.

'Grayson allows himself a half-smile now that the pecking order has been restored. He lifts the folder with his fingertips and passes it back.

'No more going back, Tom.' He smiles. 'We don't *do* the past here.'

'No, sir.'

Grayson tilts his head to one side. It is supposed to be a gesture to show some concern; he did a course a while back on showing empathy to your team. So he tries to practise it when he can. Step one – tilt your head. 'This hasn't been the best of years for you so far Tom. I do trust that you have fully recovered?'

How delicately put, Tom thinks. 'I am fine, sir,' he says.

Step two – nod a lot to show you have heard what they have said and you appreciate their point. Grayson nods a little too enthusiastically. 'Good, because I really want you back at the head of Ares – if you are up to it. If not, then DI Thorsen did a great job while you were gone and she would make an excellent permanent head of Ares.'

'You're right sir, she would. I taught her everything she knows.'

Grayson smiles. He knows what an asset Tom is to the force, and how loyal his team are to him. He would like to keep the band together, however, he has known Tom for twenty years and in all that time Tom Bevans has never shared anything personal with him; the man is an enigma. And Grayson doesn't like that, doesn't like a copper who isn't transparent. Doesn't like a copper who is too clean, it isn't natural.

'So are we clear?' Grayson asks.

'Clear,' Tom replies. 'No opening the Spall/Mason/Penn cases.'

'Thank you, Detective Superintendent.'

'No problem, Deputy Commissioner.'

*

The green folder should have gone back down to archives, but Tom had made it quite clear that it had been requested by Deputy Commissioner Grayson and he might hold onto it for a while. Then Tom had shrugged a *what can you do – he's the boss* shrug and had shaken his head sadly. He had also taken a packet of chocolate Hobnobs down to sweeten the deal, knowing it was Deirdre's day in the cold case files room and she loves a choccy biccy. Now the file sits in the briefcase between his feet as he rides the tube home. It is gone 9 p.m. so the carriage isn't full to bursting but every seat is taken. He runs his eyes around the inhabitants, none of whom make eye contact with him. There are thirty-seven men and women. Statistically, three will be gay; double that number will have committed an infidelity in the last year. A dozen will have cancer at some point in their lives and at least seven will die from it; another one will die a violent death at the hands of another human being. Of the eighteen women he can see, three of them will be victims of sexual abuse and— he stops playing the statistics game. It is too depressing. I-spy is almost as bad. He looks at the young people around him; each one is either staring into a phone screen or is bricked inside a wall of sound with thumping ear buds stealing them away from the world. He totally understands their introversion – it is always a risk to interact with the real world.

'Don't blame you.' He suddenly feels his skin redden, as he realises he just said that aloud. He looks up. For the first time four people are looking at him; they make eye contact for a split-second then look away. They think he's crazy. Maybe they are right.

He gets home a little after 10 p.m. In one hand he holds a Styrofoam container. He puts his briefcase down and opens the take-away box. Inside is a greasy looking doner kebab. There is nothing like the flavour of this meat; he loves it. He opens a cupboard and pulls out a wok. He drizzles in some sesame oil, adds a splash of teriyaki sauce and a flick of rice wine vinegar. He fires up the burner below the wok and puts the kettle on. In the fridge there is a spring onion, a couple of dodgy looking cauliflower florets, a stick of lemongrass and a heel of ginger. He chops them up and throws them into the wok – they sizzle on contact. He turns the gas down a little and reaches for the kebab. He tosses the stale pita into the bin and picks out the lettuce and tomato, then scrapes off the congealing humus and chilli sauce until there is only the wonder of doner meat. He drops it into the wok; it spits viciously at him. He opens a packet of mushroom-flavoured noodles and drops them into the kettle; they fizz slightly. The packet of mushroom-flavoured monosodium glutamate that came with the noodles gets opened and sprinkled into the wok. He mixes it all around and adds some low-sodium soy sauce. Then he fishes the noodles out of the kettle and drops them into the wok and stirs it all together. It actually looks good and he can feel saliva start to build in his mouth. He carries the wok to the table, no need to dirty a bowl, and starts to dig in with long fine chopsticks adorned with Hello Kitty. He is ravenous now, but forces himself to eat slowly and chew each mouthful fifty times before he swallows. After he finishes the noodles he eats his salad, the rescued lettuce and tomato from the kebab. It tastes only of water. So much for his five a day.

After dinner he makes a quadruple espresso, pops two ibuprofen, and clears the table. It is an old Formica one, pink with tiny white squares, which his Nan left him when she died a hundred lifetimes ago. He snaps up the two extra leaves to make it as big as it gets, then lays out a roll of craft paper, marker pens, scissors and a glue stick – just like it's a day at pre-school. He then goes to the green file he has stolen, well, borrowed at least, and slides three photographs out from a plain brown envelope inside it. With the first, he dabs glue at the corners and then gently sticks it down. One dead girl.

Her photograph is a blurred snapshot from a cheap camera, taken just a couple of weeks before she was killed; a pale girl with long, bottle-blonde hair and smudged features. She stands defiant, her legs firmly planted, arms crossed over her chest, staring into the camera. It is difficult to tell from the low quality print – but she seems to be scowling. Behind her is a taller, older man who has his hands on her waist. She is half-wrapped inside his leather coat, leaning against him in a stance that seems proprietary. Under the photograph Tom writes: *Heather Spall. 16 years old. Died 19th October 2006*. Body found on a piece of waste ground behind a community centre in Leeds.

The second photograph is daubed with glue, then placed alongside the first. Two dead girls. This photo is clearer, professionally taken by a school photographer. She is in a spotless grey and green uniform, smiling for the camera. It looks genuine; she appears care free and happy. She wears no make-up, has blonde hair that does not look as if it has been augmented and is on the attractive side of normal. Her teeth are very straight. Below this photograph he writes: *Tracy Mason. 16 years old. Died 5th November 2006*. Found at St. Mary Magdalene independent school. He stops for a moment and then draws a line from the photo, as if he is constructing a family tree. At the end of that line he writes: *secondary victim Allison Stokes. Alive*. But he remembers her flayed skin.

He picks up the third photograph, runs the glue stick along the edges, his hand shaking a little. He turns it over and sticks it down. The third victim. Sarah Penn looks back at him with her oh-so-striking blue-grey eyes. Her skin is bronzed; the photograph had been taken in Ibiza the summer before she was killed. A sly smile plays across her lips – her face so full of life and more than a little mischief. Tom feels his heart skitter slightly, he would like to have seen that spirit for himself, but all he has is this photograph. A stolen moment from a short, short life. All he has? No, not quite, he has his memories of the day she was found – when he stood over her dead body in the rain; her normally curly hair smeared into the mud and her skin reduced to a pale porcelain, as her life essence oozed out of her, into the drowned earth. Even in death he had thought her beautiful, her eyes had seared into his brain. That day he had wept over her, his tears had linked up with the raindrops and danced down his face. Under her photograph he writes: *Sarah Penn. 19 years old. Died 13th February 2007.*

Then he takes the pen and connects the three photographs together with a straight black line. Above all three he writes, *Beautiful skin.* He takes the length of craft paper, and with a roll of tape he fixes it to the wall. Then he sits back, in the least rickety of his three dining chairs, so he can see the whole page. The entire waste of life: Sarah and Heather and Tracy. A trinity of the dead. He remembers …

Back then

Tom signs in. There is no one there to offer him the visitor's book, but he finds it in the security cubby hole. He looks at his watch. It is gone midnight, now it's Wednesday 14th February

2007. He fills out each little box and makes himself up a plastic badge, which he clips to his lapel. As he does so, his fingers brush against something that is pinned to the underside of the lapel, invisible, hidden from sight, but he knows it is there. It is a CND badge. Policemen are not meant to wear any political affiliation, not on their sleeves, T-shirts or lapels, but it has massive sentimental value and it saved his life once – so what can you do?

He pushes through the 'authorised personnel only' doors and into the morgue. It is dark – mostly. Here and there, small points of emergency light shine the way, warning you not to crash into important machines. It is empty of life, even though Tom knows there are human bodies only feet from him. He runs his hand along the wall and – yes. He flicks the main bank of switches and they crackle. He hates strip lights, they make everything look vomit-green for twenty minutes. He quickly finds the log and sees where the two bodies admitted today are stored. He is looking for Sarah Penn. She is in drawer e4. He opens the bag he has brought with him and fishes out a hat, scarf and gloves. He puts each item on and then moves down to the body storage – it's damn cold in there. He stops, there is a sound. He listens for a few seconds before he realises it was him, whistling.

'Cut it out,' he tells himself. 'There's no one here to know you're afraid anyway.'

The drawer slides open. The body is intact – he had thought the autopsy may have been done this evening – that would have been much worse, to see her like that. In some sense the victims of autopsies feel more dead, but that's absurd. How can you be more dead than dead?

She looks calm, actually more peaceful than she had looked that morning, naked and cold in the mud of the allotment.

He moves his hand to touch her hair; it is dry now but no one has been there to comb it, so it is clumped with mud and blood. Up close he can see the ragged edge of her skull where the hammer blow struck, arcing from the back of the head – through hair, skin, fat, bone and brain, and out through the forehead. He leans down to examine the wound and to his eye it looks just like Tracy Mason's wound. He avoids her eyes and scans down her face to her mouth. He parts her lips and takes a sniff. He can catch a bitterness – tobacco and maybe a spirit, maybe a barbiturate, tests will reveal the truth. Then he looks up into her blue-grey eyes, still open. Earlier that day they implored him to help, now they seem to burn with scorn. 'Fourteen hours gone already – what do you know? You promised you would avenge me.' He had, in the rain he had promised her so much. All that has happened since then is that she has been put into a drawer, like a coffin. He can't help it. A tear worms from his eye and runs down his cheek. It falls and lands like a summer shower on her skin.

'Christ, Tom.'

'Fuck.' Tom jumps out of his skin.

Marcus Keyson slides out of the darkness, grinning like the Cheshire cat. 'You can't cry on the bodies, there's DNA in tears you know. We don't want you getting arrested for this, do we?' Keyson takes a spray and a wet-wipe and cleans Sarah's skin. He does it with care, but roughly, not like she's a human being but how you might clean a stain from a leather sofa.

'Were you sitting there in the dark all the time?'

'I'd been working, checking a few things – thinking time is so important and we don't get a great deal of it in this job.' He smiles. 'Do you want a drink? There's some rubbing alcohol.'

'Marcus. Jesus Christ.' But he can't help the slight trace of a smile cracking his firm-set mouth. 'And what the hell are you wearing?'

Marcus looks down at his big towelling dressing gown. He opens it to show Tom that he is fully dressed underneath.

'I sometimes sleep here, so I have some home comforts. Oh where are my manners? Coffee? I've got some biscuits.'

'It's a morgue, Marcus.'

'It's my office, Tom. I've got an espresso maker.'

The two men settle down on either side of Sarah Penn's body; they drink coffee and eat custard creams. Marcus puts the plate next to Sarah, on the tray. Tom goes to tell him not to, but maybe she would like the normality of coffee and biscuits with friends. Who knows? Tom finds his pathologist exasperating most of the time but he can't deny he likes the company. Tom Bevans doesn't have many friends, doesn't really know what a friend is anymore; the word has been so devalued these days. He can't do small talk, actually he can't really do big talk – unless it is about death. The thing that draws him to Marcus Keyson is the fact that he is not a policeman but he knows and appreciates that life, and he under-stands what makes Tom tick, he knows all about the Sad Man, all about Dani. It makes him feel close to this man. This friend.

'You should dunk.' Keyson breaks into Tom's reverie and with a broad smile dips the custard cream into the hot coffee. Tom watches him, in his head counting: one, two, three, four, five, six, sev— the biscuit is withdrawn. It has soaked up the bitter coffee. Marcus pops it in his mouth. 'Yum.'

'You think she's the same as Spall and Mason?' Tom asks, dragging them back to business.

'Oh, is it time to talk shop again?' he pouts. 'Is this the best way to spend Valentine's day?'

It almost makes Tom smile; he had forgotten the date. Romance barely registers on his radar.

'I've had worse,' he tells the pathologist, and he has.

'Have you got a hobby, Tom?'

'This isn't twenty questions.'

'Is that a no then?'

Tom sighs. 'I have no hobbies.'

'Interests? Literature, sport, music? You must like music.'

Tom says nothing. He is lost with any music past the eighties, partly due to growing older and partly because Dani died in 1989. 'No,' he tells Marcus. The truth is that what excites him, really the only thing in life that holds a genuine interest, is finding a killer and making sure he will not hurt another woman. That moment – when he is caught and Tom can see in those trapped eyes that he knows it's over, that is the best feeling. Euphoria. That can keep him going for months. 'Do you think Sarah Penn was killed by the same man as Heather Spall and Tracy Mason?'

Marcus sighs a little and knocks back the final dregs of the coffee. 'I can only be sure with Mason because I've seen the body. With Spall I can only go from the notes.'

'I understand the caveat, so can you tell me if Sarah Penn was killed by the same man who killed Tracy Mason.'

Keyson pauses. 'Nothing is one hundred per cent, but based upon the evidence I think, in all likelihood, she was. There are too many points of convergence to make me think these are two separate cases.'

'And Spall?'

Keyson makes a snorting sound. 'The Leeds pathologist didn't do a very good job with our Ms Spall.'

Tom nods: the Leeds police had written her off from the moment she was found. They thought she was a whore, turning tricks to fund a drug habit and was killed by a punter. End of story for them. They let the investigation slide, did the bare minimum and then filed her away in the 'who cares about a dead whore' file. He has written to the Yorkshire force to ask the officers involved be suspended for incompetence. Not the way to build a career but—

'Okay, let me go through the points of convergence on all three girls.' Marcus rubs his hands together and grabs a large pad of paper. 'We know that Mason and Penn were drugged before their murder. They were both given the same mix of haloperidol and suxamethonium. We have no toxicology report on Spall.' He sneers. 'Let's assume it is the same in all three. We then see that the killer waited until they were fully under and their clothes were cut away from the body – I would hazard a guess at dressmaking scissors. The cut lines on the clothes of Mason and Penn are identical. Spall's clothes were burned but there are three crime scene photos that show the clothes were cut away and the edge looks similar, but without fabric samples it is all guesswork – none of which would stand up in a courtroom.'

'I understand,' Tom says with a growing concern that these girls will never get the justice they deserve.

'All three girls were then laid out and spread-eagled, their limbs tied with looped plastic ties; the kind that are used on building sites to lash scaffolding poles together. They were splayed and then raped. Quite brutally.'

'While they were unconscious?'

'*I believe so.*'

Tom pauses to take the last fact in. Rape was mostly about power; the men who force sex on women generally take pleasure in having physical control over the women, enjoy their struggling or pleading. So what is this man thinking; what gives him his kicks? '*Are we dealing with one man?*' *Tom asks.*

'*There's no semen. No hairs, no saliva. I would be speculating.*'

'*There are bite marks, there must be something.*'

'*The killer wipes or douses the areas he bites with some cleaning product after. Bleach based. He is careful, these are planned – there is no opportunist element here.*'

Tom sighs with annoyance. '*Damn. Okay. The murder weapon.*'

'*A claw hammer swung from above with some force, almost like a golf club. It enters at the back of the skull and exits out through the forehead, just above the eye socket. Death would be instantaneous.*'

Earlier, when Tom had met the parents and the mother had folded into him and wept salty, mucousy tears onto his chest, they had asked if their daughter suffered. He had told them 'no'. He is glad to discover he hadn't lied to them. Tom stands and moves to the head of the tray and once more he looks into the face of Sarah Penn. '*Is there anything else, Marcus? We really need a breakthrough in this.*'

'*Maybe.*' *He smiles an '*I am so clever*' smile.* '*I may be on to something. I'll call you.*'

But Marcus hadn't called and there was no breakthrough in the case. Two days later Tom had gone to visit him at his home, unannounced, and seen someone there, someone who should never have been there and … and then it all came tumbling down.

Marcus Keyson fell from grace, the department was dragged down and Heather, Tracy and Sarah were lost. Tom and Operation Ares forgot all about the beautiful skin murders. There was nothing in four years. Nothing, until after Durham; after Tom discovered the truth about Dani Lancing, and after the guilt and shame broke him. Then, at his lowest point, the ghosts came; demanding he make good on his promise to avenge them. And that is why Tom has to go back to Ares, has to go back into the world – to avenge the girls he made promises to.

THREE

'Franco, I need your help on this.' The man is sweating profusely, starting to smell like a shaggy old dog. Franco has spent the last twenty minutes listing to this fat man whine about how another gang is selling dope on his patch. It is boring him.

'I can't let such a slap in the face go unchallenged. I need you to send them a message.' The fat man pleads.

Franco stands impassive, nothing can be seen in his cruel, dark eyes. The fat man giggles nervously. Franco scares him, like he scares most people. 'You want me to protect your interests, is that right?' Franco asks him and he nods. 'You want the money that should have been yours to be returned to you. And their pushers to leave your turf alone?' He pauses. He can see by the way the man's lip trembles that he wants more. This is a greedy man. 'Then what, what else do you want?'

'I want reparations. I want someone to pay.'

'How?' Franco's voice is like ice. 'Money, or are you asking for something more, are you asking for blood?' The man in front of him shrugs, Franco finds the gesture repellent – weak. The man is a coward.

'Whatever you think right, Franco. You're the boss.' He smiles; his teeth are eroded, too much sugar and crystal meth, making them brown, pitted stakes. Franco despises him.

'Go home. I'll let you know what I decide.'

With an obsequious bow, the man leaves. Franco feels like he needs a hot shower. He looks at his watch, *shit*, almost 7 p.m.

'Is everything ready in my apartment?' he asks one of the men by the door, who nods.

Franco takes the lift to the top of the building and inputs the code to reach his penthouse. Once inside the apartment, he goes to his desk and from a locked drawer takes a small box. On it there are two words: Frank Light. He opens the box and removes a hair elastic and pulls his dreadlocks back and slides the rubber ring around them. Then he puts on a pair of glasses and places a gold wedding ring onto his finger. He looks completely different, but it is not from the glasses or ring or hair tie. It is because he looks happy. He is Frank Light again.

'Are you ready, Dad?' Pia asks, a little impatiently.

'Hang on, hang on I can't find the sieve.'

'Hurry up, we don't want mushy pasta.'

Frantically Frank looks around the kitchen; somehow the counter tops are totally covered in flour and jars and towels and bags and – there it is, half hidden under an oven glove. 'Got it,' he tells her, 'I'm ready.'

'Then five … four … three … two … one …'

Together they pour the saucepans of boiling water and spaghetti into their strainers. Steam billows up, his glasses are enveloped and turn to white smoke. 'I can't see a thing,' he laughs and spreads his arms out like a zombie and lumbers forward. Pia laughs at the white eyes, and underneath all she can see are his white teeth and big grin. *How does he smile all the time, he must be exhausted,* she thinks.

Slowly Frank's glasses clear and he can see his daughter once more. She is only as big as his thumb. She sucks up a shoelace of spaghetti.

'Mine tastes great,' she tells him. 'How about yours?'

He picks out a length, a few pieces still clumped together and much too chewy. 'Perfect,' he tells her. That's the joy of eating together on Facetime; she can't see what a terrible cook he is.

'Okay,' Pia reads a few lines from the cookbook she has open in her kitchen, 'So throw the pasta in with the sauce and toss it around.'

Frank's sauce is lumpy; he should have chopped the peppers finer and the onion is pretty much raw. Oh well. The chewy pasta is thrown in and sauce spits up over his shirt and the wall. He doesn't stop smiling. Nothing will detract from the joy of spending time with his daughter – even if it is only virtual time.

Together they slide the pasta onto plates. She has a hunk of grana padano, which she grates over her pasta. He has a plastic shaker of dried parmesan that won't come out, no matter how hard he whacks the base. He looks on the side; the sell-by date has been and long gone.

'Garlic bread,' she trills and opens the oven in her kitchen some 220 miles away. He can see the steam curl up as she gets it out – it looks a golden brown. When he retrieves his, it is black on the top and still frozen in the centre.

'Delicious.' He says it like he means it.

She pours herself a glass of red wine and he has milk. They settle down at their tables, each one with an iPad and they chat – just like they do every Tuesday night. This has been their ritual since she went up to university in Edinburgh, almost three years before. Now she has nearly finished, the time has flown by ...

now things will change. For a moment his smile freezes as a breath of fear touches his skin.

'So, am I actually going to see you – not just on a screen?' Frank asks.

'Well, you could have come up here any time,' Pia teases him, though there is a little barb in there too. In three years he has not come to see her. It does hurt.

'Mmmmm. Scotland.'

'But I will be in London on Friday.'

'I can't do—'

'I know you told me, work thing.' *Always work, isn't it?* she thinks but does not say aloud. 'Then I'm in Brighton for Saturday – at the Royal Pavilion, and then home to James and Hettie's.'

'On Sunday?'

'Late Saturday night. I'll drive home after.'

'After the party.'

'It's not a party, Dad, it's work.'

He makes a small snorting noise. 'You're not getting paid.'

'I'm an intern but it's still work.' Kind of a white lie – it really doesn't feel like work.

'How late will you be coming home?'

'Midnight probably. I think the event goes until 11 p.m.'

'Would you phone me then, just to say that you are on your way home and …' *safe*. He tries to keep the anxiety out of his voice. He knows Brighton, he's seen its underbelly, seen death there – a horrible memory. 'Just humour me, okay?'

She sighs dramatically. 'I suppose.'

'And tell me what it's like in a royal place for a prin—'

'Lalalala,' she drowns him out, stretching her hand out to cover the iPad camera so her dad can see nothing but black. 'Not the *P* word, okay,' she tells him sternly.

'Okay, okay. I won't use the P word. I 'romise.' She groans at the lameness of his joke and pulls her hand away from the camera. 'So I'll see you on Sunday – just like old times.'

Pia pauses before she answers. The last few years have been great; she really feels that they have connected on a far deeper level, now that she is an adult. But she can't forget all those years of seeing him only on a Sunday – and even then he would miss weeks with no notice, or turn up for an hour and be gone, leaving her in her fanciest dress with no one to play with. The Sunday-only years were too hard. 'Yes, just like old times,' she says with sadness. A tear threatens to break through her defences but she sucks it back up and changes the subject.

'I ordered my gown this week; it's crazy, black and blue silk and all lined with fur. You're screwed if you're a vegan – you haven't forgotten have you? Graduation is on 20th July. You are still coming?'

'Of course I am, wouldn't miss it for the world.' Except he won't be going, too many cameras, too public an event. There's no way to manage the exposure and there is just the faintest chance that someone would recognise him. He can't take the risk. What if he was arrested, there in front of her? He couldn't bear that. No, he can't go to her graduation. The truth of it makes his heart shrivel. He has missed so much of her life over the years – so many successes. But he can't tell her now that he won't be there. Instead he will call on the morning of graduation and plead some terrible accident or mishap. She will be upset, of course she will, but she will have Hettie and James, and all her friends there. And he has let her down so many times in her life, that a part of her will be expecting it. He will try to make it up to her; he has already arranged for a stretch limo to pick her up from the flat and stay with her all day. It will be full of champagne and chocolates and big enough for the whole class to fit inside.

'I'm looking forward to it,' he says with a smile.

They talk VSO next, while they slurp and chew. She is so looking forward to going after graduation. She has requested, he knows what she will say before she says it – *Zimbabwe*. Home. Where he was born. He has told her stories of the motherland her whole life, so it makes complete sense that she would want to go there to see for herself what the country is like and to do some good there. He is so proud of her, but he will miss her, he has missed her for these last three years. He has missed her since the day she was born, he wishes he could have been there – not just a Sunday father. But wishes mean nothing, dreams do not come true.

They finish their pasta and then each goes to their own fridge and pulls out a tiramisu. His is shop bought. Hers is home-made. They slowly spoon the dessert into their mouths – both knowing it is almost time to end their dinner together. The mouthfuls get slower and slower.

'Time to go,' Frank finally tells her with a deep sadness that settles in his chest, but he cannot let her see that – and he cracks his whole face open with the biggest smile ever; his teeth so white, his skin dark like chocolate – not the light cinnamon of her own. Pia can do nothing but smile back; it is infectious. She knows her father is handsome. Over the years her friends have called him a blend of Denzel and Idris with a dash of Usher, and one time long ago Janey Haugh said he was a FILF. Of course, Pia had no idea what Janey meant and agreed, not wanting to look stupid. She looked it up an hour or so later, she blushed for a week. He is handsome, and he looks strong but she worries, really worries about him – which seems crazy because on the outside he is such a powerful man, but inside she sees he is so lonely. He needs looking after. *What is he gonna do without me?* she thinks as she blows him a kiss.

'Goodnight Pia.'

'Night Dad. Ready? One, two, th—'

Both their iPad screens go blank. Frank stands still for a moment, the smile frozen to his face and … slowly it begins to melt, like a snowman thawing under the first rays of a new day's sun. The smile crumbles, collapses and slides from his face. Below it his mouth is hard. Around his eyes the laugh lines fill in and the twinkle in his eye begins to gutter and burn out. In seconds his face is transformed from light and charming to hard, brutal. Not an atom of love remains. He removes his glasses; they are only clear glass after all. He takes the elastic from his hair and it springs back into its regular shape. Lastly, the gold wedding ring. Pia's father has vanished. It isn't a disguise; it would be about as useless as Clark Kent's. They are props, to remind him he is Frank Light, that when he is with Pia he is a different man. It is a fiction. He sighs. Time to bury Frank once more, at least for the moment.

He will call someone to come and clear all this mess up, the jars of olives and passata, the towels and broken lengths of spaghetti. They can take the pots and pans back to the kitchens on the ground floor; he only has them here for their dinners together – they are also mere props in the fictitious life of Frank Light. But before he can summon the staff, he must clear the room of anything incriminating. He plucks a framed picture of Pia from the wall behind him, and a tower of coloured sand she had brought him back from a school trip to Devon. He had placed them in view for Pia to see, to simulate a home and a life that does not exist. Lastly he picks up the iPad and squidges a piece of blu-tack over the camera. Then he slides the sim card from the back. Time for it all to go back in the box.

At his desk, he opens the top drawer and, in a deft movement, slides the fake panel of wood away and opens the safe. The combination is her birth date 26/01/90 and when he keys it in the secret compartment is revealed, an Aladdin's cave. The resting place of Frank Light, and his memory-box of Pia.

It is packed full of photos of her, every birthday and Father's Day card she has ever written him; there are reams of financial papers, chequebooks, statements and copies of bank accounts in her name with various stock portfolios. Lastly there are all the proofs of his life – his other life: passport and driving licence, credit cards and bank statements all in the name of Frank Light – real and yet unreal.

He moves to close the drawer but his eye is caught by a flash of silver-foil. He reaches in with two fingers and pulls out a small folded crown. Inside, if he were to unfold it, there is a message in a spidery scrawl. *A crown for a King.* He should slide it back inside, but he hesitates, his fingers dwell for a second, then another, then another. They move to a stack of papers – they are odd shapes and sizes, some of them yellowing with age, others stiff and claggy with paint and wax crayon. It is her art, from the age of about eighteen months to seven or eight years old. Matchstick people, Godzilla-like cats and angel-winged fairies. He has saved everything, all hidden away. With effort, he returns the crown and pulls his hand from inside, closes the secret compartment and locks the drawer. *Do not dwell in the past*, he tells himself, *there are too many ghosts there*. Frank Light closes his eyes and counts ten, nine, eight, seven, six, five, four, three, two, one. Zero.

Franco opens his eyes. They are bright, they burn with intelligence and ambition. He is possibly the most wanted man in London, probably the most hated – he is known as the Dark Wolf and he has been called the devil. He cannot recall all the men he has killed. That is the prerogative of a monster – to forget. Now, at least for a while, he must forget Pia. Franco has no daughter.

FOUR

Yesterday Tom spent the day reading reports and fencing with Grayson, getting up to speed on everything that had happened while he was gone; while he was on leave. Today he actually has to interact with people, make decisions and deal with the consequences of actions. There are always consequences. He looks at the clock, watches the second hand crawl around the face, waiting for 8.30 a.m. and the first briefing of the day. It has been a very long and slow morning so far. He had woken at 3.13 a.m., knowing there was no going back to sleep. He had pottered around for a while, flicking through the green folder on the dead girls but his head was too cloudy, too full of ghosts. At 6 a.m. he had walked to Greenwich Park and picked up a coffee and a Danish and then gone to his bench. From there he had watched the birth of the day. It had been beautiful, no indication that today a girl might die or a plane might fall from the sky or a child might blow themselves up in the hope that heaven on earth may come a little quicker.

Now it is time to see the team again. He is nervous. At least Jane won't be there; he has avoided DI Thorsen all these months even though she left dozens of messages, sent a get-well-soon card and even a box of food – like a care package. He ignored her because she had been the one to find him in his flat, when he had been at his lowest. He hates that she saw him like that. Hates it.

He takes a deep breath and walks back inside the Ares operations room for the first time in six months. It is open plan, there are something like fifty desks, each one covered with reams of paper burying a computer screen and phone; plus dozens of whiteboards and room dividers, most of which are covered in papers pinned to them or drawings – some of them pornographic, others just graphic. One of the walls is floor-to-ceiling glass, the others are wall-to-ceiling victim photos, autopsy reports, witness statements, surveillance results and countless lists and questions. Some smart-arse called them *the wailing walls* a few years ago and the name stuck. Completing the furniture of the room are three coffee machines and two vending machines full of fruit. Some report had said that police officers were amongst the unhealthiest professionals in Britain and were all vitamin C, D and E deprived. Hence the availability of little pots of pineapple & mango, strawberry & blueberry and melon & grapes. They had been fresh and colourful once, but now they are all green, with sell-by dates long gone. At some point they had started to smell and someone had gaffer-taped the slot at the bottom closed. It had solved the problem of the smell but made sure the machines would never be used again. Someone was supposed to be getting them removed – but it was never clear just who that someone was. Into this steps Detective Superintendent Tom Bevans.

'Welcome back, guv!' There is a ripple of applause, mostly from Fat Eddie but Jenkins too and an assortment of DSs. Clarke keeps his arms folded over his chest. Tom sees that Jane *is* there, at the back, even though she is officially off today. He will have to run out of there as soon as the briefing is over; he can't talk to her yet. His eyes run around the place, the Ares operations room – this is the house that Tom built. Thirty-five men and women look back at him. Some he has known for years, others only a short while and two are new. Trust needs to be rebuilt and bonds forged. Summertime – but the living ain't easy.

'Okay, first up. Anything overnight? Eddie?'

'Big case, guv. CID busted a dealer and searched his flat. They found a huge collection of sex dolls, some of 'em chopped up – there was a box of vaginas and,' he can't keep his face straight, 'a forest full of cocks.' Tom stares at him coldly while Eddie almost wets himself laughing. This is going to be a long day.

Tom was right – it was a long day, and he spent much of it avoiding being alone with DI Jane Thorsen, though he felt her eyes on him whenever he was in a public place. By the time 6 p.m. rolled around he felt waves of tiredness wash over him, but he couldn't go home. There was something important to do first.

He had begun the day in Greenwich Park, watching the dawn arrive, and that is where he returns to, just before 7 p.m. The staff are different at the café but it is still open – one of the joys of summer life. He orders a double espresso with just a slurp of extra hot water and sits at a table in the watery sun. It feels good as the early evening sun massages him, maybe it can thaw the final shards of ice in his heart, left from this last awful winter. The coffee is gloriously bitter. He finishes it and then reaches for his phone. He can't put this off any longer. He dials a number he has known the whole of his adult life. It rings for about thirty seconds and then the answering machine kicks in. He knows she is home; he could just go and knock on the door, it's only round the corner. He doesn't leave a message but hangs up, waits a few seconds and dials again.

'Hello.' This time a real person answers, and she sounds annoyed by the interruption.

'It's Tom, could we meet? I need to talk to you about something.'

The pause is long. 'Where?' She sounds guarded, not pleased to hear from him.

'The café in the park by the Observatory, I'm here already.'

'Why?'

He does not answer that question. 'Please.'

'Okay. Ten minutes.' She pauses and a harder edge creeps into her voice. 'Just me?'

'Just you.'

Tom slides the phone back into his pocket and then reaches for the briefcase that lies by his feet. It was his grandfather's case, his initials carved into it. Tom doesn't remember him; he was dead before Tom even went to school. Cancer. He has never even seen a photo of the old man. There seems nothing left of that generation – Tom's parents just didn't do nostalgia, or affection. But he has the case; that is something at least. He opens it and takes out the green folder and places it on the table. He puts his empty coffee cup on top, doesn't want it to blow open and show pictures of dead girls to the world.

He sees her, almost from the moment she enters the park. Patricia Lancing. He watches as she skirts the brow of the hill and follows the path. She is dressed to run, black figure-hugging sleeveless shirt and leggings. Tom guesses she will probably head off after their meeting. She is lean and fit. If you didn't know she was sixty-five years old you would put her in her early fifties. It is only when she gets really close that the lines of loss and grief, etched into her face, are clear. But she looks good, more relaxed than he has seen her in— since Dani died. More than twenty years.

He has known her since he was a child, since he and Dani started school together at the age of five; though they rarely played at that age. Back then they had been from very different worlds, but they had become great friends at secondary school and – he had fallen in love with her. The one-and-only love of his life. Unrequited, he now realises. Totally unrequited. He had always loved the time he spent with her family; as a teenager he was at their house a lot – really a lot, he thought Jim was amazingly interesting and Patty was like a second mother to him.

Now, in the park, she sits down opposite him. No smile. 'Tom.' She is cool, not cold. At least that's something, he can work with that.

'Hello, Patty.' He is warm.

'What did you want to see me about?'

It's strange – he cannot see Dani in her face, as he could when they were children. Dani had the colouring of her dad, but the mouth, the way she arched her eyebrows and so many facial expressions – they were from Patty. But now he cannot see her in the older face before him; more than twenty years of grief has hollowed Patty out, burnt her hazel eyes to deep soulless black, twisting and thinning her mouth. She reminds him of Cruella de Vil, there is such a hardness to her. But she is still brilliant, still tenacious, still a mother – she is who he needs.

She had been a crime journalist, one of the very best investigative writers in the business, until Dani was killed. Then she left writing and spent more than twenty years trying to track down

Dani's murderer, and she never let go of the bone. Even when it cost her a husband she loved, a career she adored and tested her sanity, she still dug and dug, and finally laid the question to rest. They know what happened to Dani. They discovered the truth back at Christmas in that long, cold winter. Now Tom wants Patty to use her skills for Heather, Tracy and Sarah. Her skills and – Tom feels a pang of guilt – her anger. He knows the rage burned her deeply, almost killed her, but he needs her to tap into it again. He needs Patty to burn.

'I am hoping you can help,' he tells her. She laughs, but there is little mirth there.

'And I thought this was just a gossip over a warm beverage.'

He lifts his coffee cup off the file and pushes the green folder across the table to her. She raises an eyebrow. He stops, it is in the middle of the table now.

'That isn't Dani's case?'

Tom shakes his head.

'Green folders are cold, why would you show me that?' She frowns but he sees the pilot light flicker, deep behind the dead eyes.

He taps the folder with his finger and offers her a half-hearted smile. 'How's Jim?' Tom asks.

A look of horror jags across her face for a second – horror and disgust. She sighs deeply. 'Do you believe in ghosts, Tom?'

'No.'

'Jim does,' she scowls. 'He says Dani is a ghost and was with him for the last twelve years. Lived with him, like they were flatmates; he says they used to go to the fucking cinema together. Twelve fucking years, from the time I left him to … ' she doesn't finish.

In his head Tom completes the sentence: *just before Christmas, when you called him to come and help you, because you had tried to murder a man.*

'Crazy, I mean actually crazy,' Patty continues, she does not smile. 'He's seeing a shrink now. Can you believe it?'

Tom says nothing; he can't judge. He talked to Dani-in-his-head for so many years after she died, he used to set her a place at the table and eat meals with her. Sometimes, even now, he wonders what she would think or feel. It helped him, and it was sort of addictive, even though he had always known it wasn't real, just him recreating her in his mind. Is that what Jim did, or did he truly believe in her? Is that crazy, or just sad?

'I'm sorry,' he tells Patty. 'I need your help.'

'The green folder?' She points to it in the centre of the table, her tone wary.

'I thought ...' he lets the explanation die. His eyes float up to the sky, it is cross-hatched with contrails as lucky families jet off to see the world. Dani and he had planned to travel after she graduated, at least they had talked about it. He should go, see something of the world. Apart from a work trip to Holland he has never left the UK. He must go, he would love to see New York. One day, maybe after Heather and Tracy and Sarah are avenged. 'There are some girls who need you.' He avoids eye contact.

'Need me?

He nods. 'Need someone to fight for them. Dead girls, Patty.'

'What the—?' Patty pulls back from Tom as if scalding water had been poured between them.

'Tea, coffee?' A waitress appears at their table. Patty's face is red with anger and her eyes flare. Tom orders another coffee and a sausage roll. Patty asks for a tea. The waitress leaves and Patty hisses angrily at Tom.

'Who the fuck do you think you are?'

'I think I am a police officer who is supposed to track down the killers of young women.'

'Then do that without me. It's your job.'

He leans forward and stretches his hand out and grips hers, squeezing it. 'Patty, I have three girls who have been failed – forgotten, and they need somebody to help them. They are like Dani—'

'Damn you.' She swipes her hand across the table; a vase with a single flower smacks into his chest, flicking water up and into his face. He lets her hand go and wipes the dirty water away.

As soon as he releases her she is gone, walking fast down the path that leads into the centre of Greenwich. As soon as her feet hit the grass she breaks into a run.

'Fuck!' Tom snaps, he played it all wrong. Idiot. He watches her dark figure get smaller and smaller until she is gone. He can't do this alone.

Told you! My mother is crazy. He remembers Dani telling him that years and years ago.

The waitress appears with a tray and sets the drinks down in front of Tom.

'You might as well take the tea away,' he tells her.

'Your friend isn't coming back?'

'No, no I don't think so.'

She puts the tea back on the tray. 'Do you want any condiments with the sausage roll?' she asks.

'Ketchup, please, and mustard.'

'We've got Dijon, English and wholegrain.'

'Yes please, and can I get some HP as well?' He smiles. She waits for a second, thinking he's going to say *just kidding*.

When he doesn't, she walks slowly to the kitchen, shaking her head slightly.

Tom picks up his coffee and takes a large mouthful – it tastes like burnt caramel. He feels lost. He sees those blue-grey eyes imploring him, the voices that sweep through him while he sleeps – the screams of pain and … then he sees that the green folder has gone.

Tom drinks his coffee and ravenously polishes off his mustard and sausage roll. He had not realised how hungry he was before then. He orders another two sausage rolls and sits there for about an hour, his mind mostly blank, until his mobile phone vibrates in his pocket. The number comes up as unknown. He slides his finger across the face to accept the call.

'Detecti——'

'Why did he stop at three?' Patty's voice sounds strained and distant.

'Patty.'

'Why did he stop at three? Is this the whole file? You aren't keeping anything back are you?'

'No, that's everything.'

She's silent for a while. He begins to think they've been cut off and then she speaks again.

'Why bring me in on this?'

'The deputy commissioner refused to reopen the case. It's dead as far as the Met are concerned.'

'Then I don't get it, why aren't you leaving it like that? Why so personal?'

He feels like a little boy for a moment, asked to explain why he pushed someone over in the playground and he doesn't know how to tell them what happened; he is unsure how to open the Pandora's Box of his heart. He can't tell her about the dreams, when Sarah Penn comes to him, slick with blood and rain and mud, begging him to come good on his promise. He doesn't tell her that he feels ashamed every day, that he can't stop thinking about the pain he has caused people in the past, that he feels a need to make amends to everyone he hurt or failed. Instead he says, 'They need us, Patty.' It isn't an answer to her question.

She laughs darkly. 'Ghosts?'

Ghosts. 'Young women who died unjustly Patty, girls who have been forgot—'

The phone goes dead.

She is sitting on his doorstep when he gets home, still dressed in her running clothes. She looks a little cold now. He unlocks the door and ushers her inside. As they enter, he kicks a black bin-bag out of the way. He worries for a second, that Patty will look inside and see it is full of Dani's things – her clothes and diaries. He stole them many years before, squirreled them away as keepsakes, to keep her alive for him. But now they are bagged up to throw away – and he will do it. He will. He just hasn't so far. He must – one day. Soon.

'Can I get you a—'

'Why did you stop, four years ago, why did the investigation stop? Ares seems to disappear from the paperwork and the CID took it over. Why?'

'Marcus Keyson was the team pathologist.'

She sneers at the mention of his name. 'Oh, your old friend.'

'In the middle of the investigation he was arrested for falsifying test reports – not for work on our cases, but we were all suspended while they investigated the spread of his infection. Our cases were given to a CID murder team. They had the case for a month – did all the follow-up interviews.'

'And they found nothing?'

'Not one lead. By the time we were cleared, the case was stone cold. The CID didn't even believe that the three cases were connected. They attributed them to opportunist sex crimes, but not the same man.'

Patty raises her eyebrow but says nothing. She has never had much respect for the investigative powers of the regular police.

'Because of that they arrested a few people close to the girls, a boyfriend and an uncle – but nothing stuck,' Tom continues. 'The case just fizzled out and when we were cleared it was easier for Ares to start fresh. New killings came in and we moved forward,' he feels his throat and face flush with shame. 'I forgot about them.' *I forgot their beautiful skin.*

Patty looks at him. She has known him man and boy – she has not always liked him, never thought he was right for Dani, but knows he is a fine policeman. Knows deep down that he is an honourable man with a good heart. She turns away from him and sees the craft paper taped to the wall, sees the pictures of Heather, Tracy and Sarah, the same ones she has in the file, the same ones she has looked at over and over for the last hour. The pictures are already branded into her brain. She has already decided she will investigate these deaths, inside she feels like a mother hen with her chicks. She will find the fox who savaged them and – if she is lucky, she will hurt him. If she is very lucky she will take his life. After six months, she is needed once more. And once again she has someone to avenge. It feels good.

'Do you have any bread in the house?' she asks.

'A loaf in the freezer.'

'Let's have some toast.'

FIVE

Pia hadn't meant to leave it so late. She should have left in the afternoon but there were too many goodbyes, and when they asked her to join them on a final trip she did, of course she did. She ran all the way up Arthur's Seat and shared a bottle of vodka and a lot of hugs. It isn't goodbye forever, not yet – there is graduation and a whole week of parties around it, but they are nearing the end. It hasn't really hit her yet but soon she will be gone and the next stage will begin. This has been the happiest time of her life and she does not want it to end. She wants to hold her breath, scream and scream until she's sick, but those are the reactions of a child and she is no longer a child. Except, she rarely feels like a grown-up – does she really have to have responsibilities now? A tear forms and runs down her cheek. *This is not sadness*, she tells herself. She cries because it is all ending, all changing.

She has stuffed her little VW bug with as much as possible: it will literally explode if she tries to cram anything more in – even a wafer-thin mint. In the street she suddenly stands on one leg and touches her nose a few times, first with her left hand and then her right. She passes the test. She should be okay to drive, she only had a few vodkas and she has sopped it up with three rounds of cheese on toast and a packet of prawn cocktail crisps.

The good thing about leaving at this time of night is that the traffic will be less, but it is at least a six-hour drive, and that is if she speeds. Eight hours if she goes legal, and she doesn't know that she should drive that far in one go. She looks at the time on her phone and sees it is already 7.30 p.m. She curses British summertime – it is lovely that it's still light, but it tricked her into thinking it was earlier. She won't get to Hettie's until 4 a.m. at the earliest. She should stop somewhere on the way, normally she'd have no qualms about pulling over and sleeping for an hour or two on the hard shoulder or at some skeezy motorway services, but that was before leather-coat guy. She saw him again today, just a glimpse but it has been at least two weeks and she has seen him at least once every day, and he is creeping her out. She has a rape whistle on her key-ring now and carries the can of mace her dad gave her when she moved to Edinburgh. The one she told him she would never use. She wonders now if that will prove to be wrong.

'Stupid,' she whispers to herself. She won't give him that power over her – fucking stalker. She'll soon be 500 miles from here, leather-coat will be long gone and she can forget about him; that will be good, as she has had too many nights of bad dreams.

'So let's get going,' she tells herself. She can stop when she gets tired and pull over, it will be perfectly safe; the car will be locked. She touches her phone in her pocket: for a moment she wants to call her dad; he always makes her feel safe.

'What does your dad do?' A voice from the past pings around her head. Anna, a friend from primary school who she thinks is now married with twins. 'He's away all the time – where does he go?' Anna asks. In fact all her school friends ask her something similar, they are curious about this mystery man who pops up unannounced, sometimes after a month of nothing, always with his arms full of treats and presents, not just for Pia but for them too. Charming and smiling, asking how they all are but you can't fool children with a smile, they see through it. 'Is he police, army, secret something?' they whisper when he's gone.

'You have to swear you won't tell anyone,' she pauses to build the drama. 'He does good all over the world – he's a superhero.'

Pia laughs to herself. A dozen years later and her father is still as much of a mystery now as he was then. She feels the phone in her pocket but she knows that if she were to dial his number all she would get would be a mechanical voice telling her: 'The mobile number you have dialled is switched off. Please try again some other time.' She can never call her dad, he always has to call her, or they arrange a time and date. Those are the rules. She slides behind the wheel, dipping her head slightly under the length of bookcase that threatens to brain her at any moment. Then she starts the car up and puts a CD into the player. Then, mirror-signal-manoeuvre and she pulls out onto the road and begins to drive.

Behind her, after a moment, a car pulls out and begins to follow her. The driver wears a long leather coat.

SIX

Jim Lancing reaches the path that leads to his home and stops. He feels sick. For a moment he thinks he could turn around and walk away, just keep going; except he looks down and sees the bulging bags in his hands, full of blu-tack, drawing pins, white-board markers, cork tiles and extra-large sheets of paper; and he knows she is waiting for them.

He pulls the keys from his pocket. Dani had made the fob for him at school, beaten and worn now, but he wouldn't have any other. He picks the bags up and heads down to the house he has lived in for more than forty years – home, and yet he feels scared to go inside.

In the hallway it seems apocalyptically empty. He looks up the stairs and shouts, 'I've got the supplies.'

'Bring them up, I really need more drawing pins,' Patty yells down to him.

Jim stands at the bottom of the stairs and feels his heart beat a little faster. He truly does not know if he can do this, not again.

'Did you get the cork?' she shouts down. 'We need more coverage.'

'Yes.' His voice is thin, and like an asthmatic child it barely makes it up the stairs.

'Bring it all up,' she shouts down, annoyance flecking her words.

He wants to tell her *no* and escape – RUN! Instead, he takes a deep breath and then ascends – like these are the steps to the gallows. At the top he sees the door has been pushed ajar; he could leave the supplies there and bolt, he could— of course he couldn't. He isn't the one who leaves, that's Patty's job. Instead he puts his toe to the door and—

He stops breathing. It was Patty's office, this room. Where for years she sat and wrote her articles and both her books. So many nights she would work at her desk and he would sit on the floor at her feet, reading or sketching. He just wanted to be near her. He would watch her work, the intense concentration, it was a place of safety and creativity for them both. He painted the walls – he put up the bookshelves that held her journalism awards, diplomas and letters of adoration from the great and the good. It was her office but their room – until Dani died. Then it became a room with a single obsession: solve Dani's murder. That was what Patty had lived for, the only thing that made any sense in what became her shrunken world-view; hunt him, find him and— Jim never admitted to himself back then, that when she did find the man, she would kill him.

More than twenty years of their lives were eaten up in the quest to find the man who killed their daughter and destroyed their marriage. The diplomas were thrown out, the letters from fans were burned and the proofs that once-upon-a-time they had been a happy family were discarded like meat past its sell-by date. She stripped the room and then built it back up from nothing. She covered every inch of the walls with all the evidence from the investigation – the witness statements, pictures of Dani's university friends, the autopsy report and – the worst things in the world: the crime scene pictures. No parent should see pictures of their child dead, her body after it had been repeatedly raped and then murdered. Those pictures were cancerous.

When Patty had left him, eight years after Dani's death, she had taken everything with her, stripped the walls and packed away the cancer, returned the room to a blank canvas. He had still stayed out though – it had become a spare room, a just-in-case room. He thought it would remain empty forever, but today – the walls of death are back. But not with Dani's dead face plastered over them. Now the walls are filled with pictures of other dead girls. He doesn't know them but he can feel the pain solidify the air in the room – standing there, the parents' and friends' grief vibrates all around him.

'Heather Spall, Tracy Mason and Sarah Penn.' Patty points to them in turn. They have a wall each and already photos of them, both alive and dead, are on the walls. She turns to him and he sees the spark in her eyes. He knows he has lost her again.

'Would you like a cup of tea?' he asks. Patty feels disappointment swell as she looks at the man she does still love, she does, she does (if she keeps saying it, it will be true), but she knows he wants to avoid this. She can see how anxious he is getting; he wants to slam the door and leave. He can do that, but she knows that is not an option for her. She will investigate these girls' deaths, with or without him. She would like it if he – oh, who is she kidding? He hides from death, that is why he invented this ghost – this fucking ghost of their daughter. Just thinking about it makes Patty so angry.

'That sounds like a good idea. A pot of tea, you could even go and buy some biscuits.' She smiles, feeling the insincerity creak in her bones. He hears it in the tone, but actually he doesn't care, he just wants to get away from the oppression of death.

He doesn't feel the need to look brave in front of her, that point passed them by more than twenty years ago.

She turns away from him and back to her desk where he has laid the bags from WH Smith. She pulls out more pins and jabs them into the first corkboard, putting a photo on the—

'Christ, Patty.' Jim winces at the horror of the picture.

'Allison Stokes.' She says the name with admiration. 'Her skin was shredded from her body, she didn't die, she was strong.' Jim stares into the picture – he cannot see a human being in it.

'What happened to her, after, I mean?' Jim asks.

There is a slight shrug. 'According to the file she was trauma-tised by the attack.'

'I'm not surprised.' Jim shivers as he speaks.

'She was in hospital for something like three months after – she had skin grafts. The hospital report says it was the equivalent of thirty per cent burns.'

'Jesus,' Jim whispers. He feels more and more claustrophobic – the air seems gritty in that room, full of ash. 'I'll get that tea.' He leaves.

Downstairs he boils the kettle and, checking to make sure Patty hasn't followed him down, he sheds a few tears. 'Fuck Tom and this damn case,' he spits, but underneath everything is his broil-ing anger at himself – that he told her about Dani; told Patty that he talked to their daughter's ghost. It was such a terrible mistake; they had found each other again – were planning to renew their vows almost forty-five years after they first made them. They were lovers again, it was everything he wanted. He was so happy. So why did he screw it up? He thought he owed it to her, that man and wife had no secrets. He told her all about Dani moving back home and how they talked together, went to the movies and took long walks. And as he spoke, he saw Patty's eyes turn black. The love for him that had been rekindled, died from her eyes. He could see that she thought him weak, crazy.

'What an idiot,' he hisses to himself. And then the kettle pops and he has to draw himself back together.

Patty sits at her desk and opens the bags Jim brought. There is something amazingly pleasing about stationery. She pulls out a pack of fine-nibbed Sharpie pens, Moleskine exercise books and some Post-it notes. She pulls the plastic wrap off the pack and writes—

Did the victims know each other?
How were they chosen/targeted?
What does 'beautiful skin' mean?
Will I leave Jim, again?

The last note she crumples and throws into the waste-paper bin. The other three she places on the wall. Then she opens the green folder and re-reads the post-mortem reports. These assess the state of their hearts, lungs, kidneys, the impact of the hammer on their brains, the loss of blood, the extensive bruising to the vagina, the bites to the breasts. It should sicken her, the violence towards these three women – yet she contains the effects by disassociating the pictures of the girls from the dry reports of how they died. It is a puzzle; that is all.

She lights a cigarette, she has completely given up on giving up. She doesn't smoke in the rest of the house but of course it does filter through. Jim hates it, but she doesn't care. It is her house again – *their* house again and she is staking her territorial claim, like a big dog who pisses in the corner of the room to show that's his place.

She finishes the post-mortems and then moves onto other documents. There is an extract from Sarah Penn's diary, which tells how happy she was, how she couldn't wait to get to Ibiza again. There are report cards and educational assessments. Heather was flunking, Tracy was excelling and Sarah was just normal.

Patty gets up and goes to look once more at the photos of the girls. Sarah is first, perpetually trapped on her holiday in Ibiza. Her eyes sparkle, she glows with health and youth and happiness. Like Dani had. Then Patty looks at Tracy Mason – she has the whitest teeth, they are dazzling. Lastly, there is Heather Spall, the first victim. There is no smiling picture of her, but instead she stands awkwardly in front of – what is that? A caravan? Her hair looks either wet or greasy and crawls across her face so her eyes are almost hidden. Her mouth turns down and she looks cold; she certainly doesn't want to be there. To her side is a man. Patty has to read a note underneath to see that it is her boyfriend, Gary Wilkes. He looks glum too, and that leather coat makes him look like a trainee Gestapo man, but he probably thinks it make him look interesting. Idiot. She takes all three girls' photos off the board and takes them over to the desk and looks at them under a lamp. She gets out her old Agfa Lupe to look closer into the photograph. One by one the faces expand, but all she can see is grain – the static of colour that makes up the image – there is no underlying truth, no clue. She looks into the eyes of the girls, enlarged by five hundred per cent, but there is nothing there to explain why they were chosen – why they died. Just like she could never see any hint in Dani's eyes as to why she had been plucked from life.

With a sigh she re-pins the pictures to the walls and heads downstairs where Jim waits for her. Halfway down she reels as a panic attack spins through her – is this it? Again? Is this another twenty years of not knowing, of searching for a shadow? She feels dizzy, grabs at the banister and feels a blackness ooze up her spine.

SEVEN

'Guv!' she calls to his retreating back. She has been waiting for him, hidden in the doorway for the last twenty minutes, she wants to make sure he can't avoid her today – not like he did yesterday. He stops and turns. Just seeing him makes her pulse jump out of synch for a second. He nods to her – for a moment she thinks he is just going to turn and walk away, but he doesn't. He waits there for her to catch him up.

'You're back.' It is not a question, it seems to be an accusation, at least in part.

'For my sins.' He smiles.

'Sins?' Her thoughts slip back to New Year's Day, six months back. She remembers calling in the team to make the announcement. She was shaking as she told them.

The guvnor will be away on leave. For the foreseeable future.'

'Has he fucking flipped at last?' Clarke asks. Eddie looks like he is going to cry. What does she say? It was only yesterday when she saw him, lying on the floor in the middle of his living room, everything smashed around him. She had been calling him for twenty-four hours before she went to his house and stood there pounding on the door. The front door had to be opened by a locksmith. When she finally got in, she thought a gang had smashed the place in but—

'*Guv.*' *She sees his body on the floor, unmoving, she thinks the worst. She runs to him, dropping to the floor and scooping him into her arms – her heart racing. His head turns, his breath is scotch and petrol; he has wet himself. He is wrecked, she wants to drop him, push him away – it disgusts her. Like her dad. But his fingers curl around her arm and pull her into him. His breath is toxic. He opens his eyes.*

'*It's all fucked, Jane. All fucked, I hurt them, I hurt them all.*'

'*Guv,*' *she whispers.* '*Tom?*' *But he is gone, washed away by a sea of booze.*

Yet here he is, in front of her again, looking spick and span after six months of nothing. She wants to hit him. She wants to hug him. 'You look good,' she tells him. He does, at least he looks better than when she saw him six months before; he is still too thin but his colour is better. He is not a handsome man; his features are too sharp and his skin looks like a mosaic of a million tiny pieces of bone china – but he has a sad, puppy-eyed charm. And Jane is a sucker for a sensitive guy.

'Are you going to tell me what happened?' Her voice is level, she tries to keep it light. 'What has been going on with you all these months?'

He bobs his head sideways. 'Grayson called me in, told me what a wonderful job you've done.' He tries to deflect the course of the conversation, but she can't let him.

'Marcus.' She looks to see if there is any flicker of hidden knowledge, but his face registers nothing. 'Marcus Keyson was found with his skull caved in.' Nothing from Tom. 'He was on the floor in Durham Cathedral in the middle of the night. Someone called it in and then ran, there were no prints and no CCTV. It was the night before you …' she trails off.

'What are you asking me?' His eyes are soft like a kindly uncle. 'Are you thinking I hurt Marcus?'

'Did you?'

'I didn't hurt him.' He doesn't tell her that he was there that night.

She nods, glad to hear it but still confused. 'What happened to you then? You told me you had *hurt them*, that day I came to your flat.'

He has been dreading this. 'I was drunk – I think I may have been talking about my parents.' It is not a good lie. 'Maybe o-others too.' He stammers. *Ben Bradman and Bix the artist*. But he cannot tell Jane that his actions against them haunt him too.

'Why did you request that we reopen the Mason, Spall and Penn cases?'

He smiles, of course it was stupid of him to think Grayson would keep it close to his chest. He must be scared one of his top men is going to publicly explode and shower him in shit.

'The truth?' he asks her.

'Please.'

'Do you remember Sarah Penn, her brains splattered into the mud of that allotment?'

She nods. She remembers the hail raining down on that pretty face.

'And do you remember Tracy Mason and Allison Stokes, do you remember the kiln and—'

'Yes.' She cuts him dead, she hates recalling that night.

'I have nightmares. I dream I am inside that kiln, that I forced myself in, filled with fear, the adrenalin masking the agony of my skin ripping off.'

'Tom.' She is afraid for him.

'I hide in the dark for what seems like eternity, but eventually I have to pull myself out, and when I finally fall to the floor, shredded – Sarah Penn is there to spit on me. *You forgot us*, she tells me. *You betrayed us. You hurt us.*'

'It's just a dream. It's just a stupid dream,' Jane tells him, she puts her hand out to touch his arm. He lets her lay her fingers there but he actually does not feel the touch, he wears too thick an armour.

'I don't believe in ghosts,' he tells her. 'I know Sarah is gone – they all are. But I need to come good on my promise to them.'

'Why now, why this case – we have had failures before, we've had plenty since.'

'Of course we have – but with the others I gave them my best shot. With these girls we couldn't, we were pulled off the case. It was a case we should have solved.' *And I promised them I would*, he thinks.

'CID investigated.'

'Ares hunts the men like this, not the donkeys in CID.' Tom's eyes flare.

You hunt them, she thinks, *that's just about all you have to keep you going*. She sighs. 'So let me get this right, you have nightmares and you want them to stop and there are people you hurt years ago and you want to say sorry?'

'That's about it.'

She doesn't believe him, not completely, she knows there are secrets here. Something happened six months ago – it is linked to Marcus Keyson and somehow it all goes back to that bloody Dani Lancing.

'Grayson offered me my own unit,' she tells him.

'That's great. Congratulations.' There is no pause, he means it. She feels so angry with him for a moment.

'I turned him down.'

'Why?' he asks like a concerned father hearing his daughter is dropping her best subject at school.

Christ, she thinks. *You're supposed to be a detective.* 'I don't want to leave Ares.'

'It is in safe hands. I'm back,' he tells her.

'Back but trying to open old cases and when the boss says no you turn to a civilian for help.'

Tom is completely thrown off guard. 'How did you know that?'

'Former investigative crime journalist, winner of 3 PEN journalism awards and author of two best-selling true crime books – and the mother of your murdered love. Patricia Lancing is on the case.' She tries to keep her agitation at bay but she can't help it bubbling up. 'Tom, this is not the way we do things. It is not the way we work. The police must—' She feels herself get so angry that she can't finish her sentence, can't stay there a second longer. She turns and walks away from him.

'Jane. Jane, wait. Jane, have you been following me?' She carries on walking away. 'Jane, have you been—'

'No!' She turns and shouts back to him, then turns on her heel and walks away. She hasn't followed him, she got Fat Eddie to do it. She carries on walking. Damn, that did not go as it was meant to. She wanted him to confide in her, to let her help him – to need her. *Damn!* In her pocket her phone starts to trill. She keeps walking as she answers.

'DI Thorsen.'

'I'm sorry. I shouldn't be keeping you out of the loop. I do need your help.'

She stops walking and frowns: this could be a big mistake. 'What's the magic word?'

'Abracadabra?'

She smiles. 'Close enough.' She takes a deep breath, she is uncomfortable with running an operation outside of the unit, but she trusts Tom and maybe he needs this case to be resolved before he can be truly well again. That is what she wants. 'What do you need?'

'Come to dinner.'

Her heart skips a beat.

'Meet Patty and Jim and see where we are with the case. About 9 p.m. Will you?'

What can she say?

EIGHT

The Sad Man watches the nurses hustle: each one has a part to play in this orchestration of the closing of life. He watches the family as they fold into each other, grabbing loved ones and pulling them into themselves – clashing beating heart against beating heart; the hard-wired proofs of their own mortality. In their glass cocoon the lights have been turned to twilight. Tom Bevans watches their tragedy through the glass – if they were to look out and peer into the shadows beyond, he would merely seem a ghost somewhere in the machine of the ward. But they are too focused on the man who is leaving them, the man they have loved, to notice anyone outside.

Tom turns back to the man in the bed in this room. Marcus Keyson. Eyes open but nobody home. He came out of his coma a few months ago, but the damage is immense. He still barely moves, cannot get himself up. Every twenty minutes the bed comes to life and some underlying mechanism tips and turns him, trying to alleviate bedsores and lesions. It is not wholly successful. It is almost time for him to be fed. Tom likes to do it. Likes? Maybe that is the wrong word, he does it as a penance.

He stands over his old friend and looks down into his still handsome face. He has the slightly haughty, cruel type of face that many women like – with pointy cheekbones. Pointier now, cadaverous even. He had lovely strawberry-blond hair but it has been shaved away for surgery and electrodes. Now it is stubble, like a cornfield burnt down at the end of the season. The bruising has lessened, that is good. For a long time he looked like Mikhail Gorbachev, half his head covered in a blue-black-purple bruise. A sea of blood under the skin that made Tom feel queasy to look at, but not as bad as the trap-door in his skull. His brain had swelled, filled with blood and couldn't fit in its box any more. So they cut a bit away – to relieve the pressure.

The door opens and a nursing assistant pushes a trolley inside. It must be 6.30 p.m. Tom doesn't need to look, he has the menu memorised.

'Shepherd's pie and jelly for pudding, lovely.' He looks into the face of the over-worked woman. 'I'll feed him,' he tells her and she nods with gratitude. They both know how feeding Marcus Keyson can prove slow and messy. She lifts a tray from the bottom of the trolley and hands it to Tom. There is the suggestion of a smile and she is gone.

'You know what Marcus, I think we should mix it up a bit, don't you? Let's have pudding first.' He takes the small control box that hangs down from the bed and pushes the large green button. The bed rumbles into life and brings the torso and head up. Tom drags a chair close to the bed and with a spoon he digs into the jelly. The spoon vibrates and then with a little sucky sound, it pops up, holding a green wedge of wobbling fun.

'So, I am back at work. We've got three cases open but they are all pretty simple, I think.' He laughs a little too hard, it feels fake and forced. 'Lots of forensics – prints, blood, semen – you'd be like a pig in mud.' Tom opens the man's lips with the spoon and manages to slide the wobbly morsel inside. Marcus has trouble making saliva, the doctors don't know why, so Tom takes a water bottle and squeezes a liquid that is a little more than plain water into his mouth. A lot of it dribbles out, but Tom can see how he is willing his jaws to work. Most of the doctors believe Marcus Keyson is a lost cause. The blow to the brain did too much damage – but Tom sees something in there, and his old friend blinks. It is contact, of a kind, he is sure of it. That is why he comes here, usually three or four times a week. It has been a mix of day and evenings, but now he is back at work it may just be the evenings now. They have even let him stay after visiting hours. Twice he has fallen asleep and slept next to his old friend.

'Oh Marcus.' The jelly drops out and falls to the floor. A mother bird chews up the food for her young and then spits it into their mouths for them to swallow and digest. Yeah right. If all this fails then there is puree, like baby food, and the last resort is a tube into his stomach. 'But we can do it can't we, Marcus? Have dinner together like the good old days? We can, can't we?' He scoops another spoon of jelly. 'So we have yet another pathologist, not in your league of course but,' he makes a face. 'I have some pretty big news. I went to Grayson and asked for an old case to be opened, of course he said no. "*Never go back*."' He does a very bad impersonation of his boss. 'Anyway, I am looking into one of our old cases. Beautiful skin.' Blink. 'You remember?' Blink. 'It was your last case with us. Heather Spall.' Blink. 'Tracy Mason.' Blink. 'Sarah Penn.' Blink-blink. He is alive in there, Tom knows it.

'The week you were suspended,' he pauses, 'Because I had reported you.' Blink. It seemed longer and *harder* than the others. 'You said there was a break in the case, you would call me with a piece of evidence, but you never did. Do you remember?' There is a long pause and then the second blob of jelly falls to the floor.

Patty has opened the window to air the room out, though there is still a hint of cigarette under the cloying lily of the valley spray Jim had used to mask it. Tom arrives at 8.45 p.m. He comes directly from the hospital, carrying a laptop and a box of files that he managed to access from CID. Ten minutes later Jane Thorsen arrives with two bottles of red wine and an Indian takeaway that consists of two pilau rice, a chicken biryani and vegetable biryani, a lamb shaslik, a chicken dopiaza and four veggie sides plus garlic naan. Jim grabs plates and cutlery and pours four glasses. They then take their food and drink upstairs into the death room.

While piling biryani onto a garlic naan, Tom summarises the case as it stands after four years of being overlooked. Patty then talks about her first thoughts after spending the day reading all the materials. While they speak, Jane's eyes dart back and forth over the reports tacked onto cork tiles around her. She has not seen any of this in four years and, in fact, a lot of the work done by the CID is news to her. She reads and drinks wine. Jim offers no thoughts about the case, he just watches the three of them, all the while feeling a growing unease. He watches them share insights, ideas, and throw out theories. He sees how Patty's enthusiasm grows. He can see it makes her feel happy, and he doesn't like it. He doesn't like the fact that he is losing her again. His hand starts to shake as she speaks about how she plans to visit the families of the victims, starting the very next day with a trip to Leeds to visit Heather Spall's family. Jim feels physically sick.

'You need to be careful,' Jane warns. 'There is still a killer out there who won't like someone poking about.'

Please don't go, Jim desperately wants to say, *please stay here with me*, but he can't.

'Don't worry. I've got a rape alarm and a pepper spray,' Patty tells them, though fails to say that they were both bought illegally on the internet years ago. The rape alarm could burst the eardrums of anyone within twenty feet and the pepper spray is Danish police issue and banned in most of the world for melting mice in laboratory tests. 'I'm fine, and I've done a self-defence course.' Again she only gives the bare facts, saying nothing about the man she left groaning on the floor. It had been her present to herself for the dreaded sixtieth birthday. The instructor was ex-army, huge and muscle-bound but dim and slow. In the first week he called Patty out from the rag-bag of a dozen old women and asked her to attack him. Before he had finished the instruction she swung her leg at him with all her might, and her aim was true.

'Mother-f—' He had turned a deep aubergine colour and dropped to the floor, rolling around groaning, clutching his groin. She was given a round of applause by the other women, then she was asked to leave the class. She got a full refund. Afterwards she had felt elated, she had enjoyed the freedom to lash out at someone – to strike with all her strength and to hell with the consequences; she didn't feel at all sorry that she hurt him. He should have been quicker.

'Still, you need to be aware and keep in touch with us, call as soon as you leave the family and don't go anywhere without letting us know first. Okay?' Jane adds.

'Is that enough?' Jim asks.

'Of course it is,' Patty snaps at him.

'I understand your concern, Jim, but don't worry.' Tom smiles.

'Of course I'll worry.' He shakes his head; he feels such an outsider in this stupid little group. 'I'm going downstairs.' And he leaves. He wants them to call him back, for Patty to ask him to stay, but it doesn't happen.

'Fine.' Patty shrugs at the closed door as he treads downstairs, then she opens another bottle.

NINE

The air is alive, a heaving mass of scuttling, thrashing molecules that fight, fuck and flee – caught in the wild flashes of the strobe lights. Franco can see each atom twist in the tentacles of the smoke, leap and dance to the music; the bass vibrating every-thing, synching the heartbeats of everyone in the room, making them surge. The music is all-consuming, enveloping the crowd, drawing bodies this way and that, like marionettes in thrall to the beat. The overpowering musk of pheromone and sweat skir-mish with the undertow of sweet marijuana and vanilla dry-ice to envelop the room and fill everyone's head. Euphoria – that is what this room is intended to induce. Just a tiny step to paranoia.

'Franco?' A man whose name he can't quite remember wiggles a joint before his eyes. Franco looks into the face, seeing how his eyes droop at the corners; the whites are a filigree of red web. Franco reads faces, he knows the tell-tale signs of the parasite – the man is a loser, nasty and manipulative. Later he must remember to tell his men to never let him into the VIP section again, but for now, smile and be the host with the most. Franco nods and the man clumsily hands the joint to him.

'You will love this shit, it's my own blend. Fucking mental Charlie.' Franco knows the man will see this as quite a coup, the great Franco sharing his shit, this was like a royal endorsement.

He could probably write on every bag: skunk as smoked by Franco. Might even double the price. Franco pulls the joint to his lips, his cheeks draw in and smoke curls around his face, smudging his fine features into an indistinct mess – he holds it, holds it, counts to ten elephants; smoke billows and shrouds his face.

'Hey, hey,' the loser mumbles and pulls out his phone. 'Can I get a picture of you, of us – you know, sharing and smoking?'

'I don't.' Franco never appears in photographs. Safer that way.

'Please.' The guy holds up the phone to snap a selfie and—

'NO!' Franco means to be firm but fair, though he can feel the menace creep into his voice.

'Okay, okay, Franco. You're the man, no hassles.' He looks scared. 'But it's good shit? I mean, isn't it the boss?'

How would I fucking know, is what Franco wants to say, but instead he nods and smiles, smoke and mirrors; tricks and illusions. He had held the smoke in his mouth, and like a modern-day statesman, did not inhale. He needs his wits. It is a trick he has perfected over many years, to appear to be wasted like those around him but instead be alert, able to act if something happens. No drink and no drugs. Twice in his life it has meant the difference between life and death – he has escaped by the skin of his teeth while other men, too high to avoid the cutting blades or blaze of guns, have lost their lives. He does not allow himself the oblivion of a pharma-nirvana, even if there are nights when all he wants to do is wipe his mind clean. He does not allow himself that weakness, cannot drop his guard; even though he realises nobody at this table is capable of noticing anything anyway. They are all too far gone. It makes him angry. He despises their lack of discipline. He passes the joint on to the next man, another non-entity who will dine out for weeks on tales of sharing a smoke with the Dark Wolf. His lip curls involuntarily for a moment, he doesn't like his nickname. For a time he tried to get his men calling him The Great Blacksby, but none of them got the reference so it quickly died and left him as plain old Dark Wolf.

The second man takes the joint and draws the smoke deep into his lungs, the tip flaring red like blood, he releases it and his body sags and flops, bones like rubber, into the chair. Wasted, body and mind. Franco steals a glance at his phone. It is almost midnight, still too early to leave, that is the curse of being the boss. After all, this is his place, so many are here tonight to receive his blessing and pay their regards, or merely to be in his presence like some dark pontiff. He used to get off on it, the power and the glory, at the start he had been very happy to lose himself in the excess of it all. Now it leaves him cold, and tonight it makes him feel physically sick. *All these fucking cockroaches hanging around him, sucking him dry, why can't they— Christ, calm down,* he tells himself.

He looks into the throng of dancing bodies; they all seem to be having such a good time – of course many of the women are paid to have a good time, and to give a good time to the wealthy men who prowl. So much is an illusion here, it is a pleasure dome and he its Kubla Khan.

'Mmmmmmm,' a hand slides down into his pants and grips his manhood tight, dragging him back to the real world. 'Nice,' she coos. 'You can put that big-boy anywhere you want.' He turns to her, she is young – eighteen, maybe even younger. She is naked, a vision of perfection, with long blonde hair, blue eyes and full, plump mouth. Her skin is spray-tan perfect, shiny with sweat. Her breasts are unnaturally large, he can see the trace of a fading scar above her ribcage and a crescent around her aureole, from where her nipple was moved to look more perky. Between her thighs she is waxed smooth, like a child. It upsets him. She is not perfection, more like a caricature of the perfect woman, like a blow-up doll made flesh.

'Not now,' his voice rumbles. She squeezes him, thinking it will rouse the tiger.

'Not now.' There is an edge to his voice. His eyes flare, she removes her hand quickly and slides away – almost immediately one of his inner guards has her in his lap. Franco works hard to keep the distaste from his face. He wants to get out of there; he stands and everyone in the VIP area freezes, ready to jump at his command.

'I just need a stretch – chill.' There are nods and slowly everything goes back to how it had been. Franco moves, and as he does so he scans the room. Does anyone look out of place, is anyone more interested in— *Paranoia*! he tells himself. No one is watching him. He walks across the room and through the dancers. There are two gorgeous women who spot him as he passes, they are dancing with large, pasty-looking men. Rich men. Callous men.

'Franco, hey Franco, come join us,' they call, almost pleading. They want to be rescued, at least for one night, from the fate of having these fat rich men paw and claw at them. Using them without care, without tenderness, using them any way they want, because they can pay for it.

'Not tonight sugars,' Franco grins and blows them kisses. Janus. The muscles of his face ache from the big toothy grins. If one of these men really hurts a girl there will be hell to pay but otherwise – the girls know the score, Franco is no fucking charity.

They get a lot of money to offer up their bodies to these men, to allow them to do things that their wives or girlfriends won't. That is the way it is. Money and power can buy you anything, and anyone. 'Goodnight *chicas*.' He sways his hips to the music and bows gracefully to the girls – but keeps moving, he must not get dragged into the undertow of their needs. He needs air, so heads up, leaving the club-room and taking his private elevator up and up to the sky. That is the only way to get fresh air, it's the thing he hates most about this building. No windows. Of course that makes it safe, no way for a sniper to shoot, but also no natural light. Two of his men have been diagnosed with rickets in the last year – fucking rickets. He shakes his head. Christ, he wants to see the stars tonight. It is one of the only times he can feel like he is connected to home, to the land of his birth, when he can see the night sky. Though, in London it can only ever be partial, not like standing in the bush and looking up. But it is so many years since he has been able to do that. So many years since he arrived from Harare with his orders. He was to join the gang led by a man they called Uncle Joe, a gang that sold drugs and ran prostitutes in London, a gang that sent all their ill-gotten gains directly to Harare to fund Mugabe. But those funds were dwindling, drying up like an old water-hole. Franco was to make sure the funds flowed once again.

'I have come to learn from you Uncle Joe, to help you. I am loyal.' The old man narrows his eyes and takes in this scrawny boy who has been sent to him from the old country. He looks so young, but the boy holds the old man's stare and does not look away. Uncle Joe can see, deep in the dark well of the boy's eyes, there is a fighter in there – a soldier. The old man nods

slowly. 'Loyalty is rare.' The old man has been in this country for seventeen years, since he fled the war. His men are from here, London born and bred, he would like to have someone from home, someone who owes a loyalty not merely to money and power, but to the land, the soil, the very earth of both these men's homelands. A loyalty to Zimbabwe, to its freedom and its unity and to the man they both hope will lead it into the light. So he allows the young man into his inner circle as an apprentice, sitting at the feet of a master.

And *Uncle Joe* taught Franco, he taught him everything he had learned in the years he had been in England. He taught him who to bribe, who to blackmail and who to hurt. Most importantly he showed Franco that crime was a business like any other and that it ran on greed and incentive. Carrot and stick – that was his mantra. He was a man of imagination. And that was why Franco had been sent to learn from him rather than just kill him upon arrival. One day, six months after his arrival, when he felt that he had learned everything the old man could teach him – and when he had won the absolute trust of the man and all his close associates – that was the day Franco sliced *Uncle Joe's* throat to the bone and bled him dry. Then he took a cup of his blood, and in front of the inner circle, he drank it. Then he had each man pledge his loyalty to him – if they did not, they would die. All swore. None of them believed it transferred Franco any spiritual power. They were just shit-scared of a man who drank blood. So long ago now.

On the roof of his empire, he tips his head to the heavens and looks for the wishing star. 'Star light, star bright,' nothing. Clouds and light pollution have erased the heavens. Instead of

Venus all he sees are the winking lights of cranes remodelling and re-forming the London skyline. So much beauty crafted by the human hand, elevating mankind to the position of gods ... but there is an almost infinite ugliness too. Always so much poverty in amongst the incredible riches, such pain within the pleasure. He sees it. He can trace a web of corruption and greed with the tip of his finger. He can point to a thousand homes, flats, pubs, clubs – inside sits a man, almost always a young man, with six, eight maybe ten mobile phones. One rings, there are a few words spoken – an address or meeting place given – and then another phone is used to call a runner who is dispatched with a bag of this or that. A bag of salvation, or a bag of death? It never ends. He can trace it around and back, this way and that, ten thousand strands and they all lead back here in the end. Ultimately they come back to him, directly into his black, black heart. He hates it, hates his role in it. He wants out, he wants to live a normal life with his daughter. He will not skulk in the dark for much longer. He will crawl out from under the rock soon, even if only for a brief time – but he will live in the sun once more. Before he dies.

TEN

Patty had not called ahead. She thought if she did, that Diane Spall would have refused to see her – she just hoped the woman would be home on a Friday lunchtime. The train from Euston arrived at Liverpool Lime Street at a little after 11 a.m. and she took a cab to the house in what turned out to be a very nice, middle-class area. After paying off the cab driver Patty stood in the street for a while. It is some time since she had done this, investigate a death, a death that wasn't that of her own daughter. She takes a deep breath and a Red Admiral flutters before her and settles on her dress. The print on the fabric is of roses, maybe they have fooled the beautiful creature. It sits there a moment and then, beating the filament-thin wings once more, it flutters away. A good omen, she thinks and moves to ring the bell. It is answered on the third ring.

'Hello, Mrs Spall, you don't know me but—'

'I do.' Her face mists slightly as she tries to pull the memory to the front of her mind. 'I do know you.'

'I don't think—'

'Lost Souls, the charity, you spoke at a meeting they organised for parents whose children had been ...' She can't say the word *killed*. 'I met you after.'

Patty nods but she can't place the woman, she has met so many Lost Souls over the years. There are a lot of murdered children out there.

'I still work for them, have done ever since I lost my daughter,' Patty tells Diane Spall, who nods. 'And I suppose that is why I'm here ... sort of. I want to talk about Heath—' The door swings to slam in her face. Patty is quick and her foot slides forward, catching the door.

'Please, Mrs Spall. I am—'

'Just go, please.'

'Beautiful skin,' Patty intones it like it is some secret password or an incantation of power. Diane Spall releases the door and takes a step back as if slapped.

'Please, talk to me. I'm like you. If you know my story then you'll realise it's true when I say that I have some understanding of—'

'What I've gone through?' she snorts through her nose. 'No, you don't, not really. Though I am sure you think you do. Just like I have no idea about you and what you really feel about your daughter. It might all be an act, you might be glad she's dead. You never know what's in someone else's heart, so don't think you know me.' Her eyes flash angrily.

Patty opens her mouth to argue, but nothing comes out, there is no appeal she can make to some kind of sisterhood. It is true that she can only really guess at how this woman has been affected by her daughter's death. Instead she says in an almost-whisper,

'Can I come in, Mrs Spall?'

The woman looks at Patty for a long while before she bows her head slightly. For a second, Patty seems to see through a crack in her skull to a writhing mass of insects crawling under her skin, then she moves and the image is lost, as she motions her inside with a small gesture, and closes the door.

While the kettle boils Patty looks around the living room. The sofas are deep and soft; you need good stomach muscles to get back out of them. The carpets thick and lush, there is no TV, which she likes, and the bookcase is full of romances in the Mills and Boon mould. There is a large framed photograph of a couple; the picture is black and white – a wedding. Patty guesses it is Diane Spall's parents. There are no pictures of ... no, that is wrong. Tucked away in the corner of the room, half in shadow, is a picture of Heather. Patty reaches up and plucks it from the shelf. She looks younger than the photograph Patty has seen, still a child, not yet a young woman. She is smiling directly into the camera, a tooth missing, and she looks happy.

The tea is weak, which Patty appreciates. There are no biscuits. This is not an invitation to stay for long.

'Can I ask you some questions about Heather, about her death?' Patty asks.

The mother sighs deeply. 'She were twenty-one recently. Would've been, I mean.'

'My Dani went missing the week of her twenty-first, we never got to celebrate it.' Patty tells her. She won't be bested in some kind of pissing contest of misery.

'Ask your questions,' the mother agrees and sits back in her chair, cradling the tea in her hands. Patty takes an envelope from her bag and opens it, sliding out a series of photographs. She holds up the first. 'Do you know this girl?'

'That's the other girl that got killed, after my Heather, ain't it?'

'Yes, it's Tracy Mason.'

'They showed it to me when they came back and actually paid some attention. It were that creepy policeman, the one with the white hair.'

'Detective Superintendent Bevans?'

'That's him. He made my skin crawl. He cried while he talked to me.'

Patty nods, she can see how this woman would not like Tom; his full-on empathy can be crushing.

'But you had no idea if your daughter knew Tracy?'

'She didn't. My daughter was Liverpool born and bred, she never went to London, she never went—' her eyes water; Patty can see the extreme force of will the woman uses to suck the tears back into her head. 'My daughter never went anywhere but school and church. She never got the chance.'

There is silence.

'Can I ask you something. Was your daughter a happy person?' Patty thinks of the two photographs – the child and the young woman.

'Happy?' The mother spits the word like it is poison.

'Yes. Happy.'

'I would have said she were very happy, up until a month or two before she died, until she met him. That …' and now the tears do come and everything she has built up is washed away. 'She had been such a good girl and then suddenly she were talking back, not comin' home, missing school and not doing any homework. She even left the choir and she loved her singing.' Patty can see Diane Spall's hand is shaking, it is so bad that she slops her tea onto the chair. It blooms on the fabric, altering the patch to a dark storm.

'She didn't come home one night, I was so scared.' Patty stretches out her own hand and the two women touch fingers for a moment, then the mother pulls away. 'It was a Saturday night. I couldn't sleep, I called the police but they said I should wait until the next day, it were too early. She came home the next morning, still wearing the same clothes and I could smell smoke on her – not cigarette smoke either. It were in her hair and her clothes. I asked her where she'd been, what she'd been doing and …' Patty can see that the memory is burnt into her head from constant replaying. 'Of course she wouldn't say, just told me she wanted to marry some man I had never met. Gary, bloody Gary Wilkes. She were too young.' She looks at Patty, her eyes imploring. Wanting her to agree that she had done the right thing back then, been a good mother. 'He were fifteen years older than her. The dirty bastard.'

Patty pulls out the photo of Heather that they had on the board, next to it is a tall man in a long black coat. She points to the man. 'Is that him, is that Gary Wilkes?'

She nods slowly. 'Looks like him.'

'It isn't a very good picture, do you have another?' Patty asks.

For a second it looks like the mother might hit her, but then she leaves the room. She returns a minute later with a photograph. It looks like it was taken the same day, at the same caravan, but is much clearer. So clear that Patty can even read the slogan on Wilkes's T-shirt.

'She packed her bags that day and left, to be with him. She were only sixteen. He ruined her, he killed her.' The mother snorts back the tears and her hand shoots out to Patty's arm, her fingers digging deep into it. 'She was pregnant when she died, it were only a couple of weeks old, not much more than a bean, but it were there. The autopsy told us that. They cut my little girl open and my grandchild was there.'

'I am so sorry.' Patty wants to get out, the woman's grief is too caustic; she needs to leave soon.

'The day she died, the police told me she were a prostitute, that she'd been turning tricks and got killed by a punter. They said the place where she died was where working girls went.' She shivers with the memory of it. 'Blow-job junction the newspapers called it.' The words bloat and stick in her throat, making her gag slightly. 'I remember how she looked, the young policewoman, when she told me it was a *notorious spot*. I could see the pity and the disgust in her face.' The mother's eyes are wild as she remembers the shame and horror she felt. 'I even believed 'em. I believed my own girl was a whore. I thought that man had—'

'Shhhhhh.' Patty leans forward and strokes her arm as she coos to her, as you would to a baby.

'I had her cremated, thinking she had gone bad. I was so ashamed of her. I gave her the cheapest funeral. I invited no one, just cremated her and left her ashes to go to the dump. I gave all her clothes to charity – all her books, her toys. I burned everything else. My whore daughter.' She stops to wipe away the tears. 'Then the second girl got killed, that Tracy. Then the third: Sarah. Both of 'em nice girls, good girls. Not the kind of girls to be found at blow-job junction. Then the police were back, with that Bevans, and my Heather was a victim of a serial killer, she was a good girl again, not a prostitute. Now, they thought her body might have been dumped at blow-job junction. The newspapers printed a picture of her smiling.' She has to stop again, to clear away the tears that have made her blind. 'She were a good girl, a good girl.'

Patty watches as the woman's face convulses with pain. 'I had my good daughter back – but she was gone and I hadn't got a second chance to say goodbye properly. I couldn't get her aunties and uncles to come to see her off, I couldn't bury her somewhere nice so I could visit her grave each week – I couldn't even scatter her ashes because I'd sent them to the dump. I gave everything away or burned it. I have nothing of her left. Nothing.'

An hour later, Patty's hand shakes as she lights a cigarette, the first in a long while. She is on the street, about five minutes from the Spall house. She smokes it down to the butt and beyond, then she pops two roprinole from her bag and swallows them down without water.

She begins to retrace her steps back to the station, all the way there she feels like something is missing. Not in the case – this is full of holes – but in her, she feels that she should cry, weep, sob, bawl for the poor girl and her tortured mother. Yet her eyes remain stubbornly dry. She remains unmoved, detached from the awfulness of what had happened. After all, she isn't here to grieve the loss of the dead but to help them, heal the families. Find him.

At the station she pulls out her phone and dials a number she was given last night.

'DI Thorsen.'

'Jane, it's Patricia Lancing. I've seen Diane Spall.'

'Did you get anything?'

'I'm not sure I did, but the boyfriend, Gary Wilkes.'

'Hang on.' Jane keys something into a computer, there is a slight pause. 'Gary Matthew Wilkes. The local police had him in for questioning at the time.'

'And he had an air-tight alibi, I remember reading that, it's just …' she pauses, already thinking that her idea is too crazy.

'What, what about him?' Jane asks.

'I saw a photo, not the one on file – the same day but a different angle.'

'Okay, and?'

'The T-shirt he is wearing is clearer – I mean I could read what it said,' she pauses. 'Jesus lived and died for you, and there was a sun with a fish in it.'

'I don't ge—'

'I've seen it before, the logo. It's an ultra-right Christian group, the kind of crazies who believe dinosaur remains are a government conspiracy, who firebomb abortion clinics, the women wear chastity belts and they all live in communes, hoarding tins of beans and toilet paper and wait for the end of days.'

'So you think—'

'I don't know. I just have this feeling. Heather Spall was pregnant when she was killed. That's like a stoning to death offence with these people. I wonder if we could look into whether the other girls were religious. Crazy religious.'

'I see what you're saying.' Jane pauses. 'I'll do some digging. When are you home?'

'About 9 p.m.'

'Okay. I will call you when I have something.'

'Good.' She closes her phone.

ELEVEN

Pia bends down to the stony beach and picks up a handful of smooth, mottled pebbles. One by one she pitches them into the water. It reminds her of pulling the petals from a daisy as a child, but now there is no *he loves me, he loves me not*. Nowadays she has other choices, other questions she would ask the universe.

She looks around. The beach is busy, there is a little too much flesh for her liking and a lot of it wobbles uncontrollably. Weather is weird, she thinks. All that snow at Christmas and then no rain for months, they're talking hosepipe bans and everything. Crazy. Global fucking warming is shit. They should put that on a T-shirt, or maybe they have. She pulls her phone out, half wishing for a message from her dad – even though she knows he never sends one at this time of day. It is 4.30 p.m. Time to get going, she needs to get dressed for the fundraiser. Of course she knows a lot of why she is there is as eye-candy, it feels a bit like *prostitution lite*, a smile and a glimpse of leg to get the old letchy businessmen to contribute. But she knows that is how the world works, she isn't naïve like her dad who seems to think there is only good and bad in the world, black and white, like in the old films.

'Fuck you.' A girl screams, loud and angrily. Pia cups her eyes and scans the beach. There is a group of students close to the shore, where the waves are breaking. It looks like they have a little bar-b-q.

'You fuckers!' The screaming girl kicks it over, hot coals spill and the others scatter. There are shouts and a slap, Pia can't see who, and then the screaming girl runs along the line of surf towards the pier. None of the other students follow and Pia watches how erratically the girl moves. Pia can't help herself, she walks towards the girl and the pier, clattering down the stones, which slide away from her. It is hard to go forward and not slip back.

As she reaches the wooden and metal struts of the pier, she can hear squeals of pleasure from above and rumbling as the rides thunder along. She can smell fresh doughnuts being cooked, maybe she should get some as a treat after this. She steps into the shadows – she is blind for a while as her eyes slowly adjust. She smells rotting fish and shit. There is movement at the shore edge.

'No!' Pia calls and rushes forward, dropping her coat and bags, she runs towards the girl who is close to the sea. The rocks slip underfoot but she leaps like a mountain goat. The girl is in the sea, she is cackling like a witch as she goes under. Pia knows the girl isn't in control, she's on something; it is obvious by the way she moves. Pia hits the surf and keeps going. She can see the girl, she's just in bra and panties. Pia grabs her shoulder, but it twists – slick. She is under again and gulping in water. Pia shoves her hands under the girl's arms and heaves as a wave hits them and knocks them both back, sliding them onto the pebbles.

'You idiot, come back.' Pia pulls her higher up the stones, in the darkness and stench of the under-pier. She just hopes there aren't discarded needles and condoms. Pia pulls the other girl up, her pale skin a mass of goose bumps. She is still laughing. Pia looks into her eyes; the pupils take up the entire globe, they are so dilated.

'I am gonna wash it away, I want to be new.' The girl laughs and twists to turn back to the water. If she lets her go, Pia knows she'll drown.

'Christ.' Pia grabs her arm and yanks her back. 'Sorry,' she says and slaps the girl hard – she can see her own palm print flare on the girl's cheek – her head goes with the blow and then snaps back to the centre like a rubber band. The eyes are dark coals … and then the tears extinguish the fire. 'It's okay,' Pia tells her as she sobs on her shoulder. 'You need to—' she reaches around and unclips her bra and lets it fall, sodden, to the ground. Her breasts are small, her nipples hard from the cold. Pia tugs at her dripping wet panties. They fall down. She has a Smurf tattooed on her hip. In a fluid motion, Pia pulls her in and hugs her, briskly rubbing her back. The shivering decreases a little. 'Come with me,' Pia says softly. 'Let's get you back into your clothes.'

She leads the girl back up the beach. The other students have gone, leaving the dead campfire and broken glass. Pia helps the girl dress, all the while making encouraging sounds and cooing to her. Pia barely notices that she is wet too, but there is a suitcase of clothes in her car parked only a few minutes' walk away. The girl is shivering, so Pia takes her own jacket and wraps it around her. She remembers she has a hat in her bag and pulls that out, twisting the damp hair inside.

'Are you okay?' Pia asks.

The girl looks blankly at her, eyes black saucers of nothing. 'You need to get home and into the warm. Where do you live, I can see you ho—'

'No!' The girl pushes past Pia and starts to run – the shifting stones under her feet make her look like a terrible mime-act, running in slow motion. Pia is caught off guard, it takes her a few seconds to react, then she goes after the girl, but slower; she doesn't want to spook her further. The girl reaches the end of the stones and skips onto the pavement. Pia sees her speed up, like an arrow, once the concrete is underfoot. She knows she won't catch her now.

'Oh well,' she thinks. 'She seems to have lost the desire to kill herself, and I can get another coat and cap.' She watches her reach the main road and—

A car squeals alongside the girl and arms grab at her, the girl screams and tears away from them and runs into—

'NO!' Pia screams as a car hits the girl. Sound explodes: squeal of tyres, horns and seagulls yell. A crowd surges forward and swallows her up.

Pia steps back, falling away from the scene and then turns and walks away. She is shaking, she is freezing – cold to the bone. She needs to get to her car and change, she feels in her pocket for her phone. 'Please call, please, Dad … Dad,' she desperately wants to talk to him all of a sudden. As she walks, she begins to cry.

TWELVE

The lift slides silently down to ground level and the doors open. Franco strides out into a grey and soulless corridor that wraps around the outer perimeter of the building. The design for it was based upon the servants' tunnels in old country houses, utilitarian pathways that threaded through the glitz and glitter of the main house, so that the gentry and their guests did not have to see the underlings and hired help. Here it also keeps the classes apart, but it is no longer clear which are the upper and which the lower. He walks through the production labs; a man in a HAZMAT suit raises his arm and waves. Franco stops and waves back, feeling more than a little self-conscious. The lab is gleaming, he still cannot quite believe how much it all costs but— one step at a time. Past the production labs there is a conference room with a viewing area. Franco stares through the one-way glass as the focus group answer question after question. 'So on a scale of one to ten, ten being the best, can you rate your experience of euphoria … did you feel violent in any way … were you stimulated sexually … would you have agreed to do anything anyone asked of you?' The questions keep coming but Franco moves on. These psychonauts make him nervous – they will try any combination of drug to take their minds to a new place – they don't care, mixing all kinds of psychoactive substances to create new highs. It is like stoner MasterChef, or the Chocolate Factory and he is Franco Wonka, bringing forth his marvellous cornucopia of medicines. As he walks away, a psychonaut begins to weep because one of the men with a clipboard won't kiss him.

He heads to the main barracks that houses the 24/7 security. From there he can check more than two hundred CCTV cameras that cover every nook and cranny of the building to make sure th—

'Franco.' A voice from the gloom behind him pings off the steel sheen of the walls, sounding as if it comes from all around him. 'Franco,' the man calls again. Franco turns and nods to the approaching man, who is a head shorter than he is, but a yard wider, and all of it solid muscle. His skin is several shades lighter, except where ink traverses it in heavy blocks. His head is shaved like a bullet and a scar runs from the corner of his left eye down to his chin like a tear. He is an over-muscled Pierrot striding onto centre stage.

'Gulliver,' Franco greets the head of building security. He has only been with them for three months but already Franco has assessed the man's skills and credentials. He has impressed him by being more than mere muscle, pretty rare among the pumped-up monoliths who usually work in security. He has an MA in business studies and seems to have an organised mind and has already stamped his authority on the team, provoking some bitterness from those who have worked for Franco for a long time. But there is something else, a factor that makes Franco feel uncomfortable around him: his cruelty. Gulliver seems to enjoy administering pain.

'There's been a break-in.'

'Here?' Franco feels his stomach clench; today is too important for anything to go wrong.

'One of our places in Peckham – three guys. The minder and his girl got stabbed.'

'How bad?'

'He's okay, she will be – she'll have a nasty scar.'

'Did they get much?'

'A kilo cooked for the street and ready to go out.'

Franco winces. 'Any leads on who?'

Gulliver laughs silkily, with obvious glee. 'Amateurs. Local customers who decided they didn't want to pay no more. Shit, they are gonna pay for it now, we got a positive ID off the closed circuit. We got names and addresses.'

Franco nods gravely, feeling the acid in his stomach begin to heave. 'How old?'

'Teens.' *What does it matter*, his eyes say, *they still have to pay*.

Franco takes a deep breath and holds it. Just stupid kids on the make, even younger than Pia. Sometimes kids do stupid things. They should get a second chance, shouldn't they? In the normal world you got a second chance. He looks to Gulliver, about to suggest they go easy on them but he sees the glint there. Second chances? Not here, this isn't the normal world. *You are getting soft*, he thinks to himself. *Softness will see you dead*. A voice threads through his head.

'You're sure you have the right names?' he asks Gulliver.

'No question,' Gulliver replies with a chilling firmness. Franco knows what is expected of him, what is demanded of him: a swift and savage response. It used to come easy to him; he knows there is no option. If they do not make an example of these boys it is a green light for every other gang to start to push at their borders, to scratch at their market – claw away at their clients; and then there would be war.

'Then go and pay these boys a visit,' Franco tells him, trying to keep any emotion from his voice. He does not say *kill them, hurt them* – or does he? It is so hard to tell nowadays.

'Aren't you coming?' Gulliver asks with a cruel smile. He has wanted to hunt with the *Dark Wolf* ever since he arrived here.

'Not tonight, too many people expecting to see me. You deal with them. I trust you to do the right thing.'

Gulliver nods. Franco thinks he sees a sneer at the corner of his mouth. 'You're the boss.' It makes Franco want to laugh: *boss*. He can see through Gulliver. The ambition, his lack of respect for the old man at the top. He understands it – that was him, twenty years ago. He cut Uncle Joe's throat to the bone and drank his blood, he knows Gulliver will do the same in an instant.

'Give the girl two g's,' he tells his head of security, who raises an eyebrow. 'For the scar. We look after our own.'

Gulliver curls his lips in an utterly joyless smile. 'I'm gonna film the interview. I'll send you a link so you can watch.' Their eyes lock. Did Franco hide his distaste? Probably not. Gulliver has a secure site he posts videos to. Other gangs have similar operations, they use them to demonstrate how they deal with informants and elicit information; how they torture and how they punish. It sickens Franco. Not the barbarity; the level of violence is probably no worse these days – a claw hammer to the knees or baseball bat to the jaw is pretty much the universal currency of pain today, as it was twenty years ago. The difference is in the level of showmanship and performance. Each gang tries to outdo the other in how they display their viciousness. It makes Franco feel like a dinosaur. He is an old man in this business, old and soft and just about on the scrap heap. Just about.

'Take four men and whatever tools you need out to Peckham.' His mouth is dry. 'Do whatever you think best.'

Gulliver smiles, then turns on his heel and marches off. Franco watches him go and—

A young man screams from far off. Franco feels it rather than hears it. Feels it in his bones. A memory. He shakes his head. *Forget it,* he tells himself. *These boys in Peckham, no sympathy for the devil, it's their own fault. If they try and rip off the Dark Wolves they must know the consequences.* He pushes the concern away from him: it is the only way to live this life, to compartmentalise everything in some massive emotional land-fill. Forget the past, ignore the present – look to tomorrow.

He moves forward – time to prepare, time to check that everything is ready, tonight is a big night. It is the first anniversary of the casino opening and the new building getting under way. He moves on past the labs and into the lower barracks which house up to fifteen men. The shift switches at 6 p.m. so they should—

'What the—?' he mutters to himself as inside he sees eight large men, dressed from head to toe in black, crowded in front of a bank of video monitors cackling and whooping like witches. They seem to all be watching just one of the screens.

'What is fucking going on?'

They spring back at the sound of Franco's voice. For a second there is nothing as the men look between themselves. 'It's Kavannah,' Carl starts. 'It's his eighteenth.' He tries to smile. 'Cake?' He holds up a piece of chocolate cake that has a single candle on it.

Franco scowls. He looks past the cake to the bank of monitors – and in particular the one they seemed to be watching. He can see a slim woman straddling a young man, riding him for all she's worth. Franco walks to the back of the barracks and hammers on the door.

'Get the fuck out here.'

On the monitor the girl topples sideways as the man springs up, stuffing himself back into his combat trousers and rushing to the door. He throws it open, face flushed. Behind him the girl struggles back into her underwear.

Franco shouts past Kavannah to the girl. 'Nikki, you know better than this. Get a shower so you don't stink, you're meant to be working later.' She nods, embarrassed to be treated like this, but takes it. Franco is too scary to stand up to. She treads delicately through the crowd of men, clutching the rest of her clothes. Franco watches her, she's been here a year. She was so pretty when she started. She looks as if she's aged twenty years since then; she is too thin. He sees her ribs as she walks away. Her mouth is taut where it used to be a plump Cupid's bow, her skin is blotchy with pimples around her mouth and her eyes are hollow. Make-up can fill them in, but she looks haunted. Her teeth are starting to discolour a little too and her hair is losing its sheen. He will have to let her go soon, six months at most. Drugs. He hates what they do. The irony is not lost on him.

'And you,' he turns to Kavannah. 'Go home.'

'But—'

'Home.' Kavannah nods, unsure if this is a present or a punishment. 'Sorry, Franco. Would you?' he reaches over to the table and picks up a glass.

'No alcohol on duty.' Franco's jaw grinds.

'Fizzy grape juice,' Kavannah tells him with a sort of smile. *A man that is a boy*, Franco thinks disdainfully. 'Please,' he asks. Franco holds his gaze. He isn't sure about him, Gulliver hired him only about a month ago. He hadn't realised he was so young. Maybe the manboy can cut it – maybe. With a nod, Franco takes the glass from him and drinks.

'Happy birthday. Now go home, and you others get to work.' They melt away. Franco waits a second to make sure they have left and then goes to the sink in the corner. He spits what is left of the juice into it and then rinses his mouth. 'Bloody fizzy grape juice,' he mutters, trying to get the taste out of his mouth. He feels his stomach cramp and churn.

Out in the light, Kavannah blinks and pulls the Puffa cap down over his eyes.

'This is a major pisser,' he hisses to himself. He did not expect to be leaving now, missing the whole shift. He hopes this isn't going to ruin everything; he still wants his money. He turns back to view the block, as he walks towards the tube station. He'll wait until he gets out of any sightline from the roof before he makes the call. There's a subway just on the other side of the estate that goes under the road, he'll call from in there. Unless it smells like piss; he hates the smell of stale piss. He should take the money and get away, maybe the Caribbean where he can chillax. He reaches the subway and pulls out the phone they gave him. It just has one button on it – shit style, he had to keep it secret because he could not be seen with such an ugly phone. He hits it and it doesn't even ring. This is not what it's like in the movies.

'Why are you calling?' a voice asks angrily.

'I got sent home.'

'Shit.' Kavannah can hear a muffled conversation going on at the other end. His contact has cupped the mouthpiece so nothing is clear. 'Does he know?' the voice asks him, clear once again.

'Nuffink.'

'Did he drink it?'

'Good as gold. When do I get my money?'

'Soon.' The connection is ended and the phone goes dead.

'Fuck.' Kavannah smiles, he can— 'What's that red dot?'

The bullet rips through his throat, taking half his neck with it. No sound, except the breath being torn from him. He falls back, grabbing at his shirt, trying to pull it harder into his throat and put pressure on the wound but it is so slippery now. His heart beats fast – pumping the blood around and out. He lies there and sees the golden beach. Happy birthday …

THIRTEEN

Pia reaches the multi-storey car-park and finds her little VW bug. There is no one else around so she takes off her wet clothes and puts on a new outfit as quickly as possible, her eyes flicking back and forth the whole time. She can't stop shivering. She feels like she wants to cry. She thinks she saw the man in the leather coat on the street, but how can that be? In her pocket her hand curls around her keys. If he attacks her— no, don't think like that. She needs to calm down. She looks around the concrete bunker of the car-park, she doesn't want to come here after midnight, so she drives the little car down the ramp and into the street and – BRAKE!

'Be more fucking careful,' a taxi driver yells as he swerves to avoid her.

'Sorry,' she yells to him. *Sorry*, she tells herself, her heart hammering. Not far. She drives down to the coast road and then left to a roundabout. It is hot out but she feels so cold. She drives around the circle and takes a turn to Kemptown. She parks on the street; she can pay for two hours of parking and then it's free. She buys the little sticky ticket, then looks at her phone for a map; a four-minute walk. She follows the flashing pin around two corners and onto … wow. India at the seaside. The Royal Pavilion is a scaled-down Taj Mahal. It is stunning.

'Excuse—'

She spins, the keys in her hand, ready to strike. It is not leather-coat, just an old man with a stick wanting to get past. 'Sorry,' she mumbles and moves onto the grass to let him get by. She walks on to the Pavilion. At the front entrance there is a security guard. She gives her name and is allowed to go in. Once inside she is shown to a room that is being used as a dressing room. She pulls the gown out of her bag – she loves the dress. She holds it up to herself as she pirouettes. She always wanted to be a ballerina, from about the age of five. She especially loved wearing the tutu, spinning and feeling it fill with air and glide up around her. She would spin for hours, or at least until she fell over. Yesterday, when she bought this dress for the fundraiser, she stood in the store and spun and spun. 'Please,' she had asked the shop assistant, 'take my photo.' She had handed her the phone and the woman had snapped a picture. It was good, a little blurry, but good. Pia had meant to send it to her dad right then, as a reminder of how she loved to spin, but she had forgotten. She types a short message and sends it now.

She shrugs out of her clothes until she is down to her underwear. It is cold in the room, and she thinks about the girl on the beach. Tomorrow she will call the hospital. She fishes glittery tights out of the bag and puts them on, then the dress. A full-length mirror is propped up in the corner of the room. She looks at herself in it. She looks like a princess.

She walks out of the room and sees that a whole regiment of black- and white-dressed staff have appeared and are setting up drinks and nibbles. Through the main hallway she can see the dining room. She walks to it, and the sky is full of dragons circling a massive chandelier. It is incredible. She stands there, her eyes drinking in the beauty and the weirdness and the excess of it all. She feels better, safer, in the buzz of the room. She can see four uniformed policemen and knows there will be others around. In a minute she should go and check in – her job for the night is to register guests and give out name badges. Nothing to be nervous about, it is not hard work. From somewhere a bell rings and suddenly a wave of waiting-staff sweep away like bees, gathering nectar. She turns to walk back to reception. If she had kept looking forward for one more second she would have seen the door to the kitchen swing open and a man in a leather coat talking to a waitress. But she had gone by then.

FOURTEEN

Franco only just makes it inside before he vomits. That bloody fruit juice of Kavannah's has really done something to him. He feels his forehead; it is clammy and damp. His heart is racing. He runs cold water into the basin, cups his hands and splashes the water over his face and onto his neck. He looks into the mirror above – his eyes like the depths of space, tar black but something moves through the obsidian depths. Franco closes his eyes. When he opens them, his reflection is gone; a young boy stares back at him. He feels his life slide backwards as he topples back and falls – down, down, down the rabbit hole.

The air is alive, an assault on the senses. It throbs with the heat, shimmers with the beat of a million tiny wings as insects swarm, and its scent is the sweetness of the blood. Carrion creatures crawl over the dead and burrow deep into the cuts and tears in the flesh of men, women and children who, only hours before, laughed and sang and loved life. These parasites have no respect for the once-was, instead they feast and lay their eggs inside the still-warm husks. They love the sweet flesh, it is like papaya. Insects are not deterred by the stink of death, or of the urine and faeces that mingle with the blood and pervade the air; they thrive on rot and decay. The scene is enough to make the toughest of men weep, enough to make the strongest of stomachs contract and retch. Except the boy does not react, he does not even attempt to swat away the flies that crawl over his own skin. He can feel some of them suck at his blood, driving their needle-like mouths through the hide of his skin to gorge and bloat on his warm essence. Other carrion insects are merely content to devour the blood that covers him, licking and sucking at the blood that has washed him – blood that is not his own.

He remembers the date, it was written on the blackboard this morning, just like it has been every morning: 14th September 1978. But he has no idea of the time, of how long he has lain there with the dead. How many hours have elapsed since the men came? At the sound of their jeeps the school had fallen silent immediately. Father Abraham had put his head around the door and told them all to carry on as normal. Then he walked into the courtyard to meet them, and as the first jeep pulled into the village he called out to it:

'We welcome you to our community. Come in peace and—' The bullets tore him up, like confetti, and scattered him into the breeze. The men had not even dismounted before they opened fire.

'Run,' his teacher had screamed. 'Run and keep running.'

Bheka did not run immediately, instead he turned to see the soldiers jump from their vehicles and fan out ... some of them heading to the huts and others to the school. He wanted to see their faces, he could not believe these were men, their bodies twisted and shook as the guns thundered death into the village, their faces seemed to shift like campfire smoke; men to wild dogs and back again.

'Bheka!' His sister Lulama screamed at him and grabbed his hand, pulling him towards the playground. It was not far to the scrub line and then into the bush. The teacher pushes

at the younger ones who sob with fear. Mbeki is at the front, he is the fastest. Father Abraham had said he could be in the Olympics one day. He had even promised they would get a TV for the day that happened. The children had been so happy. Greased lightning Mbeki is almost at the line of the bush when the roar of the gun begins and he folds, curling to the ground, as if he has just gone to sleep. Behind him, others start to crumple. Bheka has only imagined such a thunderous sound at Judgement Day, but souls are not rising from the earth, instead they fall around him like seeds scattered from a farmer's hand. With a sigh Lulama stumbles, her chest suddenly a mass of red swirls like on that dress she had seen in the catalogue. Bheka does not understand. She never got that dress. Her mouth is open but he cannot hear her words. She smiles – at least he thinks it is a smile – and then she floats to the ground, not releasing his hand but dragging him down with her. Behind, their teacher trips, his head suddenly half the size it had been, like a roasted squash half eaten, and he falls onto them both, trapping Bheka. The boy hits the ground and ...

The memory tears at his stomach, making him double up. *What the hell is happening?* He has not thought of the boy he once was in so many years, and his sister—

Do you tell stories of me? Lulama asks him. *Sing of us?*

Franco swings around in the bathroom – there is only him there. His sister is dead, long ago dead.

You promised you would sing of me.

'Shut up!' he yells. 'You're dead, we buried you.'

I watched. I always watch you.

'No. No ghosts.' He screws his eyes shut. 'I am not a child. Bheka is dead.'

You are not dead my bro—

'Fuck the past,' he digs his thumbnail deep into the flesh of his palm – the pain sweeps him clear for a second. 'I am Franco.'

Your language Bheka – what would Jesus say? Lulama asks.

'Fuck Jesus.'

Oh my brother.

'I am not Bheka. I am Franco.'

He feels the nausea rise again as the bathroom door opens and someone enters; the body shifts like smoke.

'Outa my—' Franco pushes him to one side and rushes past, back into the club – the sea of people and the wall of sound. The beat grips his heart and fills his chest with anxiety. Fucking ghosts. In the crowd he sees Lulama and his teacher and Mbeki and – Jesus Christ, his heart is too fast – it is going to burst. He must get away. A man in the crowd bobs up for a moment, Franco can't tell if he is real. He looks like a corrupt ex-policeman who once worked for him, but is it really DI Nathan Dent or another ghost? The man smiles and winks, his face is friendly but it makes little Bheka shiver. Franco turns and heads for the far wall, walking quickly. He can't catch his breath.

Dent watches Franco, notices the sheen of sweat on his forehead and the unsteady way he moves, weaving as if on the deck of a pitching ship. The drug is working; a little top-up will send him over the edge. He moves to follow Franco through the crowd, and as he does so he reaches into a pocket, inside there is a hypodermic. He grips the plunger as he zeroes in on his man. Only a few feet. He pulls the syringe clear and reaches to take the small plastic sheath from the tip. Ahead Franco has stopped – that makes it easy. A few seconds. He is ready to stri—

'Sorry.' A couple sway into him, almost knocking the hypodermic from his grasp.

'Watch where you're fucking going,' Dent hisses at them. The man, who might have been in a boy band when he was a teen, lashes out with his arm to push Dent back.

'You watch out, you old fuck.'

Dent would love to break his perfect boy band nose, but he is too busy. With a snarl he twists back to Franco – who is still just standing there at the wall. *Easy fucking peasy*, Dent thinks and steps forward just as Franco punches a code in, and a section of wall slides to the side and—

'Shit!' Dent faces a blank wall. *Like a fucking ghost*, Dent thinks. He slips the syringe back into his pocket and turns. He needs to find where he's gone. Franco cannot leave the building – not alive.

Franco slides through the escape door and takes the lift one floor up. His hand is still shaking but his vision has cleared and his heart has slowed. Something is up, he needs to find Gulliv—

'Damn.' He remembers, he's on his way to Peckham and Drew's gone with him. He tries to remember who is on the security team tonight. He needs a sweep of the building, he feels something big is happening. Like the day the soldiers came. Like the day Bheka hid among the corpses. The lift door slides open and Franco walks through into one of the gaming rooms, the high roller room; in the centre there seems to be a crowd around the roulette wheel. He recognises a few people from television and a senior police officer, he shakes a hand or two and air kisses a senior QC. He feels like a politician, should have a baby to hold. At the table a tall redhead winks at him. She is a regular on a soap opera. Last time she was here she had offered him a blow-job. The next morning he had seen her with her three kids on daytime TV talking about her amazing marriage. Christ, the air seems so stale in here. He smiles, he must not stay – wave, kiss and get out.

'Next time,' she mouths and licks her lips. She means it provocatively, but it makes him feel nauseous. He recalls her on TV, kissing the top of one of her children's heads. He can't breathe.

'Please, I beg of you.' A scream threads through Franco's head. To the side of the actress there is a man on his knees, his face merely a pulp of blood and soft flesh, begging for his life. A gun is pressed to his temple and the head explodes, brains all over. The finger on the trigger is Franco's. When? Fifteen years ago? The wall has had about eight coats of paint since, but he can still see spots of blood like rust splattered over it. The brains in the carpet, like maggots in spoilt fruit – it had to be replaced, it was replaced. They had learned a lesson that day. Now, they put plastic sheets down if they plan to kill someone in the building, though it does ruin the element of surprise. Franco feels sick, he feels he is drowning in blood. Every drop of blood he has ever shed swills around his ankles, an ocean of blood. He is shaking. He needs to get away from people before the next steel barrier – he types in his key code again with hands that will not keep still, and he is through to a chill-out room. Some sort of electro whale song fills the air and Bugs Bunny and Elmer Fudd run across the walls singing opera. Chasing, always chasing. 'Kill the wabbit.' He is looking for the security team, why aren't they around – where is everyone? There is a shudder, a vibration through his bones. He thinks it is the carrion insects crawling across his body to eat his sister's flesh and lay their eggs in her. He feels nauseous, disoriented, his memory shifts once more – back to Zimbabwe.

He lay in that blazing sun all day, all day with the corpses of those he loved. Seven years old and he lay with the dead. Even when he smelled gasoline and they burned the school – he did not flinch. Even when he heard the roar of their jeeps speed away, he still lay there. He had promised Jesus he would wait until nightfall. Even then, he lay still among the corpses long after the sun left the stage. Finally he squeezed Lulama's hand for the last time and released it. With all his strength he managed to crawl out from under his teacher's body. He kept crawling until he was clear of the bodies. Then he stood, slowly and painfully after more than twelve hours and—

A gun cocks. His seven-year-old heart shatters, all a waste.

'Stay where you are. Do not run.' A booming voice calls out.

So long ago.

Franco closes his eyes and shakes the memories of the boy he once was from him. They fall to the ground like dust. He is himself again. It is not carrion insects, the sound is his mobile phone on vibrate. He pulls his phone out and sees the incoming message is from Drew – one of the men who went to Peckham.

'What?' Franco asks.

'Franco, we tried,' his voice cracks, gives way to a moan of intense animalistic pain. Franco knows that sound, a man dying. 'It was an ambush, Gulliv— arrrrhh,' he screams and the line is dead.

'Drew!' Franco yells but it is too late. The phone is dead. Blood pressure spikes, nausea grips him again, his vision blurs, the walls seem to concertina away from him, and straight lines blend and bend. He has to reach out to the wall to steady himself, breathe, heart rate slowing – he starts to walk unsteadily on. He has to get to his office and the phone, his life-line to her, to Pia. Pia, he must speak to her, warn her, no one is safe. Pia. Pia. PIA!

FIFTEEN

'Peckham is a fucking shit-hole.'

'I grew up round here.'

'Fucking shit-hole.'

'There are nice pl—'

'Fucking shitty fucking hole.'

Silence descends. The sleek, grey van powers on, cutting through the dark night. Gulliver is alone in the front and smiles as he drives. Behind him four men sit: Drew, JB, Dagga and Beau. It has been something of a wild-goose chase so far – three addresses, all of them a bust. Now it is late and the air in the van has moved from anxiety and excitement to boredom and impatience. This is the last stop.

Of the four men, Drew is the longest serving of Franco's men. He has been with him for fifteen years and remembers when there was nothing but violence. The other three men have been in the *Dark Wolves* for two or three years and have known only a time of comparative peace. Gangs no longer fight amongst themselves – although there are minor transgressions. Mostly it is fights over women, occasionally over money but the old wars of territory are over. Franco has brought peace amongst the many groups who run drugs, prostitution and extortion in London. It has been a good time for business, and a good time for his men. They have grown a little fat, a little complacent perhaps. They are used to reacting to situations in the club or casino, drink-, drug- or jealousy-fuelled fights mostly. These men are not used to taking direct action. Tonight they are on the offensive, walking into the lion's den. The expectation is that these kids are amateurs. But they can still be amateurs with knives and guns.

Gulliver drives at the speed limit and with the utmost care. It would not be good if the police stopped them. It would be difficult to explain away a box of surgical grade scalpels, several handguns, ammunition and two automatic rifles. On the seat next to him sits his phone, directions streaming to it as he drives. Occasionally his eyes flick down to make sure he is still on the right track. He feels it vibrate for a second and he looks down and smiles.

'New information, they're at a club. We are going to go to the house and pick up the minder there. He can ID the kids at the club.' He tells them over his shoulder. 'This should be fun.'

'What's the plan?' Drew asks.

'We go in as a pack and chase them down. Pick each one off.'

'At the club. Do we want to make a scene?'

'How long have you been with Franco?' Gulliver asks him, his eyes flicking to the rear-view mirror. He watches Drew stiffen.

'Fifteen years, almost sixteen,' he answers.

'Long time.'

'I have seen a lot of shit go down with Franco. We're brothers.'

'And you are very loyal.' He makes it sound like an accusation.

'Franco would not question my loyalty.'

'No. I am sure he would not. You are all his,' a pause. 'Brothers.' The other three men grunt yes. Each of them may have been with Franco only a few years, but they either have brothers, fathers or uncles who served him loyally for almost two decades. Gulliver's face creases a little at the corner, it could be a smile – hard to tell. 'You don't get loyalty in gangs very often. I applaud you. I applaud you all.' Then the car falls into silence.

Twenty minutes later the truck slides into an alleyway at the back of an industrial estate. Gulliver kills the engine and they sit in near darkness. Gulliver picks up his phone, cupping the screen so that light does not spill into the cab, and dials. It is picked up immediately.

'We're here. Open the side door.'

From somewhere close by, a heavy metal door starts to screech as it swings open on partially rusted hinges.

'JB, come with me. You others wait here until I signal.' Gulliver slides out and his feet hit the ground. There is a horrible wet squelch as his foot sinks into the mud a little. Shit, his shoes are gonna get fucked. He pulls a gun from a shoulder holster and moves forward. JB follows, also pulling a gun. It feels incredible in his hand. He has never drawn a gun with the intention of firing it; he really hopes he gets to shoot someone. Quietly the two men disappear through the open metal door.

In the van, Drew opens his kit bag and pulls out a heavy silver Maglite. A gun is all well and good but you need to see what you're shooting. Then he, Dagg and Beau slip out into the night. Cold, it has turned really cold while they have driven all over fucking creation searching for these kids. Drew is annoyed; his place is at Franco's side, just like it was a year ago at the opening. He has been close to Franco for years, he can see his game plan: clearing away a lot of the hate and in-fighting, making it all more of a business – and a business about pleasure rather than sleaze. He's like a drug-land Walt fucking Disney. He can make you see talking mice too. Drew stamps his feet as the cold has gripped his toes.

'How long we gonna wait D-man?' Dagg asks.

'Shit. Let's give him another couple of minutes and go in,' Drew tells them. Dagg and Beau nod. And all three look to the door Gulliver and JB entered almost ten minutes ago. Drew doesn't like this new guy, Gulliver. He knows he wasn't chosen by Franco but orders were sent over from the old country. Drew has seen it twice before, but he doesn't get how it works. Somehow the gang has links with Zimbabwe. That's where Franco comes from and he owes some kind of allegiance to his old home. A shitload of money is sent there every month, Drew knows that – a fuck of a lot of money – but that's all he knows. Knowing more might prove dangerous.

Drew was born here, London boy through and through – they all are, except Franco. Africa, fuck, it's just a foreign land that's full of poor kids dying. It's not some ancestral home, no fucking way. Even the slightly civilised bits like South Africa are fucked with corruption. He wouldn't go even if he won the lotter—

'There he is.' Beau interrupts his thoughts and points to the open door. It is only slightly open, a thin slice of light cuts into the muddy ground before it and a silhouette stands there. It's hard to make out, but it looks like Gulliver is signalling for them to come over. Drew waves toward the shadowy figure and walks towards it. As he does so he takes the safety catch off the handgun. Something feels wrong. As they get closer, the figure steps back and is swallowed by the darkness. Drew reaches the doorway and peers inside – totally dark. He takes the Maglite and shines it into the darkness, it does little as the room inside is so huge.

'I'll go first,' he says and heads forward. 'This will—' He trips – something large is on the floor and he goes sprawling over it.

'Fucking hell,' he spits and swings the Maglite back to see what he fell over.

JB's eyes stare unseeing, his throat is open to the bone. Dagg and Beau stand in the door, incredulous. Drew sees the red dot of the laser-sight appear on Beau's chest.

'Get ou—' Drew screams but two flares of light send Beau spinning back, a bullet through the throat and head. Drew pulls his own gun, a Glock, in front of his face but he can't see anything, he can only gauge where the laser-sight came from. He fires three rounds into the darkness, the sound is deafening, the bullets spinning off metal. Drew is up on his haunches and then off and running. It is only three long strides to the door, but he knows he'll be mown down if he tries. Instead he breaks left, swinging the beam of his torch around like a ride at the funfair – trying to confuse the shooter with the rifle. Something burns the air by his head, buzzing like a wasp – but far more deadly. He sees the laser-sight on a wall ahead and veers to one side and – 'Shit.' He slips and falls. He rolls and is up again, he feels a twinge from his ankle but the adrenalin keeps the pain at bay. Two bullets explode into the ground around him; one hits a post he did not see and chips of razor-sharp concrete fly around him, slashing his cheek and cutting deep into his neck. Where the hell is Dagg? He swings the Maglite forward and – there is a doorway. He runs through it and is in a loading bay. It is too far to get to the front, a hundred yards at least, and he is no Usain Bolt; the shooter is right behind him. He spins and fires three more quickly at—— Dagg falls, a bullet through his head. From somewhere there is a laugh. It echoes around the huge room. Drew stops moving. He is out in the open, nowhere to go. He lifts the gun above his head, while he does so his other hand moves quickly to his pocket and feels for his mobile phone. He flicks it out and hits the contacts page as—

'Ah!' A bullet shatters his ankle, almost amputating his foot. He falls, hard to his left side. The phone starts to ring, he shields it with his arm.

'Christ.' A bullet shatters his elbow, his arm swings uselessly as the phone is answered.

'What?' Franco hisses.

'Franco, we tried,' a bullet hits his shoulder, 'It was an ambush, Gulliv—'

A bullet hits his arm, almost takes it off and the phone spins in the air and smashes to the ground – case, battery and sim card each spiralling away from the other. Drew yells in pain and slides back; he can feel blood pulse from both shattered arms. He will bleed to death quickly if pressure isn't applied. His vision is already woozy. Gulliver kneels down beside him.

'All over,' he tells Drew and takes his thumb and digs it into the shattered stump of his arm. The pain rifles through him like an electric shock.

'Why?' Drew manages through gritted teeth.

'You said it yourself. You're loyal to Franco.' He grabs the shattered arm and pulls. Drew screams with the pain, then slowly falls unconscious as the last of his blood weeps from him.

'You are such a baby,' Gulliver laughs. He grabs what is left of the arms and pulls the dead man around and drags him back to the main entrance. It is difficult as Gulliver's hands are slick with blood. He drags the body alongside JB's, then he goes back and gets Dagg's body and drags that to the entrance too. When they are all there, he finds the main light switch and puts it on. The room looks like an abattoir. Gulliver looks down at his clothes; he is splattered with blood and mud. He starts to strip off. Under the shirt his arms are like iron. He pulls off his pants and his penis springs up. Killing the men has made him hard with the excitement. In the corner of the room is a small suitcase he had placed there the night before. He opens it and pulls out a change of clothes – identical to those he wore before. He changes into them. He has no new shoes. Instead he pulls out a little shoe-shine kit and carefully cleans them. He looks at his face in the toecap and is happy with the result.

He looks at his watch. He is running late. Damn, he needs to speed this up. There is a metal staircase in the corner of the entranceway; it leads up to the caretaker's flat. Gulliver heads to it and scales it, two steps at a time. At the top is a plain white corridor. There is a door at the end with a touch-screen entry system. He taps in a key code and the door opens.

'Jesus Christ, you took your time,' an angry voice greets him as the door slides open. The room has two inhabitants. A man who is tall and thin, with stubble and greasy hair which is slicked back in a ponytail. Behind him, sitting on the corner of a bed, is a woman. She is addict-thin and incredibly pale with spots speckling her mouth. Gulliver walks inside, ignoring the man's outburst.

'Has everything gone according to plan here?' Gulliver asks the man.

'Of course, the boys have been downstairs for hours. They've probably pissed themselves by now—'

'The names we agreed?' Gulliver interrupts him.

'Of course we got the boys you wanted – we did everything just like we agreed. We aren't retards.'

Gulliver smirks a little at this. That was the exact word he had used about this man only hours before. 'Of course you aren't, you have been most efficient.'

'Fucking right we have.'

'And now you want your money?'

'Twenty grand; that was the deal.'

'Sure.' Gulliver pulls his gun, the silencer still attached, and fires a single bullet through the man's skull. He falls back onto the bed. The woman looks at Gulliver with scared eyes like a rabbit caught in headlights.

'I am very disappointed in you. I am feeling so fucking horny and you just don't do it for me.' He fires again, and her lifeless body folds over the man's like Juliet's over Romeo. Gulliver takes a cloth from his pocket and carefully unscrews the silencer and replaces it in a pocket on his belt. The gun then slides into the hidden holster in the small of his back. He pulls a mobile phone from his pocket and scrolls through an address book until he finds the name he needs. The phone rings a few times and is answered.

'My business is concluded. Can you meet me at the address I sent you? Ten minutes, perfect. Do make sure you bring everything you need.' Gulliver ends the call and slides the phone into his pocket.

After ten minutes a car arrives and pulls into the parking area alongside Gulliver's van. A young man gets out: he looks about eighteen, with large black-framed glasses that look like 1980s NHS free frames, but are actually incredibly expensive designer eyewear. He has a wispy black beard and he wears a chequered shirt, black Puffa jacket and a baseball cap. He leaves the headlights on the car blazing, as it is the only light available. He squints at the industrial building before him.

'Hello,' he calls out in a slightly trembling voice. 'Hello. It's Adam. You asked me to meet you here for—'

'Please turn off the headlights, Adam,' Gulliver calls out from the dark.

'Erm, okay,' he yells, his voice showing some concern as he does so. Gulliver flicks on Drew's giant silver Maglite and walks over to the young man.

'Mr Johnson?' the young man asks.

'That's right.' Gulliver smiles as he extends his hand and grips Adam's, hard. 'I'm glad you could make it.'

'Oh I'm excited – very excited by the opportunity to shoot with you.'

Gulliver grins. 'Can you tell me what you've shot so far?'

'My credits you mean?'

'Exactly Adam, can you list your credits for me?'

'Well, nothing professional, you know. I got a *highly accomplished* in the Virgin shorts competition for a movie about zombies breeding with girl guides, and a couple of pop videos for this indie band, *I am Victor Kiam's Love Child*. I also made a mockumentary about a chugger who worked for like twelve different charities in one week and at the end had all the diseases and syndromes and shit that he was collecting for – it's like satirical and stuff. I've got a disc with my show reel on – or I can give you a website to go to.'

'That won't be necessary. Who are your favourite directors?'

'Woody Allen, especially the later, serious ones. I love Wes Anderson.'

'Do you like John Woo?'

'I, I'm sorry I don't know who that is?'

'Tsui Hark?

'I—'

'Chan-Wook Park?'

He looks blankly at Gulliver.

'Okay, no big deal. What have you brought with you?'

Adam smiles and runs to the back of his car and opens the back. 'My college has great equipment, so I got a Panasonic X3. It's HD with crystal-sharp images in dark rooms – you said low light, right?'

'Very low. And what you shoot can be uploaded to the internet immediately?'

'In a flash.'

'Perfect – do you have a tripod or do you plan to hand-hold?'

'I got a brace so it's like a steadicam vibe, very Paul Greengrass.'

'Good. Then I think you will do nicely, Adam.'

'Great.' Adam looks pleased. 'So who are we filming exactly, the ad said it was a well-known performer? I was thinking comedian but—'

'All will be revealed in a moment. One last thing, before we talk details of the shoot, I need you to sign a non-disclosure agreement and a waiver of all rights to copyright of the intellectual property of your filming this evening.'

'Cool.'

'And I need an address, phone, email and your social security number. You brought a photo too?' He nods and starts to fill in the form Gulliver hands him. 'And do you have family in London?' Gulliver asks.

'My mum and two sisters live in Wimbledon.' Adam starts to fill in the forms.

'Great.' Gulliver smiles as he waits until the final signature is in place. 'Okay, I think that is all.' Adam hands back the completed forms.

'Follow me then.' And Gulliver strides away, taking the light with him. Adam grabs a silver camera case from the car and follows. Gulliver gets inside the large metal door and shines the light back along the path so that the film student can see his way inside.

'So who is it? I was thinking Frankie Boyle.' Adam gets through the door and Gulliver swings it closed.

'Have you ever seen a dead body, Adam?'

'I—'

Gulliver swings the torchlight down to the ground and onto JB, Dagg and Drew's corpses.

'Shit.' Gulliver grabs him as Adam projectile vomits and tries to twist away from the bodies.

'Good boy, Adam, get everything out.'

'Please let me go.'

'Adam, you are in no danger, as long as you do what I tell you.'

'Please just let me go.'

'Now, Adam, this is your fear talking. You're freaked out I can tell, seeing a dead body can do that. Once you get over this you will realise that this is your chance at the big time – straight out of college. You are one lucky mother-fucker.'

'I just want—'

'Fame, money, awards?' Gulliver smiles.

Adam tries to control his shaking. 'What do you want me to film?'

'Good question and a better attitude. I like that. Let me confess that there is no well-known performer. That was a little white lie. Downstairs there are three boys tied up. I am gonna go down there and fuck them up, then I will kill them – and you are gonna film it.'

'I don't want to—'

'I hear you Adam. I hear you, it's crazy shit – but with or without you I am going to kill those boys. With you – well we have an internet sensation. I predict it will go viral very quickly and you will become a household name. Without you – I still kill those fuckers in the basement, but I also kill you and cut off your cock-sucking head. After that I go and find your fucking mother and two lovely sisters and show them what's left of you before I rape and kill them too.'

Adam vomits again.

'Good. You need to get all that out – we don't want you chucking when you're meant to be filming. You know I am thinking Oscar bait tonight.'

Adam starts crying, snot pouring down his face. 'Hey hey, Adam,' Gulliver says soothingly, putting his arms around Adam's shoulders. 'This is the beginning of a beautiful friendship, kid.' And he leads the boy to the top of the stairs.

'So the filming should always be showing the victims, I will wear a mask but try and not get me in shot as much as possible and while we're in the room you don't speak, especially not on film and do not say my name. You got that?'

'Okay, Mr Johnson.'

'Not Mr Johnson. Tonight Adam, I will be known as Franco.' He grins and leads the sobbing boy down the stairs. As they walk down into the underworld, the phone rings in his pocket. He looks to see who it is. The caller ID says: Mr Pink. It is his idea of a joke.

'Excuse me, Adam.' Gulliver leaves the still-snivelling kid halfway down the stairs and walks back up to take the phone call.

'Dent, everything has worked well here. I ...' Gulliver listens for a few seconds – his entire body stiffens. 'What do you mean he's not there? There's no way out.' His face turns a deep purple as he listens to the excuses. 'Jesus fucking Christ. The drug should have turned him into a raving lunatic hours ago. What the fuck went wrong? Oh Jesus, well we need to— he is too dangerous to be left in the game and I am meant to be drinking his fucking blood in a couple of hours. Fuck! Use the girl, smoke him out.'

SIXTEEN

Pia tries to hold on to herself. She can feel her body and mind peeling away from each other, her senses dimming, her mind floating free, she—

'Think, Pia,' she hisses to herself, pulling her retreating mind back. 'The date, it's,' a curtain of darkness seems folded into her brain, she tries to push through it. 'Saturday. It's Saturday.' she feels proud of that little magic trick, plucking the day of the week from the fog. 'It's the … ' a wave of nausea sweeps over her. Too much wine, no, something else, something in the wine.

Be careful, her father's voice rumbles through her head. Always such a worrier that man.

'Oh Dad, I am so lost,' she tells him, trying to keep the fear at bay, and stay awake. 'I need help, Dad.'

Think, Pia, he urges her. *You need to fight, fight back!* That was his advice when she was being bullied at school – Joanne Pullinger. Pia gave her a bloody nose; funny that she can recall these memories from more than a decade ago but this very evening is darkening, fading from her. A shadow seems to be moving through her head, spreading a blackness, smudging and smearing the last few hours, making them formless – she can't remember. Just shades in the corner of her mind, she wants to turn on a light, shine a spotlight, but her mind slips and the memories slide away. Shadows dance. Panic starts to build.

'You need to remember,' she tells herself.

'You should feel right at home then,' a voice seeps through a crack in the darkness. A voice from earlier that night comes back to her, maybe an hour or two ago, or has she lost all track of time? Who said it? *Think!* It was someone she had wanted to impress. She remembers laughter, laughter at her? No, with her – she had told them her name, her secret real birth name and they laughed. Under the dragon's wing she told them. A shard of memory slices through the dark curtain: she stands with five men who wear tuxedos, she is in an evening gown.

'25th June 2011. That's the date, it's Saturday 25th June 2011.' Nausea again. She can't feel her limbs, floating in nothingness, like she's fallen down a hole in the earth, and all her body wants is an oblivion of sleep. She could just— 'No!' She bites herself, hard. 'Don't fall asleep.' She knows the danger she is in, knows it and yet can't feel it, she and her body are divorced. All she can do is look dispassionately on. A ghost at her own funer—

Pia! Her dad shouts, and her cheek stings for a second, did he slap her? Is he there? No, he can't be. 'Saturday 25th June 2011. Brighton.' She can feel the drug in her system suckling at the edges of her memories, erasing them – the last few hours want to fold in on themselves, like a house of cards collapsing in slow motion, wiping the hours away – minute by minute. She must try and hold on – Saturday, 25th, Brighton, by the sea, the girl in the sea and the car hit her.

There is a flare of light like headlights, catching her in their beam, her head feels like it might implode, are her eyes open or closed? Closed. She tries to open them, they feel like the lids are glued – she forces them, tears them open – there is nothing. Shapes? Maybe. She sees a dark blob that must be her hand, she tries to focus on it. 'Dad will be so disappointed in me,' is all she can think. *Never disappointed in you, sweetheart,* his voice seems to vibrate in her chest. She digs her fingernails into the heel of her palm and the pain makes the two images coalesce – a hand of five fingers, the nails are freshly painted, Hettie did them when, her vision splinters again – everything swims and she falls.

'No. I need to—' She touches the floor to steady herself – but feels nothing, her touch is faulty, her hands seem to float away from her, she almost laughs, but stops herself. This is no laughing matter – there's danger here; she knows that, but – it's so hard to care. It's hard to care about anything. She slides onto her haunches, like a sprinter. She feels the disconnection sweep her body and she topples sideways. Arm out, catches herself – pushes back, why can't she just roll over and sleep? Where is she? Brighton, on the beach? No, later in the day, it's the evening and she's at a fundraiser – is that an actual word? Her synapses are not firing as they should, she remembers insects – weird, crawling from the wood. The fundraiser, she is there, was there, am there? An internship – she went … she told them her real name and they laughed because she is in a royal palace. Brighton, the Royal Pavilion. A palace of the East – by the seaside in England. And she was the Princess in the palace, they had all laughed. She was embarrassed, it was like school, these were big braying voices, but the laughter wasn't at her but she still felt small. She so rarely tells people her real name – not Pia.

Princess, her father whispers.

She left the tuxedo men braying with laughter, puffing up their chests like animals attracting a mate. Animals. Dragons breathing fire – everywhere; on the ceiling, the wallpaper, curled around the curtains – in the paint and the wood. Can she hear breathing?

'Who's there?' She strains to pick out sounds from the dark. Nothing now, except the sound of her heart beating. Fast.

Come home safe, her dad tells her.

'I will Dad, you don't need to worry about me.'

But that was wrong wasn't it?

'Help me, Dad,' she asks.

'There are private rooms, too, maybe you would like to see them?' The voice had been warm and friendly. It had seemed so innocent, and that mouth was so kissable, and – and she was lightheaded. Two glasses of wine, surely that wasn't too much. She had eaten too, to sop it up. Such a nice mouth. Even as she thinks that, she can feel the memory of the mouth erase itself as the lights are going off all over her brain.

'It's called the Saloon Bottle – it was the private rooms of King George. Like his private den, a games room and it is where he made his conquests.' Smile – *I want to kiss that mouth*, Pia thinks. 'Later on he got so fat and riddled with gout he couldn't make it up the stairs – but he had a winch installed. Maybe he had them winch him up. Would you like me to show you where a Prince takes his Princess?' She feels the heat flush her cheeks and her far more private places warm and tingle.

'Lead on.' Her dress flows and spins – she loves being dressed up in this beautiful place. She feels so special. If the mouth moves close to her she will kiss it.

'This way,' the mouth says. 'The palace is full of secret corridors – mostly for the servants, so they can scurry from room to room but not be seen by guests.' A door opens, a jib door – a secret door, hidden from the public eye. Pia's pulse begins to race, she moves through the entrance and into the gloom of a dark and secret place – she can just make out a spiral staircase;

two flights of well-worn slats that curve up into the sky. She reaches out to a hand that squeezes her own. Dizzy. Dark. They corkscrew up, holding hands. She longs to be kissed. As they ascend, Pia lays her free hand against the wall. Her fingertips can feel hundreds of years beneath them – layers of the finest wallpapers overlaid and stripped away in places. In patches there is graffiti. Her nostrils fill with the musk of decay. She was expecting opulence, like the finery downstairs; possibly a canopy bed where she would be laid down. As they get to the final steps, she stops. She grips the other hand tight – dizzy. Was the staircase twisting in the wind? She feels tired all of a sudden, wants to rest, maybe go back down – but the hand she holds softly tugs her forwards. A whisper: 'Just a final step and then into the pleasure dome.' A laugh that is so sexy, Pia can't resist but moves forwards again, into the secret pleasure room of—

She can see that time has not been kind to this secret place. The windows are amazing, Moorish lozenges that float in the air, allowing streaks of milky moonlight to flash on the walls and floors – but that is enough to see it is derelict and dirty.

Careful! her father whispers to her.

'I want to go back downstairs.' She tries to pull her hand away, but now it is held tight and her arm is wrenched, she feels the earth move as she is thrown down. She hits the floorboards hard and rolls, her bag is lost somewhere. Somewhere over the rainbow.

From the darkness there is breathing again, she is not alone. Her heart rate spikes. What if she screams? She feels the wave of nausea – ride it out Pia, don't go under, don't fall asleep. The memories are tumbling down – there is an image of a mouth – then it is gone – where the hell is she? Why can't she just lie down and sleep. She can't feel her legs now, as if she floats clear of the floor, worked from below like a hand-puppet. She hears the sound of fabric ripping, tearing. *NO!* Someone is cutting her beautiful ballgown off of her. *But I love this dress. It was all my money for a month.* With a tug the dress is pulled away and she lies there in just her underwear. I'll get cold, she thinks. She is rolled over onto something hard or, at least to something different, the sensation is too difficult to tell.

'Just let this be over soon. Let this be over soon,' she repeats to herself, trying to keep the shame away. What will her dad say? Will he blame her? Then real fear fills her for the first time. *I can survive this. I can survive this*, she repeats as a mantra in her head. She feels her hand taken and held by her father, he grips it tight.

'Oh Daddy.'

My Princess.

Bloody Princess. She's told him time and time again: 'Call me Pia, I won't talk to you if you call me Princess.' But now, tonight – she will be his Princess. Just for the night, she will let him call her by the name she was baptised, even though she hates it.

I love you, Princess.

'I love you too, Daddy. I am so sorry.'

Shush – you never have to say sorry to me. You can survive this, her father tells her, holding so tightly to her hand.

I can survive this. I will survive this, she tells herself. *I must not sleep.* She pinches her arm, hard as she can. She barely feels it. Her vision flares, is that the door ahead? She could bolt for it, she's fast. There must be someone downstairs, if she could get to the door and down the stairs, she could save herself from something awful. The mouth is waiting in the dark for her to fall asleep, to be totally and finally lost in the darkness of non-memory and then, when she can't fight back – then the shadows will come to take her. Dad always told her to be careful, that there were monsters in the dark, but she never believed him. The biggest wave of disconnection sweeps her body up and tosses it high. The drug has her – she only has one chance. She launches herself forwards – toward the light flare, her legs are lead but they move, they move and suddenly she is a bolt of lightning, she can feel the wind in her hair, the freedom in front of her, the door is there – her dad's there in front of her waving her on.

Run darling, run like the wind. You can do it, you are almost there. I love you. I love you.

'Dad.'

She runs headfirst into the wall and crumples. Blood springs from a gash and runs down into her eyes – she feels herself become fully uncoupled from her body and her consciousness floats into the air.

Lying there she looks so much like the boy, so much like little Bheka as he lay amongst the dead. Lulama watches her, would weep for her niece if she could. Instead she can only watch as the shadows engulf the girl.

SEVENTEEN

Franco throws the door open and streaks inside, heart pounding – his head full of Drew's scream. Everything is crashing around him, the Dark Wolf is being hunted; but none of that matters, the only concern he has is Pia. At his desk he keys the numbers into the keypad and the safe slides open. He pulls out the phone and slips the sim card into it, almost dropping it. His fingers feel clammy and slimy, hard to hold onto the tiny card. But he slots it home and the face lights up. 'Please,' he whispers to himself. He slides his finger over the glass and her picture appears. Taken a year ago, on the top of Box Hill. Her curls, stolen by the wind, stream out behind her. Her simple-cut dress is red and orange – so warm and sun-like. Her face is beautiful – sculpted and fine as if in polished marble, with skin the colour of cinnamon and eyes that are an amazing green. Yet it is the smile, full of laughter and love that steals his breath away. Beneath the picture the legend reads *Princess*.

He taps her face and it moves to the left – a map slips out from behind her with a flashing green beacon. Brighton. He taps the map and it zooms in. Royal Pavilion. She's still there. The event was due to end at 11 p.m. – then there might have been cleaning up to do but it's almost midnight now; she should be heading back to London, maybe already driving her little bug of a car. He always tells her not to answer the phone while driving, but not now, tonight, break the rules. Just tonight. 'Answer please, this is urgent,' he begs the phone, but it just rings and rings. He wants to pray for her, but he has forgotten how to.

Dear Lord, hear my prayer. Lulama begins for him. He opens his mouth, but at that instant her picture fills the screen; his beautiful daughter. She has answered. Relief floods in – he had been full of such fear for her. He jumps in quickly, before she can berate him for being such a control freak.

'Sorry. I know it's like a police state and I am a dreadful man – I just had to talk to you – tell you I love you. I'm so proud of you and … Pia? Pia?'

There is no voice.

'Princess?' Normally, using her birth name would make her scream at him. But there is nothing.

'Darling.'

Nothing.

The fear washes in and he feels himself shrink smaller and smaller. 'Pia?'

'Beautiful skin,' a voice rasps. A voice that sounds like nothing he has heard before.

Cold fear. 'Princess?'

'No more Princess. Do you want to see how beautiful I have made her? You should come find her. Find me. Find me, Daddy.'

Franco hears a dull scrape, as the phone is put down. He strains to hear, but there is only the tread of footsteps retreating, echoing and fading. Then nothing. A hell of nothing. And then he hears a dull crack – like a watermelon being struck with a hammer.

'PRINCESS?' he screams through the handset. But there is nothing; maybe he hears a laugh, he can't be sure. He can't be sure of anything. He taps her face and the phone locator flashes green at him. He has to get there, get to her even though he knows the worst has happened. He will never see her smile again. His stomach contracts and he vomits onto the carpet. He opens his mouth and screams her name.

'PRINCESS!' he howls like the Dark Wolf he is and then his face twists into a snarl. Drew warned him, this is an all-out attack. He needs to leave, the truth of his situation hits him hard. He thought, if the time came, he would have weeks to plan – that he would be rewarded for his years and years of loyal service. No. He needs to get out of there now. He opens the safe and dips into the pile of passports, he takes two. There are books of stocks and bonds, he has it all copied on a key drive, which he takes. He grabs some cash – as much as he can carry – but most stays inside. Easy come. Lastly he runs his hand over her artwork, he feels the tears spike at his eye sockets, he needs to keep it together for just a while longer. Later he will have the freedom to grieve. He takes one piece, a portrait she did of him when she was nine. Goodbye to the rest. He finds a match, lights it and holds it to a potato print of the Incy-wincy spider. The paper catches and flares, there's no rain to wash the spider out this time. He throws it inside and the drawer begins to burn.

He turns back to Frank Light's phone, eyes glued once more to the flashing map-pin, making sure she has not moved, he fumbles in his pockets for his other phone. He opens the contacts and scrolls down to a number he has not used in some time. He calls it.

'Talk to me,' a voice says.

'I need you to blow a secure channel, an airwave *officer down* signal. I want every cop within fifty miles there as fast as possible.'

'Where?'

EIGHTEEN

'... officer down, I repeat, officer down. Every unit respond, airwave activation from the Royal Pavilion. I repeat ...'

The siren screams into the night and the foot grinds down on the pedal. The car hits ninety mph in seconds, hurtling down Grand Parade. The two men steel themselves and look ahead. Who is down and dying, someone they know, someone they've slept with? The pleasure pier is dead ahead, blazing with lights of all colours, Vaughn fixes on it as he floors the car, forcing it ever faster. Then, as they burst past the war memorial, they can see that to the right stands the Royal Pavilion – dark. It should be lit up in garish purple spotlights, it was when they passed it less than thirty minutes before. Vaughn notes the darkness that has swallowed the building and the gardens all around it. To his side Dexter reaches for the radio.

'CR14 responding. ETA ... we're there.'

Vaughn slams the brakes, squealing onto the pavement and just missing a life-sized statue of George IV, the mad bastard who almost bankrupted the country to build this Taj Mahal by the seaside. As the car rocks to a stop, both doors swing open and the two policemen race. Dexter has his stab-vest in his hand, no time to swing it on; he should have been wearing it but it is getting too tight and he doesn't want to ask for a new one, he can't risk the taunts of *fat-boy*. Vaughn is already ten yards ahead and extending his lead – arms pumping. He is almost there, he looks over the expanse of the building, dark throughout, he swings his hand to his belt and grabs his *fuck-off* Maglite. He switches it on and the beam cuts through the black, lighting up the entrance and catching a man in the beam, whose eyes flare.

'Police, raise your arms,' Vaughn yells. The unknown man in the entranceway swings a torch beam at them and Vaughn is blinded for a second.

'Drop the torch or I will Taser you.' He scrabbles at his side to draw the yellow gun.

The silhouette stops moving and calls out with a gravelly voice, 'Pavilion security.' He lowers the beam to the grass, illuminating the path towards him. 'The power's out. I was just looking round.'

Vaughn draws level with him and plays his torch over the man, noting his uniform. A long way back, Dexter is now walking, holding his side.

'Who called you?' the security guard asks.

'Airwave panic button – officer down.'

'Shit.' The man's face drains of colour. 'I'm ex-force. If I can—'

'Our control called your ops room but no answer, why?'

'Power's out all over the building.'

In one synchronised movement, both men shine their torches across the entrance and up to the main dome and down. It looks like the haunted house at a funfair.

'What happened tonight?'

'Private party, some fundraiser for Labour.'

'Who's inside now?' Dexter asks.

'Just security, nobody else is here, the last of the Labour lot went an hour ago. Cleaners left just before the power went down.'

'Police officers?'

'There were six most of the night, four stayed to sweep the building but they're long gone.'

'Is there a log of all attendees, was it checked?'

'We always count 'em in and count 'em out.'

'When was the power cut?'

'About ten minutes ago – everything went dark.'

'Did CCTV go out too?'

'All cameras and all comms.'

Vaughn nods; something feels wrong. In the distance he can hear sirens, an ambulance will be here in seconds and he can already see another unit pulling up on the west side of the gardens.

Dexter is talking to someone on the radio, might be ops one. He calls over to Vaughn, 'Armed response will be here within ten minutes, we should wait.'

'No. I'm going in now,' he calls back, then turns to the security guard. 'You, wait here and tell other officers what's going on. Keep the paramedic here until we shout. Nobody else in or out – got that?' The security man nods.

Vaughn holds the Taser for a second like he's posing for a James Bond poster, and then moves to the dark maw of the building and is swallowed up. Dexter watches him walk inside. 'Fuck,' he whispers to himself and follows Vaughn in.

Vaughn moves forward, his whole body tense as he flows into the darkness. He aims the Taser ahead, the red dot of the laser shines on the pillars to the side of the main door and then into the heart of the darkness. It's funny, he's lived in Brighton his whole life, but has never been inside. His school came here once but he bunked off the trip and went to the pier instead and blew his trip money in about five minutes on slot machines. History – never cared for it.

'Police!' Vaughn calls out, his voice echoes around the room, making it hard to tell if there is any other movement in there. 'Police are entering the premises, we believe an officer is down, please make yourself known.' The torch beam flares off glass and Vaughn moves it to the floor, the Taser dot moves ahead and onto a face—

'Police, show me your—' It's a model of an ancient Chinese man. The breeze from the open door catches him and his head begins to nod. *You are too late – they are dead,* the figure seems to say with a smile.

Vaughn feels his heartbeat race. He moves on, down the corridor. In the dark, shadows stretch around him, playing on the walls that are covered in leaves and bamboo, like a jungle. He heads down the longest corridors; to either side there is a wide staircase, but between them large double doors lead into … *Christ!* The laser-sight flies around the walls and then up into the air and, *there be dragons*; curling and crawling across the ceiling, hunting for meat. *It's like the Lord of the Fucking Rings up there*, he thinks.

'Can anyone hear me?' Vaughn calls out. Behind him he can hear shouts from other officers arriving at the entrance. He needs to be the one to find the injured officer. He moves forward, faster, his torch beam weaving around the floor; Taser dot threading ahead. His senses are alive, can he smell blood? He starts to jog, he knows someone needs him, he can feel the pull in his stomach.

'Police. Is anyone here?'

He sees the bamboo stairs and sprints up, three at a time. The air is thicker up here, something is there with him. He feels it. He moves ahead, almost missing the movement – but arcs his torch back. A door swings, still moving. Is it a breeze or has someone just been through it?

'Police. Make yourself known.' It is covered in the same wallpaper, almost invisible – a secret door. He reaches out to stop it swinging. Like a gallows rope. Then he slowly opens it. Dexter is with him, finally.

'Where does it go?' he asks. Neither of them know.

They slowly move through the doorway, one by one, Vaughn first. It is a small door and opens to a larger hallway. Pitch dark, except a little moonlight seems to diffuse in the air above them, making it seem like silver glitter floats over their heads. They make a criss-cross pattern with their torch beams, shafting up. They see the mistake; they are not in a hallway, not a room, it is a vestibule with a staircase that leads up, corkscrewing over their heads into the heart of the onion dome that sits atop the palace. It is the Saloon Bottle, the secret pleasure dome of George IV.

'Armed officers are almo—' Dexter starts.

'Too late,' Vaughn tells his partner in a whisper. Then he takes a step to the foot of the stairs and yells up into the silvery dark. 'Police officer entering. I am coming up. I want to see arms in the air – if you do not comply I will Taser you.' And he starts to rise. In the harshness of the torch beam this all seems so different to the opulence of the rest of the building. There is no carpet, here the floorboards are worn and creak as he steps on them. The walls have had their rich papers ripped from them and hundred-year-old graffiti stains them. Vaughn curves upwards, step by step, his nostrils flare with the scent of blood; something is here. Death is here. His stomach clenches.

'Is anyone injured?' he calls, he is almost there. He steps onto the final stair, his torch swings onto a door ahead.

'Dex, there's a door up here. It's closed. I am going in,' he calls down.

There is a crash from the room ahead.

'Jesus fuck!' Vaughn drops his torch, it clangs down the stairs. Darkness ahead. He points the Taser forwards, cutting into the darkness before him. He feels a ripple of air brush his face, it is full of decay, must and fresh blood. He hears a wheel spin and then a thud from the room ahead. He roars and kicks at the door. It splinters and bursts, the lock ripping from the wood and spinning in the air.

'Police coming in,' he yells and rushes in, his heart screaming with adrenalin; the red dot of the Taser dances. He runs in, the room confuses him, it is round, with a corridor wrapped all the way around it. Incredibly ornate windows are cut into the walls; almond-shaped glass that throw shafts of the silver moon in and—

'Christ!'

He trips. The floorboards are pulled up in one area, he falls forwards, his hands spread out to cushion his fall, and they drop into the blood, it is warm, still warm. His head fills with the scent of it all – sweet like a rose but earthy too, the undertow of corruption bites through the sickly sweet. His hands are coated, slick and sticky and warm. He feels stomach acid boiling and rising into his throat, but he fights it back down.

'Dex, there's a body.' He turns his head and yells back the way he had come to the officer who stands terrified at the foot of the stairs. 'We need medical attention, NOW.' The scent of blood is cloying and all-pervasive. 'I heard someone run, I think. I mean, I think that they're running. There must be another exit. Radio it in.' He calls over his shoulder to his colleague. Then he crawls forward and … she is dead. He knows in a second that she is dead. Her head. *Oh Christ the blood*, it fills the room. She is dead. He wants to weep, she is dead. But everyone knows the story of the mother and the two girls. They looked dead and the bodies were left for twelve hours while SOCO took evidence. Then, when they went to move them, the youngest wasn't dead, she was covered in blood but she was alive. With a shaking hand he reaches forwards, for her neck with its sweeping curve. He touches her, feeling for life, but there is nothing. He pulls his fingers away and sees his own fingerprints left on her neck, in her blood.

He staggers back, feeling the contents of his stomach draw up to his throat. He pulls air into his lungs – *don't throw up, don't throw up*. When this shift is over he wants to walk down to the sea, it will be freezing, but he wants to strip down to his pants and dive in. Have the shock of the ice water clean him; sweep away these memories and— he hears something. He freezes. It sounds human. It sounds like—

'Danny,' the second policeman calls from outside the room.

'Shut it, Dex. Quiet,' he yells.

Quiet. He strains into the darkness, reaching out with his senses and … he can hear strangled sobs. Where is it coming from?

'Who's here, show yourself.' He swings the Taser around, the red laser being the only illumination. He skittles the dot across the floor and it picks out a small black square. The sound seems to be coming from it. He takes a pair of latex gloves out of his belt pouch and puts them on, then picks up the phone. He touches the screen and it lights up. Dad, the legend reads over a picture of a handsome, grinning man. Mid-thirties probably, with a strong lean face and dreadlocks that are plaited back over his head. Her father is on the line, sobbing.

'Sir. Sir, can you hear me?'

'I …' the father snorts back a sob. 'Is she—'

'Where are you? How long have you been hearing this?'

'Please tell me, can you do anything for her?'

'Sir, I need to know your n—'

'Please. I beg you, tell me.'

He pauses and looks back to the girl on the floor. Suddenly clouds move away from the moon outside and a silver light cuts through the lozenge glass into the room, making her skin sparkle. Her eyes are open, but they are lifeless.

'I am so sorry, sir. Your daughter, she's gone.'

'Thank you. Thank you for that.' His voice cracks as sobs tear his body into a million pieces. 'I love you, Princess,' he calls out to his dead daughter. 'I am so sorry I didn't keep you safe.' And the image of him fades as the phone turns to black.

The tears fall and splash onto her image, blurring her beauty for a second, turning her into a mermaid. He remembers her loving Ariel when she was seven or eight. One day he bought her the book, it was supposed to be a big treat – but he made a mistake. He had bought the Hans Christian Anderson original, not the sanitised Disney. She was angry, kept telling him it was the wrong one, but he read it to her anyway, and by the end they were both in tears. Together, sharing the sadness … 'My Princess,' Franco breathes. Then he turns the phone around in his hand. He digs his pen into the back and opens it, removes the sim card and drops it to the floor. He stamps it into oblivion. He must not forget, he must stay free if he is to do anything to avenge her. But before that he must see her face again, one final time. Nothing else matters. Nothing. But to do that, he must find the man who can help him; possibly the only man who can help to make sense of this nightmare. A man who owes him, who a long time ago swore a bond of friendship. He needs the Sad Man.

NINETEEN

Sergeant 'Fat Eddie' Matthews's head lolls on his desk amidst the detritus of the night. Chocolate, biscuit and cake crumbs, used scratch cards and a pile of scrunched-up Kleenex. He snores a low rumble. It is just past 1.30 a.m. He should be awake, he's the night officer for Operation Ares, but it's been quiet. No dead girls tonight, at least none that fall under the remit of Ares.

Around Fat Eddie the large room is mostly in shadow, just his desk is lit by an orangey glow. This was a part of the appeal for Eddie Matthews to work all alone on the graveyard shift. He could eat his crisps, biscuits, cake and chocolate without getting the evil-eye from some young copper with a six-pack. Plus he didn't feel like he was in a massive petri dish being watched all the time by pen-pushers and bureaucrats. At night the enormous room of desks and dividers could almost feel cosy. Of course the other part of working nights was that his wife had kicked him out and he basically lived in the ops room now. In the gents he has a suitcase with a couple of changes of clothes and a mug with his toothbrush. Under his desk he has bedding. Everyone is happy that Eddie does it each night and nobody else has to work the shift. Even if most nights it is like the grave and—

Suddenly Eddie's awake. He sits up, chocolate-chip acne pebbles his face. He's lost for a second, not sure why he's awake.

Probably the lack of pillow, somebody had filled it with – well actually he doesn't want to think about what they filled it with as it smells disgusting and—

'Jesus fuck.' He stabs at the panic button but misses it completely and sends a stapler spinning to the floor. A hand grips his wrist. Eddie tries to pull it free but the man holds him like a vice. A second hand strikes, like a snake, wrapping around the fleshy chin of the sergeant. Forcing his face up, towards the intruder, until they are nose to nose. Eddie tries to pull away but the other man's grip is too strong; his fingers flash into the policeman's throat and force the larynx closed.

'You know who I am?' Franco calmly asks, his voice barely above a whisper.

Eddie's eyes flare, first with recognition and then with fear.

'I see you do.' Franco's fingers dig deeper.

Eddie fights for breath, he tries to use his bulk to break the grip, twisting one way then the other. Instead the intruder lifts him up off his feet; the pressure in Eddie's head builds. He tries to drag breath into his lungs from somewhere, anywhere – his chest burns.

'I could hold you like this for a few minutes Sergeant Matthews, I am sure you understand what the result of my doing that would be. Blink if you do.' Eddie blinks. 'Good, I see we are on the same page. You understand that it would be very easy for me to take your life, however this is not the night for you to die – assuming you follow my instructions to the letter. Two blinks for *yes I understand*.' Eddie blinks twice. 'Excellent. Sergeant Matthews, I am going to release you. Should you attempt to raise the alarm again, I shall render you unconscious and be gone before your colleagues arrive. There would also be repercussions from such an action. Do you understand?'

Blink.

He releases Eddie, who collapses back into his chair with such force that it wheels away into the centre aisle. He folds, coughing from deep in his belly, desperately trying to draw breath back into his burning lungs. Franco stands over him, watching as the big man slowly calms and becomes quiet again. When the coughing is all done, and Eddie Matthews can give his full attention once more, Franco speaks.

'I want you to call your boss.'

'DI Thors—'

'Not DI Thorsen. Your real boss. Detective Superintendent Thomas Bevans.'

'Can't – he's off.'

'I don't care who is supposed to be on call this evening, you will call him and you will tell him I am here and will meet with him in his office.'

'I—'

'Sergeant Matthews. You know me. I believe you know what I am capable of, at least by reputation. You will call Detective Superintendent Bevans and invite him to come to see me, you will not tell another soul I am in the building. You understand.'

'What if he won't come? What if he can't?' Eddie's voice is thin, scared.

'You will tell him that I am here and remind him that he is in my debt.'

Eddie's eyes flare, he jumps up. 'That's not poss—' Franco shoots out an arm and pushes him back down into his chair. 'Tom Bevans would have nothing to do with a man like you,' Eddie snarls.

Franco smiles. 'Your loyalty to your superior is good, and I understand your concern. But be assured Sergeant Matthews,

Detective Superintendent Bevans does owe me. It is an old debt, a private matter. Consequently, it is not something to be repeated – to anyone, is that clear?'

'The guv'nor wouldn—'

Franco moves like silk in the wind; a foot snakes under the chair and lifts it effortlessly, despite the bulk of the sergeant. As he topples out, Franco's arms are under him, one in his back, the other on his chest, he is not so much slammed as dunked to the floor. Almost a dip, like a tango, but there is no love here. Franco's hand is on the big man's chest, directly above his heart. Eddie has hardly a second to react as the fingers dig down.

'Christ.' That hurts, so much. Eddie stares into the man's dark eyes, saying nothing. Franco increases the pressure digging into his heart. Eddie's eyes grow larger, like a toad's. Franco releases the pressure slightly. 'You will get Detective Superintendent Bevans here, soon. Do you understand me?' This time Eddie nods. Franco releases him and stands.

'Sergeant Matthews, I have told you something in the strictest of confidence. Tom Bevans and I once had an arrangement. However, he would not be keen to make that one-time association common knowledge, and neither would I. In fact it is a secret known only to ourselves. So, if the fact were to become common knowledge,' he pauses. 'I am sure I do not need to spell out the potential outcome of such a slip. I expect to see Bevans within the hour.' He stops and half turns towards the lift, then is reminded of something and faces Eddie once more. 'Rachel. Your wife's name is Rachel isn't it?'

Eddie nods, feeling cold.

He tries the landline first. It rings for the longest time before he gives up. 'Get a bloody answering machine, guv,' he almost sobs into the phone. Then he tries the mobile, an electronic voice tells him the number he has called is unavailable. Sergeant Eddie Matthews has no idea what to do next.

'Who the hell made me the night controller?' He can feel tears pricking behind his eyes. He joined the police so he didn't have to make decisions. He begins to dial DI Thorsen's number. He gets halfway through before he stops himself. Rachel, he needs to keep her safe.

He tries to remember the training day he attended before he got this position. There was coffee and croissants first thing. Lunch laid on, it was fish and chips with home-made tartare sauce, sticky toffee pudding for afters, and coffee and biscuits all day. But what the hell did they talk about?

'Christ on a buggering bike—' then a flash of inspiration: personnel files. He knows he can access them on the computer but he's too scared to remember passwords and all that typing crap. He runs into the shadows of the Operation Ares room and flicks on a bank of overhead lights. They crackle and fizz for a few seconds before settling down to burn a blue-white light. He pulls a drawer open and fishes inside; it is the paper trail of everyone in the department. Right at the back he finds the one he needs. He pulls out the file and scans through it. Father and mother dead. No siblings. No immediate family. Lists of citations and—

'Christ.' He can hardly believe it. There, scribbled in biro, is a phone number for next of kin. No name, just a number. It could be a decade old, but it's all he has. Fat Eddie looks at his watch, it's 1.49 a.m. Then he looks up at the glass wall before him and sees just one light burning in an office above. Inside is a man who makes his skin crawl. A monster. With a fat finger he dials the number. The phone rings for a long time. Eddie is about to put it down when—

'Hello.' The voice is male, gravelly with interrupted sleep. 'Jim Lancing.'

'Bloody hell.' Fat Eddie knows exactly who he is speaking to, bloody Dani Lancing's father.

'I need to get hold of the guv, Detective Superintendent Bevans. You're listed as next of kin.'

'Who are y—'

'Sergeant Matthews. Eddie – I need the guv'nor. It's urgent,' he pauses. 'Life or death.'

'Haven't you tried—?'

'I tried everything. Do you know where he might be?'

'I'm sure—'

'He's threatened my wife.'

Jim says nothing. The unease he has felt for the last few days is turning to ice and running through his nervous system. He knew something terrible was going to happen.

'The guv needs to call into Ares. It's serious, I …' Eddie is lost for a moment. 'He's come to collect on a debt. That's what he told me, that the guv'nor owes him big time and it's time to pay up.'

'Who?' asks Jim, his voice barely above a whisper.

'An evil bastard. The worst.' Jim can hear the fear in the man's voice. 'Tell the guv it's Franco.'

Five minutes later they stand on the doorstep. Jim leans forward to kiss Patty but she turns slightly, offering only her cheek.

'Call me if you find him,' she says.

'Patty—'

'Don't say it again, Jim.' She holds her hands up like a wall, ending the discussion. 'I'm going to search the park, you go to the hospital.'

'Okay,' Jim says, his voice washed with more than a little frustration. He can see there is no arguing with her, and he knows that it makes sense to split up. It's just that, it's *Franco*. Tom had told them a little about him six months ago: he had helped Tom find Dani all those years ago, but more importantly Tom had told them that he was dangerous – the Dark Wolf. Jim has felt scared since Sergeant Matthews said the name. 'Have you got your phone?' he asks Patty.

'You asked me that upstairs. Yes. And it's fully charged,' she says quickly, seeing the question flit across his face, she knows him, she can read him like a book. 'Don't worry,' she smiles and turns to head to Greenwich Park.

'Take care,' he calls after her, but either she does not hear, or she ignores the entreaty. He watches as she walks towards the darkness, illuminated by the sodium orange of the street lights. She flickers light-dark-light-dark-light-gone. He sighs, feeling the ice creak in his veins. He watches where she was, where a Patty-shaped hole exists in the darkness and he thinks for the millionth time – how long? How long will he get with her? But the air holds no answer.

At the car he fumbles with the keys, his fingers a little numb from the cold, and they fall to the pavement. He stoops to retrieve them and notices his shoes as he does so. The left is black, but the right is brown. 'Great.' That's the problem when you get dressed in the dark.

Inside the car he turns the ignition and sits a moment while the engine warms up. When he has regained the feeling in his fingers, and the car is starting to get toasty, he finally pulls down on the handbrake and pulls away from the kerb to head out into the empty streets. He hopes, at this time of the morning, it will be plain sailing through into the centre of the city. He is heading for St. Bart's hospital. He hopes that is where he will find Tom Bevans.

'Franco,' Jim whispers to himself.

'Franco,' Patty whispers to herself.

She gets to the end of their road; to her left is Dani's old school. Before her, purple-black, is the entrance to the park. She stands under the last streetlight before the dark expanse that spreads out before her. In the distance she can see a red light winking on the top of the observatory. Around her the air seems to shimmer, but the park is just dark. She puts her hands into her pockets and feels the alarm and spray, and potentially of more practical use, there are two Rennies, four ibuprofen and her roprinole, in case she gets the shakes. She enters the park.

Patty stops and listens. Around her the chill wind plays through the trees, which stand like skeletons swaying in the embrace of a tempestuous lover. From somewhere far off there is the sound of traffic but nothing else, nothing human. Good. Being alone is good. She wishes – but wishes are for children, aren't they? For those who have no control over their own lives. She is a grown up and can make her choices, choose her own path, can't she? She yawns. Tomorrow her plan is to visit Ellen Stokes and, hopefully, see Allison. They aren't far away and Patty hopes they can see her, though if she is up all bloody night she'll be in no fit shape to do anything. She walks on.

Patty reaches the brow of the hill and looks out over London. This is the most beautiful view of the city. Years ago she and Jim held hands here as newlyweds. In the dark they made love the first night they moved here, something like forty-five years ago. With Dani as a toddler they played ball, hide and seek – threw snowballs and sledged. Together they watched the seasons rise and fall.

Careful, she tells herself, *dont get pulled down into the maudlin sea of nostalgia*. She knows that the past is quicksand and can suck you down.

Find Tom, she hisses to herself. *Find Tom and then ...* A thought swims up out of the quagmire of her brain. It is a thought that she has had over the last six months but never seen a way to act on; until now. *I can use Tom to get to Franco. I have a question for him.* She didn't realise that was the plan until this moment, but she does have something she desperately needs to know. The thought triggers a tremor. She fumbles in her pocket for the roprinole, takes a small pellet and places it on her tongue. It will dissolve. She closes her eyes and three faces swim before her. Tom, Franco and Jim: the Sad Man, the Bad Man and the Saintly Man. From somewhere a laugh floats through the air, a voice she recognises. *Not real.* She doesn't believe in ghosts.

Suddenly she feels clear, clearer than she has in months. She will ask her question of Franco. She will then follow the burning fuse wherever it leads. And at the end of it all, she will leave Jim. Again. It does not matter that he is a good man, she will hurt him. That's all she has left now – the ability to hurt.

She turns towards the dark shadow of the Royal Observatory and walks on. Below it is a bench; she cannot see it yet, but knows where it is. When Dani went missing, all those years ago, Tom would sleep there, so he was close to their house when Dani came back. Of course Dani never did come back. These last months Tom has spent many nights here. She knows that because he sometimes comes to their house after dawn to get breakfast, and a few nights Jim has sat here with him and shared a bottle. Patty crests the hill and starts down the other side. She reaches the bench. Empty.

TWENTY

'Wolf!' she laughs.

Jim holds her paw as they walk down the street. At number 41 they stop and Jim knocks on the door. A round, bubbly woman opens it. She sees Dani and her smile fades a little.

'Oh. You must be—'

'The big bad wolf,' Dani grins. 'Little pig, little pig, let me come in.'

Jim lifts a gift bag up and offers it to the mother. 'Pick her up at five?'

The mother half-nods and Dani runs past her. Jim wonders if the blood matted into the muzzle was a bit much. As he walks away he hears a Princess scream and little Red Riding Hood beg for her life. The mother might regret a fairy-tale themed party.

Jim parks his car in the extortionately priced car-park that surrounds the hospital and pumps three pounds into a machine before he heads inside. It is 2.17 a.m. by his watch. His stomach is twisted. Inside the head trauma unit is a man who— Jim can't even admit it to himself. He hears the sound again, the dreadful crunch of his skull as the brass censor struck it. It almost killed Marcus Keyson, may still do so, and Jim Lancing had been the one who let it go. Him and Dani, his daughter's ghost.

'There are no such thing as ghosts,' Patty yelled at him. His psychiatrist agrees. Everyone *real* agrees, the only ones who believe him are crazies on on-line forums and he can't keep going to them, that way madness lies. Except he's mad already, isn't he? Crazy because he misses the ghost of his daughter, he misses her so much. And that night in Durham, the night when together they almost killed a man, that was the last time he saw her. It was also the last time he saw Marcus Keyson, the man who is now little more than a vegetable, and that is all his fault. His alone, if Patty is right.

'I am looking for a patient. Keyson. Dr Marcus Keyson,' Jim asks, when he finally finds the reception desk at the ICU head trauma ward. Sitting behind the desk is a thin-faced, tired-looking nurse who blinks at him, like a newborn seeing the sun for the first time. Jim flashes his biggest smile, she narrows her eyes in response; suspicious of anyone who can appear this awake in the middle of the night.

'He's here, but only family are allowed to be with the patients out of visiting hours. Are you—'

Jim shakes his head. 'No. Not family and I fully understand the rules. I actually don't want the patient; I'm looking for a man who visits him a great deal, who also isn't family but a friend. You let him visit after hours I believe.' Jim lets the little dig sink in. 'I'm looking for Detective Superintendent Bevans – Tom.'

She nods, her face crinkling with compassion. 'The poor man, he is such a good friend to Dr Keyson. So devoted, and so affected by the accident – so sad.'

'Indeed,' Jim agrees with the nurse.

'Can I please see Tom Bevans? It is of a most serious nature. I don't need to go into Dr Keyson's room – I will stay out here.' *Please let me stay out here*, he thinks.

'I suppose you can go in. That's fine,' she pulls herself up and leads Jim to the room. He thanks her, and watches as she walks away. He looks inside, the lights are low – most of the room is in shadow but there, in the centre of the room, is a small pool of light which shows the bed, on it lies Marcus Keyson – at least what used to be Marcus Keyson. Coloured pads and wires are attached to his chest and snake down into the sheets. Jim knows that he came out of his coma months ago but with brain damage. He cannot feed himself or move unaided and Tom has been here three or four days a week for months, helping as much as he can. Trying to come to terms with the guilt he feels. Jim understands that, it is Tom's fault that the pathologist was there. Keyson had been trying to get back at Tom for reporting him to the authorities, and was determined to wreck Tom's career – but it didn't work out like that. Tom thinks it was an accident that left Keyson in this state, he has no idea that Jim swung the brass censor that smashed his head. Of course Jim did it for Patty – Keyson threatened her. But, if he could wind back the clock …

If only, if only – that's for losers, Patty had told him once. It is true.

There are two chairs in the room, the closest to the bed has an occupant, Jim can see it is Tom and, for a moment, he would have sworn a figure was curled around Tom's feet; a human figure, maybe a child. But it must have been a trick of the light, a shadow from somewhere, because it is gone now. Jim watches the younger man sleep for a few seconds; he looks painfully thin, pallid, uncared for. Franco will eat him up. Jim feels a shiver run through him.

'Oh, Tom,' Jim sighs, and he stretches forwards to huff and puff and blow the door in.

'Tom. Tom. Wake up.'

Tom's eyes flicker. For a second he looks like he'll panic, his face creases in worry – then it clears as he recognises the older man, his face lights up for a moment. He looks so young again. 'Jim. Is Dani—? he remembers. His face cracks once more.

'Why are you here?' Tom asks, shaking his head to wake himself.

'Sergeant Matthews called me.'

'What, why?' His hand goes to his mobile; it is turned off. He powers it up and sees that there are two dozen missed calls from Eddie.

'Franco,' Jim tells him, his voice full of unease.

Your word is your bond, Policeman. Tom remembers his velvety voice from twenty years ago.

'Franco is at Ares.'

Tom blanches.

'Franco told Matthews to tell you he is calling in his debt.'

'What the hell is going on, Eddie?' A minute later Tom stands in the gents' lavatory on the fourteenth floor of the hospital.

'You need to get over here now guv. He's in your office, he threatened Rachel.'

'Are you sure it's him?' he asks Eddie.

'It's Franco, I know that bastard.'

'And he said—'

'You owe him, that you owe him big time and he's here to collect.'

Tom feels hollow. This is it, Franco will be the final nail in his coffin. 'I'll be there.' The voice is so tired. 'About twenty minutes.'

'Shall I offer him a coffee?'

'For fuck's sake Eddie.' Tom sighs, he knows he shouldn't drag Eddie into this – but it's already too late. 'I need a gun Eddie, but you can't sign one out, too much paperwork.'

'Guv?' Tom can hear the tension building in him.

'Can you go down to the evidence store and—'

'I'm not sure.'

'Eddie, I will return it – I just need some insurance. It's Franco.' There is a pause that Tom thinks lasts for an eternity.

'Okay, boss. Should I get any ammo?'

'What do you think Eddie? And I am going to need a vest too. I'll be there quick as I can. Keep this between ourselves; nobody else is to know he's in the building, okay?'

'Guv.'

'And, Eddie. Be bloody careful with the gun.'

Eddie hears the line go dead. He grabs a Snickers from his drawer and waddles off to break into the evidence store.

Tom slides the phone back into his pocket and walks out into the hospital corridor. Jim stands there looking expectant.

'I spoke to Matthews. I need to leave.'

'Do you need a lift?'

'No. My car's downstairs in a special operations bay – a perk of being a copper.'

The two men stand and look at each other, neither sure what to say, or what the other needs to hear. 'Do you want me to come to Ares?' Jim asks. Tom appreciates the gesture.

'No. I need to face him, alone.'

'What might ha—'

'Jim.' He stifles the question at birth. Tom can't afford to ask himself what Franco could want. After more than twenty years it will be big. 'Bye.' Tom turns and in a second is gone. Jim watches him disappear. He should follow suit, get back to Patty – she will be home by now, and then the two of them can go to bed. He should do that. Instead he walks back to Keyson's room. He hovers by the door for a few seconds before he pushes it open and steps inside to view the man he almost killed.

'I am sorry. I wish I could take it back,' he whispers to the prone form. Then he turns to leave and—

Wait. There's a whisper. Was it actually in the air or just inside his head? It stops him, not sure if it was real or a memory or … He turns, and from the twilight of shadows, a shape emerges.

'Hello, Dad.'

'Dani.'

TWENTY-ONE

Tom pulls into the car-park and looks up at the building before him. It is a nondescript grey brick and glass monolith. There are a thousand office blocks like it in London. It has always saddened him, the anonymity forced upon his team. He had said this once, to Grayson.

'What the fuck do you want, a bloody palace?' Grayson had barked back at him, with a look that said they should feel damn lucky they weren't based in the sewers. It made Tom angry then, tonight he doesn't care anymore. Franco is inside and he will bring it all tumbling down. Tom should have stayed on leave, then he could have just faded away. That option is gone now.

Time to face the music.

He gets out of the car and heads forwards. It is ten storeys high, more than a hundred offices, mostly black at this time of night, but there is a band of light in the centre where the night officers work. There are also a few other scattered lights here and there – maybe conscientious officers, more likely forgetful ones who don't care about global warming. He takes a deep breath. When he breathes out, it curls like a miasma in the air around him.

He walks to the entrance, slowly, like he drags a lead weight behind him. He can see Fat Eddie on the other side of the revolving door, pacing about. He looks scared.

Franco's voice reverberates in his chest. *One day you will repay this debt, Constable Romeo.* Tom had agreed. But that was more than twenty years ago. Suddenly, Eddie sees him and pushes through the door and bounds down the steps like an enthusiastic puppy happy to see his master.

'Guv. I am so glad to see you.'

'Nice to see you too, Eddie.' Tom wants to tell him that he looks like the cowardly lion, but he holds his tongue. 'Where is he then?'

'He's in your office, guv.' Tom nods and then slowly walks to the door, pulling his swipe card out and then thinking again.

'Eddie, you'd better swipe me in. There can't be any record that I've come in tonight.'

'But you're back now aren't you, guv?'

'Yes but, this might be bad.' Tom regrets the words. He sees how Eddie's head droops. 'Let's see what Franco wants.'

'Guv. He said you owed him, owed him big. What did he mean?'

Tom hesitates. 'I met Franco a long time ago, when he was a kid, and he helped me.'

'Your girl?' Eddie says in little more than a whisper.

'Yes.' Tom pauses, unsure how to proceed with Eddie. He can't tell him that Franco helped him frame an innocent man.

'Christ, it's hard to believe he would help anyone, let alone a copper.' Eddie remembers when he was in vice. They found a girl, sixteen. Her face had been smashed to a pulp and she had been burned, between the legs, with a red-hot brand, an 'F'. She was the property of Franco and he had killed her as a warning to others. Killed her and mutilated her – to make a point. Seeing her like that, her skin vivid and raw from the heat, it still made him feel sick, even though he had seen so many others dead since then, but she had been his first. His first dead girl, and still the most horrific. He had hated Franco since that day, not just wanted to see him locked up but wanted to see him hurt, beaten, tormented – just like that poor girl had been.

'Was this before he, you know?' Before he was a butcher of young girls is what Eddie really means. He desperately wants to picture a Franco who is not a blood-soaked monster, not for his sake, but for Tom's. He cannot bear to think of his guv in league with such a man.

Tom shakes his head. 'He had taken over the Dark Wolves about a year before I met him. He told me that first day that he had killed his uncle and drank his blood.' Eddie's face creases up in horror. 'He said that was how they transferred power in his tribe – back in Africa. I don't know that I believed him back then. I have heard many stories since.'

'What did he do for you?' Eddie asks.

'Gave me an address, it turned out.' Tom stops. 'It was a dead end.'

'So you don't owe him nothing. Call a SWAT team out.' His eyes are full of fear. 'They can wipe him out like he's a fucking cockroach.'

Tom shakes his head. 'Let's go Eddie, time to see a man about a wolf. You need to book me in as a brief or something, no pass issued, only visiting for a few minutes to drop something off. No photo, I haven't been here.'

'What about how he just appeared at my desk.'

'Fucking security, I don't know. Just don't mention him. We'll have to find out how he got in later and plug the bloody hole.'

'I'm off shift in—'

'You are not off-shift today. You just pulled a double – triple if needed.'

'Guv.'

'You've only been sleeping anyway. Nap in my office until I call you.'

'Won't you—'

'Not staying, too bloody dangerous here. I'm gonna take him out through the back. Remember Eddie, he wasn't here, I wasn't here.'

'What do I tell DI Thorsen?'

'Nothing. I mean it, Eddie, tell her nothing.'

Eddie nods reluctantly.

Eddie swipes his card and the door pops open. As Tom goes to push through, Eddie grabs him by the shoulder. 'You ain't gonna do what he wants are you?' He sees the ragged F burnt into the most sensitive part of her flesh.

'I don't know, Eddie. I need to hear what he's got to say. Whatever happens, Rachel won't be harmed.'

'And you?'

Tom would like to kiss him for his loyalty. *I am lost already,* he thinks. 'Don't worry about me.' He smiles. Together the two men enter the building and take the lift to the fourth floor, one storey below his office. When the door opens Tom walks out, turning to Eddie.

'The gun.'

Eddie hands over an Asda carrier bag. Tom looks inside, and nestled in a sea of empty crisp and chocolate packets is a folded Kevlar vest, a box of ammo and a small handgun.

'Thanks.' Tom nods and then starts to walk up the back stairs. Eddie goes back into the lobby and calls a lift.

Tom stops in the stairwell and takes off his shirt. He puts on the vest and curses Eddie for finding him an XXL. It swamps him. He puts the shirt back on over the top. He feels like the Hunchback of Notre Dame. The gun slides into one pocket and three shells into another. The rest he leaves in the Asda bag. Then he pushes the emergency door open and steps out onto the floor. His office is just a little way ahead. He takes a deep breath and walks forward.

He pushes his office door open and steps inside. Sitting behind his desk is Franco.

TWENTY-TWO

Franco's eyes flick up as the door opens. He pulls himself up from the chair, feeling a creak in his hips and legs – his head is splitting – but he does not want to be seen like that, on-the-ropes, beaten down. They cannot both be Sad Men. He draws himself up to his full height as Tom enters.

'Detective Superintendent Bevans.' He greets him formally.

Tom feels heat flush up his body. 'I am not your bloody—'

Franco kicks the chair away from him, sending it crashing into a bookcase. His face flashes murderous anger. 'You made a promise to me Detective Superintendent, do you not recall it?'

'Of course I do, but it's more than twenty years ago.'

'There was never a time limit on your pledge.'

Tom feels his jaw grind and the taste of blood enter his mouth. He had spent years waiting for the call from Franco, a demand that he lose some evidence or inform on a colleague, but it had never come and he had slowly lost the fear. He had forgotten that one day he would have to pay. 'I expected you to call in my debt before now.'

Franco smiles, but it is feral and cruel. 'Did you think that I would make you my bitch?' Tom says nothing, just holds the man's gaze. 'Did you think I would turn you into my spy in the police? I did not need that; I had my spies already.'

'DI Dent.'

Franco laughs a genuine laugh. 'Among others. Did you think I would use you like Dent? To do my dirty work.'

'I thought …' Tom dries up. The truth is he never thought, he had never asked himself what he would do, how far he might bend to Franco's will. The question was always too scary.

'Friend Tom.' Tom starts at the name Franco had used all that time ago. 'I did not intend to call in your debt—'

'I don't understand,' Tom interrupts him.

'I need—' The energy seems to drain from the man and Tom sees him visibly sag.

'I cannot help you, Franco. I won't hel—'

'It is my daughter.'

'I can't.'

'She is dead.'

'I …' Tom can say nothing. From nowhere, pain pours from Franco and sweeps the room like a tsunami.

'She was murdered.'

'I'm sorry.'

'Tonight.'

'Christ.' Tom cannot help himself, he steps forward and lays his hand on Franco's arm. Franco grabs his wrist and squeezes it.

'I need you.'

'I can't.'

'I need you, Friend Tom.' A wracked sob erupts from his mouth and he slides down to his knees, still gripping Tom. He buries his head in the policeman's chest and sobs. Tom folds down with him, until he is also on his knees and grips the other man's shoulders. Through the sobs, Franco manages a few words. 'He killed her, while I was on the phone with her. He killed her so I could listen.'

'Christ, Franco.'

'I heard it, heard her die Tom. And then he spoke to me – he spoke to me, crowing about what he had done. He was so fucking arrogant, taunting me. She was killed to attack me. My wonderful daughter, desecrated by that filth and he laughed and he said she had beautiful skin bef—'

'What! What did he say, what exactly?'

'Beautiful skin.'

Tom feels the ice rush into his veins. *Beautiful skin*. He sees his hands covered in blood, sees her skin scraped away – sees three corpses.

TWENTY-THREE

Jim looks at her incredulously. 'But I want coffee.'

'Hit the hot chocolate button. Trust me,' Dani tells him with a little laugh – his daughter's ghost laughs.

'Okay.' He puts his pound in and hits A5, hot chocolate, and watches as—

'Oh.'

'You see.' She grins as syrupy black coffee pours into the little plastic cup. It is so hot that the plastic sags a little in the middle. He pulls it out gingerly, just holding the thin plastic lip.

'So what do you get if you actually press the black coffee button?' he asks.

'Tomato soup. Cold.'

He nods his head as if it makes sense. 'Do you want one?' Then he remembers. She is so real to him, it is difficult to recall she is just smoke and memories. 'Sorry.'

'No, don't be. It's great to be told I look alive. Do you think I've lost weight too?' She twirls around, then laughs.

'You look great.'

She smiles. She wants to tell him how much she has missed him, but that is a guilt trip she isn't prepared to lay on him. 'Are you happy, with you and Mum I mean? Back together.'

He smiles something that looks more like a grimace. 'I am ... happy.'

Dani's face clouds over. 'I thought you'd be more enthusiastic than that.'

He stares at her for a moment; he can't tell Dani that her existence is the wedge that has been driven between them. He can't tell her that he has been seeing a shrink – trying to exorcise her from his life. His stomach is so twisted. How can a person be so happy and so miserable in the same moment?

'Why did you disappear after that night?' he asks her.

'I didn't want to Dad, I … it's a long story.'

Jim nods to his daughter. Patty will be back at the house by now, as she didn't find Tom in the park. He should text her, but what does he say: *Found Tom. Dani here, too.* And what reply would he get? *You are broken my love and I won't fix you.* 'Tell me what happened.'

'I'm trapped here.'

'I don't understand.'

'With Dr Keyson. I can't leave him. This is about as far away from his body as I can go.'

Jim shakes his head slowly, this is crazy. It is actually crazy to think his daughter's spirit is trapped, somehow kept away from him.

'Do you remember that night in Durham, when you helped me swing the brass censor and it hit him?'

The memory makes Jim wince, the sound of his head like a watermelon hit with a hammer and the way Keyson's body fell.

'When the paramedics came and rushed him to hospital, I had to go too. I was literally dragged along, like my spirit was glued to him.'

Jim feels his legs move, against his will, like a marionette worked by a master puppeteer. He can't – he can't stay here. Can't listen to this insanity. He wants to, wants to hold her so much and have it back as it was. The three of them together, a family again, that is all he wants but his head is pounding like it will explode. 'Oh hell.'

'Dad, Dad what's wrong?'

'This is.' He keeps retreating from her. 'Dani, it can't be real. You can't be—'

'Please, Dad. Stay. You can't imagine how lonely I am. Day after day sitting with someone who is like a corpse.' Jim retreats from her, walking backwards until he reaches a set of double doors. 'You aren't real, Dani. You're just in my head. I talk to you because I miss you so much. I love you so much but, but you're gone. You are dead.'

'Dad, please.' She stops abruptly, just before the double doors and her image darkens. 'I can't go any further.'

'Tell me something I don't know,' he asks.

'What.'

'Tell me something you have seen, anything, anything I don't know.'

'Dad, I'm scared.'

'Something I can't know, that only you know.'

'Dad, I see others like me, they scream and cry and it drives me crazy. The dead won't shut up. I am going mad. I nee—'

Jim pushes back through the doors, which swing back and forth, cutting away the vision of his daughter. No, his imaginary daughter. They swing half open and he sees Dani as a child. The door cuts her away and then opens again and she looks a thousand years old.

'Please, Dad,' she calls through the doors.

'For God's sake tell me something,' he whispers. 'Otherwise you can't be real.' In his head Patty and his psychiatrist start to clap. He wants to be sick.

'Dad.' Her voice is barely there. He walks back two more steps and then turns and runs to the nearest toilet.

'Mum has Parkinson's,' she says feebly. 'I saw her medicine; it's roprinole. She takes it in secret. I saw it at Christmas before all this happened. She hasn't told you, has she? Has she? Dad … Dad?' But Jim hears none of it, he has gone. 'I'm not just in your head. I'm not. I'm not.'

TWENTY-FOUR

They are in outer space, a void of nothingness, as they speed through the Sussex countryside on the grey ribbon that man has folded into the earth. There is barely another car on the road and no lights except their own headlights that carve into the shadows ahead. Franco drives. Tom offered – he can't believe a man who has just lost his daughter wants to drive, but Franco insisted. The distraction may be what he needs, who can tell what a shattered heart needs to keep it going. Tom's mind is spinning; *beautiful skin*. How can Franco have anything to do with murders from four-and-a-half years ago? What can it mean?

Tom sees the speedometer breach 120 mph, but the car purrs. It is a Jaguar, better than any of the souped-up police cars in which he has sped to crime scenes, driven by spotty nineteen-year-old boy racers. Normally his nails would be biting into the flesh of the seat, desperate to hold on, but he trusts this man next to him – at least he trusts him not to kill them both. Not before he sees the body of his daughter. After that, well, Tom thinks all bets are off. He remembers something he read once, about a Native American tribe. They had been deathly afraid of the trains that came to their country as they believed the human soul could only travel at the speed of an animal. Anything that sped faster than a horse, disengaged the soul from the body and left it behind, like a giant streamer flailing behind. When the body stopped moving the soul was reeled in at the speed of the horse, but for those hours or even days that the body and soul were cleaved apart, the man or woman is left amoral. With no centre and no control, they are free to do whatever evil they want. Tom wonders if that is why Franco speeds through the dark – is he trying to distance his body from his soul?

Franco faces forward, the last of the drug Kavannah slipped him is working its way out of his system, he should be back to normal, except the ghosts are still there. He can see them on the periphery of his vision, caught in the hinterland of the headlights' searching glow, they stalk after him led by Uncle Joe. Franco wants them gone. He switches off the headlights and plunges the car into the pitch of black.

In the dark he remembers … remembers Bheka …

The gun cocks. 'Stay where you are,' rings out across the dark expanse of scrub that radiates from the charred remains of the village. Bheka knows he is dead, he closes his eyes again. Lulama sighs in his ear, she will not be remembered by a single living soul – none of them will.

'You lay dead for more than half a day,' the man's voice snakes from the black. 'Was that cowardice?' Bheka says nothing. 'My men would say you hid like a girl.' Bheka chews at the inside of his mouth. This man does not deserve his attention; instead he must prepare himself for death. He closes his eyes and recites to himself the Lord's Prayer. He recites it fully twice before the man speaks again.

'Should I kill you?'

'You should kill yourself,' Bheka spits out.

The man laughs a deep hearty laugh. 'You are no coward, boy.'

Slowly, Bheka turns to the man. He is tall, angular and lean – perhaps forty years old. He wears tattered camouflage trousers and jacket over a T-shirt that looks almost shredded by wear. A gun belt traverses his chest and on his head he wears a brown beret. A single strand of grey wiry hair emerges from underneath. His face is grimy with sweat and dust. His skin is dark except for a crescent-shaped scar that runs from below his left eye down to his mouth – it is pink, like a newborn piglet. 'I am impressed that you had the strength to lie still for so long, that took great courage.'

'Jesus, what are you doing?' Tom panics. Black invades everything, forcing into his eyes and mouth. He lashes out towards the middle of where he thinks the steering wheel is and the column that sets the lights, but Franco's hand slaps him away. The dark is everything, they are moving at 120 mph – they will die. 'Franco, for Christ's sake put the lights on.' The headlights snap back on as the car thuds onto a rumble strip, Franco compensates and the car is back on the motorway. Tom's heart is sawing at his chest.

'Fuck. Fuck.'

Franco hears the man laughing … General Ndela of the militia for the liberation of Zimbabwe. It is warm and inviting, he misses it … after all these years.

'You bloody—' Tom feels icy cold, sweat trickles down his back as anger rises. 'If you have a fucking death wish then stop and let me out now.'

Franco's eyes do not leave the road. 'I am sorry, Friend Tom, forgive my—'

'You are not my friend. Fuck, Franco. Friends! Christ, you helped me once and I am grateful for that but,' he feels nausea from the fear, it loosens his tongue.

'I have read the files. You beat a man to death with your bare hands. You've cut the tongues from men's heads who have spoken against you. You sell young women into hell and—'

'Don't you dare judge me, Sad Man.' Franco snaps his head around to look at Tom, his eyes flare anger and his voice is caustic. 'Rumour and hate – are you asking if they are true? This foul and dirty gossip – is that what you would hold against me, Detective Superintendent Bevans? Are you my jury, are you finding me guilty? Are you calling me evil?'

Tom's mouth shudders with unasked questions, but is silent. Both men look forward through the windscreen into the dark. Tom sees the figure of a man twist in the shadows at the edge of the headlights, he knows him, his name is Bix.

Franco's deep voice rumbles from beside him. 'We have both done wrong. Are you an evil man, Friend Tom?' Tom does not answer. Instead he remembers the glass in his hand as it carved Bix's face, a handsome face. The scream. They both hear screams.

'I do not need a judge and jury to find fault with my life.' Franco speaks softly into the night. The two men sit in the dark and silence, and Franco recalls the man who destroyed his village. He remembers General Ndela.

Bheka runs at him, pulling back his fist – the blow lands with a dull thud – the boy's arms are spongy, but the man does not try to defend himself. Bheka strikes and strikes and strikes. A wail forces itself from his mouth as he continues to punch; hitting again and again into the man's stomach and legs. He punches and then kicks. He lashes out with every ounce of strength he has – he expects a bullet in his head any second but he does not care. He would welcome death. The soldier does nothing except absorb the blows and the anger, taking all the force Bheka has, until the boy is worn out, and slumps down at the man's feet. Ndela leans down and in a gentle motion, he scoops the boy up in his arms, like he is a rag doll, and begins to walk back to the village. Bheka does not struggle, there is nothing left in him.

'Close your eyes if you do not want to see them,' the soldier tells him. Bheka closes his eyes and within seconds he is asleep in the man's arms.

'Tell me about her, your daughter,' Tom finally asks.

There is a pause and Tom isn't sure if he hears a sigh seep from the other man's chest. 'Princess. Her name is Princess. Christ, she hates that name.' A big laugh explodes from him. 'Pia, call me Pia – that was all I heard from about the age of eight, they teased her at school. Princess was not a cool name, so she became Pia.' Tom cannot see the memories that wash through Franco but he knows they are there.

'How old was she?'

'She wa— is twenty-one. She's about to graduate.' He is not ready for her to be in the past yet, he has not said goodbye.

Tom nods. 'Then she was born only a year or so after—'

'Yes, and I might hold you responsible,' he tells Tom, and it is only part joke.

'I don't understand.'

'No.' His face creases for a moment. How much will he tell this man he hardly knows? This man who thinks the world is black and white, he should tell him only what he needs to know, and yet – the world stopped spinning tonight.

'I was born in 1970 in Zimbabwe. My parents died when I was young and my sister and I were taken in by missionaries. We were happy, until I was seven years old. Then I was reborn, baptised in blood; my entire village was gunned down, victims of a bloody war: *The Chimaranga*. I held my sister's hand as she was shot, my teacher's head was blown half off and he fell on me, protecting me from the bullets and machetes of the men who came for us. They had come to kill the nuns and priests who lived with us and taught us – and who spied for the British to defend the land they called Rhodesia and we would call Zimbabwe – our promised land. The soldiers spared no one, but me. And that was an accident. Luck.' His lips curl in what Tom thinks is half-smile, half-snarl. 'Lucky me.'

'Seven.' Tom cannot imagine the trauma inflicted at such an age. 'What did you do?'

'I did what any other seven-year-old boy would do, I became a killer. I joined the soldiers who murdered my sister.' Franco recalls the first man he killed, six months after Lulama died. He killed a priest – of course it had to be a priest.

Ndela gathered all the boys together and then presented the man for Bheka to kill. He was fat and sweaty and smelled; Bheka slit his throat without a flicker of hesitation. Together, Ndela and his boys watched the life-blood pump away while the priest flailed his arms – it looked as if he were trying to catch his own blood as it sprayed into the air, as if he thought he could return it to his body and live. It made the others laugh as the priest clutched at the air, like a deranged marionette, his lips moving and moving, reciting something none of them could catch, until he finally gave up and sagged to the floor, then toppled sideways into the dirt. The other soldiers clapped as if they were at a show. Franco remembers there was no pride, he just did what Ndela asked of him.

'You joined the men who killed your whole village?' Tom asks incredulously.

'He buried my sister, dug her grave himself. I saw his hands split and crack as he hacked into the hard-baked earth. He let me say a prayer over her. I have not spoken one since. Tonight I tried to say one for Pia, but I could not. The words stuck in me.' Franco pauses. 'He taught me to read. Every night we read together and he shared his schooling with me, shared his intelligence and his love for our country. He clothed me, gave me a reason to live. He named me. I was reborn and re-baptised. Franco. I called him Papi.'

Tom shakes his head. 'Why are you telling me this?'

Franco is silent as he contemplates his response. The simple answer is that after years of keeping all this inside, he just wants to let it out as he is almost at the end, and Tom just happens to be there.

'I was sent to England in 1988 to join the Dark Wolves, kill Uncle Joe, the gang leader, and take over the business.'

'Who sent you?'

Franco smiles. 'It is hard to give names and be exact. The Dark Wolves may have been based here but their allegiance was to Zimbabwe and to the Zanu-PF. The gang was a fundraising operation, nothing more – at least at the start. By 1988 so much of the civil war was funded in our country by the drug sales here. But revenues began tailing off as Uncle Joe was becoming less patriotic, forgetting the cause. I was sent to take over.

Ndela selected me and presented me to Mugabe; I was to be his man over here. You cannot imagine the pride I felt to be in his presence. Back then he was a giant, Nelson Mandela and Mother Teresa rolled into one.'

'You told me once you slit your uncle's throat and drank his blood.'

'I did.' He remembers the warm, thick, iron taste. 'And that first year after I took over was one of disgusting excess and depravity.' He shudders at the memories of that time, he is ashamed of himself. 'And then at my lowest ebb you came to see me, all full of love and with no regard for your own safety. All for your Dani.'

Tom remembers. He remembers he was all fire and brimstone, ready to defend Dani and her reputation at all costs.

'Around me all I saw were people who wanted more for themselves. I was already becoming sick with it all and then you made me think – about love, loyalty and hope.' He laughs at his own naïvety. 'The gang had a woman, we shared her – took whatever we wanted from her. There were always women we shared. I thought I wanted one of my own, a girl who was less drugged up than the others, who I could talk to.' He laughs. 'I wanted a girlfriend but that was just impossible. Men like me can't have that kind of normal life – you know, just can't.'

'What happened?'

'I got me a girl, pretty, from a good family and smart. A girl who had fallen through the cracks and would sell herself for some rock. I liked the look of her, so I kept her for myself.' He sighs. 'There was no love, apart from her love for the pipe. We never had discussions about life, the future, but she fell pregnant.'

Suddenly the car turns the corner and the darkness becomes diluted by high arcing lights that illuminate the highway with pulses of orange. Franco slows a little, as the road becomes a single carriageway for the last section. It is 3.45 a.m.

'You raised a child in that environment?'

Franco laughs, though it sounds tinny and hollow, there is no fun in that sound. 'Do you ever go to a park on a Sunday, in the summer especially?' Tom shakes his head. 'It is full of fathers with their children. Many are dads who work all week and only see their kids at weekends, others are men who no longer are a part of the family but have a few hours a week to try and win their child's love, or buy it.' He pauses, the driving needs a little more concentration now. 'That was me. It was more than I could have hoped for.'

Tom turns and looks out of the side window. An old, old daydream comes back to him. He sees himself pushing a child in a swing – Dani's child. A child they raise together.

'When she told me she was pregnant,' Franco continues, 'she wanted the money for an abortion.' His jaw grinds and his knuckles turn white on the steering wheel. 'I had never considered a child. I was already bored with this woman, with this loveless sex and …' he trails off.

'Dani was pregnant,' Tom tells the darkness, rather than directly addressing Franco. 'Twice. The first time was a violation and he paid for it.' Tom feels the broken glass in his hand once more and hears Bix's screams. 'Then, just before she died she was pregnant again. I thought that if I scared away the man who she was with that I could replace him. We could be a happy family.'

'Everything changes when you become a father,' Franco says in a whisper that Tom can barely catch. His words are like a sudden hailstorm, they fall and cut the two men in half, and then are gone, leaving merely a breeze to lick their wounds.

'I forced the girl to keep the child, paid her to keep clean and put her into a sanatorium, more like a five-star hotel, while we waited for the child. But I knew I could not raise it, not in the world I inhabited. So, after Princess was born, I paid the woman off and she disappeared.'

'You never saw her again? She never saw her child again?'

'Never.' There is no hint of regret in his voice. 'I built a life for my child. I found a couple who would act as foster parents. I bought them a house, I paid them each month and in turn they raised my child. They did a fantastic job and they gave her love.'

'Did they know who you were?'

'No.'

'What you did?'

'No.'

Tom looks astonished. 'What did they think?'

'I did not lead them on.'

'What did they think you were?'

'They thought I was a spy, they thought I worked for the British government and travelled a great deal.' He pauses and a sad smile breaks across his face. 'They thought I was one of the good guys.' Tom cannot help but snort with laughter. Franco is quiet; he stares ahead into the darkness.

Tom leaves him in peace for a few minutes, but he can see that they will soon be in Brighton and there is one question he needs answered.

'So do you think this is an attack on you?'

'I thought Pia was a secret, but somebody has found her and I believe this is a *coup d'état*. I am being ousted from my position and Pia was the lever.'

'Why not just kill you?'

'I think they want to know where the seventy-five million pounds are first.'

'You've stolen seventy-five million from them?'

'Invested. I invested seventy-five million.'

It is just after 3.50 a.m. when the road from London finally peters out and turns into a roundabout. *Welcome to Brighton* is written into the grass with beautiful flowers that proclaim the gateway to London-by-the-sea. Though, in the sodium-lit darkness, the colours are merely muted greys that seem sinister. More like a warning to retreat.

TWENTY-FIVE

His hand is in his pocket, his thumb slides along the edge of his laminated warrant card. It reads Detective Superintendent Tom Bevans. Metropolitan Police. Operation Ares. He can feel his body tense and sweat is breaking out on—

'Don't,' the man beside him says in the calmest of voices. Then he reaches out a hand and lays it on his arm. The fingers squeeze, then release. 'Calm,' Franco tells him.

Tom nods. They stand on the path and look forward. They know Pia's body has been found but there is no ID yet. They also know the first officers on the scene have cordoned the building off and set up a perimeter. The crime scene is at the top, a path has been secured inside by a small SOCO team and guards have been posted to keep the room secure. Now it is clear and the initial responders are waiting for a senior investigating officer to arrive with a full forensics team. It is 4.15 a.m. and they will be here any minute. Tom has told Franco how the investigation will go. Once the team is in place Tom can turn up and ask to speak to the commanding officer. He can request for the case to be placed under the remit of Operation Ares. He can ask to see the body. The answer will be no. He can go through proper channels – that will take at least two days.

'You said once the team is in place?' Franco had asked.

'Yes.'

'And that will happen—?'

'Any minute now.' Tom takes a deep breath; he does not make eye contact with his companion. 'So I need to go in now and act like I am the SIO – like I own the place.'

'We.'

'No.'

'We both go in.'

'Franco—'

'Both. Tom, we both go in.'

It was no use. Tom knew it. So they stand and take a breath, then stride forward, Tom slides his thumb across the laminate. Two steps more. He grips it and pulls it out as they reach the guard.

'Detective Superintendent Bevans.'

The PC pulls up out of his slouch.

'This is my DI.'

'Thorsen,' Franco finishes, his voice deep and steady. Like he dares anyone to challenge him. The laminate card curves forward, Occam's razor in motion.

When has my pass ever been checked by a guard? Tom thinks. *Once*.

'Who found the body?' Tom asks, to distract.

'PC Vaughn and myself.'

'You are?' Franco asks.

'Dex—' He looks into the DI's face and Franco sees the eyes widen. This PC knows him, maybe he isn't totally sure, but he recognises Franco. Dexter stiffens, he is shorter than Franco but he draws himself up to almost the same height. Tom feels the danger, they need to move.

'PC Dexter. Please log DI Thorsen in too.' He pulls a pen from his pocket. 'Where do I sign – you are keeping an entry log, aren't you?'

He doesn't take his eyes from Franco. 'DI Thorsen?' he asks.

'We need to see the body ASAP – this is part of an ongoing investigation, we are looking at multiple victims. Chop, chop, constable.'

Dexter wilts a little under Tom's authority and offers him the clipboard. On it is a poorly photocopied form that is at least a hundred degrees of separation from the original. Tom signs and pushes past.

'Thorsen – with me.' He orders, almost like you might command a dog to heel. Franco's eyes flare in annoyance but he does as requested and follows, feeling PC Dexter's eyes on him all the way. As they walk, Tom hisses to his companion, 'He knows you.'

'He thinks he does, but he's not sur—'

'He knows you. Fuck, Franco. We need to be in and gone before the real SIO gets here.'

Franco says nothing. They walk through the empty ticket office. It is dark, there is still no power. In the gloom they can just about make out police tape flapping ahead of them like a trail of breadcrumbs leading the way to—

'Who's there?' a voice calls and then a beam of light catches them. Tom raises his warrant card and shields his eyes.

'PC Vaughn, I assume? Can you move the light? I'm …' Tom's voice dies in his throat as the torch beam is moved out of their eyes and they can see the man before them. Blood smears his chin and is swept through his hair. His uniform is soaked – deep and dark and Tom knows it is blood.

'What?'

'I attempted resuscitation, sir, but it was no good. She was already gone.' His eyes are dead. Tom nods.

'Good to try, son. There have been cases …' His voice falls away and all he can do is nod again. He can see the young man is in shock. 'I'm the SIO, Detective Superintendent Bevans and this is DI Thorsen.' Franco has started to shake, next to him – it is the blood. He knows it is Pia's blood. Tom thinks he has a few seconds before his companion explodes. 'We need to get in to see the body. I understand from PC Dexter that a path of least contamination has been cleared.'

Vaughn nods.

'Do you have suits yet?'

'Gloves and foot covers at the bottom of the stairs.' He turns and his hand moves to a solid wall and, click – a secret door opens. On the floor are gloves and what looks like a pile of shower caps. Tom slips two over his feet and then snaps on gloves. Franco follows suit but his eyes are glassy – he is totally on automatic pilot. He needs to see his daughter's body.

'Can we take your torch, lad?' Tom asks. Vaughn hands it over. Tom takes a breath and he and Franco walk forward, leaving Vaughn in the darkness at the base of the steps.

They move into a small vestibule, behind them the door clicks into place. Tom shines the light ahead – there is a staircase which spirals upwards, winding like a corkscrew. It leads up into the giant onion dome at the heart of the building. Tom looks to the left, where there is a passageway – it was once for servants to scuttle through to attend to the king. This whole area behind a false wall so the staff could go about their business but be invisible. Above them were secret rooms for the king – a retreat, a pleasure dome. Once, long ago and now it is a murder room.

'You can wait he—' Tom starts but Franco drifts forward, like a sailor hearing the siren call and unable to stop himself.

Franco slowly starts to climb the stairs. Tom shines the light ahead so he can see. It looks like no one has been here in a very long time. Tom follows Franco up. They both move slowly, the wood creaks and bows under their weight, the treads are buckled and slope to the left. As they climb they begin to see some silvery light, as lozenge-shaped windows throw a little hazy moonlight onto the stairway and illuminate graffiti and spider webs. As they approach the top, Tom can feel the nervous energy flowing from Franco. He is grinding his teeth – it sounds like a field of grasshoppers. Suddenly he stops and dips his head. His large hands go to his neck and he delicately removes a St. Christopher pendant.

'It was my mother's. The only thing I have left of her. I won't take it into the room.' Tom nods, he understands.

They reach the top of the stairs. Before them is a circular corridor, wrapping around the main room. They can see the room is full of windows, Indian shapes and designs, lozenges of glass that reflect the style of the Taj Mahal. They move slowly, the air is thick like mud. Tom sees a foot. There is no shoe, no sock. The foot bone's connected to the ankle bone, the ankle bone's connected to the leg bone, the leg bone— There is a naked body. The head hidden by a filthy mattress.

'Princess.' Franco is one thousand years old. 'Noooooooooo,' he bellows, leaping forwards. Tom reaches out to stop him. There is a path cleared, but Franco does not care. He kicks through the tape, kicks at the blood markers and is bending to her. His grief is all he knows – all there is. Like fire it burns, white hot, enough to burn time itself, destroy civilisations, end all life on earth. He pulls at the mattress and sends it flying into the wall.

'Damn it, Franco, you are destroying evidence.'

Franco does not care, he just wants to get to Pia. The mattress is ripped away and— Time freezes. Tom watches the father see the dead girl. Pain flares and then, it morphs into a laugh. A laugh that sounds like joy.

'It isn't her. It isn't Pia.'

'What?' Tom jumps over the carnage Franco has created to get to the body. He kneels down, the blood has congealed to gore, like almost-set raspberry jelly. Tom takes the sight in and, 'Oh my God.' His brain reels. The woman is spread-eagled, she has been nailed to the floor through her feet and hands. Her legs are spread wide, like a cheerleader doing the splits and she looks red and raw between her thighs. Her breasts have been bitten and a claw hammer has crashed through skull and brain. It is the same. Heather Spall, Tracy Mason, Sarah Penn and this girl. *Beautiful skin*. This is another beautiful skin murder.

'It isn't her. It isn't her.' Franco is ecstatic – for a moment, but then another realisation sweeps him. 'So where is she? Where is Pia? Tom, where is she?' He looks frantic, he had given up until a few seconds ago, he believed life held nothing more than revenge for him but now; now there is no time left for discussion. A loud voice suddenly fills the room.

'The two men at the crime scene, the men who called themselves Bevans and Thorsen.' Tom immediately recognises Vaughn's voice being amplified through a megaphone. 'Come down the stairs with your hands over your heads.'

'Damn,' Tom spits. The noise Franco made has totally smashed any chance they had of brazening this out. Dexter is going to tell everyone he thinks the number one wanted drug lord is contaminating the crime scene and— *Christ*. Bang goes Ares, bang goes everything. 'Franco, we need to go down and—'

'I need to find Pia.' Franco's eyes are wild. 'I can't be arrested. I can't.'

Behind him, Tom can hear men advancing slowly up the stairs. He needs to calm Franco down or they are both going to be Tasered.

'We have no choice, I'm sorry but—'

'No, Friend Tom, I am sorry.' Franco picks Tom up like he is a toothpick and runs with him to the door to the stairs. Tom looks behind him, and for a second he can see a flash of the stairs as Vaughn and Dexter are about halfway up, they both hold yellow Tasers and Dexter has the tell-tale flash of red on his jacket to show they are filming this.

'Oh Jesus,' Tom says, before Franco launches him like an Exocet down the stairs and into the two policemen.

'Chri—' Vaughn attempts to duck but Tom hits him full in the chest. Both men sprawl backwards. Tom tucks his head in as he smashes into the wall and bounces down – tumbling head over heels. He slams into Dexter, knocking him to his knees but keeps going. His head strikes the bannister and Tom blacks out.

Vaughn pulls himself up and runs down to the crumpled heap at the bottom of the stairs. 'Get medical assistance, officer down,' he yells through the jib door and then moves to the body, warily. He kneels and checks for a pulse. Unconscious, but not dead. He looks up the spiral staircase. Dexter believes the man up there is a terrifying killer. He looks around but can't see either Taser. 'Crap!' He steps over Tom's prostrate body and heads up the stairs.

'Police. Give yourself up and you will not be harmed.' He

feels in his pocket, no Taser, no pepper spray – not even a baton. Damn. He goes on, up into the Saloon Bottle. As he reaches the top stair, there is a loud crack from inside. He says a one-line prayer, then pushes forward, a little anxious about what he might find. And, truth be told, he doesn't want to see her body again. He enters the Saloon Bottle. Everything has been trodden through and fucked up – Christ the SOCO team are gonna have his guts for garters.

'Fuck.' The body is still there, but surrounding it there is a whole mess of bloody footprints, proof that at least one crazy guy was up here, but now, there is no one in the room. No DI Thorsen or Franco or whoever he is supposed to be. Vaughn is the only man alive in that room.

TWENTY-SIX

The phone rings a little after 9 a.m. Jim scowls, but Patty picks it up and walks into her office with it.

So much for a relaxed breakfast, Jim thinks.

'So, I looked at the crazy Christian angle.' Jane Thorsen doesn't have any time for pleasantries, she is right down to business. 'I couldn't find anything in Sarah Penn's life, no church links of any kind. Tracy Mason went to a church school, but nothing hardcore, they look like one of those families who go to a ten-minute service once a month so the school accepts them; hypo-Christians, but I can't see that there is any mileage in it as a link for the victims.'

'Okay.' Patty feels a bit deflated; she had thought she was on to something.

'Sorry to be the bearer of bad news.' Jane senses how much Patty needs to make a quick break in the case. 'So, any stuff happen yesterday?'

'I called Tracy Mason and Sarah Penn's families and they are both free on Monday, but I haven't spoken to Ellen Stokes yet. I was thinking I might try and see if she's free today, I thought I might call her later.' She had been thinking of calling at about 11 a.m. to see if she were in church. 'I want to see Allison, I want to know if there's something more than a faceless man saying "beautiful skin".' She sighs, spoken aloud it all seems like such a mountain to climb. Four years – will she remember anything now?

'Great, keep me in the loop,' Jane tells her. 'Have you heard anything from Tom? I tried to call him but just get his voicemail.'

'No … I … no.'

Jane hears the frost in the voice and knows there is something wrong. 'Okay, well let me know when you do.'

'I will.' And Patty puts the phone down. Damn, she hates lying to Jane and isn't really sure why she did. She just somehow thinks that Tom would not want Jane to know about Franco. For a second, concern jags through her mind, but Tom is a big boy who can look after himself. She has another job to do. She has three girls, who could not look after themselves, to help. She picks up the phone again and her eyes rest on the death wall. She sees the pictures of Tracy Mason – alive in one, dead in the next. She dials, not caring that it is only 9 a.m. on a Sunday.

'Hello?'

'Is this the Stokes residence? I am calling for Ellen Stokes.'

There is a slight hesitation. 'Speaking, but I was just about to—'

'I am not cold calling you Mrs Stokes. I am not trying to sell you anything. My name is Patricia Lancing, I have been asked to contact you by Detective Superintendent Tom Bevans – do you remember him?' For a moment there is nothing. Patty can only imagine the anxiety creeping through the poor woman, to have it all dragged up again must be awful. Awful. But she must, for the three dead girls. 'Tom Bevans, he heads Operation Ares, they looked into—'

'I … I … yes. My daughter's … yes. I remember.'

Of course you do, Patty thinks. *You don't forget your daughter's skin being scraped off.* 'I would like to come and see you.'

'Has something happened?'

'I was hoping to meet with you. I was also hoping I might see Allison.'

'It's been four years.' Panic is seeping into her voice.

'There is nothing to worry about, please let me assure you this is merely in accordance with procedure, at this stage we are just assessing the situation of the case.'

'There hasn't been anything. Not another girl?'

'No, we have a legal obligation to look at all open cases every four years – it is just routine.' Patty is proud of her ability to lie so easily.

'I see. I suppose I could—'

'I can come to you – it won't take long.'

'Allison doesn't live here.'

'I understand – can you give me a number for her.'

'No, no I can ask her to be here, so we can both …' she trails off. 'When?'

'Is today too soon?'

'I … I need to do some shopping. Maybe you could come later, say at 2 p.m.'

'And you will ask your daughter to be there.'

'She can't talk – you do know that, don't you?'

Patty takes a deep breath. That answers her biggest question – there are four victims in this case. 'I will treat your daughter with total respect but, please let me be honest, Mrs Stokes. Your daughter, without realising it, may hold the key to this case, these three deaths, and if at all possible—'

'She is only just getting her life together now, all this time later. I don't want it to be raked up again. She's delicate.'

'Mrs Stokes. Let's meet, just you and I. Then I will tell you what I want to ask your daughter and you can decide.'

The woman on the other end of the line thinks for a while before she speaks. 'Okay.'

Patty reaches the top of Ellen Stokes's road very early for their meeting; it is only 1.20 p.m. A little way down, she can see her walking towards her house, carrying two large bags of shopping. Maybe she's got cake for them, how classy. Politeness would dictate that she let Ellen Stokes get home and freshen up for a few minutes before she arrives, but Patty has never been that polite. Instead she walks briskly on, so they both reach the path to the front door at the same time.

'Mrs Stokes?' Patty asks, though she recognises her from photos in the file.

'Erm ...' she looks flustered, a little dazed.

'Patricia Lancing, we spoke this morning Ellen.' Patty smiles and holds out her hand, Ellen Stokes looks at it for a moment and then grips it.

'Sorry, of course, yes,' she looks at her watch quickly and a flash of annoyance runs across her face, then is gone. 'Please come in.' She turns and Patty sees that her mascara has run a little, tears have tracked down her cheeks. Patty follows her down the path to the front door and into the house.

While Ellen Stokes freshens up, Patty stands in the lounge and waits. The room is spotless; if anything it strikes Patty as too clean. It reminds Patty, uncomfortably, of the flat she lived in until last year – until she returned to the family home to live with Jim once more. It had been a sterile apartment. She spent her time living off pre-packaged foods and wallowing in her fantasies of revenge. She didn't clean much, but everything was spartan – like this. No art on the walls, no family photos – nothing to feed the grief, nothing to provoke memories of happier times, because that is just fuel for the hate and shame. She sighs, and begins to look around once more.

The bookcases are full, but it is bland paperbacks and what looks like a five-year run of *Reader's Digest*s. None of the spines are broken, they look like the books you'd see in a furniture showroom, there to give the impression of – of what? Not intellectualism or erudition, more just a feeling of connectedness with the world. She looks around the room, no TV. What does Ellen Stokes do with her time? Perhaps she just cleans.

Patty looks into the back of the bookcase and there is something wedged at the back, behind the yards of unopened volumes. She leans in and fishes out a photo album. *The Wedding of Ellen and David, 2nd June 1987*. She flicks through the pages: it is a compendium of snapshots taken by family and some professional portraits. The couple look so happy – he is handsome and she is a world away from the woman upstairs, making herself look presentable and washing the tear streaks of mascara from her cheeks.

She flicks forwards through the book and sees a marriage told in a visual shorthand. The honeymoon, the first home, a new car and then a child is born and they beam at a bundle in their arms. Patty suddenly has a flash – an image she saw in the files; Allison Stokes wrapped in gauze and streaked red with blood, her face flayed, featureless, like a newborn mouse. Patty pushes the image back, it is not helpful. She turns more pages, there is a christening, birthday parties, a father with his daughter on his shoulders – he looks so happy. And then the happiness is burnt away, the images thin out. There is more time between each picture and the smiles have lessened. Instead the faces are overshadowed by a darkening storm-cloud. Patty can see how it trips across Ellen Stokes's face. Her husband stops appearing in the photos – bang, just like that. Now it is just Ellen and her child. There are no more smiles.

Patty hears movement in the hallway and stuffs the album back behind the books, slides the glass back into place, and sits as Ellen Stokes walks in.

Patty can see she has made an effort; it is probably some time since Ellen entertained. Her hair is down now and brushed, with little clips that Patty thinks are too young for her. It is mostly grey but here and there she can see the original red flecked through it in places. Her face is lined and pinched, her mouth thin and tight – it is hard to believe she is the carefree beauty from the wedding photos, though Patty is fully aware that many have said the same of her in the past. Grief dries and hollows you out and Patty is only just starting to realise that Mrs Stokes has had a lot of grief in her life.

'Tea, coffee, hot chocolate?' Ellen asks, keen to please.

'A glass of water would be great.'

'Still or sparkling, oh and I have herbal and fruit teas.'

Patty smiles. 'Do you have peppermint?'

'Oh.' She looks panicked and runs off to check. Patty follows her into the kitchen. Of course, it is spotless, and looks barely used. Patty runs a finger over the oven hob; two of the flame controls still have their little plastic covers on them to keep them clean. She probably only uses the front two, maybe she just heats up soup or boil-in-the-bag meals. To the left of the oven there is a spice rack, which is empty, just a tub of low sodium salt and some sachets of fake lo-cal sugar. This is not a place for fine dining.

'Yes, here we are – I knew I had some.' She holds a peppermint tea bag she has recovered from a dusty box of assorted flavours.

'Lovely. Thank you.' Patty tries to sound genuine.

The two women sit at the kitchen table. It seems less formal than the living room.

'Thank you. I don't want to take your entire afternoon, but I have some questions.'

'Of course. Do you want the bag left in?'

Patty nods. 'Did you speak to Allison?'

'No, not yet. Sorry, I wanted to talk to you first.'

'How has her recovery been?'

'Physically it has been tough, but the doctors have been just great. The skin grafts have taken.' She frowns. 'People still look at her but – you know.'

Patty nods, understanding how being stared at wears you away. 'You said she has no speech?'

'They say she can speak, I mean physically, there is no actual damage, she just doesn't. Trauma, it can close down the part of the brain they said …' she dries up. Patty can see the strain in her face.

'Were she and Tracy Mason friends?'

'I don't know. You know what kids are like, best friends one minute and then hair-pulling and spite.'

'Did they fight?'

'No. No, I didn't mean that. They had known each other for years of course. They started school together at five. They were always in the same class and a couple of times there were play-dates and birthday parties, but I wouldn't say they were natural friends. They were very different.'

'They wouldn't have been together that night?'

'I doubt it. Allison often had classes after school and we did after-school clubs as I worked full-time.' She looks at Patty with eyes that scream *I know I am a bad mother*. Patty can't be bothered to contradict them.

'It was Bonfire Night,' Patty reminds her.

'Remember, remember the 5th of November—'

'Gunpowder, treason and plot.' Patty finishes the rhyme for her. 'Did the school have fireworks?'

'Not in the school itself, but there's a playing field that the school owned and there was a bonfire there. Allison said she was going to it.'

'Would most of the school have gone?'

'Yes, it was free and there were hotdogs and burgers and—'

'Alcohol?'

'Not officially, but, you know teenage girls.'

Patty does. She remembers a time when Dani was about sixteen. She was out at a party and called to say she was staying with her friend Izzy. She was obviously drunk. Patty demanded the address to go and get her and it turned into World War Three. The happy times. 'Do you think some of the girls snuck back into school to drink after the bonfire?'

'Maybe.'

'I would like to ask Allison about that.'

'She may not remember.'

'Why?'

Ellen Stokes pauses. 'She never …' she wants to say *talks about it*, but of course her child doesn't talk, not about anything. 'She never writes about that night, she uses an iPad and a phone to communicate. I think she might have just erased what happened. To Tracy and to her.'

'She looks in the mirror.' Patty did not mean it to be cruel but she sees how it cuts into the woman's heart. 'I did not mean that to— I am sorry it was insensitive.'

'I think I need you to leave now.' She stands.

Patty stays sitting. 'Beautiful skin. Your daughter told Detective Superintendent Bevans that the killer said those words.'

'I am sorry but I must insist—'

'She heard his voice, we know that at least. That night she wanted to tell someone, but she was too ill to be questioned.'

'That was four years ago.'

'I can't believe anyone can forget, not that.' Patty's voice rises – she is, of course, an expert on not forgetting.

'I thought it was over,' Ellen Stokes says in a tiny voice.

'The pain is over, your daughter is recovering – she is damn strong. But there are three other girls who are gone forever and their parents and families need to know that person will never hurt another young woman again.' Patty stops as Ellen Stokes sits back down and begins to cry. Patty wants to lean over and stroke her hair, tell her that all will be well, but that is just too weird and creepy. 'I'm sorry Ellen, we—' she stops at the sound of the front door opening. Together Ellen and Patty rise and walk into the hallway. There at the door, in a long raggedy coat, is Allison Stokes. Her hair has grown back, it is long and wavy and covers a lot of her face. Her skin is deathly pale and Patty can see the tracery of scars and tiny blood vessels.

'Darling.' Her mother's voice is soft, comforting, like soup on a winter night. 'This lady is here to ask a few questions ab— about the attack.'

Her eyes flare. Patty sees fear in them. 'I don't mean to scare you—'

Allison Stokes opens the door and is gone.

TWENTY-SEVEN

Franco's hand shakes. He needs time to think – needs somewhere to keep low and work out what he is going to do, because so far there's been no thought, no planning; he has just acted on adrenalin and reflex. That can only get you so far and he's reached the end of the line. He looks up at the sign: *Brighton Pier*. Earlier it was lit up in hundreds of tiny light bulbs, but now they are cold and the sign is dark. He looks to both sides of the sign and all around the entrance – there's no CCTV. He takes a deep breath and then jumps; in a flash he scales the metal fence and perches on the top like a seagull, then he leaps at a striped awning that announces the most delicious doughnuts in Britain. He hits it hard, feeling it tear under his weight, his legs slide through but it slows him enough – he hits the wooden deck with a jar to his knees, but nothing worse. He looks around, no sign he has been spotted. Limping slightly, he makes his way down the pier and is soon swallowed up by the darkness.

As he walks, the heartbeat of the water lapping at the pier begins to calm him. It has been the worst night of his life. Christ, how can it only be one night?

He escaped the Saloon Bottle the same way the killer must have gone. There was a service room off the circular corridor; he was looking for a window but he found a trapdoor. Old

King George had used it to winch up his billiards table, then himself when the gout got too bad. Franco dropped through it, down three floors into the basement of the pavilion. A dusty old mattress had been left there to break someone's fall and it worked equally well for Franco. He found himself in a servant's passage, they ran like a nervous system through the body of the house so anything the rich desired could be delivered to them, it was almost like being home. The only light came from the shaft above. Except, as his eyes adjusted there was a door that was not quite closed. He pulled at it and— clever. It opened into a secret tunnel that led under the gardens and into the old stables that now form the Brighton Museum. It took Franco a few seconds to run through it and as he reached the old stables, he could see that the power was out there too – so no alarms or CCTV. He just pushed through the front door and out. He could see a gaggle of police forming at the entrance to the Pavilion, soon they will search the grounds and set up a perimeter; but by then he will be long gone. Seeming to have no care in the world, he walked out of the palace grounds and onto marine parade. Where, where now? He had to think. And then he saw the pier.

The wood clicks as he walks. Along the promenade there are signs telling him to get married there, have a party there – the best place for stags and hens. The thought makes him cringe. At the end of the pier there is a fun-fair. He should have come here when Pia was a child – she would have loved Brighton. It is a place for children, if you don't look under the surface. He reaches the fun palace at the end, even in the dark it looks pretty shabby. It has a lame-looking ghost train, an old-fashioned helter-skelter and a flume ride that would only be exciting for ants. But what he does like is the old steam-driven carousel. It is hand-painted and in the pre-dawn light the horses look demented. He climbs aboard and sits on a horse called *Lorna sucks cocks*, according to the tag felt-tipped on its neck. That would be a good place to watch the dawn break and thank the heavens he is alive. He is starting to realise the extent of the attack and how it had been planned. His empire is gone, wiped away in a flood. But he doesn't care … in many ways it is a relief. He has wanted out for so long, but he thought it would be on his terms. That was why he had *re-directed* the seventy-five million. He thought he had been so careful, about the money and even more, about Pia. *Oh Christ, Pia*. His stomach cramps at the thought of her, scared and alone. But at least she is alive. Alive, but they will use her to get what they want from him. For now, he has a small amount of leverage – small. Miniscule. But it is something.

He sits there, on Lorna, and wait for it, wait for it … a blood-red shimmer signals the new day. *Red sky in the morning, devil's warning* echoes through his head. As the first rays of sun slide across the sea, Franco takes out his phone and its sim and battery. He slots them together. If they are as organised as he thinks they are, they will know he ha—

It rings. It is an unknown number but Franco swipes to accept.

'You are one lucky mother-fucker,' a voice begins.

'Gulliver, good to hear from you.'

'I am sending you a photo.'

There is a *ping* from his email. Franco does not want to open the message – he is afraid of what he will see.

'We have her – the beautiful Pia. She is one fine—'

'What do you want, Gulliver? I am turning this phone off in forty-five seconds.'

'We want our fucking money. We want the seventy-five million you stole.'

'What do you think of me? Seventy-five million, that's just the cream off the top. I took you for more like two hundred million. You bunch of stupid fucks.' He laughs – he needs to up the ante, goad Gulliver and force him to make a mistake. He needs to make it personal.

'You mother-fucking cocksucker,' Gulliver screams into the phone, then pauses as the greed sets in. 'This is the deal. You will come to us and bring all the bank codes for the money, every fucking penny of that two hundred million. We will take it all back and you will say sorry for taking it. Then, and only then, we will release your daughter. She will be allowed to go free. You will not. In front of all *your* men I am gonna slit your throat and drain you slow, like a pig, before I drink your fucking blood. That is non-negotiable, Franco. We got your little girl.'

'But you don't have me.' He drops the phone on the deck and crushes it underfoot. Then he vomits. 'Oh please forgive me, Pia.' This is the biggest gamble of his life. From the other end of the pier he can hear a cleaning crew arrive and begin to open all the stores and kiosks. Time to go. He slides off the carousel horse and begins to retrace his steps. As he nears the entrance he realises he never looked at the message Gulliver sent him. He can imagine what it was.

TWENTY-EIGHT

Tom paces the small room. It's about 2 p.m. Still Sunday. Christ, thinks Tom. Sundays used to be so boring. All you'd get was over-cooked roast lunch and *Alias Smith and Jones* or *Bonanza* on the TV before everyone fell asleep. Now you can fit in 120-mph motorway dashes, dead bodies, being chucked down stairs by drug lords, going to hospital for concussion and being thrown in a cell, all before lunch. And he bets there won't even be a lunch. He could murder one of his Nan's roast chickens – even when the veg had been on the boil for forty-eight hours and the bread sauce was congealed and dry like filler. It would still be better than this.

'Is anyone there?' he calls out. *Nothing*. It's been an hour since anyone had poked their head around the door. He feels humili-ated and … what a bloody mess. No one is telling him anything, he feels like he wants to explode. Did they get Franco? Have they identified the body? Was someone coming down from London? Was he going to be held long? Was he going to be charged? But more than that, the question that was going round and round in his head was: Is this the fourth beautiful skin murder? Is the killer back?

Christ! He kicks at the cell door, over and over. 'I am a senior police officer – I do not deserve to be treated like this.' He kicks the door one final time and then goes and sits down on the squat block in the corner. His head is killing him from the tumble he took down the stairs and he asked for coffee more than two hours ago and – nothing, not even a crappy instant. *What a bloody mess*. That is all he can think, that he will be lucky to get out of this with a dishonourable discharge.

Suddenly the cell door swings open with a crash and a voice barks out, 'Stand up, Bevans.' A small, dark woman enters, about fifty-five years old, her hair short and spiky. She has dark, deep-set eyes and a thin face. Attractive but hard, her skin looks as if it has been toughened by decades of smoking and stress. She is dressed in a sophisticated-looking black trouser suit and has expensive-looking jewellery liberally spread over her neck and hands. 'I am Chief Superintendent Fiske, and you are a pain in the fucking backside, Detective Superintendent Bevans. Either you're stupid or you're a fool – which is it?'

'Neither, ma'am.' Tom's voice is icy. He does not appreciate being talked to like this by a fellow officer.

'I find that hard to believe as I am not the one with a huge fucking bruise on the side of my head and looking at a list of twenty disciplinary actions and a suspension from active duty – at the bare minimum.' She glares at him. 'Come on, walk with me.' And she turns and leaves the cell. Tom follows after her like a toy poodle.

Fiske leads him down a corridor and into an interview room.

'Sit down,' she barks.

'Chief Superintendent Bevans.' He reminds her of his rank.

'Tom, you will call me Chief Superintendent Fiske or ma'am, anything more familiar and I will crush your balls – do you get the fact that I am more than a little peeved to be here. I am supposed to be hosting a charity lunch for—' She waves her hands in annoyance. 'I forget what for, but it was going to be a damn sight more fun than spending time with an idiot like you.' She drops a sheaf of papers on the table in the middle of the room and glares at him.

'I had asked for coffee.'

'You don't always get what you want, Tom.' She strikes her palm on the table for emphasis. 'You attended a crime scene, you were not entirely truthful with the idiot on the perimeter.'

'I did nothing wro—'

'Shut up! I don't want bullshit. Have you any idea what kind of trouble you are in?' She pauses and arches an eyebrow. Tom sighs; he finds these demonstrations of power a bit tedious, but keeps his mouth closed.

'You had another man with you, who signed in as DI Thorsen. I have now seen a picture of the very attractive DI Thorsen. How is your eyesight, Bevans?'

'He was not DI Thorsen. He abducted me at gunpoint from my home at approximately 2.30 a.m. and—'

'Really, that is the best you've got?' Tom can see she doesn't believe a word of his story. 'One of my officers, PC Dexter, has identified the man you signed into MY crime scene as Franco, a London drug lord.'

'Yes, that is the man who abducted me.'

Fiske's eyes are black stones but they twinkle like they belong to the wicked witch of the west. 'I am not recording this inter-view, you may have noted that.' She pauses, then sighs. 'I know you Detective Superintendent, I attended a talk you gave a few years back at the academy. I know all about Ares and what you do there.' She leans in close to him and says in a low voice. 'I'm on your side Tom. Just tell me why you allowed a—'

'I was abducted at gunpoint.'

'Bloody hell. I don't want to hear that shit, Bevans.' She cuts him dead, her voice is like a steam shovel slamming him into his place. 'I know you've been on leave for six bloody months – *sick leave* on the record. Off the record I hear you cracked up, gone a little loony tunes?'

Tom feels his hackles rise. This is not the way to talk to a senior officer. 'You're right, I have been away. But I am back.'

She snorts. 'Why in my fucking city?'

'This is the fourth victim.'

That stops her in her tracks. She looks him up and down once more. 'What case?'

'Beautiful skin.'

She thinks for a few moments. 'Okay, I'll bite. Tell me more.'

Tom tells her all about Heather, Tracy and Sarah.

TWENTY-NINE

Pia wakes cold and hungry. Her mouth feels like a rodent crawled inside and died. She tries to stand but— Jesus. Her ankles are tied together. She is just in her underwear. Fear sweeps across her and she starts to sob, she is so scared. Something awful has happened. She wants her dad.

'Is someone there?' she calls out, though without much volume. 'I need the toilet.' Nothing. 'I'm cold.' She wonders where her gown is. Her teeth start to chatter, as much with fear as with cold. 'Please,' she says, though it is little more than a whisper.

She rolls herself against a wall; it is brick and rough to her skin. She uses it to sit up, even though she feels it scratch and tear at her back. Once she is sitting she thinks she can use the wall to lever herself up to standing and – then what? Suddenly there is a grinding sound of metal on metal and a door swings open. The sudden glare of a bare light bulb burns Pia's eyes and she covers them with her arm. A shadow enters the room, blurred by the glare of the bulb. She struggles to see and feels her legs being pulled. 'No, no please,' she shrieks. Then feels her legs pushed apart. 'Oh Christ.' Her hands spring down to her thighs to protect herself but nothing happens. The shadow moves away. Pia's eyes start to adapt and she can see it is a man, he is stocky like a body builder. His skin is a tone darker than hers and his bald head has stripes of ink banded across it. The light is blotted out by something landing across her face – in a panic she pulls it away. It is fabric, a shirt. She puts it on even though it scratches her a little. Then a plastic bucket lands at her feet with a clanking bounce.

'I'm hungry and thirsty too,' she tells the shadow.

'Don't fucking push it,' a thick, guttural voice slides from the dark.

'Please, you must have the wrong—'

'Pia. We have the right girl.' He walks back to the door and starts to close it. 'Pia, have you ever fantasised about being gang-banged? Think about it now.' And with a laugh he walks out and pulls the door closed.

As he walks away he can hear her sobbing. Good, he likes them scared. When the time comes she will be a snivelling wreck, and he will make Franco watch his little girl defiled, and he will be first. He promised Franco that he would let her go – and he will, but he never said what state she'd be in. He laughs. It is time for the hunt.

THIRTY

The train is just about to pull out as Tom hurtles into the station. No time for tickets, he flashes his warrant card at the barriers and jumps aboard just as the whistle is blown. It is 8.49 p.m. and he has spent the last five hours with Fiske and her team, looking at the girl they found that morning. Still no ID but Tom is convinced it is the same MO as the others. But he is no closer to knowing why, and what the link with Franco is. At some point Grayson called him and shouted for twenty minutes. Tom held the phone at arm's length until the storm of abuse passed. He is due to see Grayson first thing the next morning. He feels so dog-tired.

He finds a seat and settles into it. The train is pretty full with revellers returning home after a dirty weekend at the seaside. Tom leans his head against the window and closes his eyes. Blood. They open, he is inside the kiln – he screams. The whole train carriage stares at him.

'Sorry. Bad dream.' He tries to smile but can't quite recall how. Instead he closes his eyes again and ... Sarah Penn's shoe in the mud swims up in his mind. Not a dream. Stay awake and remember. Remember!

FUCK. His eyes spring open. He is back on the train, he has been drooling on his shoulder. He looks around. From the way a couple of women look at him he realises he was whimpering.

He does that, in his sleep. He whimpers. Christ. He doesn't have time for sleep. He pulls out his phone and looks at the time. 9.40 p.m. He has two bars on his phone so checks the train line app and finds that his train gets into Victoria at 10.24 p.m. He texts the time to Jane Thorsen and asks her to meet his train. Then he stares out of the window and watches the dark landscape clatter by. All is shadows. *Where the hell are you, Franco?*

In London, at the headquarters of Operation Ares, the night shift is running around like a chicken with its head cut off. For the second night in a row, Eddie Matthews is wondering who the hell put him in charge. The phone is ringing off the hook, everyone is calling for Bevans and he doesn't know what to tell anyone. At 9 p.m. that night a video was uploaded simultaneously to YouTube, Tumblr, Vimeo, Facebook and a dozen other mainstream sites. Torture porn, with the emphasis on torture. Three young men are killed slowly by a shadowy figure who introduces himself to his victims as Franco. As of yet no bodies have been found but one of the boys has been identified as the teenage son of a Conservative MP.

The video has created a shitstorm and the prime minister is due to be in New Scotland Yard in ten minutes to ask questions. It will be a night like out of the bible, and not in a good way. No fish sandwiches and wine, but floods and fire and brimstone and apocalypse. It will be: find Franco and crucify him in the full glare of the press. There must be blood, and the breaking news is that the last person he was seen with was Detective Superintendent Tom Bevans, and that they gate-crashed a murder scene. It is all crazy, and is making Eddie feel more and more uncomfortable. Because the worst thing is, that he has watched the video a lot of times, it has a time stamp on it and Eddie remembers that Franco had his hands around his throat at exactly the time he was supposed to be torturing three young men to death. The man in the video is not Franco. Something is very wrong – even Fat Eddie knows that much.

Tom Bevans feels the train shudder to a halt. With some effort he pulls himself up and looks out of the train carriage window. On the platform stands DI Jane Thorsen. Christ, something is happening in his chest. He is so glad to see her. As soon as the doors are released he slides them open and jumps onto the platform. He almost runs to her.

'You're alive then.' Her voice is wary, brittle. In the unnatural light of the station Jane Thorsen looks hard and on edge. He can see movement around her mouth, as if she is holding something at bay.

'It's good to—'

'You need to get into Ares right now, it's big.'

'I found a fourth girl, a fourth Beautiful Skin killing,' he tells her.

'Fuck, Tom.' She shakes her head. 'That is going to have to wait. The son of Tristan Farthing, a bloody Tory MP – he's been killed and it has been seen by about two million people.'

'What! Jesus, but what has this got to do with us?'

'Not us – you. The murderer is someone you supposedly are pretty chummy with.'

She turns and storms away. Instead of following her he lifts his phone and types in *MP son killed*. Most sites have already taken the video down, but he finds it on an illegal, off-the-grid site. Not official internet, this is the underbelly of the world-wide web, the dark net. Tom watches just a couple of minutes before he feels too queasy to carry on, the level of violence is too disturbing – even for him. This is the zenith of a plan to destroy Franco, and it takes character assassination to a whole new level. Tristan Farthing is very rich, very influential and he is baying for blood on every TV news show and in the pages of all English-speaking newspapers in the free world. He will whip this up into the biggest manhunt of all time. Christ, these gangsters must want the money Franco *invested* at any cost. He puts his phone away, he needs to think. This will hurt him. He and Franco are linked. Chief Superintendent Fiske will have passed on all the details about this morning and – this is bad.

Tom manages to catch Jane up just by the underground station outside the main concourse. She is standing there talking on the phone. When she sees him her face clouds over.

'That was Grayson, he's spitting blood. He wants you in.'

'I haven't slept or showered in—'

'Every available officer is on it – Clarke, Jones and me, all reassigned. I shouldn't have come to pick you up but …' She leaves it unfinished.

'Christ.' He thinks today can't get any worse.

'He must have gone crazy, to kill in such a public and vicious way, and to identify himself. I always thought Franco was—'

'Innocent. Jane, he didn't do it. It's all linked up with the Beautiful Skin killings somehow. Now I am caught in the web right along with Franco and—' he pauses. 'He has a daughter. Last night she was kidnapped, they will kill her if we don't stop them.'

'Is that all?' Jane asks, chewing her lip as she walks down into the underground station.

THIRTY-ONE

Franco sits in a twenty-four hour internet café trying to breach the firewall around the Dark Wolves intranet. He cannot make a dent in it. He hides his trail by using a string of dark net sites but it is all a waste of time. Then he contacts customers and colleagues all over the world and they all say the same thing – they heard he was dead.

He checks the regular news sites but the body in the Pavilion has yet to be identified. There is no report of men found dead in Peckham, but there is news of a fire that burned out the top floor of a maisonette block in East London. He expects everything he once owned is gone. He has nothing, except some cash, a key drive and two passports. But somewhere out there he has a daughter – he has Pia. At 9 a.m. he logs off the computer, no closer to knowing what has happened. He is still only half a mile from the crime scene, but he doubts that the police will be looking for him here. They will have expected him to run back to London. It made sense to stay in Brighton. But he needs help with his next step and he cannot call on the Sad Man now.

He has not been in Brighton for years. He had thought he would not come back after last time. He had come down to deal with a former employee, James Daniel North. The man had set up business on his own, and that could not be tolerated. So

Franco had travelled down with five men, including Drew, and an ex-policewoman called Sylvie Dance, who had worked undercover narcotics in London and Brighton for years. She worked for whoever paid her and Franco always paid well. It took a while, but they finally tracked North down. The man was a parasite. He would find a vulnerable woman, get her hooked on him and the free drugs he gave her, then when she was under his thumb, would move in and make her place his own. After six months or so he would move on. If the woman was lucky, she still had a home. Usually there would be nothing of value left in it, as he would have sold or wrecked it. A few times the woman found herself in prison. One woman awoke from a bender to find her baby dead in the bed alongside her. It was North's bad luck that it happened the day Franco found him; actually it was everyone's bad lu—

He senses movement behind him rather than seeing anything. Idiot, letting his mind wander off on worthless thoughts when he should be careful. Christ, he is getting careless. He carries on walking. He can't look back; he needs to use any mirror or glass he can find to try and catch a glimpse of his pursuer. He needs to know if it's police, or a more dangerous enemy.

Franco stops; he is coming up to the centre of town. It is too early for many people to be up and most shops are closed, but the cameras will still be working. Brighton is pretty sleepy at the weekend, and you're more likely to see people who haven't been to bed yet than early risers, so it will be impossible to get lost in the crowd. There will also be full CCTV coverage. A door opens to his right, and just for a second there is a flash of leather coat and long blond hair from behind him, then it is gone. A Nazi hit-man? Well it isn't police, that's for sure. For a second Franco stands there, unsure where to go or what to do and then he feels the rush. He can't believe leather-coat is going to do it here, but the man is hurtling towards him. He almost wants to wait and feel the blade enter his flesh. He was cut once, a razor slash to his chest – it didn't hurt for ages, the wound was so clean and neat and the adrenalin shot him into the sky like a firework, but he came down eventually and – it needed a lot of stitches. He could wait for the blade, but there is Pia to rescue.

He drops to the floor like a stone, at the last possible second. If he had tried to feint left or right the man would have moved with him and struck like a heat-seeking missile. As he falls he feels the blade whip over his head and leather-coat hit him hard, trying desperately to stop, but the momentum flips him up and over with a grunt. Franco can't see the knife. *Just take the risk*, his brain screams. He grabs leather-coat by the neck and hauls him up – Franco is taller and stronger but leather-coat twists and turns like an eel. Franco clings to him and runs into the road – he didn't look to see what was coming – he is too high on rage and endorphins to know. On the other side is a community church and little garden. It slopes down from the road with a stone wall at the top. Franco pitches leather-coat over the wall, arms and legs windmill in the air, and in his hand Franco sees a blade that glitters silver with blood. Franco looks down to see his side is punctured and bleeding profusely. Franco jumps. It reminds him of those fat wrestlers he used to watch on a Saturday afternoon, the ones who would stand on the ropes and – Geronimo! – jump onto their opponent. It was always so fake, you can really fuck someone up if you jump on them with all your weight. Just like he does now. Landing on leather-coat with all his might, he feels the snap of a rib. Together they slide down the incline, leather-coat on the underneath trying to tip his rider off, Franco riding him like a bucking bronco, holding the arm with the blade, desperate to keep it from flashing at him. They come to rest at the bottom of the slope. Leather-coat has a used condom in his hair: Franco almost laughs. He leans down, trying to knock the blade away – if he releases the pressure for one second, leather-coat will stick him with it and it will be all over.

'Why are you following me?' Franco screams into his face.

'So I can kill you.'

His hand is rising; he is younger than Franco and while he doesn't have the bulk he has an intense wiry strength.

'Where is my daughter?'

'In hell where she belongs.' Leather-coat's eyes flash and he gives a whoop of delight, his hand is free. 'Fuck you!' he spits at Franco and slashes upwards. Franco throws his head forward – the knife would have pierced his eye but instead it slices through his ear. Franco's forehead lashes down and head-butts leather-coat – he yells in pain but the knife is poised to flash again. Franco can't grab the arm – his side is tearing open, he feels the blood soaking his shirt. He lunges forward and he sinks his white, white teeth into leather-coat's throat with all the tearing force he can. Blood erupts into his mouth, pouring over his chin. It is salty and hot and he wants to vomit. His ears are thudding with his own blood – he can't be sure who is screaming. He bites deeper and harder, mucus and tears join the blood that keeps pumping. The body below him thrashes. Like a wolf he shakes the throat as he bites. He keeps biting, harder and deeper – harder and deeper – harder and deeper.

You can stop now, my brother. Lulama touches his shoulder. *He is gone, you have won.*

Franco releases his jaw, which aches with the effort and falls to the side of the dead man. What has he won? He wants to cry – that was the most disgusting thing he has ever done. His soul is so steeped in blood.

For your daughter, for Pia, Lulama whispers.

'For her.' Franco sits up and goes through the man's pockets. He finds a mobile phone inside and scrolls through the contacts. There are only a dozen names – but there are two he recognises. Gulliver and Nathan Dent. He stands and looks around, but he sees no one. He grabs leather-coat's feet and drags him towards some bushes. He rolls the body inside, it will do for now. Then he stands up and—

'Zombie!' There is a drunk in a sleeping bag calling out to Franco. Around him are three or four empty two-litre bottles of cider. 'Zombie, good on yer mate. I fuckin' love Zombie day. Brains. Brains.'

Franco stares at him. It takes him a second to realise that to this man, he looks exactly like a zombie. He is covered in blood, his mouth especially. With a grunt Franco lifts his arms and stomps off like he's on the set of a George Romero film.

'Brains.'

THIRTY-TWO

Patty is not sure why she has come, especially on a Sunday when the trains are terrible and the last part of the journey was a replacement bus that smelt of fried food and wet nappies.

Now, in the early afternoon haze, she stands on a piece of abandoned wasteland watching as a woman fellates a man, both only partially hidden behind a crumbling wall. Blow-job junction – aptly named, she thinks. She is amazed it is so open, blatant even. It is an industrial area behind the railway tracks, and only a couple of roads away it is bustling and busy with shoppers. But here there is just an expanse of nothing, like a shell crater that was never rebuilt after the war. Men drive into the side road and amble over to what is almost a taxi rank. Now there are three or four women waiting for a client. Then money changes hands and the couple walk behind a wall. Patty is fascinated. She can imagine David Attenborough doing a voice-over, explaining how the lesser-brained human seeks release without procreation. In her pocket she has a pile of snapshots she had done at Snappy Snaps yesterday afternoon. She has twenty copies of the picture of Heather Spall and another twenty of Gary Wilkes. She is waiting for the current transaction to complete before she approaches the woman to show her the photos. She wants to know if she has ever seen Heather. She is sure the answer will be no, but she does wonder about Gary Wilkes.

'Working?' a voice from behind her asks. Patty turns to see a tall, quite attractive man in his late forties standing there. 'Twenty for unprotected? Well?'

Patty looks shocked for a second and then says, 'Okay.' She nods towards the wall and starts to walk there. The man follows; he has a nice suit. When Patty gets close to the other couple she sees that there are mattresses laid on the ground. They look filthy and soiled, they are for the women to kneel on – like hassocks in this priapic church. The man leans against the wall.

'Let me see it then,' Patty purrs. He unzips and pulls his penis out; it is already engorged. 'Great,' she says. And from her pocket pulls a can and maces his penis. With a scream he drops to the floor, his groin on fire, the skin already blistering. He rolls on the ground, sobbing. Patty watches him with some satisfaction – it feels good.

'What the fuck?' The woman who had been on her knees a few seconds before, bursts around the corner. Patty can see her customer running the other way, trying to tie his belt as he runs. The woman looks down at the man on the floor.

'Oh, him.' She laughs. 'That'll teach ya for taking liberties,' she yells at him and kicks at the ground, showering him with little pebbles. She looks across to Patty. 'You alright, love, do you need some Listerine?'

'No, no that's fine. I think I might want a cup of tea.'

'Oh, well, there's a transport café in the next street. You'll probably do alright, there's usually a nice bloke in there who wants a bit o' company in his cab. He likes to be mothered.'

'Great.' Patty smiles. Behind them, the maced man is crawling back to his car, still whimpering. 'But actually I'm not working right now, what I wanted to do was ask about a girl.'

Patty sees the other woman immediately turn frosty. 'I don't know nothing.'

'I'm not police or anything. I just wanted to ask about my niece.' She pulls out the photo of Heather. 'She's dead.'

'Don't know 'er.' The woman turns to go.

'She died here.'

The woman stops.

'Right here.'

The woman turns back and nods to say she'll look at the photo. Patty hands it to her. She looks into Heather's face for a long time. 'No, sorry. Never seen 'er.'

'She was found over four years ago. October time, 2006.'

The woman nods. 'I worked here then. I've been here eight years.'

Patty keeps her face neutral. Inside she feels sick to her stomach. 'How busy is it here?'

'Like Piccadilly Circus some nights.'

'Even in the winter?'

'Blokes always want their cocks sucked, same in an anorak or Hawaiian shirt. Christmas night is one of the busiest – they like to come after midnight mass.'

Patty can't help but sigh, she doesn't mean it to be judgemental but she sees how the woman bristles. 'Now you go back to your fucking nice house and leave me to get back to work.'

'I am sorry,' Patty tells her, reaching out to her arm. 'Please, one more minute.' She reaches into her pocket and pulls out the second photo. 'Do you recognise this man?'

'Him. Oh yes.'

'How often does he come here? Did he visit girls back when my niece was killed?'

'He ain't no client. He's a fucking menace. Preacher Gary, that's him, isn't it? Fucking holy bastard. He comes to teach us about hell – like us working girls need to be told about hell. All he fucking does is scare the punters away.'

'Where does he come from – what church?'

'Up there.' She points to a green painted, squat building on the corner of the wasteland.

'The community centre?' Patty asks.

'It were once, been one of those loony churches for years now. Bloody menace it is.'

The woman keeps on moaning about the church but Patty has stopped listening. All this time she has been wondering how Heather could possibly have died here – out in the open, it made no sense, especially when compared to Tracy and Sarah's murders, both of which took time and required privacy. Now it was obvious – Heather was killed in the community centre and dumped out here.

THIRTY-THREE

'Why are you covered in blood?'

Franco looks down; he hasn't got very far from the park where leather-coat's body is hidden.

'Why are you dressed up?' the boy asks: he looks about six.

'I—'

'It isn't Zombie day. No matter what that man said. That's in September, I know, I get to join in at the beach. Last year we made spaghetti and tomato sauce and called it spag brains. My dad lets me watch all the horror films, so long as I don't let my mum know.'

'Oh. She wouldn't let you?'

'I'm not old enough. My dad lets me do anything. I want to live with him but my mum says I can't. He isn't trustworthy. He's a no-good mo'fo.' He smiles.

Franco tries very hard not to laugh. 'Oh. How old are you?'

'Eight,' the boy tells him. Franco thinks him a small eight, undernourished perhaps. 'I'm Harry,' the boy tells him and lifts up his coat. His T-shirt says *Harry*.

'Nice shirt. I should get one that says Frank.'

'Is that your name?'

Franco hesitates for a second before he nods. 'Yes. I'm Frank. Pleased to meet you, Harry.' They shake hands. Franco looks around. Apart from the boy, the street is empty.

'Are you by yourself?'

'No, I'm with my dad.'

'Where is he?'

'In there.' The boy points to a bookmakers. 'He has,' Harry screws up his face, trying to remember his father's words exactly, 'Business to conclude. They let him in before it opens.'

'Oh,' Franco winks at the child, 'shall we go over and see your dad?'

The boy smiles broadly, happy to have an excuse to enter the forbidden territory. Franco puts his hand on the boy's shoulder and leads him over. The sign says closed but the boy is right, the front door is unlocked. Franco pushes the door open and walks inside with Harry.

The hoody doesn't quite fit. Franco's arms and neck are bigger than Harry's dad's, but at least it isn't covered in blood. His trousers were no good, far too skinny, but the bookie had a much larger girth, so Franco took those. Even with the belt biting deep, the trousers feel voluminous, like a clown's. But beggars can't be choosers. As soon as he saw the dad, Franco knew he smoked crack. It was the teeth, also the posture and the fear. He stank of it. A terrible father, but the perfect informant. He knew who Franco needed to find. The person he had put in charge of the Brighton operation, the ex-policewoman, Sylvie Dance.

He feels bad about Harry, but what other eight-year-old will be able to regale his classmates with a story of being locked in a cupboard by a criminal, with his dad trussed up in another room. The CLOSED sign on the front door will keep them from being discovered for a few hours but after that – Franco needs to be quick.

*

He reaches the flats in twenty minutes; the instructions were clear. The lift is broken so he climbs the stairs two at a time. The flat is at the very top, he might laughingly call it the penthouse suite. He doesn't knock. He knows the deal, he will have been on CCTV from the minute he entered the building. If they were happy to see him, the door would be open. It isn't. In one motion, his leg is up, boot aimed and— Crack! The lock splinters, the metal casing shoots off somewhere and the door swings open.

'Jesus fuck!' a voice comes from inside.

Franco pushes it open hard and storms in – all in one fluid action.

'Keep away from me Franco, you psychotic fuck.' She has a gun, but is shaking so hard it waves all over the place.

'Chill, Sylvie, all I want is some—'

'I will call the police. I know what's gone down, you fucking monster. Keep out.'

He doesn't take any notice. He figures it isn't loaded, he almost doesn't care. Even if it is, he doubts she could hit him, she is shaking so much. He pulls the gun out of her hands with such force she tumbles to the ground. He turns the gun over – empty. From behind her there is a scream. A girl, eighteen at most, is struggling into her clothes; she's got her knickers on and a shirt. On the shirt is a big badge: *Lose weight now, ask me how – I'm Charlotte.*

'Shut up, Charlotte,' Franco yells at her. 'You will be fine if you shut up and sit down. And you,' he looks down at Sylvie Dance, 'never pull an empty gun on someone.' He reaches around and pulls the gun he stole from Tom from his waistband. 'I could have shot you.'

'I really need—' Charlotte starts before she collapses into tears. He sees that she's wet herself with fright. When can he stop being a monster?

'Sweetheart, just sit down and relax. Sylvie will find you some clean clothes in a minute.' His voice is soothing and the girl, though still shaking, sits and sobs quietly. He reaches down to Sylvie Dance and offers her his hand. She refuses it. Her eyes are just full of fear.

'What? Sylvie, I need help. I really need your—'

'I know what you've done, Franco. I've seen it. You sick fucking bastard. How could you?'

Her eyes are wild, dancing with genuine fear. He doesn't understand, the last time he saw her they were good, they had gone through a nightmare – Drew, Sylvie and him, but they had come out the other end. They had lived. He thought Sylvie knew him, trusted him.

'What, Sylvie, what do you think I have done?'

Sylvie shows him the video.

There are credits. Just that fact amazes him. The screen is black then the camera slowly moves onto brick, with red text that creeps across the frame: He who steals my bread – a lesson in morality. Then the camera stalks around the room: it looks professional, the camerawork is so smooth.

'Oh, Christ,' Franco breathes, he wants to lean forward and slam the laptop shut. Charlotte has closed her eyes already and Sylvie is smoking like it's the coming apocalypse. He has to watch.

On the screen three young men stand in troughs of water. They have sacks over their heads, but apart from that they are naked. A chain is looped around each of their necks and is attached to the ceiling. It allows them just a fraction of movement – any more and it will tighten around their throats. If they sag, they will strangle themselves. Franco can see that at least two of them have relieved themselves down their legs and into the troughs. All three are red and covered in goose bumps. The room is hauntingly silent.

A film by Adam Holt-Granger.

From out of shot a stream of liquid, which looks ice cold, suddenly shoots over all three boys. They scream. The room is suddenly full of whimpers and cries.

'Help, help us,' the boy in the middle begs.

'Please, please, we have done nothing wrong,' the boy on the right squeals.

'They a-a-asked us to s-s-stay.' The boy on the left stammers. 'She said she w-w-wanted to party, we—'

'Shut the fuck up,' screams an unseen man. Unseen, but Franco recognises the voice.

Gulliver.

'I am not here to rescue you,' Gulliver laughs as he pushes at the middle boy, just his hands are seen on the video as the camera zooms in. The body moves just an inch and the chain bites into his throat. The boy croaks like a toad as the metal claws at him. The other two boys squeal with fright.

'Shhhhhhhhhh,' Gulliver whispers.

The boys force themselves to be silent, though each of them shakes with absolute fear. Gulliver's hands appear on camera, holding a silver case. From it he takes out a cattle prod, a knife and a hammer and shows them to the camera.

'Now boys, tell me your names.'

'We have done noth—' Gulliver jabs the cattle prod into his groin. The boy screams and convulses. The chain closes on his neck.

'Oh fucking Christ,' Franco feels the bile rise. These are the Peckham kids. He sent Gulliver after them – what is this fucking madman going to do?

'You good ol' cracker boys seem to be under the impression that you are here 'cos you were staying around to fuck the girl upstairs ...'

'We—'

'SHUT UP!' Gulliver screams, and the words echo around the room like a bullet ricochets. 'You are here because you stole from me.'

'We never di—'

Gulliver jabs the cattle prod into the boy's side, the scream makes Charlotte start to cry again. The pain makes the boy sag and the chain bites – the camera zooms in to catch every detail of the choking boy. Franco feels his hands shake. This is his fault, he allowed that psychopath to go after those boys, he signed their death warrant.

Gulliver lifts the boy up, the chain loosens and the boy claws air back into his lungs. 'Christ kid, don't throw in the towel yet – you might still live. We are gonna play last man standing. Two of you are going to die for stealing from me. One of you will live. You just need to keep standing while we play the knock-out rounds.'

The camera pulls back again to show all three boys. Adam Holt-Granger has switched off his brain. He is Ernest Hemingway, he just records what he sees. No comment, no moral judgement. Just film. Just film the torture of young men his own age.

'Now, I want to know your names and what Daddy does, because I hear that one of you naughty boys has a dad who is a member of parliament. Who would that be?'

Franco suddenly understands what this is. What a fucking idiot he has been, this is part of the attack. Last night was an assault on all fronts. Physical, emotional and an attempt to destroy his name and reputation, and they have succeeded.

'Josh. It's Josh,' one of them speaks as snot and tears run from inside the sack over his head and down his neck and chest. 'His dad's in the government or something.'

'Great. Thank you. And if you want to know my name – it's Franco.' And he swings the hammer.

Franco leans forward and slams the laptop shut. He doesn't need to see any more. 'That was not me,' he says to Sylvie. He can hear how pathetic he sounds but he is desperate for this woman to know and acknowledge the fact. Someone needs to know, anyone. They are painting him a monster before they kill him. He can't have that happen. Sylvie grinds out her cigarette and lights another; this is the only thing that keeps her hands steady.

'They all die. It takes about an hour. He does terrible things to them, makes them do awful things to each other. In the end the three of them are all dead. It's disgusting.'

'You don't believe I would do that?'

She shrugs. 'I don't think that is you on the screen, not now. But it's the Dark Wolves, isn't it? It's your men. You gave the order.'

He opens his mouth to deny it, but the words stick, stale and mealy in his mouth. Three more ghosts to fill his head.

'It makes *Saw* look like the *Teletubbies*,' Charlotte's thin voice comes from the other side of the room. 'It's like they chainsawed Po.' Sylvie agrees.

'How did you get it?' Franco asks.

'It's everywhere. I got a text at about 3 a.m. from a dealer in Manchester. He heard about it from someone in St. Ives. It's viral. The police shut the YouTube version down but it's everywhere else – every dark net site.'

'It can only have been a few hours.'

'Have you heard of the internet?' Her voice is venomous with sarcasm.

Franco nods, the reality of his situation still breaking over him.

'What was the name of the director?' He leans forward to the laptop.

'Do you no good. He's dead.'

'What?'

Sylvie opens the laptop and drags the cursor across the timeline – taking the film to the end. Now the camera jerks, the lighting is different.

'Oh no.'

There is a boy. He really does look little more than a tall child. A wispy little beard shows how young he is. But he won't be getting any older. His throat has been sliced open. On his chest is a card, it reads: Directed by Adam Holt-Granger. Then the camera whips away and walks into another room, and the action makes Franco feel seasick. Then the camera stops on two more bodies. A woman in her late forties and another who looks like a teenager. They are dead. The Holt-Grangers are all dead.

Franco sits for minutes, saying nothing – lost somewhere. Sylvie smokes nine more cigarettes before he speaks again. 'I need some cash, a car and a clean phone. I ask you to please keep it a secret that I came.' Sylvie looks coldly at him, she says nothing. 'And, I think you are going to need to clear out. I think the Dark Wolves are being dismantled and they will roll up the whole network. I think everyone I ever dealt with is in danger.' She laughs at that.

'Not us. Someone else is running the show, but it is just like before.'

'Who?'

'No name yet. We were just told there would be a break and then business as usual. I'm on holiday.'

Franco takes her car, a white sporty Lexus, and drives out onto the coast road, making sure Sylvie sees where he is heading from her eyrie in the sky. As soon as he is out of sight, he stops and gets out. With the butt of the gun he cracks both number plates, making them illegible. Then he gets some dirt from the side of the road and starts to make the car look like shit. He pulls the hubcaps off and throws them into bushes. Then he cracks the back window with the gun butt. Once all that is done he drives on, taking a long, winding country road that loops back to Brighton. It takes about forty minutes to get back into the centre of the town. He parks the car in a multi-storey car-park and leaves the keys in the ignition and the driver's side door ajar. If he's lucky it will get stolen quickly. He walks out of the car-park. It is still just 11.30 a.m. He walks towards the pier. There are going to be people watching out for him all over. Sylvie will let them know he has a car, there will be people posted at the train station and Gatwick. So, he is taking the slowest, most shitty way out of Dodge. He heads to the coach station.

When he gets there he's a little disappointed. He hoped it would be busy so he could melt into a crowd – but there is only one old woman with a stack of bags and boxes and a Japanese student. There is no café, just a ticket area and a tiny waiting room. His stomach rumbles and the marrow in his bones calls out for caffeine. He pays for a ticket to Leeds. He chooses Leeds because the coach is leaving in five minutes. When it pulls in, he gets on last. The woman with the bags and boxes takes more than five minutes to get on and takes up about a third of the available seats. The Japanese girl gets on. Franco watches her, wondering if she could be part of a gang. Paranoia – that is his life now, or at least it is until he can find Pia. That is the only goal he has now.

Only three passengers, he doesn't like that, he wishes there were more. He could really do with some more black faces to get lost among. If questioned, they will all remember him. He needs to be invisible for a while. The engine starts up, the coach judders – he really hates coach travel; it is just for the poor and losers. For now, he is a poor, shit-sucking loser.

The first stop is Gatwick. He gets off there and walks into the North Terminal. Within a moment he is swallowed up by the thousands of people who are jetting off to follow their dreams. He goes with the mob, into the heart of the terminal and then finds a little oasis of calm. He stops there, remembering Pia. He is taking such a risk with her life, he knows that. It makes his chest burn. As he sits there, for the first time since all this happened, he has time to think and tears begin to run down his face – unbidden, unwanted but unstoppable. They are for Pia, but also for Lulama and Bheka, the boy he had once been. He also weeps for Papi. He has not thought about the old man for a long time and yet, he misses him. Misses their time together. The hours, weeks, months he took to teach little Bheka to read; Jason, Sinbad and Robin Hood. Powerful role models for a child of war. Later, as Franco grew up, the two men played chess at night, and they talked about strategy – and the future. Of a time when the land would be theirs again and the wounds of all this fighting could heal. They spoke of themselves being the men to salve the land, heal the country – once it was won.

Franco leaves the main thoroughfare; he knows he should stay submerged in the sea of humanity, but he finds he cannot. He can't abide the pressure of the world bearing down on him as bodies flash past like a stroboscope of beating human hearts pulsing around and through him. He needs air, space, to be alone. He finds a small area of seats wedged between a crappy sandwich place and a fancy shirt shop. The area is empty, so he sits there and lets his memories soar free. He holds Pia's hand and sits at the feet of his Papi. It is the perfect place to get lost for a few hours while he dreams. And he forgets the roving eye of CCTV.

At some point, maybe two hours later, his mind falls back to earth and returns to his body. Immediately hunger laps at him, he needs to eat. He walks around in a little circle and weighs up sandwich shop A versus sandwich shop B. He goes with B, though when he bites into his choice he finds he can taste nothing, there is no pleasure in the food, as if his tongue is numb. He eats because his stomach growls and he knows he must. He needs energy if he is going to be revenged upon Gulliver and Dent. He finds it hard to believe that the man who used to run his errands like a dog is now hunting him, but his name was in leather-coat's phone.

In a chemist's shop Franco buys a toothbrush and toothpaste and takes them straight to the toilets. It makes him feel a little more human to be able to clean his teeth. He sniffs at his body; it's pretty gross, though not really him. It is mostly that the stolen hoody smells really bad, crack-smoking mo'fo bad. He goes back to the chemist's and buys a deodorant, which he covers himself in – both under his clothes and over them. That should be enough. Then he looks at himself in the mirror. He does not recognise the face that looks back. He is not Franco, not Frank Light – not even Bheka.

He goes back to the main part of the terminal and sits in the departures area, watching as thousands of people flood through. He has a passport, he could leave. But he can't, not without Pia.

After a couple of hours he walks back to the coach station and buys a ticket to Edinburgh. It is a city he has always wanted to visit. The coach changes at Victoria. As in most things, London is the heart. Again he pays in cash. Then he returns to the airport terminal and sits. The coach is due to leave in thirty minutes. From his pocket he takes the bag he got from Sylvie. Inside is a phone, with its sim and battery taped to it. He assembles it, writes a text, but does not push send. Instead he watches the ebb and flow of humanity. From the outside he looks like a man meditating, possibly deep in prayer. He waits and he watches as the thirty minutes until the coach leaves tick away. When only eight of them remain, he sees what he has been waiting for: a tall, strong-looking black man, about his build and shape. A decade younger, but that does not matter. He watches him join the line for a flight to Florida. Franco looks down at the text. *I am going abroad for a while, so you will not be able to contact me directly. If you need to get a message to me, the man to trust is Detective Superintendent Tom Bevans.* Franco reads the message back to himself a few times and then presses send. Then he slowly walks towards the target, who is being asked questions at the security barrier. Franco squeezes up to them and slips, stumbling heavily and falling into them.

'Sorry, sorry guys,' he holds up his hands, 'really sorry.' He rights himself and walks onwards, still offering up his palms and then holds up two peace signs. 'Love ya,' he calls out and turns and slips into the crowds. No one saw him slip the phone into the man's luggage. He feels a slight pang of guilt, knowing he will be stopped and questioned. At worst, the plane will be diverted en route and landed in Iceland, but probably he will be taken off when they reach their final destination and he'll be quizzed for a day. They'll soon work out he isn't Franco, but they'll keep asking. He'll get compensation, which isn't the worst thing for the guy. Really, it could have been so much worse.

Minutes later Franco sinks down into a seat on the coach bound for Edinburgh. It is about half full, mostly students and an older man that smells slightly of urine. He closes his eyes and falls asleep.

THIRTY-FOUR

Christ, I need my bed, thinks Tom as he walks from the tube station up to New Scotland Yard. He had hoped that Jane would collect him in a squad car, but she was too upset with him for that. He had left her on the Victoria line – he should call her in the morning, if he makes it to then without Grayson tearing his heart out.

As he gets closer he can see Grayson on the street outside the main entrance lighting a cigarette. He sees Tom and waves him over.

'It's fucking crazy that I have to come out here for a cigarette. When I retire I am going to spend the first month of it just smoking. Morning, noon and night; one after another. Bliss.' He takes a long drag on the one in his mouth and holds it in his lungs – then lets it out in a long breath, like it's a mindfulness practice. 'You lied to me, Bevans.'

'I did not—'

'You tried to sell me that beautiful skin crap, and I asked you if you had any reason to believe there would be another victim, after four bloody years, and you said no.'

'At the time—'

'Zip it. Less than a week back on the job and you force your way into a crime scene, taking Britain's most wanted with you.

And what do you know, a victim with all the trademarks of your pet killer. Tell me what the fuck is going on.'

Tom knows his career hangs by a thread here. How much *truth* can Grayson handle?

'Franco broke into the ops room and forced Sergeant Matthews to call me in.'

Grayson looks at him with amazement, then drops the cigarette to the pavement and grinds it under his boot. He takes a phone out and dials.

'Get Fat Eddie from Ares to my office, now.' He hangs up and turns to Tom. 'Then what?'

'Franco had a woman, she had been missing for a few days. Saturday night, someone called him from her phone and when he answered, they killed her so he could listen to her die. On the phone they said "beautiful skin".'

'On the phone?'

'Yes.'

'Christ. This is such a fucking mess. You've seen the video. A bloody MP's kid.'

'It isn't him. It isn't Franco.'

'You know him that well? Recognise his voice, what – do you get together a lot?'

'The first time was on Saturday night, and that was also the time he was supposed to be killing three young men. The man on that video is not Franco.'

'Oh, don't be so naïve. The video time code was faked, then he went to you to get an alibi.'

'I don't believe that is true, sir. He—'

'Are you bent, Bevans?'

'Sir—'

'Crooked, are you bought and paid for, does Franco cock a finger and you go running?'

Tom wants to hit him. He can't admit that he owes Franco a debt from more than twenty years ago – that would break his career. He trusts that Eddie will say nothing, especially as he called Eddie twenty minutes ago and told him what he could say. 'Deputy,' he pauses a little too long for Grayson's liking, 'Commissioner Grayson, I am not disloyal.' The two men glare at each other. 'But the man who came to me was in pain and all he wanted was to see the body of someone he loved.'

'Oh boo-fucking-hoo.'

'He just used me to gain access to the crime scene.'

'I don't buy that, Bevans – why you?'

'I think Franco came to me because I have a reputation amongst the women he trades.'

'That fucking Sad Man shit, give me a break. Bevans, I don't know what the deal is but I don't trust you. There is something going on. I am putting you on suspension.' Grayson turns and walks to the door.

'Fine, sir. I will write up my notes, stating clearly that I advised you a week ago to reopen a murder enquiry and you refused, allowing a fourth victim—'

Grayson turns, his face an absolute storm. He strides back and his finger stabs towards Tom's face, making him pull away. 'Don't play politics with me son. You will not win.'

Tom pauses and then, in as calm a voice as he can muster, says, 'Then, I request to remain on active duty so I can bring this killer to justice, sir.'

Grayson sneers. 'No, you are on temporary suspension. I want you in my office Wednesday morning and we'll set the date for your disciplinary and dishonourable discharge. I won't do any paperwork before then – but I don't want to see you anywhere near this case.'

Tom nods slowly, he sees that he has been given a life-line. Or is it enough rope to hang himself with? Either way, he has two days to find the evidence he needs to change Grayson's mind and keep himself as the Chief of Ares.

'Two days, *Mr* Bevans.' From his pocket Grayson pulls a packet of mints and chews on one as he walks back inside the building.

'Stupid melodramatic bastard,' Tom mutters under his breath as he watches the figure enter the building and disappear into the brick and glass. Then, feeling that his whole body is tingling, he walks back to the tube station. *Time for bed*, he thinks. He can't wait. Then his mobile rings.

'Tom. I think I've got something.' It's Patty. 'Can you come over now?'

He sighs. 'I'll be there in twenty minutes. I am going to need a really strong coffee.'

THIRTY-FIVE

The three of them sit, looking despondent. Tom has told both Patty and Jane about the conversation with Grayson. Two days and that is it. Patty has the door open and is smoking, blowing the clouds of nicotine and tarry goodness into the hallway. The office had, once upon a time, had a little window, but after Dani died and the room was turned into a murder enquiry room, it was boarded over to make space for pictures of the autopsy, removing all natural light. The last thing Patty had wanted to see was sunlight dancing in the room; it was for mourning, not for life.

'I just don't …' and Jane Thorsen dries up. They have been over it all again. How does this new body tie into the other three cases?

'Maybe it just doesn't,' Patty says. 'A copycat perhaps.'

'But why … and why drag Franco in?' Jane asks.

'He thinks it is an all-out attack on him, he stole seventy-five million from the Dark Wolves,' Tom tells them.

'Christ,' Jane mutters, more to herself than the others. She shudders. The images from the video are still rummaging through her brain. She would like to make them stop, file them away in a box, but they are too raw and livid still. She is scared, that level of violence makes her want to curl into a ball. 'So who was the victim?'

'He didn't know her, at least I don't think so. He had expected it to be his daughter, Pia Light.'

'So have Brighton identified the victim then?' Jane asks angrily.

'No, not yet.' Tom yawns, his body starting to close down with absolute exhaustion. Jane clenches her jaw.

'Can we forget the fourth victim for a moment?' Patty insists. 'What about Gary Wilkes and the church connection? I tried to get into the building today but it was locked up and it looks like it is only open for services two days a week. It could be where Heather was killed. We need to get the CSI team in and—'

'It's four and a half years. There's no point in a forensics sweep. Not of a public place like that.' Tom tells her as his eyelids fight not to flutter closed.

'I am going to get a cuppa,' Jane announces, her voice heavy with annoyance. She pushes past Patty and heads downstairs.

'Is Daphne causing trouble, Fred?' Patty asks when she thinks Jane is out of earshot. She follows it with a wonky smoke ring.

'It isn't funny, Patty.'

She tips her head to one side as if she thinks he's wrong. 'She's a bit overwhelmed by the breaking news. And, I have to say, so am I. Franco scares me. You being involved with Franco scares us both. At least I know why you're tied to him.'

'You think I should tell her that he helped find Dani?'

Patty shrugs. 'That depends on how far you want to go. She will ask what he did, how he helped. Are you going to tell her that he helped you frame an innocent man?'

'For Dani, I did it for Dani,' he tells Patty, though he knows how frail the excuse is. He shattered a man's life, but he needs to set that aside for now. One day he will try to make amends to Ben Bradman. One day. Not today.

*

Downstairs, Jane stands in the hall by the front door. She is shaking a little. A part of her wants to walk through it, she should go and see Grayson now, ally herself to him. Tell him that Detective Superintendent Tom Bevans has gone outside of the department to recruit a vigilante ex-journalist who may be unhinged and—

'Oh, I'm sorry. I didn't realise.' Jim has almost walked into her in the dark.

'No I was just standing here. Bit stupid really. I came down to get a cuppa.'

'The kitchen's in here. I'm hiding in it, can't go upstairs, not into that room.'

'Oh,' Jane says, and follows him into the kitchen.

He makes himself a coffee, strong enough for a spoon to stand up in, and makes her a tea. Earl Grey with a drop of milk. She doesn't really want it, but it will be nice to hold something and give her hands a job to do. They sit at the kitchen table. Jane sees how tired he looks. She had thought him a very handsome man when she first saw him – what, only a few days ago now. He looks like he hasn't had a second of sleep since then.

'She told you about today?' he asks.

'Yes, it's a really good lead.'

'She sprayed a man with mace, on his private parts. Mace that is illegal in this country – it melts rodents.'

'I—' She has no idea what to say. She can feel the waves of fear that wash off him. 'She may have exaggerated.'

'I doubt it.' He drops his head, Jane thinks he is about to cry. Oh, what the fuck does she do – she is not equipped for comforting people. Snapping the cuffs on someone, chasing down the bad guys and swearing like a trooper. Those are her strongest attributes. *Please don't cry*, she begs him in her head.

'I talk to my daughter.' He looks up, into Jane's eyes. No tears but a wildness there. 'Did Tom tell you that?'

'No.' She shakes her head, a little lost. 'Your daughter, I didn't realise you had another child.'

'No, we don't, just one. I talk to Dani. She talks back. I saw her yesterday,' he laughs. 'It's crazy, isn't it? Crazy.'

She opens her mouth to speak. There is nothing to say.

A short while later Tom walks down the stairs and pushes the kitchen door open. He feels a sudden rush of sentiment hit him. For the briefest second it is like Dani and Jim sitting chatting at the table – a scene he remembers so well from his teen years. Then they both turn to him and it is blown away. Jim is not the man from thirty years ago – time has taken a toll, and Jane is not Dani. She is harder, grittier, but solid and dependable. She is alive.

'Patty is going to try to see Allison Stokes tomorrow. I'm going to call Sarah Penn's mother and try to see her. I was thinking … Would you go to see Marcus?'

'What?'

'He blinks.'

Twenty minutes later, Tom gets to the bench. His bench. His and Dani's bench. He stands there, staring at it. He had come here to sit down and think, try and work out what is going on with this case, and with Jane. The way she looks at him, he can't tell what is going on with her. She seems to be fighting inside. Sometimes she looks at him with such disappointment and it makes him feel like crap. He looks at the bench, just a metal frame with six planks of wood, yet it is full of pain for him. Why does he come here? Dani's gone, he tells himself. Get over it. He walks backwards for a few steps and then slowly turns and heads away, towards the observatory, where his favourite tearoom is. He wishes it were open; he would love one of their hearty bowls of boiling hot soup. He feels so cold.

When he gets there, it is an empty circle, no seats set out, but there is a low wall he can squat on and look at the statue of Yuri Gagarin.

'There was a man who travelled,' he thinks with a pang of jealousy. He was going to travel, a long time ago. He and Dani talked about seeing the world. He had imagined them marrying on some tropical beach, but she never thought about them as a couple. Life is never what you think it will be. *Que sera sera*. Maybe. Maybe Grayson kicking him out will be the best thing that could happen to him, if not, he could be trapped as the Sad Man forever.

'What the hell?' a voice behind him yells.

Tom turns to see Jane jumping down off the wall and heading towards him. He feels the skin on the back of his neck stand up.

'Blinking,' she yells, then holds up a manila file which she waves in the air.

'What?' he asks excitedly.

'I just read through the official file forensics on Penn and Mason.' Her tone reeks of disappointment and anger. '*Examination journal: Date 16 Feb 2007, Time: 18.30. Examined Sarah Penn again. Then checked with the cadaver of Mason. She is the same. I am now going to check the photos and examination notes from Spall. I am pretty sure will be the same. Eureka, all is revealed.*'

'I don't—'

'He'd worked it out. That smug bastard had a link for all three and knew what was going on.'

'But he can't have, he must have checked the notes from Spall and seen whatever he thought was wrong.'

'But he was arrested within days.'

'You don't think he'd keep a major clue to himself because—'

'He's a control freak and a vindictive bastard. I can see him keeping secret the fact that Hitler was alive if it worked for him. I'll make him fucking blink what he knows.'

'Don't go in so angry. He will just clam up.'

'Don't worry, I'll ask Jim to go with me. He's a pretty calm influence.'

Tom feels his mouth go dry. 'That isn't a good idea.'

'Why?' she asks.

Oh crap, he thinks, *is it time to tell her the truth, the whole truth*? 'Jane—' he starts and then his attention is drawn to the small red dot that has appeared on her throat.

'Jane,' he shouts as her body jolts back with force, like she has been hit by lightning, and she smashes into the ground.

'JANE.'

Her body slams into the dirt, convulsing. Tom makes a move towards her but a hand spins him around. A gun is pointed between his eyes. The man holding it is stocky and powerful looking, dark skin made even darker by the bands of thick ink that cover much of his arms, neck and shaved head. His eyes are hard and cruel.

'Don't fucking move or she will get another charge.'

Tom flicks his eyes back to Jane: he can see the tendrils of the wires, their barbed hooks secure in her flesh. Her eyes are wild and dancing, drool flecks her chin and she has blood on her lips.

He guesses she has bitten her tongue. Tom knows the Taser is set far higher than is safe.

'And I think she wet herself on that first go, so it will be really painful in certain parts to get another big shock – if you know what I mean.'

'You bastard,' Tom snarls at the man.

It is all he needs. Even though Tom made no movement towards him, he squeezes the power and Jane's body jerks off the ground.

'Stop it.' Tom holds up his hands and takes a step back. Too late he sees the pleasure in the man's face. 'Please,' he asks in a small voice, collapsing in on himself, supplicant to the man with his finger on the trigger. The man with the Taser smiles and releases his finger. Her body drops, breath smacked from her.

'Fuck you, copper.' He presses the trigger again; Jane spasms uncontrollably. It tears the heart out of Tom. 'Say sir.'

'Please, sir. Please stop, SIR.' Tom drops to his knees, submissive, showing he is no threat to the man. The man grins at Tom, and releases his finger. She drops again. Blood is running freely from her nose and mouth now.

'Good, what a good little piggy you are,' the man smiles. 'If you're a really good boy I might let you play fetch before I cut your fucking heart out. Now I am going to ask you one question. If you lie or don't answer I will barbecue this fucking bitch. Do you understand me?'

'Yes,' Tom tells him in a voice that is slow and deliberate.

'I'm not sure I believe that. I want to hear that a bit louder – and call me Mr Gulliver.'

Tom closes his eyes tight for a beat and then answers, 'Sir. Yes, sir, Mr Gulliver.' Tom's heart sinks, Gulliver has given up his name, it can only mean one thing, the bastard plans to kill him no matter what he says. He will kill them both.

'Good.' Gulliver grins. 'Old man, this is the question – and remember when you are formulating your answer, that I can do this.' He theatrically stabs at the trigger.

'Nooooo.' Tom falls forward into the dirt at his feet. Gulliver hoots with laughter.

'Jesus man, you are one sorry sack of spineless shit. I think it would do the bitch a favour to waste her so she doesn't have to be around you anymore. Should I?' He waves the Taser around in the air.

'Please leave her alone.'

Gulliver laughs. 'Is that it? Leave her alone. Are you really the high and mighty Sad Man I have heard so much about? Our girls fucking rate you. Why?' Gulliver puts his boot onto Tom's head and pushes it down. The earth bites at his cheek. Gulliver could crack his skull, grind his bones to make his bread. Tom's heart races. He prays. He is rusty, but he lets out a prayer to any god that might be listening. *Save her. Please save Jane.*

'You are pathetic.' Gulliver lifts his boot from Tom and steps back. 'No wonder this country is fucked with the likes of you keeping the streets safe. Jee-sus.' He laughs a deep hearty laugh. Tom pushes himself slowly up from the ground and onto his knees. His arms slide back, looking like he is supplicating himself even further, but his fingers find the thin metal baton in his belt. Gulliver spits on the ground in front of him.

'You look like you're ready to suck my cock,' Gulliver sneers. 'You probably would. Fuckin' coward.' Tom steals a glance up to his face and then drops his head again. Gulliver looks disappointed, like he wanted a real fight.

'So here's the question, Detective Superintendent Cock-sucker – fuckin' look at me.' Tom looks up into the cold eyes of Gulliver. He tries to keep the hate from his own. He must look soft and scared. Hopeless. 'Where's my man, Franco?' Tom feels the man's eyes burrow deep into his skull. 'Don't fuckin' think about lying to me boy. I know you and Franco are close and I hear that you are the only man in Europe that he trusts. So hard luck to you.' He levels the gun at Tom's head and theatrically raises the Taser with the other. 'You are going to tell me where he is right now or I am gonna fry her fucking brains like KFC.' He smiles so wide, Tom can see the gold fillings all the way in his back teeth. 'If you tell me, she will live. You won't of course, I will still kill you, but the plus side is that it will be quick. I will put a bullet through your head. Don't tell me – and she will be in pure agony before she finally dies, cursing your fucking name for putting her through so much. And the truth is, that after all that shit, you will still tell me what I want to know because I will crush every bone in your body – but she'll be dead and you'll be well and truly fucked. So, I advise you to take a moment, and then tell me, mother-fucker, where is Franco?'

Tom holds his gaze, as behind his back his fingers fasten around the baton. 'Franco. He's right behind you.'

Gulliver sucks in air through his teeth, his eyes flaring with anger. 'Oh guy you are totally fuc— aaaaaahhhhhhhhh,' he screams as a blade rips through his shoulder, thrust from behind by his former boss, ripping tissue and muscle apart. The gun drops from Gulliver's hand as blood fizzes from the wound. At the same time Tom pulls the whip-thin metal baton from his belt and brings it crashing onto his wrist. The Taser flies away as the bone snaps. Tom is over to Jane in an instant, carefully taking the Taser clips from her and pulling her into him hard, so glad she's alive. She is out cold, but her pulse is strong. Tom looks back. Franco has his arm around Gulliver's neck, choking the life out of him, while Gulliver lamely tries to bat him away. Both men are slimed with blood that leaks from the shoulder wound. Franco tightens his grip around the stockier man's throat and lifts him off his feet. Gulliver tries to say something but there is only a gurgle.

Franco bends his head forward to his ear and whispers, 'I thought you wanted to hunt with me, Gulliver. Thought you had what it takes to be a Dark Wolf.' Franco laughs softly as the man gets weaker and weaker; blood loss and a lack of oxygen to the brain dragging him down. Franco feels the flutter of his spirit knocking at his chest and he lowers him back to the ground as Gulliver gives up the ghost and loses consciousness. 'I guess you just played at being a wolf – boy,' Franco tells him while he counts to ten, all the time keeping his grip on the carotid artery firm – starving the man's brain until he is fully unconscious, another thirty seconds and there will be no coming back. But that is not the plan. Instead Franco releases him, and like a dead weight, drops him to the ground. Alive. Just. He looks to Tom, who is cradling Jane Thorsen. He walks over to them and kneels down.

'Is she okay?'

'I think so.' Tom does not look up to Franco, his eyes full of concern for the woman in his arms.

'You stabbed him in the shoulder, the arm with the gun.'

'Yes.'

'You should have stabbed him in the arm holding the Taser.' Tom turns to look at the man, his face is red with fury. 'You put her in danger.'

'I didn't know she would be here.'

Tom looks up at Franco. He holds eye contact for a few seconds, then goes back to Jane. Her eyelids flutter and eyes open. Tom is a little overwhelmed by the rush of happiness that surges through him.

'Jane. Jane, can you hear me?'

'Fuck, that hurt. I am really going to have to think hard before I ever Taser anyone.'

'Can we get her to her feet?' Franco asks.

'Franco?' she asks. She has only seen photographs. He is much more handsome in person, and his eyes are far crueller.

'DI Thorsen.' Franco offers his hand to her. She doesn't take it. 'I don't blame you,' he tells her as he withdraws it. 'And I am responsible for what you just went through, not Tom Bevans, but for the next forty-eight hours I am going to need your help and I ask that you do not arrest me in that time. After that, when my daughter is safe, then you can decide what you want to do.'

She nods slowly. 'I think you are scum.'

'And I thank you for your honesty.'

'Forty-eight hours.' The same time limit Grayson gave Tom.

'For my daughter. She is an innocent in all this.'

'How can any child of yours be innocent?'

Franco sighs, but does not answer. Instead, he stands and walks over to Gulliver's body and begins to go through the pockets.

Jane looks to Tom. His eyes are soft, he seems to have faith in this man, this killer. 'Tom?'

He nods.

'Okay.' She rolls to one side and tries to rise, but wooziness spreads over her so she sits down again. 'So what happened?

Who is this guy?' She points at Gulliver. Her teeth chatter slightly, from the shock.

'Well, the first bit is easy. What happened is—' he points to Franco. 'We were live bait.'

'You, Friend Tom. I sent a text to someone I believed had betrayed me, saying the only man I trusted was you.'

'Then you watched me until—'

'Yes. I am sorry.'

'A sacrificial lamb. Never mind that they could have killed or tortured the people I love.'

Franco's eyes flick to DI Thorsen. Her pupils have flared at the word *love*. 'I didn't believe I would put anyone else in danger.'

'Just me.'

'Just you.' The two men's eyes lock. 'These men are professionals. I expected a threat and an attempt at bribery. I did not believe Gulliver would attack a senior police officer. I just needed him to show his hand.'

'You didn't think they would send the psycho torturer.' Jane is angry, not for her – but the threat to Tom. 'He's the guy from the video, isn't he? This is the "Franco" that tortured and killed those boys?'

Franco's jaw tightens so hard it looks like it might snap as he recalls the abominations done in his name. 'I underestimated the risk. I thought I knew him better. He was my head of security.'

'The job centre screwed you,' Jane barks with a little laugh.

Franco looks darkly at her. 'Not the job centre, but you're right.' His eyes narrow. 'I was set up.'

'Okay, so this man Gulliver was sent to find you – what if they'd sent a dozen men?' Tom asks.

Franco holds his gaze. 'I thought it unlikely, these men attempted an almost bloodless coup. My four most loyal lieutenants were killed and they would have made an example of me. They have used stealth so far, but if a lot of men had come to question you then I think I would have left you.'

Tom watches Franco's face for a few moments. 'Probably the right decision.'

'Tom!' Jane is incensed.

'It's okay,' he tells her, then turns to Franco. 'I understand.' Tom knows what a man will do to save the thing they most love.

'Are we good?' Franco asks. Tom pauses.

'We're good. But never endanger those I care about again.'

Franco nods. 'Yes, Friend Tom.'

'And your word is your bond,' Tom tells him. Franco smiles a bitter-sweet smile, recognising the irony of Tom's words. 'So now what?'

Franco bends back down to Gulliver and carries on searching his pockets. He finds his phone and slips the battery and sim out. He finds two secreted knives and a gun, and pockets these. 'We need to secure Gulliver and hold him somewhere for a day or two. Is there somewhere, someone you trust?'

'I—' Tom wavers, he can only think of one place. He knows Patty will be fine with it, probably really enjoy having a killer in the house, but Jim, he is not sure about him. 'There are friends who will help, but do you think it's safe for them?'

Franco makes a face that is something between a smile and a grimace. *Safe* has become a very malleable word lately. 'I think it will take a while to link them to you, but they will eventually. I think we have some time before your friends become targets.'

'Let's take Gulliver there,' Tom decides. 'There's no CCTV along the edge of the park, but there is in the street by the school. We carry him the long way and hope no busybody is watching.'

'Thank you, Tom,' Franco tells him. Jane shakes her head slowly, her teeth chattering even more than before.

The two men help lever Jane to her feet where she wobbles like a newborn giraffe, still lacking the motor control the electric charges deprived her of.

'I can carry Gulliver. Can you help Jane?' Franco asks Tom.

'Of course.' Tom holds his DI around the waist, puts her arm over his shoulder and walks her forwards. There is something about their closeness, their hips clapping together, that he likes. Franco bends down and with great effort, picks Gulliver up and slings him over his shoulder. As he does so he feels the wound in his side tear open again.

Then, together, they head to Patty and Jim's house.

Twenty minutes later Tom pulls the duvet around Jane, and pats it into place. She is already asleep. He has never, in his entire life, tucked another human being into bed. He suddenly feels an enormous emptiness open up in his chest. He wants to kiss her forehead, goodnight sleepy head, he could say.

He had carried her upstairs and stood outside the door while Patty helped her undress and wash. The Taser had totally wiped her out; she couldn't even hold a washcloth without help. Then Patty put her into an old pair of Jim's pyjamas and into bed. She had fallen asleep as soon as her head touched the pillow. Patty left the room and Tom stayed. He wants … shit, what does he want?

He watches her for a few minutes and then leaves, switching the light off but leaving the door ajar so that some light spills inside the room from the hallway – like a nightlight to keep her safe if she wakes.

Tom leaves the room and walks into the operations room, the walls of death room. The desk has been taken out. Franco has laid cardboard and newspapers and crushed egg cartons across what had once been a small window, and has gaffer-taped across them. Sound proofing. In the centre of the room is the heaviest wooden chair in the house; Franco carried it up from the living room. To get it through the door he ripped one of the arms off it. In the centre of the seat, a channel has been cut. Sitting in the chair, naked and handcuffed from both wrists, is Gulliver. His chest and arms are tied to the back of the chair, and he is forced forward, which looks uncomfortable, and then taped with gaffer. His mouth is covered too. Under the chair, at the bottom of the channel, Franco slides a bucket. Tom sees that it is to catch urine and faeces that flow down the channel. Gulliver is too dangerous to release from the chair to use the bathroom. He can piss and shit where he sits. Around him are the pictures of the dead girls Heather, Tracy, Sarah and – Franco has put a picture of Pia on the wall. One he has carried in his wallet all this time. Christ she is beautiful, thinks Tom. Then he remembers she is being held somewhere, she may already be dead.

Franco pulls at the gaffer tape – that sound – the tear of fabric. It makes Patty gasp. Tom hadn't seen her there, in the corner of the room. He looks to her, thinks he sees fear in her eyes for a moment; but he looks again and sees she isn't afraid. She is excited.

'I need a pillow case. Patty.' Franco's request snaps Patty from her reverie.

'Yes, of course.' And she disappears to find one.

Franco turns to Tom. 'Almost done,' he tells the policeman.

'What's the plan?' Tom points at the man in the centre of the room who is still out cold.

'We leave him for a day. No food or drink and no bathroom. We do not talk to him or let him talk. Darkness and quiet. That should soften him up and then tomorrow night we question him.'

'Question?' Tom knows it is a euphemism for something far, far nastier. He closes his eyes for a moment to steady himself. 'And are you going to—' he can barely bring himself to ask the question, 'Are you going to treat him in the same way, the same way he treated those boys, to get the information?'

Franco feels the blood around his heart turn to ice. 'For my Princess? I will do anything.'

Jim is asleep. At 4 a.m. he is woken. 'Patty?' he whispers.

'Shhhhhhhh.' She curls into him, naked. She kisses him and he rouses. She pushes him onto his back and releases him from his pyjamas, then she rolls onto him until he is inside her. There's very little light in the room, just enough to see her eyes and the smile that flicks across her mouth. They lay still, he feels the beat of her heart. They two of them seem to synch together. She kisses him and softly and slowly moves on top of him. Their hands interlace.

'I do love you,' she whispers.

'I know you do,' he replies, and lets her make love to him.

Jane Thorsen awakes. She thinks she hears sex sounds coming through the walls, but maybe she is still asleep. She twists round in the bed. There is only a little gloomy light from the window but the door is open and a crack of electric light falls across the room. She sees a figure in the chair opposite. She knows who it is, even though she cannot see a face. She pulls the duvet back and slides across to him. The floor is cold. It only takes two steps to reach the chair. Tom is in it, wrapped in a blanket. She takes his hand – he wakes with a start. She pulls him up out of the chair and across to the bed. Together they fall back onto it. She pulls the duvet over them both and wraps him in her arms. Together they sleep.

Franco stands in the doorway and watches the captive man. He awoke a few hours ago, thrashed around for about forty minutes like a snake in a box and then fell back into unconsciousness. Franco never said a word to him. He looks at his watch. At 8 a.m. he will wake the others. There is a great deal to do today.

THIRTY-SIX

Jim makes breakfast. Bacon, eggs and toast. He also makes a packed lunch for each of them, except for Franco who says he never eats lunch.

This morning they have made their plans.

Patty has spoken to Ellen Stokes and she is seeing her that morning; she hopes Allison will be persuaded to meet them too.

Jane is heading to the Operation Ares briefing room and will try and discover everything she can about Gulliver and the shadowy ex-DI Nathan Dent. After that, she is going to try and track down the mother and brother of Tracy Mason and then at 5.30 p.m. she is going to visit Marcus Keyson for dinner. Tom will spend most of the day talking to Brighton about the body there, hoping they don't know Grayson has suspended him from active service. At 5 p.m. he will interview Sarah Penn's family.

Jim is to act as jailer to their prisoner. He has been told to stay out of the room unless Gulliver makes such a noise he has to intervene. If he does, then Jim is to use the Taser on him. The thought makes Jim sick.

Franco will not say exactly what his plans are – only that he is going to see the person who betrayed him to Gulliver.

Breakfast is a pretty sombre affair. There is little or no discussion. Patty has barely a few bites of toast. Tom and Jane eat slowly and do not make eye contact, both feeling awkward after waking alongside each other. Franco looks as if a storm is building deep inside.

Finally, only Jim is in the house. He clears away the breakfast things, washes the dishes and puts everything away. When he opens the fridge he finds three packed lunches sitting in there. He wants to cry. Suddenly from above there is a thump … thump … thump … Gulliver is stomping in the room upstairs. It continues for twenty minutes, the steady drip, drip, drip of stamping torture. Jim thinks he will go mad if he has to listen to it all day. Franco has told him only to go up there if the noise can reach the street but Jim can't stand it. After all, he's handcuffed, what can he do?

Jim walks up the stairs, slowly. He can still hear the thud but it is muted here, not like it is when he is directly under it. Jim can see through the slats in the stairs as he goes up and up – he can see through to the room. The door is open; he thought it was meant to be closed. He stops. Thump … thump … thump …

Jim takes another step, he can see into the room now and the chair isn't there. It was right in the middle of the room but it's gone. Thump … thump … thump … What is going on? Thump … thump … th— crash!

'Christ.' His hands shake as he climbs the final few steps and walks to the door. He pushes it all the way open and looks inside. 'Hell.'

Gulliver is face down as the chair has fallen forwards. He lies pressed into the floorboards, one shoulder torn loose from the gaffer tape as he thrashes about, like a shark on a line – putting all his energy into tearing himself free.

'Stop moving,' Jim shouts with all the authority he can. Gulliver stiffens and the room becomes perfectly still. 'I'll stand the chair back up. Don't try anything.'

The chair has tipped forwards. To lever it up Jim will have to kneel down and use both arms to push it back onto its legs. He'll need to be careful, but only one of Gulliver's shoulders has loosened and the handcuffs are still in place.

'Okay, I am going to move you back so the chair is upright. Stay still so I don't hurt you, okay.'

He kneels down and feels for the bottom slat of the chair. With Gulliver sitting there it will be very heavy. He will have to get very close to the man. He slides forward. The smell from the bucket under the chair is foul, makes Jim want to retch. He looks to Gulliver – the pillow-case over his head makes it hard to tell where his face is. Jim imagines he is smiling, but it must be a trick of the light. He feels sweat trickle down his own back, he doesn't like to be this close to such a dangerous animal.

'Okay.' His fingers find the slat and he leans into the chair to lift it, his face almost touches the pillow case and— 'Aghhhh!'

Gulliver's head punches forward in a vicious butt. He catches Jim on the ridge of the nose – there are fireworks and an explosion – he feels one side of his nose cave and blood spurt across his face. Gulliver pulls back and strikes again, like a snake. He has almost no room to move but he is pistol quick. The second butt hits Jim in the eye and Jim feels the socket crack. The pain is tremendous. He calls out and feels himself topple back – immediately he understands the danger. Gulliver pushes forward. He is trying to get on top of Jim, and if he does he will use the weight to crush the life out of him, he must— 'Aagh.' A third head-butt hits his chin and into his throat. Jim feels blood run down his nose and well in his gullet, he will drown in his own blood. Gulliver forces forwards – he is winning. Jim slides back, the weight of the chair forcing into his stomach and groin – *Christ, it hurts*. Jim feels his life on a see-saw. 'Dani,' he calls, but she is not there. 'Patty.' He will die alone.

The fourth head-butt. It is the worst, but this time it is Jim who smashes his forehead into Gulliver's face. It hurts Jim's forehead but; he feels something break. Immediately the white pillowcase is stained with blood. Gulliver howls and whips his own head forward, but the pain confuses him and he misses Jim. The force of the butt over-balances Gulliver and Jim rolls out and away as the chair crashes forward and Gulliver yells in pain. He thrashes about, trying to loosen the tape. Jim sees it coming away in places. Suddenly Gulliver's chest is free – the man bellows and strains more. Jim is up. Blood runs down his face, his eye burns and he can feel it is swollen badly and getting worse. He runs out of the door and into the hall. The desk is there and on top is the gaffer tape. Behind him he hears the chair grate on the floor. Jim grabs the tape and rips a piece from the roll. He goes back in. Gulliver is undulating, a lizard flicking this way and that.

'Stay still, damn you.' Jim kicks at him. His foot presses him back into the chair, then Jim quickly loops the tape around his neck and starts to run it around, to cocoon the writhing Gulliver. He keeps going until the man is literally a ball of gaffer. When he has finished he closes the door. Silence.

Jim strips off his clothes and puts them into a plastic bag, which he will burn at some point. Then he goes to the bathroom and runs the hottest shower he can bear. He steps into it and begins to weep.

THIRTY-SEVEN

Franco looks down at the house through binoculars. He can't see anything to worry him – though, to be honest, he wouldn't until they decided to swoop down on him. They are professionals, and he is supported by – who? A policeman who cannot stop crying, an angry love-struck policewoman, a mother with some kind of death wish and a man who runs with ghosts. And Franco himself? He must be Timmy the dog. They are the Famous Five. He smiles, remembering reading stories about them to Pia. Pia.

He slides the tablet he bought that morning out from its packaging and fires it up. While it is booting-up, he takes the pay-as-you-go phone and sets a personal hotspot for the tablet. Then he logs into the house's security cameras, having set them up so he could operate them remotely from wherever he was. He never used it to spy – okay, that is a lie. When Pia was a teenager, he did check she was home from a party two or three times, but he never checked if she was with someone. He did pay her that much respect. Now he goes through all the cameras in the house. Hettie is home, working at the back and James is in his small office in the converted garage. Franco sees nothing else to worry him. Okay, time to pay them a visit.

He had chosen them to act as foster parents when he was just nineteen years old. He did a good job. They were a married couple who, at that time, had run a small recruitment company specialising in the catering trade. A year before Franco hired them the business had crashed and burned. They owed a lot of money to some pretty nasty people. Franco could clear that debt and keep them safe. They were ideal in one other respect too. Hettie had three stillborn births, and doctors advised her against trying again. They were desperate to be parents. They seemed the perfect couple to entrust his child to. He set them up with this house and paid them very well to raise Pia. Franco paid for all her schooling and sent the three of them on educational tours of Europe, starting when she was five years old. Franco lived vicariously through her.

There were rules too: Hettie and James were always to be clear they were foster parents and employed by Franco. They were never to be called Mum or Dad or even Uncle and Auntie, only Hettie and James. If they ever wanted to leave his employment then they had to give six months' notice and they could not contact Pia after that – not for anything. Within a few weeks he knew they were safe and would never leave. They loved her, almost as much as he did. They raised her well.

When she reached eighteen, Franco paid them off with a very large golden handshake and gifted them the house he is about to break into. Franco bought Pia her own apartment and her little bug car. It had seemed ideal. Seemed.

Franco deactivates the alarm and censors. At the gate he punches in a five-digit code that overrides the security protocols and opens all doors in the house, even the panic room. Then, on purpose, he triggers the silent alarm. Flashing lights will now go off in the corners of each room in the house. They are subtle: unless you are looking for them you can't see them but Hettie and James will know. They will make their way to the panic room and lock themselves in. The silent alarm sends an SOS directly to the police and a private security company – or it is meant to. Franco has disarmed that too. He watches on the tablet as they both see the alarm and panic; he thinks Hettie will have a seizure, she is crazy. They run to the panic room and seal themselves in. Good. Franco uncouples the phone and tablet and takes the battery and sim from the phone. He packs them into his bag and heads down to talk to the couple.

The text he had sent from the airport had been to the two of them, the text that had brought Gulliver crawling out of the woodwork. One of them, or both of them, has sold him out. It was the only thing that made sense of what had happened, using Pia to get to him. He feels the anger build, but he must keep control.

He pushes open the panic room door – that first instant tells him all he needs to know.

'Mr Light, sir. Come in and close the door quickly. The alarm has been triggered and the police—'

'It's okay, James, the alarm's false.'

'But the police, sir?'

'They are not on their way.'

Franco looks to Hettie. He saw the panic streak across her face the instant she saw him and there again when she heard that the police weren't on their way. He feels like he wants to die, it would have been so much easier if James had betrayed him. But Hettie. He feels the gun in his pocket. It will be easy to kill them, here in this panic room. He could just seal the door and leave their corpses to rot. In the garage there are cans of petrol. He could slop it around the house and torch it. He could not burn them alive but he could burn the house down with their bodies inside – he could, couldn't he? Shouldn't he?

'I don't understand, sir.' James's face twists, as if he is beginning to feel that something is terribly wrong. 'I thought your text said you were away.'

'Yes. Yes it did, but I'm not. It was a trick.'

'Trick?'

'Yes a trick. I am very sorry.' He looks past James to Hettie who has shrunk into the corner. 'How did you find out, Hettie?' Franco's eyes are like burning coals. Hettie whimpers and shrinks further back.

James steps between Franco and Hettie. 'Find out what, I don't—'

Franco places his hand on his shoulder and exerts a small amount of pressure – enough for James to know that Franco could drop him at a second's notice. 'This is between Hettie and me.' The man looks totally confused and turns to look at his wife.

'What's going on?' he asks her, but she says nothing – just looks at Franco, full of fear.

'She found out who I was. What I was,' Franco tells him, though his eyes remain fixed on Hettie.

'What you are, I don't understand. You work for the government.'

'No,' it is little more than a whisper from the woman. 'No, he doesn't.'

'She's right.'

James looks from Franco to his wife, and back again. 'Then what are you?' His voice is starting to get scared.

'Drugs,' Hettie spits out like poison. 'He sells drugs.'

James can't believe it. 'You're a drug dealer?'

'I'm sorry,' Franco tells the man and means it.

He looks back to Hettie. 'How did you find out?'

'A photo. One of the nannies in the park saw a photo from a club. It was of her boss and some tart at a club. His arms were all over her, but there was a mirror behind them and there you were.'

Franco nods. He would have guessed it would be something stupid like that – it's the fucking camera phone. It used to be that you could ban real cameras from the club – but these fucking phones. 'Then what?'

'She told me she saw you in the photo – she recognised you from when you used to pick up Pia. I told her she couldn't be right.'

'You didn't tell me,' James says in a quiet voice, lost in the middle.

'She brought me the photo the next day. There was no doubt.'

Franco can imagine the pain Hettie must have felt in discovering the truth after all these years, all the lies. 'Did you tell Pia?' He feels sick asking the question.

'No.' Some of the fear has washed away and Hettie stands up a little taller. 'I wouldn't do that, not to her. She loves you. You're her father.'

'But you told someone.' Anger bubbles into his voice.

'How do you live with yourself?' Her eyes flame with righteous anger. That is why he had chosen her to keep his Princess safe – she is a good person. She has faith and courage.

Hettie looks like she wants to spit on him. 'Drugs, corrupting children. Is that what this house was built on?'

Franco looks around at the house Pia grew up in. 'Yes,' he tells Hettie. 'This is the house that drugs built, like every penny I ever paid you. It was all filthy drugs money, blood money.'

'Jesus Christ.' Tears run down James's cheeks; he is totally overwhelmed by this. 'Mister Light, I'd—'

'Franco, my name is Franco.'

'Why, tell me why?' James yells. The sound fills the room, forcing all other sound out. The three of them stand in silence as *why* ricochets from wall to wall.

'Freedom,' Franco says, and it makes Hettie laugh.

'Freedom? You are joking.'

Franco drops his head. For a second he sees Lulama fall, twisting into the earth and then he feels Papi lift him into his arms. The sun is on him and the feel of the earth in his fingers as they sprinkle it onto her grave. The soil of his country, his home. 'Joking? I think I must be.' And he closes his eyes, shaking his head to suck back the tears and snot that threaten to rush out and drown him. He raises his head once again. 'Who did you tell, Hettie?'

She slowly pulls herself up, straightens her spine, all the while keeping eye contact. 'I called the police.'

'What?' Franco feels the air punched out of his chest.

'I called the police,' she repeats. Franco's head swims. 'I called New Scotland Yard. They took my details and an hour later a policeman came to call.'

'He interviewed you?'

'Yes. He brought a file on you, all about you. What you do and—' she can see the pictures again in her head, dead children – drug death. 'You are a monster.'

Franco does not respond, he just blinks as if a thousand flash-bulbs have gone off in his face. 'And yesterday, when I texted you, did you call him and tell him what the text said?'

'Yes.'

'What was his name?'

'He said he was a Detective Superintendent Bevans, Tom Bevans.'

Franco feels the world shift around him slightly. 'Can you please describe him?'

'I don't know, about fifty, not too tall, lean – kind of a hungry look, brown hair. A thin moustache, greying. He sounded a little like a Geordie maybe.'

Not Tom. The man was Nathan Dent. Ex-Detective Inspector Nathan Dent.

'He asked about how I knew you and—'

'You told him about Pia, you told him I had a daughter.'

'I—' she sees the horror and the anger and the sadness in his eyes.

'Pia?' the woman asks, feeling a dizziness begin to grip her.

'They came for me. They tried to get to me through her.'

'Pia?' The room spins.

'They found her.'

'PIA?' She starts to fall.

'They have her, Hettie, they have our little girl. You gave them to her, you wrapped her up with a fucking bow and handed her over. If you think I am a bad man, then you know nothing about the world. You have delivered her to hell.' She falls forwards and Franco catches her; he holds her and leans in to whisper. She struggles but he holds her tight. 'You did this, Hettie. Pia has been taken and another girl is dead. All because of you.' Hettie begins to shake. 'But we have one slim chance to get our Pia back. One possibility to see her smile again and hold her again. One chance!' He lets her go, and she whimpers and curls away from him into a ball. James kneels down to comfort her. Hettie's eyes are full of fear but they are latched on to Franco.

'What? What can I do?'

'I have one of the men – one of the leaders of the gang who took her. I want to offer them a trade, a life for a life. I need you to contact this policeman who called himself Bevans. You need to make an offer, to trade their man Gulliver for her – can you do that for me? Can you do that for Pia?'

Hettie nods.

Half an hour later she has spoken to Nathan Dent and there is a plan. Franco thanks Hettie for her help, then he takes the phone from her. He frisks them both to make sure they have no other phone, then he leaves them in the panic room. He should kill them. The old Franco would have done, betrayal warranted a death sentence. But she had held Pia as a baby, had changed her and cuddled her; laughed with her and loved her. Hettie and James love Pia every bit as much as he does himself. If he gets Pia back then he has twenty years of lies to heal, and she will need her other parents. He cannot deprive Pia of their love, not now.

He locks the panic room door and finds heavy oak furniture to build a barricade across the entrance. Inside they have tinned food and water for a month. He cuts all communication from the room and makes his way out of the house. In a few days he will alert the police and they can rescue them. Until then, he needs them to keep a low profile. He heads to the—

'DAD.'

He turns, there is nothing. He imagined it. 'Dad.' He hears the call again. Maybe it is a child on the street somewhere, its cry carrying all the way into the house. But it sounded like Pia.

THIRTY-EIGHT

The two women stand together. It is only a few days since Patty last saw Ellen Stokes but she feels as if something has changed. Possibly it is the setting, but it feels as if there is something deeper. The two women are walking along a shaded avenue; the trees are tall and elegant with a canopy of lush green leaves. Wild flowers have forced their way through cracks in the paving stones, which undulate as tree roots creep below them.

'She lives independently, has been there for two years. There are four young women in the block, all with problems. A warden lives on the ground floor if needed. The flat is small but nice, lots of light. Allison draws and paints. She's always been creative, artistic.' Patty nods but lets Ellen Stokes do all the talking. 'There's a common room on the ground floor, opposite the warden's flat. That's where Allison will be.'

'She knows I want to ask her about—'

'She knows.'

They carry on walking. From a street close by Patty hears an ice-cream van. Its jingle is happy and catchy – it's whippy time.

The two women reach a small red-brick block. Patty thinks: *municipal building*, straight away. Ellen Stokes pushes a buzzer and then leans over to say her name into a grille that has had two blobs of chewing gum forced into it and the word *EVIL* written in marker pen across it. There is a pause and then a buzzer sounds as the door clicks open. They go through and pull the door closed with a heavy *thunk*.

Patty follows Ellen Stokes through a short, dark entranceway and then into a hallway with two doors. Patty notices that she seems nervous now, and wonders if it is still a shock to see her own daughter. Ellen knocks lightly on the door. Without waiting for a reply, she opens it and leads Patty inside.

It reminds Patty of a hospital visiting room, the way the chairs are placed along the walls. In the centre of the room is a long table, but beyond the room is a lovely looking walled garden, almost a secret garden. Patty can see through an open doorway directly into it. Light streams into the room, mostly through net curtains, which throws a diffuse light onto the white walls. Only one person is in the room when they enter. She stands, backlit for a moment, so that it appears there is a halo around her head. Patty can see nothing more until she steps forward, eclipsing the sun and – Patty can't help but take a quick breath and bite on her lip. Even after all this time, the skin looks pasty and uneven, like a patchwork that almost matches but not quite. The stitches have long since dissolved but they have left their marks, like a join-the-dots-dot game of odd freckles.

'Allison, thank you for agreeing to talk to me.' Patty steps forward and holds out her hand. The girl drops her head. Patty reaches for her hand, taking it softly. 'I am so excited to see your art.'

Allison lifts her head, she really does have the most alert and wonderful eyes, Patty thinks. The girl curls her lip slightly. It is the closest she can get to a smile.

'Let's sit, maybe you could show me what you are working on.'

Allison attempts a smile again and picks a pencil off the table. She points at Patty, then at the sketch book.

'Do you want to draw me?'

She nods.

'I would be honoured.' Patty tells her and then sits down for her portrait. Ellen Stokes looks so pleased. 'I'll see about some tea.' And she leaves.

Thirty minutes later Allison puts down her pencil and turns the pad around to show Patty.

'I love that,' she tells the girl, genuinely impressed. Allison tears the paper from the pad and hands it to her. 'Thank you so much.'

'Allison had some pictures up at the library a few months ago – we were so pleased, weren't we darling?' she asks her daughter, though Allison ignores her.

'Could I see some of them?' Patty asks.

Allison nods and opens the pad. At the back there are a number of pieces in laminate pouches. She hands them over. Patty looks at the first one. It is good, she can see the talent there. The colours are so vibrant, especially the reds. 'I wanted to come and see you to talk about something else too,' she looks across the table, into the young woman's crystal blue eyes. 'The night it happened, do you remember it?'

There is a pause and then the girl drops her head. There is the slightest of nods.

'You were incredibly brave that night.' Patty turns the pictures over – there are some still lifes that are pretty good, and a lovely nude from a life drawing class. 'I hoped you could be brave again and talk to me about it, do you think you could?'

Again, there is the smallest nod of the head.

'The man who caused all of this. You heard his voice?' Nothing. 'You told a policeman named Tom that the man said *beautiful skin*, do you remember?'

Nothing.

'Allison, I would like to know if you saw him, saw his face. Did you see him?' Nothing. Patty has reached the end of the stack of pictures. In one pouch there are a number of charcoal sketches. She pulls them out, one makes her gasp. There is a man hanging by his neck. Patty looks up, she feels the blood drain from her face.

'B … b … b …' Allison's lips quiver. Ellen Stokes stiffens, watching as her daughter attempts to speak to someone else for the first time in years.

'Take it slowly, Allison,' Patty tells her.

'B … b … bew …'

Patty looks at the picture, the man being hanged. 'Is this him?'

'Bew … ti … f … f … f …' she tries, her lips drooling and shuddering.

Patty dives into her bag and pulls out a folder. She grabs a photo and drops it onto the table alongside the picture of the hanged man. It is of a man in a leather coat.

'Is this him?' She stabs her finger down on Gary Wilkes's face.

Allison screams and her mother throws her arms around her. Patty has him.

Patty is a runner, so she runs. There is a train in twenty minutes. She could have got the tube or a taxi, but that is no good for her, not what her body needs. She runs. She will make the fast train to Leeds and tonight there is a church service. She has a date with Preacher Gary and in the bag that swings on her hip, she has the can of mouse-melting mace.

THIRTY-NINE

Tom stands on the doorstep with his finger poised to ring the bell. He has a flashback to 2007. He rang this same doorbell then. That day he told a couple that their daughter was dead, that Sarah Penn was gone. He sees their faces again, from that day – the pain in them, the anger. He rings the bell and waits.

It swings open and— the breath is stolen from his lungs. Sarah Penn stands there. She looks just like she does in his dreams. His mouth opens, incredulous.

'You bastard,' she hisses as she swings her hand – it is half slap, half punch. It stings and sends him reeling back. 'You promised, you swore you would get him.'

'I … I am sorry,' he tells the ghost girl, who is already in floods of tears. Her mother appears behind her and puts her arm around the girl and leads her back inside. It is then he sees how the girl limps; one leg is twisted and withered. Emily – he remembers her now, it is Sarah's sister. Four years younger than the dead girl and now she looks so much like her. So much like Sarah looked when she died. Tom watches mother and daughter withdraw into the darkness of the house and after a while, he follows them in.

It feels like a dream. Emily scowls at him, her face shifting through anger to fear to grief to loss. She remembers him from the funeral, remembers him telling her mother he would find the man responsible. She believed him then, he had been so sincere and he looked so upset. He cried for Sarah. But it was a lie. Her sister rots in the earth and the man who put her there walks freely upon it. Her eyes burn him with shame. Tom feels as if a huge insect is wriggling in his chest. He doesn't want to stay here; he is starting to feel panicked. Her mother, Gabby, sees Tom's discomfort and Emily's anger. She doesn't really care about how Tom feels, but she does not want her daughter upset even more.

'Em, can you go and make us some tea – then how about you do your homework?' The woman smiles at her daughter, and ushers her out with a little sweeping motion. Emily sneers but does as her mother asks. Once the door closes the woman goes back to her chair and sits opposite Tom.

'She's a good girl. It's been hard.'

'I understand. I am sorry to bring this all up again. Your husband—'

'Gone. Two years ago, already got another baby, with a girl not much older than Emily.'

Tom feels the sadness pervade the room. He must not get caught up in it. He opens his case and pulls out a folder. From that he slides a photograph that was emailed to him from Brighton. He places it face down on his knee. 'I want to show you a photograph. To be honest, I really wish I didn't have to – it is all we have and—' He turns it over. It is obvious the girl is dead. 'Do you know this girl?'

Gabby Penn clearly doesn't want to look, but she forces herself – taking deep breaths as she wills her eyes to look at the photograph. 'Has he killed someone else?'

'We aren't sure.'

'I thought it was all over.'

'I'm sorry. Can you tell me if you've ever seen her before?'

She screws up her face and then takes a peek. He can see the relief pour across her face when she doesn't recognise the girl. 'No. Never seen her.'

'Okay. Thank you.'

'Is that it?'

He remembers Patty's question from a few days ago.

'Was Sarah ever active in church?'

'No.'

'Even a community club where they had bible stories or something?'

'No.' Gabby Penn shakes her head. Tom nods and a sigh escapes. It was a long shot. He closes his eyes, feeling so tired all of a sudden. At that point Emily walks back in with two cups of milky tea.

'That was you Ems, wasn't it?' she says to her youngest daughter. 'You did the church back then, for a while.'

The girl nods and hands the tea over to Tom.

Tom looks up at her. 'Can you tell me about it?'

The girl shrugs. 'It was a year or so after my accident.' She nods at her leg. 'It was good, helped a lot. They were kind. Not everyone is so kind.'

'Was it a regular church?' Tom asks.

'No, it was all a bit happy-clappy wasn't it, Ems?' her mother says.

Emily nods, a little embarrassed to be the centre of the conversation. 'I liked the singing, and the trips.'

'Trips?' Tom asks.

'They were free. We would go to other churches and stay there for a night or two.'

'Like a jamboree in the Guides,' Gabby Penn says helpfully.

'Sarah went with me sometimes. When I needed help, when my leg was bad,' Emily told him. He feels his breath turn to ice in his lungs.

'Did she take you on a trip shortly before she—' he pauses, 'before she died?'

Emily nods. 'About a month or so. It was in Somerset I think – Cheddar Gorge. We went in some caves and told scary stories.'

Tom opens his folder and takes out a series of pictures. 'Did you ever see any of these faces on that trip?' He holds his breath.

She looks at the pictures. 'Yes. Her, her and him. That one was seriously creepy.' She points to one of the pictures.

Oh Christ, Tom thinks.

FORTY

Franco stands before the grey shutter. It is covered in the ragged black tags of spray can illiteracy. In some parts of the country there is real street art: here – there is nothing but a dirty protest. He looks at the shutter edges. They are streaked with a smear of oil and a pattern of small cross-hatched nicks – that's good. He did that the last time he was here. If anyone had opened the shutter he would see the story in the oil, and walk away. But nobody has been inside apart from him. He has a small key that he uses to open a metal cover that slides to one side. Under that is a key-pad. He types in the code and waits a second before the machinery gears up and the shutter judders upwards. When it is halfway up, he bends down and slips under it, grabbing the shutter lip and pulling it down hard. The motor grates for a second, the cogs biting themselves, like a dog with fleas gnawing at its own tail, then the shutter slides down and Franco is in darkness. He fumbles in the dark for a second, before finding the camping lantern and flicking it on. It has a long-life bulb so it takes a good minute to warm up to anything approaching enough light to see by. He waits.

Once he can see again, he starts to open boxes – this is his life, Frank Light's life and Bheka's life. He did not bring much with him from Zimbabwe, apart from a small suitcase that held all his clothes – none of which had been warm enough for England. He had brought a few books – the books he had learned to read with: *The 1001 Arabian Nights,* he loved the stories of Sinbad the sailor the most. *Around the World in 80 Days* and a *Boys Book of Greek Myths.* Especially beloved were Jason and his Argonauts.

He only brought one other thing from Zimbabwe: a picture frame. Hand-carved with diamonds of dark and light wood, it was made by his father, a man he never met. It is the only thing he owns that his father had touched and crafted.

'Damn.' His hand goes up to his throat. He left his mother's St. Christopher pendant in that charnel house. A wave of anger and self-loathing washes over him. 'Stupid, stupid, stupid.' For a second he feels as if he will drown in all of this. 'Get a grip. Control yourself. Pia needs you. She needs her father strong,' he tells himself.

Suddenly Franco drops down onto his knees, something he has not done since— really, it is something Franco has never done. Bheka was the one who prayed. Now he falls down and tries to remember— but the words won't come. He has not said them since he and Papi buried Lulama. He misses his sister, and the man who came to be like a father.

'The Lord, he is my shepherd.' He hears her beautiful voice reach out to him and he repeats the words. 'He makes me lie down in green pastures,' brother and sister intone together. 'He leads me to the quiet waters where we drink.' He feels her hand on his head.

'Please forgive me, Lulama.'

I love you, my brother. It's all she needs to tell him.

*

Later, once he has completed the hymn and remembered the words to the Lord's Prayer, he opens the first of the boxes that are piled in the corner of the lock-up. In one he finds a newspaper from almost twenty years ago: on the front page Robert Mugabe grins out at him. Standing beside him is General Ndela and tucked behind them both, just sticking out, is Franco. Below the picture, the three of them are named, the newspaper has called him Franco Ndela. He had forgotten there was a time when he was like the old man's son. So long ago. Franco scratches his finger through Mugabe's head and tears him from the picture. Now it is just Papi and him.

In another box he finds all the financial documents he needs, everything he has squirreled away over the years for Pia. It is a good sum, it will give her a start in life if – if she still has a life. The thought makes his stomach twist, he must not think like that. He must have faith.

He opens the final box, though it is more of a crate. On top there is a sea of shredded paper. He leans over and pushes his arm into the box, parting the waves of newsprint, stretching down, down and down, until his fingers touch the cold metal of what he has been searching for.

'Yes, that will work.' He is pleased.

The light burns her eyes as the bag is pulled from her head. She drags oxygen into her lungs, fills them fit to bursting so her head spins a little; she is just so glad to be breathing in air that is not stale with sweat and dried vomit. She tries to open her eyes, to look around but she can't – they hurt too much. Through the semi-closed lids she can make out shadows, probably artificial light, so she can't tell if it is day or night. She isn't even sure what day it is. She aches all over, and she smells. She smells really bad. She would like to wash; just to feel human again for a few moments would be wonderful. That is all she wants, can't she have something so simple?

'There's water and food,' the voice tells her. It is the same man she has heard before – not the deep-voiced man but the nasal one. He sounds Northern, but the accent is weak, as if he has lived away from his roots for some time. She tries to open her eyes but they hurt too much, after all that time in the dark they cannot bear the light. Suddenly she is tugged forwards and—

'There.' He unties her hands. 'Eat,' he tells her.

She kneels down. She can smell the food. She reaches out her hand.

'Hope you like vindaloo,' Nathan Dent laughs.

Her fingers probe into something warm, she brings them up to her mouth and licks them. Her tongue burns from the depth of heat in the sauce, but she is too hungry not to eat it. She feels around but there is no knife and fork. She picks up a handful of rice and spicy meat sauce. She puts it into her mouth. Her tongue goes numb with the heat and she has to force it down her gullet. It burns, acrid and stodgy. She feels around for the water she was promised. She finds it and takes a large glug. It helps but as soon as it washes down her throat the acid of the chillies is back. But she has to eat, and so she forces mouthfuls down, trying not to chew but just swallow the food so she has some energy. Her eyes are running from the heat. When she thinks she has eaten the whole plate she drinks the water down in one long continuous draft, just hoping her stomach can keep the food down.

'Bravo.' Dent is full of admiration and he claps a little. 'I didn't think you'd be able to eat it. That was the strongest they do – I am impressed though, of course, I would have thought the daughter of Franco would cope with pretty much anything.'

'Who?' she calls out. At last there is some chink in the curtain, some reason in this madness. 'You have the wrong person. I don't know a Fran—'

'Frank Light, Franco. He's the same man. I have got to hand it to him, to get away with such a massive con for so long, very impressive.'

'My dad is the best—'

'Drug dealer and death merchant in London, maybe Britain – even Europe.' he chuckles.

'My dad—'

'You don't know him, darling.' The man sneers. 'I worked for your dad for years. Did all the shitty jobs he thought were beneath him. I paid bribes, greased wheels to sort out his problems. Traded in smack and shit and pussy and cock. Planned honey-traps, took incriminating pictures and I'd break people's legs if they didn't toe the line. So I know your dad, sweetheart – far better than you do.'

'My dad's a good man.'

'Your dad's a killer.' He laughs. 'You have no idea, do you?'

'He works for the government.'

'What? With Santa and the Easter Bunny, are you really that dumb?'

She feels sick, no idea if it is the food burning its way down her throat or the lies this man is pushing onto her. Her father is a good man.

'Anyway, in a few hours you'll be able to ask him yourself.'

'You're releasing me?' Her heart soars; she feels tears build like a storm cloud behind her eyes. 'I'll be free?'

Dent weighs up the potential endings for tonight's meeting. In reality he doesn't give her much chance of coming out of this alive. 'You're bait, darling. Whether you end up as cat meat or live to see another day depends on your dad.'

'You are making a huge mistake.'

'No, no I'm not. I think you were the mistake darling – the great Franco has an Achilles' heel – a secret daughter. You are the answer to a dream come true.'

'Franco,' she mutters to herself, under her breath. *Franco*.

FORTY-ONE

Jane approaches the room with trepidation. By her side is a nurse who is tiny, Thai or Filipino perhaps. Jane can't believe such a small woman could work in the NHS; she couldn't possibly have the strength to roll a patient over in bed, or deal with any trouble.

'Here,' the tiny nurse tells her and, with what looks like a little bow, she walks back to the nurse's station, leaving Jane at the door. The advice is usually – if you are nervous imagine the audience naked, except she doesn't need to imagine. She has seen Marcus Keyson naked, many times. They dated for a while, and it even got serious enough that he met her mother and, of course, he charmed her. He could charm anyone. But it all turned sour and after he was arrested she didn't want to see his face. He tried to talk to her but she cut him dead, and now she needs him. Ares needs him. She takes a deep breath and pushes inside.

That same breath is knocked from her lungs as she sees him. 'Oh, Marcus.' He is so thin, withered by inaction. She can still see the handsomeness in his face but it has been hollowed out and whittled to almost nothing. She moves to stand over him, leans forwards and presses her lips to his. He had been a great kisser, once. Now it is merely the lightest of touches. His lips are so dry, so she extends the tip of her tongue out and licks them, then with the slightest *pop* their lips separate. His eyes open and Jane thinks they swim with fear, but as they focus on her they seem to calm. He sees her, knows her … he blinks. Three times quickly.

'Hello Marcus.' It is little more than a whisper, for his ears only.

Blink-blink-blink.

She drags a chair over to him and sits by his side, taking one of his large hands in hers. 'I didn't realise you were …' she tails off. It is not true. She could have come before now. She is only here because she needs his help.

'Are you tired or can we talk?'

Blink-blink-blink.

'I came to ask you something.'

Blink-blink-blink.

She wonders if this is real. Is he actually communicating with her, or does he just blink in bursts – is three blinks just some synapse misfire?

'Blink four times if you remember Sarah Penn.'

Blink-blink-blink … blink.

'Do you remember she was killed? It was your last case with us?'

Nothing.

'Do you remember she was the third victim?'

Blink-blink-blink-blink. He closes his eyes. When he opens them again he looks even more tired than he did before. She should go, he is too fragile to be questioned like this. But there are the dead women.

'I need your help Marcus. There has been a fourth victim. A fourth beautiful skin murder.' He closes his eyes hard, then opens them in one angry blink, his eyes seeming darker.

'Can you …?' His left eye twitches, his lip is curling slightly at the edge. It looks like a mini seizure.

'Christ, okay maybe we should stop this.' His eye goes crazy. 'What, Marcus? I don't know what you need.' She can see he is trying to concentrate, to stop the fluctuation.

'Let's stop this I don—'

BLINK! With an enormous effort of will his twitch stops – but she can see the strain as his mouth tightens and she can see the veins stand out on his head.

'Okay, calm down, rest.' She takes a pen and pad from her bag. 'We have all the time in the world Marcus, no hurry,' she tells him in a sing-song voice, one she normally reserves for infants. 'I read your notes for those last days, you seemed to be onto something.'

Blink-blink-blink-blink.

'You told Tom you thought you were about to make a breakthrough – did you?'

Nothing.

'Marcus.' She sees something new in his eyes, something only there in these last few seconds – hate. Who would he hate? Tom? 'Marcus, this is nothing to do with Bevans. I run Ares now and I need your help.' His eyes soften. She can see there is some pretty bad blood between those two men. 'I am asking this question for me and those girls, for Heather and Tracy and Sarah. Did you discover something?'

Blink-blink-blink-blink.

'Could it solve the case?'

Blink-blink-blink-blink.

Anger spikes at her for a second. She lets go of his hand, it falls down and his whole body is tugged to the side – she sees the electrodes attached to his chest move a little as they are dragged. *Why did you keep evidence to yourself Marcus?* she thinks. But she knows that if she asks, he will not answer. She lifts his hand again and squeezes it.

'Marcus, I am going to go through the alphabet. Please blink when I hit the letter you need. Blink four times if you understand.'

Blink-blink-blink-blink.

Then she begins to slowly go through the alphabet, watching him blink. It is slow and they keep stopping when his eye twitches uncontrollably. After twenty minutes they have three words – and Marcus Keyson has turned grey with the strain.

Jane reads back the words: 'Not. Rape. Dad.'

The two of them sit in silence. Her thoughts swirl around the room, filling the air like the milky-way does the night sky, but nothing coalesces into an idea. It is all barren rock floating through space. She has no idea what this could mean.

'Marcus,' she whispers and his left eye opens. He begins to blink frantically.

20-15-13. He pauses, 4-9-4. Then he opens his right eye and Jane whimpers. It is filled with blood.

'Nurse! Help needed, nurse!' She tears the door open and yells down the corridor.

FORTY-TWO

Patty watches the man lay his palm on the woman's forehead. She screams and gibberish pours from her lips as the congregation gasps.

'Hear her speak in tongues,' a man calls loudly from the row behind and the room answers him.

'Praise be to God,' sixty men and women call, raising their hands up and spread to heaven – Patty almost laughs at their sincerity. She looks around the bare room, lit only by thick votive candles that give off a slight scent of burning souls. It is a pretty humble place, but she can feel a raw power in the room, though it seems centred more on desperation than any real spirituality.

The Preacher moves on to the next woman who is already on her knees, rocking back and forth with a stream of unintelligible babble erupting from her throat. He lays his hands on her and she swoons to the floor, and quickly two men spring to help and place a cushion under her head. Patty shakes her head sadly as she watches Gary Wilkes move the entire way down the line laying his *healing* hands on the congregation. *Mass hysteria*, she thinks. Perhaps this is why he finished killing after three victims – he found a new way to get what he wanted; these idiots are his new victims. Patty sits back, all alone in the last row of the small community centre on the edge of the wasteland. She wonders how these people are taken in by him. How could Heather Spall have grown to trust him – be made pregnant by him, and then let him kill her? Was it somewhere in this room, on the wooden floor before the pews? Did they run with her blood? Did he find out she was pregnant, that she would ruin his scam by revealing he was a hypocrite? Did he rape her and then take a hammer and – the blood. The blood.

'Please stand to sing "Joy to the Holy Dancers".'

Patty opens and closes her mouth for the next five minutes, no sound escaping as her lips merely saw at the air. It is a song she doesn't know and hopes never to hear again. She watches Gary Wilkes stand in the makeshift pulpit, his arms open and aloft, like a pound-shop Jesus. It makes her nauseous. She puts her hand into her coat pocket and feels the can of mace nestled inside. In her other pocket she feels the sheath of the knife. It is sharp, capable of killing a man; as is Patty tonight.

As the service comes to an end, the congregation flocks forward to shake him by the hand, touch any part of him or his clothes, and put money into the boxes that are carried around by the other members of the church. Patty melts back into the shadows and waits. She is hungry. She knows she should have called Tom or Jane as soon as Allison Stokes saw his picture, but they would have told her to wait for the police, and she can't. She wants this on her terms. She needs this to salve something deep that bites in her chest. She can't hide it and she doesn't want to fight it. The truth is that she wants to catch him and she wants to hurt him, to punish him for Heather, Tracy and Sarah.

And for me. A voice calls from twenty-two years underground. And for Dani.

*

It takes about thirty minutes for the room to clear, leaving only Gary Wilkes and two other church officials. Patty slides out into the night and waits on the corner between the road that links the community centre and the wasteland. In the distance she can see the headlights of cars weave around the turning and stop. Then the doors open as women get into their cars, or the men exit and walk to the line of women Patty knows are there. She feels useless. She can see what a vicious cycle is being perpetuated here but can do nothing about it – nothing. She slides the knife from its sheath. She loves to hear that little sound it makes, as the blade pulls out into the air and the metal sings, so glad to be free. It feels good to hold the knife. She feels strong, powerful. She waits for the Preacher to have completed his final rituals.

Gary Wilkes leaves the church with one other man. Patty follows them at a distance. A part of her had expected Wilkes to leave the church and walk over to the wasteland and the queue of women – but he walks the other way. She watches how he walks, swaggering, with his chin high like a peacock strutting; she hates him, he's a parasite. She follows the two men, hoping the other man will leave while Wilkes is still in these empty backstreets.

'Come on,' she whispers to herself, 'come on.' She keeps walking behind them, quiet as a mouse and always in the shadows. She is good at following, she would make a great stalker.

Suddenly the two men shake hands and part. *Good*, she thinks. She waits a few seconds and then follows the larger figure of Wilkes. She slides her hand into her pocket and retrieves the mace. Up ahead she sees the lights of a main road – damn, it is far closer than she had thought, he is almost safe.

'Help me,' she calls out and falls to the ground. Up ahead Wilkes stops and turns, unsure that he heard anything. 'Help me,' she cries in as pitiful a voice as she can.

'Where are you?' he shouts into the darkness.

'Here. I can't get up, can you give me a hand?'

He walks back to her; the night is so dark – so many of the streetlights have been shattered by vandals and not replaced by the cheapskate council. 'Where?' He calls before he sees her, an old lady who has fallen in the street. 'Do you need an ambulance?'

'No,' she cries and snaps up to her knees as he reaches her, his arm outstretched to pull her up – she extends her arm with the mace and squirts it. Instead of a billow of cloud it streaks out a single concentrated stream that almost misses him, just slicing into his cheek and below his eye.

'Ahhhh!' he cries out and staggers back. She jumps up. He can see that her finger is flexed on the trigger again and, as she sprays him once more, he spins around and pulls his leather coat up high, taking the brunt of the hit on the shoulder and collar; though he yelps again as fire whips across his neck. His cheek burns and he can feel his eye begin to swell, but he can still see through it. He needs to get away. He runs, back to the main road – he can hear the woman follow him, tears streaming down his cheek, he can't run straight, the pavement isn't flat – shit, he slips and falls. Half down onto his knee, he feels it jar and the joint immediately begins to tighten. He must get up and regain his speed. He needs to— 'Hell.' Mace spits at him again, like a snake striking; shooting venom. Most of it sails past his head but the edge of the mist scrapes at his forehead – burning him. He opens his mouth to call for help, but it's a woman, an old woman at that. He can't cry for help to be rescued from an old lady. He just needs to make it to the main street – there he will be safe, there he will—

Patty is faster than him and she is not in a panic, she is in control. As he jumps off the kerb she throws her handbag at his legs, and the straps curl around him like a bolas. Normally he would have just shrugged it off, but tonight is not a normal night – he is in pain and afraid, so the bag somehow tightens around his legs and—

'Noooo.' He falls. He can feel grit and gravel scraping at his face. He feels blood, metallic and sweet, slide through his mouth and ooze out onto his chin. Momentum takes him some way until he slides into a heap in the road. Patty is on him in a second. He rolls over, his face full of fear. She can see the blood and the tears and the snot that crusts him, like a feral child. She swings the can towards his face, expecting him to bring up his hands to try and protect himself.

'Please tell me why,' he says. 'How have I hurt you?'

'Not me. Heather. Heather Spall.'

'Heather,' he repeats, almost with a reverence and then he opens his arms and tips his head up to accept the cleansing fire of the mace.

Her finger is on the trigger, she can write her name in acid on his face, wipe that smug charm away forever. She can. 'You killed her.'

'Heather, no. I loved her. I wouldn't have hur—'

'What do you take me for?' she sneers at him. He is only going to lie to her. The only person to trust is Allison Stokes, and the fear in her eyes when she saw his photo. That is all Patty needs. She draws up the mace; she will fire the whole can into his face and wash it away like it is a righteous flood. Her finger tightens and—

'Arrrgh!' She is thrown sideways as something clubs into her shoulder, the can spills from her hand and hits the pavement, spinning there. Patty slides to her side, not hit hard enough to go reeling. She lunges towards the can but a boot kicks it away. Patty goes for the knife but arms snake around her and hold her tight. She struggles, but whoever holds her is much stronger than she is.

'Let her go, Kendra,' Wilkes tells someone behind Patty's head and the arms release her. A young, dark-skinned woman steps from behind, her eyes shooting daggers at Patty. Wilkes puts his hand on her shoulder and squeezes. 'I'm okay, thanks Kendra, why don't you go back to the church?'

'She tried to—'

'And I'm fine. Please go.'

Kendra leans her face into Patty's as a warning, and then she walks off angrily. Gary Wilkes bends down and picks up the mace can. Then he swings it around so it is pointing directly into Patty's face.

'You think I killed Heather?' he says calmly. Patty stiffens. She feels every atom in her body contract – she needs to run, but she is paralysed. He smiles, then turns the can around and hands it back to her. She takes the can, her hand shaking. She drops it, she tries to pick it up but she can't, her fingers won't quite do what she wants them to. She can feel a ripple building in her, so she fumbles in her bag and finds the roprinole. The maximum dose is two tablets every six hours – she takes five, all she has left. She swallows them down. Finally she turns to look at Gary Wilkes.

'I know you killed them.'

'What makes you think that?' He does not sound angry at all, just inquisitive.

'There was a witness, she identified you.' She expected something, a gasp or a thunderous look; thought he might run. But there is nothing.

'Heather and I met through the church.' His eyes mist over. Patty sees him fall through time as he remembers her. He is lost in his memory for a few seconds before he talks again. 'I was too old for her. I had never been interested in any of the young women at the church and some of them did pester. I could have had a number of them – sexually I mean, but I didn't. Then Heather came along and … she was different.' He looks into Patty's eyes, back in the present. 'I loved her, and she loved me. Her family hated me, of course they did, thought I had stolen away their little girl – but they stifled her and she was bored by her life and the role she was playing in their insular world.' His face creases with pain. 'She would have done something amazing. If she had lived.' He stops.

Patty thinks the pain in his eyes looks real, but it doesn't matter; remorse can't erase what he did. 'When she died I fell apart. They, the police, put me in the cells. I was petrified, because I had no faith, not a real faith. That was what I learned there in the cell, that my faith was nothing, frail and ephemeral like dew in the early morning.'

'Beautiful skin.' Patty sneers.

'I'm sorry?'

'You said it as you killed Tracy Mason.'

'I killed Tracy Mason.' It is not a question, though it isn't quite a statement either.

Patty tenses, feeling the pressure build between them, something needs to blow.

'Maybe I did.'

In her pocket she grips the knife – she could slice it into his throat, she could – she really could. 'I rolled over in that cell, like a hedgehog, and was deaf, dumb and blind. I should have screamed about innocence, not only mine but Heather's. Instead I just dropped out. The police and the newspapers painted a terrible picture of her, said she was a prostitute. I just let them, never said a word in her defence. They held me for days, hardly even bothered to ask me anything. They thought she was worthless and I was guilty. They didn't even try to look for anyone else. Finally they let me out on bail. I got bail because they thought all I'd done was kill a whore – not a *real* person. What they said made me feel sick, but I was just so happy to be out of there, I said nothing. I just kept my mouth closed and went to the church. They let me sleep there. It was my sanctuary.' He shakes his head. 'Then the next girl was killed. Suddenly it all changed and they finally accepted that Heather was a victim of something more, bigger than a prostitute killed by her boyfriend or a punter, that she was kind and sweet and good and—'

'Tracy Mason,' she almost spits at him.

'I don't know her.'

'It was Bonfire Night.'

He nods. 'Oh yes, the second girl. I am sorry I didn't remember her name. That was very disrespectful, I should know that. Remember, remember—'

'Her parents remember her.'

'I'm sure she left a hole in their hearts that is impossible to heal.'

'Even by the laying on of hands.' He does not rise to the bait. 'Where were you the night she died: 5th of November 2006?'

'I was at the church. I never left it after I got out on bail, didn't feel safe anywhere else.'

'That's no alibi. Your congregation would lie to save you.'

'I wasn't a preacher then, I was a mere penitent,' he sighs. 'But the police checked the film that night.'

'What do you mean?'

'A news crew were there, from the BBC, they filmed a report on anti-Guy Fawkes celebrations. The church built a *guy*, a straw man, but did not burn it. One of us washed its feet and anointed it with oil. I wasn't on the TV personally but they did catch me on camera. The police viewed all the tapes, you can check.'

Patty's head swims, she remembers the CID report, it just said *verified*, his alibi was verified, not that he was filmed there at the time. He must be lying, he must. She reaches into her pocket, her eyes hold his, and she pulls out her phone. She calls Jane. It rings but all she can hear is the blood thumping in her head.

'Patty, how did it go with Alli—'

'Gary Wilkes.' She cuts Jane dead. 'Heather Spall's boyfriend. He had an alibi for the night Tracy Mason was killed. The CID report just said it was verified. Can you see what it was, how tight it was, did they check it?' Her voice drops to nothing. 'Is it real?'

'Okay, let me bring that up.'

Patty can hear her fingers working on the keys. She looks deep into Gary Wilkes's eyes. They are calm. Patty doesn't need to hear what Jane is going to say – she knows what Wilkes said was true. Her head begins to swim as Jane's voice curls through the undertow.

'Tight as it gets, a film crew—'

The phone slips as she doubles over and vomits bile onto the street like a teenager after a vodka binge. It pours out of her; there is little food, it is mostly hate and rage and stomach acid. She falls to her knees with her stomach spasming until she is totally empty.

Gary Wilkes bends down and picks up the fallen phone. The face is shattered, a mosaic of splinters held in place by the metal frame. Behind the broken glass is a black and white photograph.

Strange to see monochrome on a phone, Wilkes thinks. It looks like it is from another era, another life. A dark-headed man, handsome, with big features and a large smile, with a teenager. She has the same raven hair as him but her face is elfin, sweet and shy. Her smile is far more guarded, almost as if it has been demanded of her and she resists. He runs his finger over the face, can feel the patina of broken glass, and the phone responds.

'It still works, that's good,' he tells her. She looks up to him, her face ashen and drool hanging from her lips. 'Here.' He hands her a tissue and she wipes her mouth.

'Thank you.' She can feel the corrosiveness of her breath; it is worse than the mace.

'Do you want to freshen up? We could go back to the church,' he asks. Patty looks away from him as the shame builds in her. *It isn't him*, but she was ready to burn his face away, even kill him. She would have done, if the girl hadn't stopped her. Will she never learn? Allison must have got it wrong or Patty had misinterpreted that look. Damn it, she had wanted so much to catch the killer, wanted so much to – to hurt him, that she hadn't done the background work. She hadn't double-checked the alibi, hadn't talked to Jane or Tom. A conflagration builds in her chest, a bonfire of her vanities.

'I could have killed you,' she murmurs, more to herself than the man with her. He deserves a real apology, but she feels too raw. 'I have to go.' She swings her bag over her shoulder and takes a step forward but her knee buckles like her legs are rubber bands.

'Let me help you.' He puts his arm around her shoulder but she flinches and cowers slightly. *Crazy*, she thinks, *it should be the other way around. He should be afraid of me.*

He moves away from her, just a step or two, and then slowly, like you would to a skittish animal, he offers her his arm. She takes it with trepidation. 'Please take me to the train station,' she asks him.

'Of course.' They walk, slowly, towards civilisation. With each step Patty feels the shame eating into her bones. As they pass under orange-red streetlamps, she can see how he limps and his right eye has almost swollen shut now. How will she tell Jim about this, how proud would this make Dani feel?

'I ... am sorry.' Her words come out sounding more like an accusation than an apology. She stops walking. 'That didn't sound right.' So hard to say sorry and mean it. Instead, she yawns, she could fall asleep there, right there in the street.

'No need to be sorry. You wanted to hurt me, but you stopped yourself. That was—' Patty dissolves into tears, falling forwards. Wilkes literally catches a waterfall of emotion as she tumbles, yelling and weeping into his arms. He does not catch much of what she says, it is all trapped within the heaving sobs. All he can make out is—

'—revenge.'

He holds her while she weeps. Finally she gets herself back under control.

'Thank you.'

'Blood does not redeem blood,' he tells her in the most sombre of voices.

'I do not seek redemption, only revenge.'

'For Heather?'

Patty does not answer for a while and then she makes a little plaintive sigh. 'Not Heather. Not Tracy, nor Sarah.'

'I don't understand.'

'That's because it's all crazy.'

'I am a good listener.' He smiles, it is warm and lazy.

'My daughter was killed. I wanted to make someone pay for that, but I failed.'

'So now you try to make people pay for other crimes, you're like Batman?'

'Christ, put like that you make me sound ...' she doesn't finish. He can fill in the blank. There is silence between them as slowly the shame and anger leaches away from Patty. Finally she is ready to walk again, and slowly they both move on, like veterans of a recent war – both injured in the line of duty.

After a while they reach the train station. There is one last train home. At the entranceway Patty stretches out her hand to his. He takes it in both of his hands, like it is a delicate butterfly he does not want to damage. He smiles and then, for a moment, his face clouds over.

'You said someone identified me. Said I killed the girl.'

Patty shakes her head. 'The poor child reacted to your photo, maybe it was the leather coat, maybe you look like someone else. Or maybe she has just been through too much. Allison Stokes has ha—'

'Allison!' he says with some shock.

'You know her?' Patty feels light-headed.

'She went to one of our churches in London. We met at a gathering. She was alone and so I talked to her. It was a huge mistake. She latched onto me, pestered me for months, she would call at all hours and even turned up at my flat once, totally out of the blue. She said she loved me.'

'When?' Patty breathes.

'Before I met Heather.'

FORTY-THREE

Eddie Matthews is the worst driver in the Metropolitan police, bar none. By the time they reach Ares, Jane is a nervous wreck. On the rollercoaster journey from the hospital she goes over what Marcus had blinked. Not … rape … Dad. She tries to forget the final two words he gave her – they are even more disturbing. Jane has decided to keep those compartmentalised – they are not to do with these killings, they are something else equally grave.

NOT. RAPE. DAD.

By the time Eddie slams the front wheels into the kerb for the final time, she knows what they mean.

'Run, Eddie,' she tells him as she hurtles up the main steps and into the building.

'Oh fuck,' Eddie pants as he trots gamely behind.

Jane races upstairs to the Ares operations hub and logs onto the HOLMES computer, which gives her access to all crime reports and all logged 999 calls going back to 1995. She cannot get access to medical records without a judge agreeing the request, and that could take days, but this should work, as long as an ambulance was called.

The blue-green glow of a monitor lights up Jane's face as she scrolls through reports.

'Tea?' Eddie asks and offers her a choice of a Toffee Crisp or a Lion Bar to go with it. Jane takes the Toffee Crisp.

It takes her about an hour of referencing and cross-referencing – but eventually she finds the reports.

'I've got it,' Jane tells Eddie and the two of them scroll through the notes. 'An ambulance was called at 6 p.m. 7th April 1996,' Jane reads.

'So how old would she have been then?'

'Eight, I think.' Jane quickly does the maths. 'Male in mid-thirties found dead at bottom of stairs, neck broken. Had been dead some hours. Call made by wife on return from work. Child found by body.'

'Allison Stokes,' Eddie reads over her shoulder. 'So her mother lied about how her husband died – she said he had a heart attack. Why lie?' he asks.

'Isn't it obvious?' Jane says, the hair on her head sticking up like the hackles on a dog.

'No.'

'The kid pushed him down the stairs.' Jane lets it settle between the two of them for a few seconds and then Eddie shivers. 'Bloody hell.'

'We need to see if anything is tagged from juvenile support,' Jane tells him and starts typing. It only takes a minute. 'Oh, Christ.'

'What did you find?' Eddie asks

'Allison Stokes half-blinded a kid, stuck a pencil in his eye – she had therapy for it but no charges were made.' She hits the desk in anger. 'Why did we never see this?'

'Keyson found it.'

'Dad.'

'And that bastard kept quiet – I can't believe he did that.'

'Some kind of revenge for Tom informing on him,' Jane says with disgust at the man she had once thought she might love.

'So NOT RAPE. What does that mean?'

'There was no semen on any of the victims, and their vaginas were heavily bruised. It wasn't rape, she used something on them, a sex toy or something. It wasn't sexual. It was to make us think it was a sex crime and not—'

'Not what?'

Jane sighs. She looks drained. 'I don't know. I don't understand her.'

Jane's mobile rings. From the ringtone she knows it's Tom. 'Tom, we think we know what happened. Allison Stokes killed her father … Tom … Tom can you hear me?'

From a long way off Jane hears a single word. 'Help.'

FORTY-FOUR

It is 9.40 p.m. It feels later, as if a century has passed in these last few days. Tom feels old and slow, far too slow. His head is a stew of half-digested information and there is a growing sense of dread that grips him as he makes his way across the city, getting closer and closer; with Emily Penn's words repeating and repeating through the cavernous recesses of his mind. 'Seriously creepy that one ...' over and over her words tumble and each time he feels more like a fool. Stupid Superintendent Sad Man.

The air is stilted, the day's heat still lazily washes through the streets – held in place by low, oppressive cloud. He knows it is warm, but he feels cold. Cold to his bones. He would love a coffee, a bitter espresso to warm him up, but nothing is open.

Finally he reaches the correct street and looks at the text on his phone to check the flat number. The phone's read-out tells him it is almost 10 p.m. He only has two hours before he should be with Franco. He hopes it is enough time to set his affairs in order, enough time to catch a killer and lay to rest three ghosts. That is all he wants.

He reaches a low red-brick block. He pushes a buzzer and waits.

'Yes,' a voice answers, someone he does not know.

'Police, please open up.'

There is a click as the main door judders and opens a crack. He takes the handle and pulls. Inside is dark. Then from one side there is a slice of bright light as a door opens.

'Is there any trouble, officer?' a middle-aged woman asks. She pokes her head around the door and Tom can see she is a little scared but intrigued.

'Please go back inside. There is nothing to worry about. There may be another officer here in a short while. Please let them in and tell them I have gone to see Allison Stokes.'

'She isn't in her room,' the woman tells him. 'She and her mother are in the lounge. It's at the back – through the corridor. Do you need me to show you the way?'

'No, thank you.' He smiles tightly. They are both here, good – he thought Allison might have run. Almost the end now.

As she closes her door, the passageway is thrown into total darkness. Tom has to edge forward, his fingertips on the wall, as he moves slowly ahead. He reaches the end and there are two glass doors. He opens one, which leads into a large dining room. There is no electric light, but a silvery moonlight does penetrate through the sheer of net curtain to create shapes and shadows. He scrabbles on the wall and finds the light switch. He flicks it and ta-da – two women are illuminated. Ellen Stokes stands by the table, her face drawn and heavy. Tom can see how her jaw clenches. Sitting at the table, with her back towards him, is the girl. Between them both sits a hammer, the murder weapon. It looks so innocuous, just a tool that can be used as easily for good as it can be used to cause pain. It is all Tom needs to close the case, to give Heather, Tracy and Sarah what he promised them. Peace.

'Allison.' It is almost a whisper, as if he is calling to a lover. She swings her head around to face him and there is a jolt of memory: the girl's eyes open as she slides, in a river of blood, from the kiln. The purity and depth of the blue against the mash of her skin seared into his brain. He has seen her in his dreams so many times, but tonight he does not know what to expect. A monster or an angel? In fact, after all this time, she just looks human. He can see tears stream down her face. On seeing him her mouth twists up to an approximation of a smile. She jumps up and runs to him, her arms open.

'Allison, stay here,' her mother barks, but the daughter runs and throws her arms around Tom, her saviour all those years ago. He looks into her eyes and then over to her mother – who seems to snarl at him.

'B ... b ... b ...' Allison is trying to say something. Tom dips his head to catch her words. 'B ... b ... bastard.' And she stabs the syringe into his heart.

'ALLISON!' Ellen Stokes screams, but the whirlwind in Tom's head steals her words away.

Allison grunts as the needle slides and buckles on his stab vest. She pushes at the plunger with all her might but cannot pierce his skin. Her fingernails sink deep in his arm. Tom pushes his hand into her shoulder and he tries to force her back but she holds on tight – like a spurned lover desperately clinging on. She is incredibly wiry and slips and slides like an eel. With an almighty effort he slams her off him, just for a second, and the syringe slides and spins from her fingers and falls to the floor.

'Bastard!' she spits, her voice grates with lack of use, her face bestial, inhuman. She leaps back at him, is all over him as she claws at his face, wanting to rip his eyes from his head, but she cannot get her arms tight around him now, he has the leverage to push her off. They spin like dancers on the spot – a whirl, her thumb digs into his cheek. Her fingernail is poised above his eye, ready to strike. He stamps hard with his boots on her toes, grinds them. She yelps, pain and anger – there is a momentary release and he slams her shoulder back with all his force. She topples back a step and ... something on the table, she grabs at it and then lurches at him, swinging the claw hammer. 'Agh,' he yells as it hits his cheek, a tooth cracks and a cheekbone snaps. Her eyes are fire. He has totally underestimated her – idiot. She swings again and the hammer catches the side of his head – red, he sees red and feels the vision on his left side crumble away. He falls back, his legs hit a chair and he topples, in slow motion. He remembers bible class, his mum used to make him go, she thought that he needed something to offset all the boozing and swearing in the house. He had hated it. When they did the story of David and Goliath he was sent out because he wouldn't stop saying how crazy it was. David would never win – never kill Goliath.

He hits the floor hard; the breath is knocked from him. He looks up at her, she looks like she's about twelve; a tiny frame but she lifts the hammer over her head and – his arm is caught up in the chair. His chest is fluttering. He is pushing himself up but it feels like he's moving through treacle. She is going to cave his skull into his brain any second. He doesn't see his life flash before him, he just sees one face. 'Goodbye Dani.'

'Bastard,' Allison screams with such hatred. She bares her teeth like a wild animal about to savour the kill and— then her eyes flare and she spits all over him; bubbles of phlegm surge through her teeth and spread as drool pours down her chin. Her head lolls to one side and she topples forward onto Tom, the hammer falling from her fingers like a leaf blown from a tree. He puts his hands up and she hits them and rolls, half onto him and half to one side. Tom sees that the syringe she had tried to stab him with is embedded in her neck, the plunger has been pushed all the way in. Tom looks up to see Ellen Stokes standing where, a moment before, Allison had stood, and she is shaking.

'Is she dead, she isn't dead, I don't want her dead? She's my baby, I can't … is she …?'

'Please call an ambulance,' Tom asks. His legs are shaking too much for him to get up. He thought he was going to die.

'Lucky boy.' He hears a voice, like a whisper though the long grass, touch his soul as it passes and is gone. He lies there a moment, listening to Ellen Stokes as she talks to a 999 operator and asks for an ambulance and police. Allison's head is on his shoulder. He can see her skin, so pale – it looks as if it died long ago, as if she has been stitched together from cadavers. He can hear his phone ringing in his pocket, but the girl's body on him makes it very difficult to access it. With two fingers he manages to pull it out and swipe the call open.

'Help,' he says in a pathetic voice, even though help is already on its way.

FORTY-FIVE

'Honestly, no one has ever complained before,' Eddie whines as he is forced to ride shotgun.

'I can't believe that's true, Eddie – you are without doubt the worst driver I have ever—' Jane trails off as she concentrates on burning rubber all the way to Allison Stokes's flat. She uses the siren sparingly, at junctions and broken sight lines, but the speedometer barely dips below 120 mph for the entire journey, which is nine minutes. Nine minutes, during which Jane feels like she is in freefall, her heart lodged somewhere high in her throat.

As they draw closer to the assisted living block, they can hear sirens. Jane slows to make the final corner and they turn into the road. Ahead there are police cars and an ambulance. Jane bites her lip. The car has barely stopped before she is out and running, her warrant card in her hand. A perimeter has been laid. Tom was so terse, he just gave her the address and said to get there. He sounded hurt. Ahead, she sees a PC, his arm already swinging out to stop her.

'DI Thorsen, Operation Ares.' She waves the warrant card, doesn't even slow but shimmies past the PC with a perfect dummy. His 'Oi' isn't heard. She hits the front step, she should sign in, should wait for gloves, foot protection, maybe a mask – she doesn't. She bounds inside.

'This is a crime scene,' someone calls out but it's just blah, blah, blah in her head. She stops in the lounge doorway and takes a breath before stepping inside. There is blood spray over the sofa and carpet – too little to be arterial, probably from a heavy blow. Impact spray – just like Sarah, Tracy and Heather. She feels her body start to shake. Shock.

A body position is marked out, white tape outlines a victim fallen, but the tape is empty. Injured, not dead. A hypodermic lies on the carpet marked and tagged and – there is a hammer. A claw hammer, and its end is bloody. There are hairs on it. The hairs are white. She sees him dead, laid out on the slab with an ankle band that reads *The Saddest Man in the world*. Where? There is a hand on her arm.

'This is a crime scene.' The PC has followed her inside.

She lifts her warrant card. 'DI Thorsen, Operation Ares. We have—'

'Are you wanting Detective Superintendent Bevans?' he asks.

She can feel all professional conduct start to fall away. 'Please,' is all she can say.

'The warder's flat, it's back through the passage and on the right,' he says with a wave.

She nods and walks back the way she had come. She smells coffee and follows her nose. The front door has been wedged open with a paperback copy of *How to Win Friends and Influence People*. She walks through and finds a small kitchen. At the table Tom sits, his hands cradled around a mug that steams. A blanket has been wrapped around him, grey police issue. She stops there, in the doorway. In part she feels like a mother who has been desperately worried about their child, but as soon as she sees they are safe, all that desperation bleeds away. But the other part, the part that is a woman, feels a desperate twist in her guts. Jane Thorsen doesn't like that second part.

There is another figure at the table, also wrapped in a police blanket, but that person's back is to Jane. Tom sees his DI in the doorway and, for a second, smiles at her, then he turns his attention back to the other person at the table. He nods slowly and kindly, his eyes crinkling – empathy washing off him in waves. Jane had almost forgotten how the Sad Man could make you feel: safe and no longer alone in grief.

Jane slowly walks around the table, keeping to the wall so as not to spook the other person. It is Ellen Stokes.

'Ellen,' he asks her, 'would you mind if Jane came and sat with us?'

The mother looks up. Her eyes seem unfocused for a moment and then they sharpen. 'I remember you,' she says. Jane nods and slides to the table. 'You helped Allison from—'

'We both did, Tom and I helped her together.'

'We were just talking about Allison,' Tom says, his voice soft and level.

'Where is—'

'The hospital,' Tom cuts in. 'She will be fine.'

'I didn't want to hurt her,' Ellen Stokes's head is bowed as she talks to the air. 'I just wanted to stop her hurting another person, I just couldn't …' her head snaps up. Her eyes are puffy and red. 'I couldn't let her do it again.'

Tom stretches his fingers out and squeezes the mother's hand. 'And you saved my life. I thank you for that.' Jane tips her head to his, her eyes widen – *tell me*, they say. He shakes his head, almost imperceptibly, *now is not the time*. He smiles at Ellen Stokes. 'Have you ever seen your daughter commit acts of violence before?'

'It depends what you mean.' She shudders. 'As a child she would catch insects and tear them apart bit by bit – but most kids do that, don't they?'

'I think lots do,' Jane tells her, hearing the guilt in the woman's voice.

'We had a bird fly into the glass doors once, it was hurt, I didn't know how badly. I was going to take it to the vet but Allison – she stamped on its head. "Putting it out of its misery" she said, but she did it so quickly. And afterwards, she kept it in her bedroom.'

'It's hardly—' Tom begins.

'She killed my—' The voice is so pitiable that Tom is unsure what she said.

'What did you say Ellen?' he asks in a low, velvety voice.

'She killed my husband, her father.'

Jane feels her breath catch in her throat. She had been right.

'I don't understand. I thought your husband died of natural causes, a heart attack I thought.'

'I came home and found him at the bottom of the stairs, his neck …' the memory makes her shake. 'We told the neighbours it was a heart attack. We moved soon after. I found him, that day, and Allison was sitting there on the carpet right next to him. She was only eight years old. She said it was an accident. She said she heard him yell and found him like that but—'

'You didn't believe her.'

'She didn't grieve. The doctors said it was shock but I saw her smile. She dressed in black for a whole year but it was because she liked it, liked the attention.' Ellen Stokes pauses, looking between the two police officers. 'I tried not to think about my fears, tried to move forward, even though I missed him so much.'

She pauses, they can both see the pain that radiates through her. 'When she was ten she pushed a pencil into another child's eye – ruptured the eyeball.' She drops her head and breathes deeply, trying not to hyperventilate.

'Take your time, Ellen,' Tom tells her.

'It was on purpose, kids saw it. She had threatened to do it first. She was expelled and we moved away – again. I asked her about it and she told me the girl was a bully and deserved it, she had made Allison angry and she fought back.' Tom stretches his hand to her arm and squeezes. 'I asked her about Dave, her dad. I asked if she had been angry with him too and she said she pushed him.' Ellen Stokes shakes, trying to keep the tears at bay just long enough to tell Tom her story. 'She said she pushed him because he touched her, she said he touched her in the bath. But he wouldn't, he couldn't, he was a good man and she took him away from me, she made me live all alone.' Tears and snot and despair flood out of the woman, a whole world of bottled-up grief. Tom is up and around the table in a heartbeat. He scoops the woman up and hugs her, she melts into him and turns to slime and sobs. Jane can only pat at her back awkwardly, like you would to a favourite dog; she has no idea how to deal with such extreme emotion.

'He was a good man. He was my man,' she wails into his chest as he holds her.

'It's okay, Ellen. It's okay.' He rocks her, as you would a child trying to get them off to sleep after a bad dream.

'It was always bad after that, between us. I hated her. I hated my own daughter.' She looks up into Tom's face. 'Isn't that awful, to hate your child?'

'But you didn't. You kept her safe – that is what a loving mother does.'

The sobs grow, the chest heaves even more and she clings tighter, deeper to Tom.

'I was almost glad when she got hurt. She needed me to look after her again, to tend her skin and take her to the hospital. All those skin grafts and injections, I felt needed. I didn't think for a second that – oh God, those poor girls.' She snorts back her tears and breaks Tom's embrace. Jane hands over a packet of tissues and she goes through half the pack before she can speak again.

'When did you begin to realise she had been involved with the girls' deaths?'

'After the third girl. I'm sorry, could I have a glass of water?' Jane stands and goes to the sink. There are some rinsed glasses there and she fills one from the tap. She sees how her hands are shaking, making the water pretty choppy and stormy.

'There you go.' She hands Ellen the glass and sits back down.

'After the third girl was found, you made an appointment to see her. She was back from the hospital then and I agreed to you seeing her. When I told Allison you had called she blew up, was in a real state, foul moods. But I still didn't believe that she was capable of—' she takes a sip of the water, more to calm herself than anything else. 'The day before you were due to come we had a call and the interview was cancelled. We never heard from you again. A few weeks later I said we should call and she exploded at me, told me to just leave it alone and not stir it up. I thought it was just the terrible memory of that night but I couldn't help thinking about her moods. And the fact that nothing happened while she was in the hospital. Three months and then when she gets home there was another death. I couldn't swear to the fact that she was home that night. She had gone to bed early and locked her door. I fell asleep on the sofa – something I never did before. I wondered if—'

'You think she might have drugged you?' A single tear slides down Ellen Stokes's cheek as she nods.

'I would wake up in the middle of the night thinking about it and I was so scared, scared of my own—' She lets the thought die and is silent for a while. 'After about a year she was on the mend, she didn't need to worry about dust on the skin grafts and, well, she could go out again. I thought she might like to go back to the church – she had liked it, but she laughed and said: *not back to those bitches*.'

'She was talking?' Jane asks.

'Only to me. Only in private. In public she was mute. She got a kick out of it.'

Tom nods. 'She had gone on a church trip hadn't she, to Somerset, sometime in the late summer of 2006?'

'Yes,' Ellen replies, but is a bit puzzled. 'There was a boy – well, a man really. He was much too old for her, but she liked him, Gary ... Gary Wilkes.'

Tom nods again. He has spoken to Patty in the last hour and knows all about Preacher Wilkes.

'She had met him once or twice before on trips. He was kind to her. I don't think many grown-ups were ever that kind to Allison – she was hard work. And, of course, she became a little obsessed with him. She wrote to him every week, letters and cards and sent him poetry. She was so excited about going to Somerset, I think she thought they would be a couple, but something happened. When she came back her mood was dark.'

'He had a girlfriend with him in Somerset, Heather Spall. Actually she was the same age as Allison and physically similar.'

The mother nods her head sadly. 'That would have hurt her deeply,' she says with a sigh.

'Their relationship was probably a secret, but it might have been that Allison pestered him until he told her about his girl-friend to get rid of him,' Jane says.

'No, I think it was something else,' Tom tells them. 'Emily Penn told me a few things about that night. Sarah had gone there to look after her sister and one night when most of the visitors were at prayer, she played a truth game with a few others who were playing hooky from the service. Sarah told her later that a girl had told lies about one of the preachers being her boyfriend. There had been a big argument and threats were made.'

'You think Heather was there and called Allison on her stories?' Jane asks.

Tom nods. 'I think Heather and Sarah were both there and they probably laughed at her and for that—' he stops, aware that Ellen has become incredibly quiet.

'I think that is probably right,' the woman says in a voice little above a whisper. She drops her head.

'And Tracy Mason?'

Ellen Stokes sighs. 'She was the perfect girl, everyone loved Tracy. She was clever and pretty and kind and … and my daughter was jealous. I think she had always hated her, since they were five years old.'

'Do you think that her success killing Heather made her want to try ag—'

'I don't know.' She folds forward and sobs.

Tom puts his hand on her arm. 'I am sorry. We can end this now and talk some more tomorrow or the day after. You should go to be at Allison's bedside when she awakes.'

'Thank you.'

'Do you want an officer to go with you to the hospital?'

'Please.'

Tom stands and walks back into the main body of the building. Jane turns to the mother.

'What happened here tonight?'

'My daughter tried to kill him. I stopped her. I am praying she is alright.' Jane's brow furrows. 'I didn't want to hurt my own daughter, I just needed to stop her. She needs help.'

Jane nods, then leaves the woman, and walks back out of the kitchen. She stands in the hallway as the PC who spoke to her earlier walks past and into the kitchen to take Ellen Stokes to her daughter. Tom strides over, still wrapped in the blanket. Jane sees the other side of his head for the first time. A large wad of cotton dressing is taped there, and above it his hair is matted with blood.

'Tom.' She stretches her fingers out to touch his head but he pats her hand away.

'I want you to stop here and take over.'

'You need to get your head looked at.'

'Allison Stokes killed Heather Spall, Tracy Mason and Sarah Penn. But she had no part in the death in Brighton.'

'I don't—'

'I need to see Franco. Gulliver knows what happened with the fourth girl. This is all a game someone is playing and I need to know what is going on,' Tom says.

'I'll come with you.'

'No, I need you with Allison Stokes. Question the girl as soon as she wakes. I do not want her wriggling out from under this. Get her nailed for all three.' He holds eye contact, sees how fierce they are for a moment, then they soften.

'Okay, guv,' she nods, looking as if she has lost something dear to her.

'Smile, Jane, we broke the case. We should be happy.' It is true, yet neither of them can scrape up a smile. 'We solved three murders. Yah for us.' He looks into her eyes and can see there is no joy there, only concern. He would like to lean forwards and kiss her. Deep down he thinks this will be the last time he sees her – he believes he is following Franco into the underworld and he won't come back. But he still can't kiss her. Coward! Instead, he turns and walks away.

Jane watches him as he leaves. There is something she has not told him, that Marcus Keyson had a massive internal haem-orrhage tonight. He isn't expected to live for more than a day. She didn't tell him because of the final two words Marcus had communicated to her: 20-15-13 and 4-9-4. TOM DID ... she thinks he was trying to tell her TOM DID THIS TO ME.

'*Did you, did you, Tom?*' she asks his retreating figure as he disappears from sight. Jane Thorsen wishes she knew.

FORTY-SIX

10 p.m. Franco has sat in Greenwich Park for the last few hours. If he has been followed from Hettie and James's house then he does not want to lead anyone to Patty and Jim's place, or to Gulliver. Only two hours until— he is ready to die. There will be only one regret: Pia. That he will miss so much of her life – has already missed so much. He has spent most of the last few hours remembering the highlights of his life. They all feature Pia. Going to the zoo, a birthday party, trip to Chessington World of Adventures, seeing a penguin for the first time ... and her hugs. Every single one is etched into his heart. He wasn't at her birth – that is where the regret starts. He didn't see her until she was two days old. Christ, what kind of father is he?

'Pull yourself together,' he tells himself. There is only one way to be a father tonight, and this is the most important fatherly act of his life. He must save her – at all costs. That is all he can do to show how deep his love for her is. No words. Action. He stands, he is ready.

Franco sees the chair pitched over and for a moment fears the worst, until he sees the man is still tied into it, though now the gaffer tape cocoons him like a fly in a spider's web. He strides in and grips the back of the chair, he lifts it off the floor and slams it back into position. He pulls the hood from the man. His mouth looks like a swarm of bees have stung it over and over. Gulliver says nothing, but his eyes blaze a dark and primitive anger. Franco leaves the room for a moment and returns with a smaller chair from the office. For a few minutes the two men sit in silence.

Franco remembers the first time his foot touched British soil. It made him want to cry, and to head back home that second. Touching the soil of another land felt wrong – his essence seemed to drain from him into the ground. At home, every step made him strong; that was what Papi had taught him. They fought for their land, for every grain of dirt. It was Zimbabwe, he was Zimbabwe. They fought the British and then they fought themselves – brother against brother, but always for the best of the land, for the long term future of their country. Zimbabwe needed to rise out of the mire and thrive. That was what Papi told him, and that was what Robert Mugabe promised them, not just freedom but prosperity for all. For all of Zimbabwe.

'Please.' Mugabe had asked him, and what could Franco say? The man was a hero, a patriot; he would be the saviour of his people. 'I know my friend, General Ndela, thinks of you as his own son,' Mugabe tells him and Franco turns to Papi and feels pride swell within him. 'But I must tell you that I feel as if you are my son too, my son and the son of Zimbabwe. Your generation will learn what it is to be free, thanks to men like you who will create the opportunities for us to win.' The great man had told him that, and Franco felt as if the future of his land rested on his shoulders. His land. A month later he left it. He has never returned.

*

'I imagine you're from Surbiton or some shit suburban hell-hole,' Franco says to Gulliver, his voice soft, keeping his anger in check. 'You were probably the only black kid in the class so you grew up with a big fucking chip on your shoulder.'

Gulliver remains silent.

'I imagine your dad's a professional. Maybe a surgeon in the old country but has to be a lowly GP here, and your mum – maybe his secretary. They never get into the golf club or the rotary, no matter what they try. No matter how hard he plays the choc-ice—'

'Fuck you.' Gulliver's voice is low and rumbles.

Franco smiles. 'So you have someone you care for, at least.'

Gulliver laughs. 'They're dead. You cannot get to me through them.'

'Who sent you to me?' Gulliver is silent. 'Who planned this – not just you and Nathan Dent.' Franco sees him wince. 'I know all about Dent's involvement.' He smiles. 'Were you to be the new lord of the Dark Wolves?'

Gulliver shakes his head sadly, like he's listening to a madman.

'Do you know what it takes to lead men?'

'Please – you are no leader. You are weak and spineless. Maybe someday long ago you were big and bad but that is the past, now you are a washed-up old fuck. You are done, have been since the day I arrived, you just didn't know it.'

'You could have asked nicely. Pretty please and I might have gone.'

'There ain't no *gone*. You get retired, you don't choose to retire.'

'You get killed.'

'I know you did it. Uncle Joe.'

'I did. I cut his throat and drank his blood. Was that the plan with me?'

'Too fucking right, you were meant to be trussed up like a sacrificial lamb that night. We were gonna film it and show it to everyone. Show what happens when a new leader is chosen.'

'Were you the one who was going to drink my blood?'

Gulliver just smiles.

'But I went and slipped out of the trap.'

'Lucky for you, but not for that pretty daughter of yours. I am looking forward to tasting that piece of sweetmeat.'

Franco burns with anger for this man, all he wants to do is pull him apart with his bare hands, but he cannot. Maybe if he's lucky he will get the chance later, if he isn't dead himself. 'Well I don't think that will happen. I've made an arrangement with Dent. I am trading your sorry fucking hide for my daughter.'

Gulliver laughs. 'You are crazy – do you think you have any chance of getting out of this alive?'

'Honestly, I don't. All I want is a chance to get my daughter out. I have no plans to survive. But before I go, I will make sure you are already on your way to hell. We leave in a few minutes – make peace with your God.'

'It is you who needs to be thinking about God.'

'I am,' Franco tells him with a smile, then he rips a long strip of gaffer tape from the roll and covers Gulliver's mouth nice and tight.

Downstairs Tom waits for Franco. His body hurts. He has washed away the dried blood from his temple but the cracked tooth needs attention. He will call his dentist in the morning, if he's still alive. If. He looks around the living room. Jim is asleep in a chair, Patty sits at the table; she has only been back about an hour from Leeds. He has filled her in on what happened with

Allison Stokes, and she nodded but said nothing. She is very pale. Not for the first time Tom thinks she looks ill, really ill – cancer ill, death ill.

'Coffee?' he asks her. She shakes her head and then they hear the sound of Franco coming down the stairs. He comes in and, despite his size, Tom thinks he looks shrunken, deflated. Before he can open his mouth Patty interrupts him.

'Franco, can I ask you something – in private.' She looks a little desperate, Tom thinks. Something has happened to her, something in Leeds. If he lives, he will ask her, but not now. Franco nods to her and the two of them walk into the hallway for a moment. Tom watches them go, he is intrigued but too tired to do much of anything. After a minute, Franco returns.

'It's time.' He pulls a gun from his belt and hands it to Tom. It is the one he had Eddie steal for him just a few days ago. Christ, that feels like a million years ago. 'I need you to cover him while I cut him free and get him ready for travel. Do you understand?'

'Of course.'

Tom and Franco walk upstairs to prepare Gulliver.

Patty comes back to the lounge, in her house – the house she bought with her husband and young daughter almost forty years ago. It holds so many memories and yet she is cold to it. Cold to the bone and nothing warms her. That is why she had to see Franco. She has asked him for a favour and he has given her a phone number. She has made a phone call and set something in motion, something that could give her some peace, warm her finally. The house seems so quiet. She looks across at the man she married forty-five years ago. The man she loves, the man who sees their dead daughter. Maybe that isn't so crazy after all, maybe she can forgive him that – forgive him his loneliness. She moves over to the sofa. She shakes his shoulder.

'Wha—?' he asks through the fug of sleep.

'Come upstairs, to bed.'

'What time is it?' he asks.

'Late. It's much too late,' she says and she leans down and kisses him.

'That's nice.'

'I don't want to be without you.'

'Nor me.'

'Let's go upstairs.'

Jim swings his aching legs from the sofa and they go upstairs and undress. Their bodies bulge in places they never did before, but nothing like that matters. They make love. They cannot tell where one begins and the other ends. At some point they fall asleep, melded together with love and sweat and tears and joy.

FORTY-SEVEN

'You are joking?'

Franco shakes his head. Tom had not thought the multiple killer beside him had much of a sense of humour before this, but he realises that he does have a macabre gallows humour.

'The school?'

Franco nods, staring straight ahead through the windscreen. 'It feels appropriate.'

Tom shrugs. He can see a kind of symmetry, to meet Dent and trade Gulliver for Pia at the school where they found Tracy Mason's body and pulled Allison Stokes from a kiln.

'But it's a school.'

'Makes it perfect, public but private too. At this time of night it will be deserted but if an alarm is raised the police will respond quickly, and as you told me before, there are lots of hiding places.'

'It's like a rabbit warren.'

'We might need that.' he pauses, 'Tom, have you seen *Butch Cassidy and the Sundance Kid*?'

'Where the two heroes are cut down by about a million Mexican guns at the end?'

Franco laughs, 'If you think we're the heroes then you are fucked up, my friend. You might be a hero in some parallel universe, but not me.' Tom opens his mouth to argue – but shuts it again. Franco is kind of right.

'But that isn't why I thought of it. Tonight might go down like Butch and Sundance.'

'The hundred Mexicans with blazing guns against just two guys scenario?

'Not necessarily Mexicans, but yes.'

'Could be,' Tom agrees.

'So I am going to go in with Gulliver and leave you in the car. We are going to need a quick getaway.'

'No.'

'Friend Tom—'

'I'm coming in too.'

'There is no reason for us both to die.'

'I agree. I'm coming in too.'

Franco grits his teeth. He has too much blood on his hands already. 'Jane—'

'What about her?'

'She is in love with you.'

Tom sighs. He can't believe it is true, even though it is what he wants. 'If we get out of this alive I will ask her on a date – satisfied?'

'Where will you go?'

'I don't know. Dinner somewhere nice. Chinese maybe, or Thai.'

'Thai is not very good for kissing – the ginger and chilli. That is why French cooking is so good for sex.'

Tom feels extremely uncomfortable all of a sudden. 'Isn't it time to get going?'

'Probably. Oral—'

'Let's go.' Tom cuts him dead and opens the car door. The night is warm and a little sticky. The moon hangs lazily above them, gorged on the day's sun.

*

Tom walks around to the back of the car and pops the boot; Gulliver lies inside. Before they left, his wrists were handcuffed behind him, his mouth taped and a weight gaffer-taped to his chest. He will find it extremely difficult to run away from them. Then a large and blood-free hessian coffee sack was taped around his torso and a smaller one over his head. His feet are bare. Franco appears to the side of Tom and draws a gun; he holds it against Gulliver's head while he cocks it.

'I am sure you recognise the sound.'

The sad sack nods.

'Good. Please be aware I will be holding this gun on you at all times. Should you hesitate to obey any command I give—' he presses the muzzle into the back of Gulliver's head, 'First I will shoot you through the left knee, then the right. Do you get the point?

The sack nods. Franco steps back and nods to Tom who helps the sack- and gaffer-taped man from the car. Franco looks at his watch. It is 11.45 p.m. He pushes Gulliver in front of him and the three cross the road to the school.

They stand before the grand old building, above the doorway Tom reads the school motto once more. *Rather death than false of faith*. In the intervening years since he first saw it he has grown to appreciate it more. They meant a religious faith, but if you replace it with a faith in friendship, a loyalty – it works.

To the right of the school sign there is a box, an alarm, which blinks every ten seconds. Franco looks at his watch. 11.50 p.m. It is time. He watches the hypnotic blinking, and then it is gone. He watches a full minute of non-blinks before he turns to Tom.

'We can go in now.'

The two men and their blind captive walk around to the rear of the building and cut through the fence into the school playground. With some effort they push Gulliver through, not caring if the sharp edges of the chain-link cut into him. He crashes through and lands headfirst on the concrete. Once they are in, Tom leads the way into the main building. He remembers the layout pretty well, even after four years. The doors are oak, old and beautiful. It takes Franco four hefty kicks to smash them in. Inside, everything is dark. Franco feels a shudder creep through him and he could swear he hears a voice.

You are brave, my little Bheka, she tells him, but he shakes his head. She is wrong, he is not brave, never has been. A brave man would have honoured the lost souls of his family and his people, he denied them – like Peter with Jesus. Lulama is long gone, but he would still ask her one last favour.

Protect Pia, he whispers to his sister's spirit.

Tom pulls two large police-issue Maglites from the holdall slung over his shoulder and hands one to Franco. Then they point them into the gloom like light-sabers and walk through the haunted school, up, up and away.

'If there was a film made of your life who would star in it?' Tom asks Franco as they walk up the stairs to the art rooms, where the kiln is.

'Owen Wilson,' Franco replies.

'Really?' Tom shakes his head. 'I thought you might have gone with someone who was—'

'What?' Franco's voice is heavy and stern.

'No, no, that's a good choice. Up here.'

Tom leads them into the art room. The moon throws a silver mist throughout the room and shadows climb and crawl over every surface. The forest of limbs has gone, Tom is glad of that, they creeped him out. However, they have been replaced by walls covered in faces. Death masks.

'Perfect,' Franco purrs.

They wait, Gulliver between them. He lies on the floor, looking more like two sacks of coffee with feet. Franco keeps looking at his watch. It is now fifteen minutes past midnight. They are late. Tom can feel the tension building in Franco as they wait. Of course that is probably what Dent wants; to make Franco volatile and more likely to make mistakes.

'Did you know that octopuses have blue blood?' Tom asks.

'No Trivial Pursuit questions.'

'Okay.' And silence falls once more.

Tom looks to his watch. It is almost 1 a.m. He wonders how long they will wait. Will they still be here when the school bell rings in the morning? He can see that the sack on the floor is shaking slightly. For a moment Tom thinks it is fear, but he realises it is probably Gulliver shaking with laughter. Butch and Sundance.

'Listen,' Franco whispers.

Tom strains into the dark, there is something. Movement below them, faint, but it is there. Franco walks back to the art room door and into the hallway; below he can see torch light. Franco listens hard. Four men and another figure, who is being half-dragged. It must be Pia. Franco leans over the bannister.

'Up here, we are up here.' His voice pings down the wooden staircase, echoing back on itself.

'We are on our way, Franco.' A voice snakes up the stairs. It is nasal and has a Geordie twang. Nathan Dent is on his way.

Franco walks back to Tom and the prostrate Gulliver. 'Are you ready?' he asks the policeman. 'The only thing that matters is Pia. If you have the chance to get her out of here then please do.'

'I understand, Franco.'

The killer grabs the policeman by the arm. 'Thank you, Friend Tom.' Then he turns to face the door as Dent walks through. Tom moves to his side and carefully places his foot on Gulliver's chest, pressing him into the floor.

Behind Dent are three large men. Two of them carry machine guns. Kalashnikovs, Tom thinks. The third holds a rope, at the end of which—

'Pia.'

The figure has a hood over her head, just like Gulliver, but Dent leans across and pulls the hood off.

'Ta-da.'

She looks gaunt. Her skin is filthy, except where her tears have made clean streaks, her hair is greasy, her mouth is taped – but her eyes burn.

'Pia.' Franco jumps forward but the machine guns are levelled right at him.

'Not another fucking step Franco or my men will cut you in half,' Dent yells, stopping Franco dead, but Tom can see how his mind is working, as he weighs up the chance of taking out all three men. Tom thinks he might go for it, then Dent changes the odds. 'Oh, and apart from the fine boys I have with me here—' He waves his arms in the air. Suddenly the air is alive with the dancing fairies of red sniper sights. Franco watches a red dot close in on Tom's forehead and rest there like a bindi. He knows a similar red mark has settled between his own eyes.

Tom watches Franco stiffen like a hunting dog who senses fresh blood. 'There are six men with high-powered rifles trained on you both. Franco, I am sorry to tell you that you will not leave this room alive. Neither of you.' He turns his attention to Tom. 'I am sorry, Detective Superintendent Bevans.'

'Don't worry, ex-Detective Inspector Dent.'

Tom looks into Dent's eyes; he has not seen him in more than twenty years. Then, Dent had been whippet-thin with oily, dark hair with a little moustache and cold, heartless eyes. Tom can see it is the same man who stands before him now, but the body is thicker these days, the hair has thinned and greyed. The eyes though – they are still heartless.

'You two together again. The Dark Wolf and Sad Man, true love is it? You know I never got it back then, why an eighteen-year-old maniac was so keen to help a love-torn copper. But I get it now, you are both good old-fashioned romantics, and there's a bit of homo-erotic action too, let's face it.' He gives Franco a leery, dirty wink. 'Who goes on top?'

'I have a question,' Tom tells him.

'Shoot. No, not you guys.' Dent waves at his men and laughs at his joke. The two henchman look like they only have a very limited vocabulary. 'Now. Tom, ask your question.'

'Beautiful skin. Why did you copy the beautiful skin murders?'

'Oh that was all theatre, intended to confuse any investigation – but it turned out to be so lucky. I had no idea that using it would get you out of the closet and back with lover-boy Franco. It was just meant to muddy the waters if something happened. Pick an unsolved set of murdered girls and add a new one – makes the new one get lost in the storm.'

'Who was the girl? The dead girl?' Franco's voice cuts through Dent's appreciation of his own cleverness.

Dent shrugs. 'New girl fresh off the boat from somewhere bleak – dreaming of a new life. She would have been disappointed, turned into a whore. Maybe we did her a favour. Don't know anything else. Not even a name.' Tom feels his chest tighten at the callousness of the shrug. It reminds him so much of his own father — that mean, drunk fuck who would hit his mum and then shrug like that when Tom asked him why. *Why did you hurt her?* Shrug. Just a fucking shrug.

'Did you kill her?' Franco asks Dent.

'Personally? Did I break open her skull with a hammer and mush her brains? No, I did not personally kill her. Actually I was at your club. You saw me there but you were pretty out of it.' Dent turns to Tom. 'Do you remember my daughter? You met her once – she was about twelve. She's thirty-four now and very attractive. She killed the girl.' He leers at Tom and then looks back to Franco. 'She was also the one who drugged Pia and lured her away from the party. You know I was shocked when I found out your daughter liked girls and not boys. That can't make a big man like you very proud, can it?' Franco does not respond. 'But it made everything a whole lot easier for me. I didn't need to bring anyone else in, just kept it in the family. You know, at the end of the day, we are just a good old-fashioned family firm – makes you proud doesn't it, the best of British.' He smiles. His confidence is supreme. 'Now if that answers your question, we have our own business to conclude.'

'I want to talk to my daughter.'

'Oh, be my guest,' Dent tells him with an absolute relish.

Franco moves to her slowly and, with a gentle touch, removes the tape from her mouth.

'Darlin—'

'They said you're a drug dealer, a killer, that you—'

He folds around her, wrapping his strong arms across her and dips his mouth to her cheek, making a clean, lip-shaped kiss on her cheek. He whispers something into her ear.

'Don't touch me,' she screams, almost hysterical. 'Don't!'

He steps back, his eyes brimming with tears.

'Was it all lies, was everything all just lies? My whole life, how could you?'

'And your mummy was one of his crack whores, don't forget that,' Dent crows.

Franco can see Dent has told her everything, filled her up with poison and bile, and it makes his heart bleed. He longs to hug her. Hug her and rip that smug bastard in two.

'He drank his predecessor's blood after he cut his throat, and he had a girl brand—'

'Shut up,' Franco screams at Dent. 'Shut the fuck up.' Veins stand out on Franco's neck. His skin is a thousand shades darker than normal, his blood is boiling and his ears are full of the pounding of it in his head. He looks at the man before him with pure hatred. Tom tenses. This is not going well. Franco turns back to Pia, and he opens his arms, his eyes are burning, the eyes of a father. He is Frank Light once more and he drops to a knee before her.

'Everything—'

'Don't you dare try to explain what you did. You animal.'

'The first man I killed with my bare hands was a priest.'

'Jesus. Jesus.' Tears stream down her cheeks and she falls.

'It's okay my darling,' Dent says to her with a soothing sing-song tone. 'We'll take care of the nasty man, you can even pull the trigger if you want. After all this monster has done to you.'

Franco closes his eyes. When he opens them they are hard and cold. The eyes of a killer. Tom can see this is all falling apart.

Any second Franco will run at them and all hell is going to break loose.

'Let's cut the crap, Dent,' Tom yells. 'We have your man, Gulliver here. The deal is still to trade him for Pia. Let us just concentrate on that.'

Franco is breathing heavily. Tom thinks his mind is gone. He needs to focus again. Tom can see the sniper sights dance over his heart as well as his head. He looks at Dent: he is wearing something in his ear, and on his lapel – there is a black dot. He is wearing a microphone. The snipers can talk to him and can hear everything. Okay.

Dent smiles. 'You're right, you have Gulliver.' He swings round to face Tom and his hand goes to his waistband. In a fluid motion he draws a gun and fires three times into the coffee sacks. Blood squirts up, covering Tom, who still stands with his foot on Gulliver's chest. Gulliver's body moves once and then stops. Tom can see brain matter through the hessian and blood is pooling around his feet. He feels sick.

'Oh look at your fucking face.' Dent hoots with laughter. Tom looks up and waits for Dent to stop laughing and push the gun back into his waistband.

'Fuck you,' Tom tells him and then grabs the buckets of paint he placed behind him and swings them with all his might. The paint arcs towards the windows and with an all-mighty squelch, they cover the windows in a riot of colour. Immediately the dancing red dots disappear. Tom shifts from where he was standing, as a bullet cracks through the glass. It would have pierced his heart a second before but now misses and rips through the intestines of one of the large bodyguards; the bullet rips half his stomach out and as he falls his finger twitches – at close range the torrent of ammunition from the Kalashnikov rips the other armed man in two.

'Stop firing if you can't see,' Dent screams into the microphone. The third guard, holding the rope attached to Pia, just stands there, eyes wide. Then Franco kicks viciously into his leg, shattering it. The man drops to the floor and Franco grabs at the gun in his shoulder holster. Out of the corner of his eye he sees Dent already has a gun in his hand. It is swinging towards him. He will fire before he gets the muzzle clear of the leather. So close. Not even enough time to close his eyes. Dent smiles, he will enjoy killing Franco almost more than anything he has ever done in his life. His finger begins to squeeze and—

'Argh!' Dent screams as a knife blade pierces his wrist. It goes all the way through and blood starts pumping. The gun drops. Dent turns, his blood arcing as he moves. His face ashen, and his eyes full of hate. *How*?

Pia is shaking. She has one arm free from the gaffer, she used the knife her father secretly gave her to cut herself free. That knife is now in Dent's wrist. She sees the blood and she vomits all over Nathan Dent. Franco rises with the gun in his hand, aimed between Dent's eyes.

'Dent, slowly spread your arms and legs and drop to the floor. Tom, call Jane. We need the snipers cleared and—'

'ENOUGH!' A voice hard with authority fills the room as a gun is pressed into Pia's head. 'Drop the phone Detective Superintendent Bevans, and you drop the gun – Bheka.'

'Papi?' Franco drops the gun.

General Ndela stands with the aid of a cane. He is tall, stately. He reminds Tom of Nelson Mandela; a gun-wielding Nelson Mandela.

'Nathan, would you attend to your wrist before you bleed to death. Then have some more of your men get over here to clear up this mess.' He turns to Franco.

'Papi.' Franco smiles at the man – he is still pleased to see him, even if it means he will die.

'You are such a deep disappointment to me.' He levels the gun at Franco and his finger tightens.

'Whoa, general,' Dent calls out as he sees that Ndela means to shoot Franco. 'We want the money first. The two hundred million.'

Ndela smiles, then he swings the gun and clubs Pia, sending her spinning and crashing into the corner of the room.

'PIA!' Franco yells but Papi levels the gun at his head once more.

Franco's eyes are on Pia. She is unconscious but does not look badly hurt. It is probably better that she is unconscious; he does not want her to see him die. He turns to Papi.

'You sent me away.'

'You had a job to do, more important than the war.'

'I thought you cared for me?'

Ndela smiles. 'I did. You were like a son to me.' The smile shifts, only slightly; he looks like a snake. 'But you have ceased to honour me.'

'Never. I have never failed in my duty to you or our country.'

'You steal from us.'

'No.'

'Two hundred million.'

Franco sighs. He would laugh if the whole thing were not so pathetic. 'Steal? You have no idea, any of you. Over twenty years I have sent you many hundreds of millions. Where, where is that money?' Ndela is silent. 'Is it in the stomachs of my people? Is it in the libraries and schools, the museums and universities we spoke of all those nights in the—'

'SILENCE!' Ndela's face blazes. 'The road is long and our enemies surround us on all sides. I thought you would see that.'

'But I do. To fund the war against our oppressors we create misery here. We destroy lives wherever we go. All our money is blood money.'

'But it is OUR bloody money. Where is it?' Dent asks. He has wrapped his wrist in a handkerchief, though the makeshift bandage is already looking rusty with blood.

'Papi, do you remember reading to me? My favourite stories were those of Jason and his Argonauts, do you recall?' Franco's voice is soft, full of warmth for those long-lost days. Ndela shrugs. 'No, oh well. Do you know what a psychonaut is?'

'Enough of these games.' Ndela points the gun at Pia's head.

'A psychonaut is a drug taker. He will take absolutely anything, any combination of psychoactive compounds. He is fairly wealthy and enjoys drugs. He is not an addict. He will not buy from an addict but will purchase on-line or in a shop. He, and she, are the future. Legal drugs, one step ahead of the law and all delivered through the mail system. Legal, less destructive, more lucrative.'

'Two hundred million?' Dent asks.

'Invested. In the basement of our building are computer systems and labs that would be the envy of any pharmaceutical giant. We have ten world-class chemists developing the range. We even run focus groups to see what they like best. We have tasting notes, which drugs are best with food, which with sex, we include Viagra in the ingredients of some of the range. There are anti-depressants in others. Some you absorb through the skin, bodily contact. I have planned a whole new massage industry – *The High Life*. Papi, it is a brave new world. A world with no more hiding in the shadows. I am tired of being a cockroach. And in five years, you will see more money than we have ever made. This is the future I have invested in.'

'Invested?' Papi asks.

'Invested. You have everything there in the building. For more than twenty years I have only taken a very small wage for myself, mostly to pay for Pia's schooling. There is a little in savings and that is all in Pia's name. That is all I have taken. It is a fraction of what a banker might have earned and there are no performance-based bonuses. I have barely taken a day away from my responsibilities to our cause, and I have raised a daughter away from the fucking hell-hole I helped to create. I have always been loyal to you, to my country. All I wanted was to stop peddling so much death.'

Dent closes his eyes. Papi lowers the gun and takes a couple of steps towards Franco, leaning heavily on his cane. He looks into Franco's eyes. He sees the truth there.

'Mr Dent. Would you kindly tell our friend what we did with his headquarters.'

'We burned it to the ground. We killed the men who worked there, destroyed the labs and the equipment,' Dent tells him wearily.

'On your suggestion Mr Dent.' Ndela's arm swings out, far quicker than one would expect from such an old man. He shoots Dent through the head. His final expression is of total surprise, and then his body falls gracefully, like a dying swan. Ndela bows his head and the room is totally still. Slowly he raises his chin; his eyes look tired and his face is pale.

'Oh my boy,' he says to Franco. 'What a stupid waste. I am sorry.'

'Papi.' Franco opens his arms to hug the man. Ndela smiles and then his cane swishes through the air. Franco sees it coming and tries to rock back but he feels the blade bite at his throat. A thin red line is drawn across the dark skin.

'Franco.' Tom screams and runs forwards as Franco falls, clutching at his neck. Blood bubbles like a spring through his fingers. Tom grabs his throat and pushes his hands down and in, applying pressure to the wound. The blood flow slows and stops, but Tom can see all he is doing is putting his finger in the dike, and very soon his hands will not be able to keep the blood at bay.

Behind them, General Ndela shakes his head sadly.

'You could save yourself, Detective Superintendent Bevans. If you want to run then go now. I will give you to the count of ten.'

'Don't bother counting.' He pushes his hands further in, not wanting to strangle his friend but needing to keep the pressure. Franco's eyes swim, his mouth opens but only a bubble of spit comes out of it. Ndela comes close and watches as Tom struggles to save Franco. He looks at the man as you would watch an ant carrying a leaf that is ten times the size of itself.

'Why?' he asks Tom.

'He's my friend. I will not let him die.'

'You are too late for your friend. All you can do is watch him die drop by drop.' Ndela shakes his head sadly and walks over to Dent's body. Then he leans down slowly and speaks into the microphone on his lapel. 'If you can hear me, I need three men over here.' Then he takes a step back and stands by Gulliver's body. He will wait while the boy he once thought of as a son bleeds to death. He will not mourn the loss. After all, Bheka has been such an annoyance these last few months. Tom feels Franco's body shudder; it is going into shock.

'Stay with me my friend,' Tom whispers to the man on the floor. He thinks there could even be the shadow of a smile on his face. His lips open and Tom leans forward to hear.

'Sundance – you took your foot off Gulliver's chest.'

'Yes, about thirty seconds ago,' Tom answers and they both close their eyes.

The explosion rips Papi in half as the landmine strapped to Gulliver's chest explodes. The snipers watching from across the street see all the windows blow out in the art block and dust envelops the building. Then the men run away.

Tom coughs as the dust swirls around him like a blizzard. The room is a total mess, cupboards have burst open or splintered in the blast. Paper, shredded like confetti, dances in the air. The floor, in places, swims with paint that is swirling together to make new colours. Franco is gurgling, which may be laughter or blood in his throat or— Tom realises he can only hear in one ear, the other is a howling void, like a storm. His eardrum has burst. Franco's lips open but there is no sound.

'Don't try and talk.' Tom keeps both hands pressed hard into his throat, but he knows what Franco wants to ask – is Pia alive?

'Oh Christ.' Blood is beginning to bubble through Tom's fingers as Franco starts to shake again.

'You are not going to die. Do you hear me, you stubborn bastard? You are not going to die.' Franco sighs, or it might be a laugh. Tom looks around, he can see the debris of exploded art supplies drawers all around him. His eyes latch onto something that could help, but there is no way to get to it. 'Damn.' He looks over his shoulder, as far behind himself as his neck can stretch.

'PIA,' he yells into the howling wind of his shattered hearing. 'PPPPPPPIIIIIIIIIIAAAAAAAAAAAAAAAAA.'

There is nothing, no movement. The dust is too thick to see through, but at least she had been thrown to the furthest corner of the room. She should be okay, unless something has fallen on her. 'Christ.' He is going to have to shift Franco's body. He will have to release the pressure of one hand on his neck and— 'Jesus, no.' Blood oozes like an oil slick as he tries to lift his hand. Tom pushes back down, desperate to stem the outpouring of the life-blood. The pressure keeps the wound closed but it is only a matter of time before it seeps out and Franco bleeds to death. 'AGH!' Tom screams into the air. 'I will not let you die. I am fed up with avenging the dead – for once let me save someone.'

A hand comes to rest on his shoulder. He looks around. Blood smears her forehead and her cheek has been ripped open – but Pia is alive. Tom feels the tears rain down.

'Glue. There in that pile, superglue.'

'No need to shout,' she mouths and moves to the drawer. She pulls out three tubes of superglue. She opens one and slices off the top. 'There, just between my fingers, squirt it slowly and follow as I move a finger away – then shoot more in,' Tom tells her and she aims it at the wound in her father's neck.

'All of it,' Tom screams. And Pia fires the entire tube, lacing it back and forth over the slice in his throat. As she does so Tom eases off the pressure. The glue gets slick with blood but it stays in place.

'Another tube,' Tom yells and Pia quickly snaps the top off the second nozzle. She blasts away, and when it is done she fires the last tube over it too.

Together Pia and Tom cocoon Franco's neck in a bandage of plastic skin. Kodak can have the glory of saving Franco's life. After three tubes, no blood is seeping out. Tom slumps down beside his friend. Pia taps him on the shoulder and mouths to him –

'Police siren.'

He nods to her. 'They can't find your dad here. We need to go.'

She hesitates. Tom can see the confusion in her eyes. 'Pia, I don't know what to tell you about your father – I expect all of what Dent told you is true. He has lot of blood on his hands but—' But what? She looks at the policeman with such hope and expectation, she wants something to believe in. 'He helped me once. When I needed a friend, he was there.' That is all Tom has. It is very little to build such faith on. 'And he loves you. He loves you, Pia.'

She nods her head slowly, then leans down and takes her father's arm. Together the friend and the daughter manage to get Franco to his feet and they stagger through the building and out into the dusty night.

It's an hour before the first fireman enters the building; he is a specialist in judging structural integrity. The air is still at least eighty per cent dust and he wears breathing apparatus. It takes him a few minutes to judge that the building is safe to enter and then the SOCO team moves in. They take with them giant vacuum cleaners to filter the air, and of course they keep it all for sorting through later. At about 5 a.m. they finally let DI Jane Thorsen through to the crime scene. She has been chomping at the bit for hours. She tries not to run, then she tries not to panic, then she tries not to cry. No Tom.

Some of the team tag and bag all they can find, and some try to collect the various pieces that once made General Ndela into a whole man. They find most of him quickly, but it takes a few hours to find his head. It isn't until someone thinks to look inside the kiln, and there it is.

FORTY-EIGHT
Almost three months later

Thursday 22nd September 2011. The last day of summer.
The weather has changed. There is a chill back in the air as
summer slips away. Flowers still line the verges of the roads and
giant baskets overfill with blooms all the way along the seafront,
but they are drooping and will not be replaced. It is the end.

From close by Franco can hear the calls and splashes of
children enjoying the final day of the late summer sun. Soon the
ice-cream stands will shut up shop for the last time this year.

Franco stands on the sea wall and watches the water shimmer
in the sun. His neck is almost healed; he still talks in little more
than a whisper but Jacks told him it is sexy, so that's good. He's
been writing – stories of his tribe. He began with the ones he
remembers from his mother, but he has been creating his own
with Mbeki and Lulama and even little Bheka. Poetry too, and
he will try and put a tune to them one day and sing them. Maybe
he and Pia will sing them together. He hopes so.

'There you go.' A hand is extended to him holding a twist of
soft ice-cream and a flake.

'Thanks,' he tells his daughter. Together they stand and watch
the water. Tomorrow she will return to London to be back with

Hettie and James. She knows everything, all he has done. They have sat together for days and days as he has told her his story, he did not try and hide a single detail from her. Both during and after his tale, there were tears – so many tears. She will never forgive him, that is what she said, but maybe they can learn to be a father and daughter in some way. He hopes so, but the important thing is that she is alive. It means there is a chance that one day she can trust him again. Together, they stand and watch as the starlings dance through the air for them. They sweep and climb in patterns that defy belief, linked and yet independent. It is magical. He laughs, and Pia turns to him and, while there is not a laugh, there is a smile. That is something. It is a start.

He looks at the clock-tower close to the pier. It is 1.30 p.m. Time to go back to the house, his home for the moment. It belongs to Ed and Jacks. They are Patty and Jim's oldest friends. It is a safe haven. Franco likes them, especially Ed. At night, by an open fire, they talk politics. The two men play games too – chess and cribbage and sometimes cards. So different to watching porn and playing Grand Theft Auto. The couple have a dog and at dusk he has his last walk of the day, along the beach, as the sun dies. Jacks walks him and Franco tags along. They call him Frank. To them he is Frank Light. Finally, Frank Light is real. He is starting to get used to it, a new name for a new man. He hopes.

When he and Pia arrive back at the house they find the guests are all there. Jim and Patty and Jane and Tom.

Patty watches Franco as he enters with his beautiful daughter by his side. She is happy for him, even though she knows there is tension between them. She sees how Franco has aged in the last few weeks. His hair has grey shot through it now and she could swear it was solid black when she first met him. But the biggest difference are his eyes. Now they are full of sadness – but they are warm. The ice has melted. Smile lines radiate from the corners. He looks happy. He is lucky, probably luckier than he deserves. Her stomach is a mess of crawling worms, she has come here not really to see Jacks and Ed, but to talk to Franco. She asked him for a favour, that night he almost died. She asked for a telephone number and she now has a name and an address. She wants to ask his advice. She needs to know the danger she could be in if she uses it.

Jane enters and stands next to her. Patty looks over at her and—

'You're pregnant,' she whispers to Jane, whose eyes widen. She says nothing, just nods a *yes*.

'Does Tom know?'

She shakes her head. 'I am afraid to tell him.'

Patty creases her forehead. 'You will make him the happiest man in the world.' She leans over and kisses Jane on the cheek. For a second she imagines it is Dani who is pregnant and she will be a grandmother. Her heart stops, she must not think that.

Lunch is full of laughter and stories, mostly from Jim and Ed. Franco enjoys hearing them but he notices that both Patty and Tom are quiet. He knows what is going on with Patty. He has advised her to forget the name and address she has.

'Can you not just go on with your life? You have Jim and he loves you,' he had told her. But he did not expect her to say yes and forget the name, or where to find the man. *Dog with a bone*, that was how Tom had described her once, and he was right.

'It is not enough,' she had told him.

'Then I wish you well. I hope you find the truth and it ends your pain.'

Franco understands her needs and her hunger for the truth. But what is going on in Tom's head? He has no idea. Ed opens a bottle of wine and starts to pour glasses.

'Only a little for Pia,' Franco tells Ed.

'Dad, I'm a grown up.'

He looks at his daughter. 'Yes you are.' He smiles at her.

As the sun begins to dip down, Franco and Tom walk on the beach as the dog runs back and forth ahead of them.

'So tomorrow you're off?' Tom asks.

Franco nods. 'I don't know for how long but I need a change of scene.'

'Will anyone be looking for you?'

'I doubt it. But if they do …' He lets the line float out into the breeze.

'Good luck,' Tom says to his friend.

'And you, something is troubling you.'

Tom nods to his friend. 'Marcus Keyson. He has been moved to a hospice. Three more strokes this week, they are amazed he has lasted this long. He could go tomorrow or—'

'You feel responsible?'

'I didn't hit him, but I put him in that room. I damaged him enough that he felt he wanted to hurt me.'

'That was Keyson and not you. He broke the law and you informed on him. Do not feel guilty.'

'No?' Tom shakes his head, remembering how he held his hands to Franco's throat and kept the blood from seeping away. 'He was my friend, once.'

Franco nods. 'Maybe. But not all friends can be saved. Friend Tom.' His words spiral up into the air. Then the two sad men look out to sea. The dying embers of the final summer sun warm their cold, damaged hearts.

On the two-hour drive back home they are both quiet. Jane is full of trepidation over telling Tom about the child growing in her womb. Tom is full of unease. As they get close to the flat they now both share, Tom speaks for the first time in ninety minutes.

'I am going to drop you off. I need to do something.'

'Oh, okay.' Actually she is relieved; she can delay telling him about the child.

He drops her off and drives. He isn't exactly sure where he is going but uses the map on his phone to find the hospice. When he arrives he asks for Marcus Keyson's room and is shown to it.

In the bed Marcus looks emaciated, a child version of the large man he once was. The doctors say they are amazed he is still alive; they don't know how he keeps going, or how long he has to go. Tom sits with him for a while, telling him how they solved the case, and how it took them nearly five years to work out what he, Marcus, had deduced in only hours.

'You really should have been a copper, Marcus,' he tells the fallen man. 'You would have been the best.' There is silence for a while and then, much to his own surprise, Tom slides to the floor and says a short prayer. Then when he has finished, he leans in close to Marcus and whispers into his ear.

'I think I was a little in love with you ... for a while, my friend.' He sighs. 'I have had so few friends, real friends. For the longest time I thought my only friend was Dani, and she was enough, but I was fooling myself. I loved her too much for it to be a real friendship. I don't think I really knew what friends did for each other. Recently, well maybe I have learned a little more. But you were my friend and I did betray that. I should have talked to you before I turned you in. I am sorry. I wish I could make amends. I wish I could be a true friend to you Marcus.' He leans across and kisses the man on the forehead. 'I will try to be your friend now.' Tom Bevans takes a pillow and slowly, like a lover, places it over the mouth and nose of his friend and holds it there until the man's pain is gone.

Patty drives like a bat out of hell. Jim winces at least a dozen times and holds onto the door handle for most of the journey. The name and address that Franco's contact gave her burns in her pocket. This is it, she can't delay this any longer.

'This isn't the way home,' Jim says with some concern.

'No,' Patty tells him, her eyes latched onto the road.

'Where—'

'Don't ask me Jim. Please trust me.'

'Okay.' His voice wavers with fear.

An hour later, Patty holds the note in her hand and scrutinises it again. A wind, from nowhere, whips at it, almost tearing the slip from her grasp – but she holds on. It reads: 18 Addlestone Lane N8 and has the name, Vincent Bale. She looks up at the building that sits between 14 and 24.

'It's a church,' Jim says.

No shit, Sherlock, Patty wants to snap at him but bites her tongue. She can see what it is. It looks old, the walls are part cobble and part brick, like a patchwork of history. She assumes it is a hybrid; partly an ancient building that crumbled away but also a more recent work. Around it a churchyard creeps but she can't see more than dark shadows loitering in the gloom. The building itself is almost totally dark, with only a single dim light somewhere in the back, which just manages to lighten a window. Has Franco's man got it wrong?

'Let's knock.' Patty pushes open the small wooden gate and heads down into the darkness. Jim doesn't move. He feels a little concerned by all this cloak and dagger stuff. He had hoped that this afternoon would be the end of it, that seeing Franco off would mean that life went back to normal. But here they are, chasing something, always chasing something.

'Dad.' Dani appears in front of him.

'Dani.' He moves to hug her but remembers at the last second – she isn't real.

'You haven't come to see me in months. You knew I was alone, all alone in that room.' She tries to keep the disappointment from her voice, but can't.

'JIM!' Patty calls from the black and he runs to her, leaving Dani at the top of the path. *She isn't real.* He feels sick.

Patty waits for him to reach her before she pulls back the enormous metal knocker and hammers on the door.

'What are we doing here Patty?' he asks, but she ignores him as she listens for sounds of life. She knocks again; she can hear the echo ricochet from the walls inside but also off the gravestones out here – pinging between the dead and strumming in the arms of the trees. There is nothing from inside. Jim looks back into the dark but Dani has not followed him. Patty pulls the knocker back and hammers ever harder.

'Dad.' She is next to him. He can't breathe. 'Keyson is gone. Dead. I'm free. I can be with you again.'

'Someone's coming.' Patty steps back, she holds her breath.

'Good evening.' The door opens a crack and a head peeks out. The man has a round face with tight curly hair.

'We were looking for number 18 Addlestone Lane.'

'Well, you found it,' he tells them and opens the door fully. He is dressed in jeans and a pale blue shirt that is topped with a dog collar. 'Come in.'

Inside it is small and quite plain. The lights are out and shadows dance around the walls from a series of guttering candles on an altar. A sign asks for one pound per candle to commemorate the dead. Jim moves towards the altar and lights a slim taper with hands that shake.

'For Dani,' he murmurs. He catches the ghost's eye and she smiles.

'You said this is 18 Addlestone Lane.'

'Sort of,' he says and smiles. 'The church is really 16 to 22 but the rectory, where I live, is officially 18.'

'You—' She doesn't know what to say. He's about forty-five years old. He would have been early twenties when Dani died, could he be the man she has come to see?

'Are you Mr Bale?' she asks him.

'I'm Reverend Stiles. Paul.'

'Do you know a Mr Bale?'

'I am sorry.' He sees the flash of disappointment skitter across her face. 'I don't know anyone of that name.'

Patty droops ever so slightly. Jim feels nausea tighten his stomach and cold creep up to his chest. What does Patty want here?

'I am sorry I can't help.'

'One of your congregation?' She is clutching at straws, she knows it. He smiles the kind of smile you keep on hand for aged relatives and neighbours with dementia. 'I am sorry.' He sounds sincere, she can see that he'd be a popular vicar with—

'Mum!' Dani cries as Patty faints.

'Patty!' Jim calls as he sees her stumble and slide sideways. She takes a table down with her, scattering guides to the church in German and Russian all over the floor. Jim gets to her and lifts her head. She is shaking badly.

'C-c-coat p-pocket,' she stammers, and Jim fishes into her pockets and finds a little silver pill-box and draws it out. She sucks down the two roprinole and closes her eyes, trying to ride out the storm.

'Could we have some water?' Jim asks.

'Of course,' Reverend Stiles says and calls out to the darkness at the back of the church. 'Vincent, can you bring some water.' Patty rolls onto her back and looks up at the ceiling. It is not the Sistine chapel, but— *he said Vincent.*

Jim watches his wife with real concern and behind him, he hears his daughter's ghost begin to sob. He turns his head to see a man emerge from the shadows with a glass of water. He is bald and painfully thin, maybe sixty years old.

'Here,' the man says. His teeth are not good, discoloured and cracked, at least two missing at the back. Patty reaches for the water with one hand but with the other grips his wrist. 'Thanks, Vincent. It is Vincent isn't it, Vincent Bale?' Electricity runs through him, his lip curls like a cornered dog and the glass of water explodes on the flagstones. He wrenches his hand free from her grasp, pulling her forwards and her hand lands in the glass. 'Ah!' she yells as her palm is sliced open.

'Vincent!' Reverend Stiles is shocked. Vincent looks to him, his face a churning mix of emotions.

'Please Mr Bale, we just want to talk with you.' Patty can see the man is about to run. 'It is our daughter, we want to talk to you about our daughter.'

Not again, not more, Jim thinks.

'I know you,' Dani whispers from the shadows, her voice full of fear.

'Your daughter?' the man breathes. He looks panicked.

'What is going on, Vincent?' Reverend Stiles asks, but Vincent does not take his eyes from Patty's face.

'Please help us,' Patty asks, as she slides her hand into her coat to pull out her wallet. Slowly she opens it and slides two fingers inside, like a magician intent on showing there is nothing hidden. She draws out a photograph. It is twenty-four years old. 'This is our daughter, this is—'

'Dani.' Vincent Bale finishes her sentence. His eyes fill with tears and he turns and runs.

'NO!' screams Patty.

'Please,' Jim yells but the man is already gone.

'I don't understand.' Reverend Stiles shakes his head. Jim turns to Dani, she has darkened, the air around her is ink black. 'Dad.' She is barely there, he can only see her outline.

'Our daughter died,' Patty tells the clergyman, 'a long time ago. We think that man was there when she died and—' A shudder of hopelessness runs through her. Jim thinks she may collapse again but she pushes him away as he tries to hold her.

'Patty, why didn't you tell me why we were coming here?' Jim feels sick. Suddenly the room is so hot.

Patty doesn't look at her husband, but instead she grabs the clergyman's hand. 'I hoped he could tell us about her death. I need to know, you see. I have to know.'

'Vincent has been at our church for the entire time I have been here – that is nine years. I believe he was here many years before that, he is a devout man, a—'

'You don't need to defend me.' A voice comes from the back of the church, from the darkness. Then a torch illuminates the flagstones as Vincent Bale walks forwards carrying the torch in one hand and a small box in the other. 'I don't want no trouble, but I owe it to her.' When he gets close he transfers the torch to his other hand and pulls a ball of cotton wool, a bandage and some iodine from his pocket. 'Let me dress your cut,' he offers.

'I can do it myself.'

He nods and watches as she dresses her own palm.

'Thank you for coming back,' she tells him as she finishes the rudimentary bandage.

'I should have talked to you before now. I promised myself I would, but I was too much of a coward,' he tells her.

'What do you mean?' Jim asks.

'Dani's death.'

'We know what happened, but I need to ask you about her state of mind.'

'I think you should sit down,' Vincent tells Patty.

'We know what happened. She lost a child and sold herself to a gang for the oblivion of heroin, and that killed her. I just need to know if she said anything.'

'No!' Dani starts to scream – the sound fills Jim's head.

'You don't know, you really don't know,' Vincent Bale says, his voice full of pain.

'What do you mean?' Patty asks.

'She was at rock bottom. She talked about the baby – she wanted to end the pain. The drugs did that, she wanted to make herself forget the child, and it worked for a couple of weeks – but the pain came back. No matter what she did.'

'Did she kill herself?' Patty asks the question that has tortured her since that night in the cathedral, all those months ago.

'No. No, she was strong. She reached the bottom and started to bounce back up.'

Patty feels the world start to shake, like an earthquake that starts in her chest. 'What are you saying?'

'She stopped taking the drugs. She wanted to start again, she was getting clean.' Vincent's eyes are filled with tears as the images flash through his mind. Memories he has tried to suppress for so long.

'But she died of an overdose.'

'She wanted to be totally clean, and she was getting there – then she decided to stop being used, she said no to sex with us, she wanted her body back, but she'd been branded, she was ours. That was what he said.'

'Who?'

'The boss, Jackson, Bill Jackson – he ran the gang and he owned Dani.'

'Owned?'

'He might have been a bit in love with her – he certainly wanted her. He said she couldn't stop. He raped her. She fought him and—'

'What?' Patty hisses.

'He broke her hip – he was such a big man and she was so slight. She was in a lot of pain and was screaming abuse at him.

Jackson was out of control, he took a syringe of shit someone had cooked up and he jabbed it in hard.'

Dani sobs as the memories rip at her. His face on her, the breath – the pressure he put on her to open her legs. 'Oh Christ.'

'He didn't know she had kicked it, or he didn't care, but it was too much. It stopped her heart.'

Patty thinks it has stopped hers too.

'He killed her. Everyone went frantic; we left the house and ran. We all ran.'

Patty has curled into a ball, but she shakes; she shakes as if she will explode. The clergyman has gone, then he comes back with glasses and a bottle of whisky. He pours four glasses and hands them out. His face is ashen.

'I never went back to that life after that day. I liked your daughter; I would never have wanted to see her hurt. Instead I found God and came here. I should have … I should have gone to you back then. I was scared. I am sorry.'

Neither Jim nor Patty know what to say. Their hearts and heads can't communicate now. Jim watches his daughter's ghost flicker, like the old TV signal he remembers from when he was a kid, and then she is gone.

'I have something that was hers. I've kept it safe. Please.' And he takes the small box in his hand and offers it to Patty. Her hands do not work, so Jim takes the box and opens it.

'She always had it with her, and she washed it more than she did herself. She loved it.' Jim pulls a small stuffed animal from the box.

'Hoppy Bunny,' they both say, remembering the first toy Dani got the day she was born.

'Bill Jackson.' Patty says his name with so much hate. 'Where is he?'

An hour later an old married couple walk into a pub. Patty falls into a chair and Jim orders for them. A double whisky for Patty, and a coffee for him. He also gets four packs of crisps.

At the table, Patty is folded over with her head resting on her arm. Jim looks at his watch. It should be 3 a.m. as it feels like the wee small hours of the morning. Instead it is only 10.30 p.m. Jim sits next to her and strokes her hair. She even lets him do it for a few moments before she gently pushes his hand away. She turns her face up to his – her eyes are puffy, red and raw.

'He killed her.'

'Patty.'

'She was coming back to us, she wanted to live.'

'Please don't.'

'He killed her.'

'Twenty-two years, Patty.'

'And we finally have his name, and we know where he is.'

'Yes, we know where he is.'

Patty draws away from Jim and wraps her arms around herself. Jim rises and looks through the large glass front of the pub. Outside, on the other side of the street, he sees his daughter. She looks pale, even for a ghost. She isn't real. She isn't – but he wishes she were. He turns back to his wife.

'He's in prison, Patty. Life for murder. He has already been punished.'

'No. No, Jim he hasn't, not anywhere close to being punished. Not for Dani, not for our daughter.'

Outside, she stands in the cold. Twenty-two years dead but still in pain.

'What do you want?' Jim asks Patty.

'Revenge.'

'How?'

Patty looks into his eyes. 'Jim, I want to kill him.' She takes his hand. 'I want to kill him. I need to.'

The old married couple look into each other's eyes. Slowly Jim nods. 'Okay. We will kill him.'

Acknowledgements

I am incredibly grateful to a bunch of people who helped me in the development of my *second, difficult* novel. Making the transition from someone who juggles work, being a new dad and writing in the early mornings and witching hour, to becoming a professional writer who can write a book in a year (as opposed to a meandering three years) has been quite a trip. I could not have done it without the support of my agent Simon Trewin and the team at WME. I would not have done it without the hard work of my editor Gillian Green at Ebury and everyone there, especially Emily Yau.

With the publication of *The Last Winter of Dani Lancing* I become a crime writer and have been amazed at the friendliness and support that community has shown me. So a big thanks to them all, especially Sophie Hannah, Mark Billingham, Stav Sherez, Mel Sherratt, Anya Lipska and Michael Ridpath.

The research for this novel has been a real joy. I have been in secret tunnels in a royal palace, police cells and speeding through the night at 120 mph responding to 999 calls. I have also walked through walls at the Royal Observatory, heard ghost stories and seen real pain and suffering on the streets. I would like to thank the Sussex police force, who have been fantastically helpful, especially Detective Inspector Vicki Harris, Inspector Andy Kille, Chief Inspector Rob Leet, Detective Sergeant Julian Deans and retired Chief Superintendent Graham Bartlett. I was lucky enough to receive help and advice from the team at the

Royal Pavilion in Brighton and I want to thank them all, especially Dr Alexandra Loske and Daniel Beevers. I also want to thank the staff at the Royal Observatory Greenwich, especially Dr Marek Kukula. Medical help and expertise has come from The Bad Doctor, Ian Williams.

I have a small group of friends who have read and commented upon the book as I wrote, and they have been great. Take a bow Finn Clarke, Ann Fletcher, Melanie Green, Linda James, Margaret McKie, Cath Quinn and Charles Turner. I also thank Emma Jane Unsworth who dared me to add the phrases *boxful of vaginas* and a *forest full of cocks* into the book. She is supposed to now do the same.

I am also grateful to my American family – The Murphys. They have been great cheerleaders, especially my father-in-law, Paul Murphy, who gave a talk about my first book at his local rural library. He told the senior citizens in the audience to buy it and not read it, too much sex and violence – but they still had to buy it. The rest of the Murphy clan – Dave and Tracy, John and Tere and Bill and Michelle, ta.

And, as always, to my sister Jools who is my great, great friend.

This book was almost entirely written under the influence of heavily caffeinated beverages and I would like to thank my favourite suppliers: the staff of the Emporium Theatre, Brighton for keeping me topped-up while I wrote.

A special thanks to Bill and Christine Gerhauser for their support a lifetime ago.

Lastly there are two people who keep me sane and happy: my daughter Arden, and my amazing wife Lynne Murphy.

P. D. Viner
June 2014